PEARL MOON

PEARL
MOON

Katherine Stone

FAWCETT COLUMBINE

NEW YORK

A Fawcett Columbine Book
Published by Ballantine Books

Copyright © 1995 by Katherine Stone

All rights reserved under International and Pan-American
Copyright Conventions. Published in the United States by Ballantine Books,
a division of Random House, Inc., New York, and simultaneously
in Canada by Random House of Canada Limited, Toronto.

Library of Congress Cataloging-in-Publication Data
Stone, Katherine
Pearl Moon / Katherine Stone.
p.   cm.
ISBN: 0-449-90829-1
I. Title.
PS3569.T64134P4   1995
813'.54—dc20   94-13176
CIP

Designed by Ann Gold

Manufactured in the United States of America

First Edition: April 1995

10 9 8 7 6 5 4 3 2

Fic.

PEARL MOON

PROLOGUE

Highland Park
Dallas, Texas
Saturday, June 5, 1993

"Stephen and I won't be getting married after all."

Allison Parish Whitaker's stunning announcement was made with soft apology to the five beloved relatives assembled before her in the great room of the Whitaker mansion. Her father and grandparents were here at her request—because, she had said, she had something important to tell them.

Every event in Allison's life was of great importance to them all. From the moment of her birth, she had been the center of their lives and the focus of their fiercely protective love. They wanted only the best for her—perfect love, boundless happiness, untarnished joy—and what they asked in return, so very little really, was simply that Allison not be taken from them as her mother had been. But despite her loving determination to honor their simple request, more than once in her twenty-seven and a half years, Allison had nearly died.

The cancellation of Allison's plans to marry was hardly a matter of life and death, of course, and yet, in a way, to her family it was. They believed that Stephen would be as fiercely protective of her as they had always been, and would love her long after they

3

were gone, and, most important, they believed that he would make no demands of her that might cause her to die as her mother had. His three brothers could add the requisite branches to the Gentry family tree, and since Stephen himself didn't feel strongly the need to ensure his own immortality through children, he would never ask of his wife that she have a baby.

The broken engagement between Allison Parish Whitaker and Stephen Worth Gentry also meant that four of the Lone Star State's greatest fortunes would never wed. But that was of absolutely no consequence to Allison's loved ones. The Parishes and Whitakers knew all too well the clichéd truth that even the most extravagant of riches could not guarantee happiness.

"What happened, darling?" Pauline Whitaker asked finally, breaking the shocked silence, her voice filled with loving concern. "Did Stephen—"

"No, Gran," Allison assured. "I was the one who called it off. I told Stephen last night."

"But why, dear?"

The gentle, logical question came from Douglas Whitaker, Allison's paternal grandfather. On his beloved face Allison saw the bewilderment that they all surely felt. From her family's perspective Stephen Gentry would have been an ideal husband, protective and kind.

But what about love? Allison wanted to ask. What about love and passion and the sharing of dreams? Perhaps no man would ever fall in love with just plain Allison, her heart not her fortune, but . . .

Somehow Allison couldn't confess to her grandfather her romantic wish to be loved for herself, nor could she admit that Stephen had seemed far more upset about the marriage of wealth that now would not occur than he had been about any loss of love.

Shrugging softly, she answered vaguely, "I just decided that I wasn't really ready to get married. I'm sorry. I know this is going to be embarrassing, especially at this late date, but I just couldn't do it."

"It's not unusual to get cold feet as the wedding nears," Iris Parish offered. "Are you really sure you want to cancel altogether?"

"Yes. I really am. It's not an impulsive decision. I've been thinking about it for some time, long before the call came from my publisher."

"What call?" Robert Parish asked. Then, smiling fondly at the granddaughter who reminded him so much of the daughter he had lost, he guessed, "They want you to do another book of photographs of Texas?"

"They want me to do another book, yes, but not of Texas."

Allison's gaze fell then, to the hands in her lap. They were folded together, ladylike as always, but Allison alone knew how tightly clasped they were. As she stared at the white knot her hands had become, she focused on the shining silver bracelet that encircled her left wrist. The bracelet was not simple jewelry, a glittering adornment worn only on select occasions. Rather, it was a necessity, worn always.

The message engraved in crimson on Allison's medical alert bracelet sent an ominous reminder of her precarious fragility. And now, as she read the familiar bloodred words, another reminder danced in her mind: telling her family that she was canceling the Dallas wedding of the decade just two weeks before she was supposed to walk down the gardenia-festooned aisle was absolutely trivial compared with what she was about to say next. They wanted what was best for her, what was safest and happiest, and if marriage to Stephen wasn't it, then so be it. But what Allison Parish Whitaker planned to do in lieu of entering into safe, if loveless, matrimony would not be perceived by those who loved her as best at all, or safe, or happy.

Allison drew a steadying breath, looked up from the silver-

and-crimson bracelet, and said, "They want me to do a book about Hong Kong."

As she'd expected, *Hong Kong* caused a fresh round of startled silence. But there was another consequence, something Allison hadn't anticipated at all. Virtually in unison, all four grandparents cast anxious, searching glances at her father.

For as long as Allison could remember, there had been a ritual to these family conferences about her life. She would state her case, and her grandparents would gently but firmly voice their concerns, and only after all their worries had been fully expressed would her father enter the discussion. In Allison's memory, neither Garrett Whitaker's parents nor in-laws had ever solicited his opinion until their own arguments were exhausted—because, almost always, Garrett sided with his daughter.

But now all four grandparents were looking at him, and they seemed to be imploring him to join what Allison knew would be their own fervent pleas that she not travel to Hong Kong.

Why? Allison wondered. Did Hong Kong have some special significance for him? Or was its meaning for him the same as it was for the rest of them, derived merely from its geographical proximity to Vietnam?

Allison couldn't read her father's thoughts. But it was clear that, as always, Garrett Whitaker wasn't going to offer any comment until everyone else had finished.

Allison waited politely for one of her grandparents to speak, but when the silence began to verge on awkwardness, it was she who finally embellished, "What actually happened was that a man named James Drake called my publisher. He's a real-estate developer who lives in Hong Kong, and he's building a new hotel there, the Jade Palace, and a month ago, quite by chance, he saw a copy of *Lone Star Serenade,* and now he wants me to take photographs of Hong Kong that will be on permanent display in his hotel."

Allison faltered then, needing a breath and suddenly finding herself in a struggle for air that was far more than simply the need to replenish oxygen following her rush of words. She was suffocating, smothered by love, so tightly bound by its protective cocoon that she would never be able to spread her wings unless she forcefully broke free. That was what she was doing now, an almost desperate act of rebellion fueled by surprising hope and not-so-surprising guilt. Her family loved her deeply, and that was wonderful, she was so lucky to be so loved, but . . . *she was suffocating.*

"James Drake," Robert Parish echoed finally. "There's an Englishman named James Drake, a land developer with major holdings throughout the world."

"This is the same James Drake."

When her quiet confirmation evoked a look of obvious surprise on her grandfather's face—amazement, in fact, that a man like James Drake would actually have selected her to take the photographs for his new hotel—Allison felt an unfamiliar quiver of irritation. Despite sales of *Lone Star Serenade* that had exceeded all expectations, the people who loved her continued to view her photography as a charming hobby, not a serious career.

Allison conquered her annoyance quickly. After all, her grandfather's surprise was no more than what she herself had felt when her publisher called to announce that the real-estate mogul wanted *her.* And, like her grandfather, her surprise had rapidly given way to amazement when, with her permission, James Drake had called her directly, on her private line in the mansion where she had lived her entire life.

The deep, solemn, elegantly accented British voice not only told her that he *wanted* her for his Jade Palace, but that he *needed* her as well. There was far more to her photography than an imaginative interplay of color and shape, he said. Somehow she captured "essence." And that was what he wanted for his hotel, portraits of Hong Kong that would celebrate its heart, its spirit, its very soul.

James Drake believed in her talent. He regarded her photographs as works of art and planned to display them amid the priceless treasures that would be housed in his Jade Palace. Allison could have defiantly told her grandfather that James Drake had confidence in her ability, even if *he* didn't. But she never would have made such a hurtful proclamation. She loved him far too much, and she knew without question that although Robert Parish might not consider her a gifted artist, he absolutely believed her to be a priceless treasure in her own right.

A priceless treasure who is going to Hong Kong, Allison vowed silently as she awaited the bombardment of objections that were bound to come. She welcomed her grandparents' worries and was determined to lovingly allay each and every one. To that end, she had spent most of the past two weeks preparing for this moment. The lavender-and-cream bedroom that had so recently been cluttered with magazines for the new bride was now a jumble of information about Hong Kong.

Allison was already fascinated by the British Crown Colony in the South China Sea—the quietly impassioned voice of James Drake had accomplished that—and as she viewed videos and eagerly worked her way through a small library of books, her enchantment only crescendoed. It felt as if her delicate wings were struggling for freedom . . . and they were promising to soar to the moon once they were free.

"You can't go to Hong Kong, Allison." It was Iris Parish who broke the lingering silence. But she did not launch the assault against Hong Kong for which Allison had so carefully prepared. Instead, her words were much closer to home. "Your doctors are here. What if something happened? What if you needed blood?"

Allison ached at the fear she heard in her grandmother's voice and was quite startled by the emotional words themselves. She had not expected the issue of her health to be raised. True, her doctors were in Dallas. But it was also true, and they all knew it, that if something did happen—if, ever again, she did need blood—it would make no difference whether she was in Dallas or Hong Kong. Both locales boasted state-of-the-art health care, of course. But modern medicine had nothing to offer Allison, nor—medically—did her family. They had all been tested, and it had been with a sense of great sadness—and great helplessness—that her father and grandparents had learned that their blood would be as harmful to Allison as the blood of a stranger.

"Nothing's going to happen to me, Grandmother," she assured gently. "I'll be very careful. I promise."

"But still, Allison," Pauline Whitaker insisted, "Hong Kong *is* dangerous."

"Dangerous?"

"There are hurricanes there, aren't there? *Terrible* ones."

"Yes, there are hurricanes," Allison replied calmly, relieved that the discussion had shifted to one in which her assurances could be based on fact—not merely on hope. "Although in that part of the world they're called typhoons. But Hong Kong is ready for them. Weather satellites identify the impending storm while it's still at sea, long before it reaches land, and by the time it arrives, the boats are in typhoon shelters and the buildings, which are constructed to withstand the force of the wind, are secure."

"You can never fully anticipate nor control a natural disaster," Douglas Whitaker said flatly. "And, Allison, what about the political disasters? Remember Tiananmen Square?"

"Of course I do, as does everyone who lives in Hong Kong. The territory doesn't officially revert to Chinese sovereignty until July 1997, and in the meantime Governor Patten is working very hard to institute democratic reforms, to make sure that the freedoms Hong Kong has enjoyed will continue to flourish after the turnover."

Douglas arched a loving eyebrow and couldn't suppress a proud smile. His granddaughter had done her homework. "But," he said gently, "there's absolutely no guarantee that he'll succeed."

"No, there isn't," Allison admitted. That was what James Drake had told her as well. Despite the Joint Declaration, the future of Hong Kong was uncertain. There could be devastation beyond imagination. Which was why, the aristocratic voice had added solemnly, his Jade Palace—and her photographs—were so very important. The hotel would be a symbol of the unique harmony that was Hong Kong, the improbable yet spectacular marriage of East and West, of mystical dragon and majestic lion. The Jade Palace would be built to survive whatever destiny had in store for the "Fragrant Harbour," a permanent monument to the splendor that once had been. Allison's photographs would be enduring symbols as well, irrevocable snapshots of history. "But Hong Kong is safe now, and it's considered by many people to be the most exciting and cosmopolitan place on earth."

"It's too far away," Pauline said with an unmistakable note of finality.

Allison knew the distance between Dallas and Hong Kong in all the conventional ways it could be measured: eighty-three hundred miles by air; fourteen hours plus one day by time zone; and, remarkably, only a few seconds by phone and with a clarity that made it feel like it was just next door.

But the way her grandmother was measuring the distance wasn't conventional at all. It was a measurement of the heart, and Allison saw in her grandmother's eyes that the anguish was evergreen still, despite the vast distance of years.

But Gran! she wanted to cry. Hong Kong is *not* Vietnam. Yes, at their nearest borders, the two are only four hundred miles apart, closer than Dallas is to New Orleans. But Hong Kong is not Vietnam, and this is now, not twenty-eight years ago, and . . . "I really hope that you'll all come visit me while I'm there."

"Oh, no, Allison. If you go, you'll just have to come back as soon as possible. Hong Kong is a very small place, isn't it? Surely you won't need to be there for more than a few weeks."

"I'll need to be there at least until the hotel opens," Allison replied quietly. And, she thought, if I don't have all the photographs I want for the book, I'll be there even longer.

"Until the hotel opens?" Iris repeated with horror. "But when will that be?"

"Everything in Hong Kong happens much more quickly than it does here," Allison explained, recalling James Drake's reply to her own surprise that a hotel that was not yet under construction, and that was going to be as grand as the Jade Palace, would be completed in less than seven months. Everything has to be accomplished faster in Hong Kong, he had told her, because its invisible clock is ticking relentlessly toward destiny. "So even though the ground breaking isn't for two more weeks, the hotel's grand opening will be on New Year's Eve . . . on my birthday."

"You're not going to be in Hong Kong for Christmas!"

"Yes, I am." There had been a little apology—but not much—when James explained to her that the finishing touches, including the displaying of her photographs, would be done during the Christmas holidays. She didn't have to be there for that, of course, but if she was, she could oversee the placement and lighting. "I'm going to be in Hong Kong for Christmas. But what I thought, what I hoped, was that we could all spend the holidays there. I've done some checking and have discovered that there are wonderful cruises of the South Pacific and Far East. There's one that begins in Tahiti on December fifth and reaches Hong Kong on the twenty-fourth. I have the brochure in my room. I know how much you love cruising."

It was true. In recent years the four grandparents, who had been close friends since before Allison's father was born, had developed a passion for cruising. They had traveled virtually everywhere—except, of course, the Orient.

Hong Kong is *not* Vietnam, Allison wanted to cry again. Please come celebrate Christmas with me, and the grand opening of the Jade Palace, and my birthday. Please, for me and for you, put your pain and your anger *and your prejudice* to rest at last.

Allison knew that her grandparents would make no concessions whatsoever today. Indeed, between now and the time she boarded the plane for Hong Kong, they would hold fast to the belief that she should not go, and they would be inexhaustible in their attempts to get her to change her mind.

In the past she had always acceded to their wishes, not wanting them to worry about her and knowing that their concern was born of love.

But this time was different.

This time Allison Parish Whitaker was going to do what she wanted.

She had to.

As a tense silence fell again Allison felt flutters of fear. Despite her own desperate need to be free, would she yield to their wishes as always?—because, after all, she loved them deeply, too.

She battled the fear with a daring thought. James had given her the unlisted phone number of his penthouse in Hong Kong and had told her to call him at any time for any reason. She could call him right now. She would confirm again that she was coming to Hong Kong, and in reply the deep, quiet, elegant voice would tell her once more how pleased he was that she had agreed to be part of his most important project.

Allison wanted to dash to the privacy of her bedroom and make that bold call. But she didn't. She couldn't. She was far too well-bred to make such a precipitous exit, and she loved them far too much to compound their worry by doing something so totally out of character.

The silence might have lasted forever, and she might have suffocated then and there, but she was rescued by the man who had rescued her so many times before, the father who had been to Vietnam and whose losses had perhaps been the greatest of all.

With a single word Garrett Whitaker could prevent Allison from going to Hong Kong. If he was opposed to her plan, she would, without protest, remain in Dallas. It was her father's reaction that Allison feared the most—and that gave her the greatest hope. More than once she had unwittingly flirted with death, but because he loved her, he had conquered his own fears to allow her life to be as normal as possible.

It was her father who had taught Allison to ride horseback, and to drive a car, and even to pilot a plane.

Now it was he who spoke.

"I think it's time for Allison and me to go flying."

"When are you planning to leave?" Garrett asked when they were high above the ground. He was at the controls and Allison was beside him. They had done this hundreds of times, when he was teaching her to fly and after, at times like this, when there were issues to discuss in private.

"A week from today."

"Where will you stay?"

"At the Trade Winds. It's a Drake hotel. In addition to the regular guest rooms there are a number of residential apartments, which is what I'll have. It's in the heart of Hong Kong's financial district and caters to an international business clientele. It should be very nice—and very safe."

"I'm sure it will be. But . . . I wonder if you'll be lonely."

Perhaps, Allison thought. But there was a difference between being lonely and being alone, wasn't there? She had never really been on her own, and now she needed to be, to spread her wings . . . if she even *had* wings. "I can call you, can't I?"

"Of course you can." Garrett smiled. "Anytime. All the time."

"I imagine I'll meet people." *I'll meet James.* The thought came without warning and once born had a life of its own: James, who is undoubtedly as sophisticated and elegant and passionate as his voice . . . and who is almost certainly happily married . . . and who, even if he's single, is not likely to want to waste his valuable time on a hopelessly unsophisticated, possible butterfly-to-be who knows virtually nothing about the world outside her luxurious cocoon. Forcing the troubling thought back into its own cocoon, Allison said, "Oh, I forgot to mention that the builder for the Jade Palace will be Sam Coulter. He used to work for you, didn't he?"

"Yes, he did." After a thoughtful pause, he added, "I'm glad Sam will be in Hong Kong, Allison. You'll like him."

There was nothing in Garrett's tone or words to suggest hidden layers of meaning. But Allison knew her father well enough to deduce his protective thoughts.

"I don't need a bodyguard, Dad! And besides, Sam is going to be incredibly busy. Even though it's apparently par for the course for everything to happen at a breakneck pace in Hong Kong, to go from ground breaking to grand opening in just over six months seems impossible."

"If anyone can do it, it's Sam."

They fell silent then, and for a long time father and daughter simply gazed straight ahead, toward the golden rays of sunlight that were fading over Texas but that already shone brightly on a new day in Hong Kong.

Finally Allison asked quietly, "Is this okay with you?"

Garrett turned to her before answering. "I get the impression it's something you need to do."

"Yes," Allison replied, her heart filled with love, as always, for her father.

Love and worry. Garrett Whitaker had devoted his life to his daughter and to the memory of his wife. He had never found a new love, and to the best of Allison's knowledge he had never even searched. To the world he seemed content, fulfilled; but Allison knew that something compelled him to fly for hours, just as she often did, solitary journeys into the clouds, chasing rainbows and dreams.

Something was missing from her father's life.

Allison feared that something was happiness.

Maybe if I go to Hong Kong, she thought, maybe if I prove that I can be safe and happy on my own, it will give him a chance to find what's been missing all this time.

But, she realized, her father hadn't yet said that it was all right with him for her to go, and as he had stared toward the horizon— toward Hong Kong—dark shadows of worry had crossed his face.

"Is there something about Hong Kong?" she asked softly. "Something I don't know?"

Oh, yes, there was something about Hong Kong, something no one knew and something far different from what his parents and in-laws imagined. To them, Hong Kong was where Garrett had been when their hearts were shattered. They blamed Hong Kong for keeping him from them, for *hiding* him when they needed him so desperately. They assumed he felt the same way.

But he didn't. To Garrett Whitaker, Hong Kong was paradise.

"Have you been to Hong Kong, Dad?"

"Yes, once, very briefly, a long time ago."

"And?"

"And it was wonderful, Allison. Magical."

"Then it's all right with you if I go?"

He would miss her, and he would worry about her, but how could he possibly say no? Hong Kong was where he had spent the happiest week of his life. "Yes. Of course it's all right."

"And you'll come visit?"

"We'll see," he answered vaguely. Then, before returning his dark green gaze to the horizon, he smiled and added softly, "I hope so."

Garrett could not promise his daughter that he would visit her in Hong Kong . . . because there was another promise of love, made long ago—but forever—to Juliana.

Juliana . . . the woman he had loved as no other.

Juliana . . . the mother of his other daughter, Allison's half sister, the child of love he had left behind.

PART ONE

CHAPTER 1

Aberdeen Harbour
Hong Kong Island
June 1960

She wasn't Juliana Kwan then, nor did she speak flawless English, nor was she at home on land. Then, at age thirteen, her Chinese name meant Tranquil Sea, and Cantonese was the only language she spoke, and not once had she ever set foot on solid ground.

She lived on *Pearl Moon*, her father's fishing junk, in the floating city in Aberdeen Harbour. Only the men went ashore, and sometimes only near the shore, just close enough to sell the fish that were their livelihood. Other goods were sold as well, piecework done by women and girls while the men and boys were off at sea. Some families supplemented their fishing income by assembling batteries, or cloisonné pillboxes, or paper flowers, or plastic dolls.

The women of Tranquil Sea's family—her mother, grand-mother, and the cousins and aunts who lived on adjoining boats—spent endless hours adorning bolts of satin and silk with beads, sequins, and pearls. The elaborately beaded fabrics, which would one day become elegant dresses and romantic wedding gowns, were sold to a dress shop on Queen's Road West, on the other side of Hong Kong Island, in a world that none of them would ever see.

Tranquil Sea knew the island only from her vantage point in the harbor. From there it seemed immense—and formidable. The jagged green peaks were far more than mountains. They were the silhouettes of slumbering dragons. She had no idea how far away the dress shop was, nor any concept of the cosmopolitan city that lay beyond the dragons, nor any expectation that she would ever journey there.

She did, however, have some idea of life just beyond the water's edge. From the deck of *Pearl Moon* she could see the fishing village of Aberdeen, the pink-and-green buildings nestled into the hillside and the constant flow of cars and trucks that traveled along the harborside road. Sometimes the cars brought people from the other side of the island, wealthy men and women who temporarily abandoned their Rolls-Royces to venture onto the water, journeying by sampan to the festive floating restaurants, or to their expensive pleasure junks moored in the most sheltered part of the harbor.

Tranquil Sea knew that she would never be a part of the life on shore. In a few years a marriage would be arranged for her, to the son of another fisherman, and once wed, she would leave *Pearl Moon* to live with her new husband's family. She would have children, boys who would fish and girls who would clean the fish—and cook and sew and one day marry the sons of fishermen—and who, like her, would never set foot on land. That was how it had been for generations. The people who lived in this community of wooden boats and salty waves disdained any other way of life. If anyone ever dreamed of living ashore, it was a hidden dream, never spoken aloud, because to do so would have been a betrayal of family, of tradition, of destiny.

But Tranquil Sea wondered about life on land, and sometimes she even allowed herself to imagine the glittering world that lay beyond the emerald dragons. She felt guilty for having such forbidden imaginings and yet the dreaming part inside her would not be still, awakening within her a dangerous longing to see the place where the beaded fabrics she created became romantic gowns, and perhaps even to see one of the joyous brides, and . . .

She never allowed such unforgivable fantasies more than a few precious moments of life before banishing them, knowing they would return again to tempt, to taunt, to beckon.

This is where I belong, she reminded herself. I am a child of the sea.

Tranquil Sea's life was one of great certainty—and of even greater uncertainty. That she would always live on water was a certainty, as was her destiny to marry the man her parents chose. But the predictable scenario that had been scripted from the moment of her birth was set against a backdrop that was wholly unpredictable and potentially devastating. The city of floating teak was in constant peril of self-destruction. An overturned oil lamp or a casually tended cooking fire could create an inferno that would consume the entire community of wooden boats—and the families that dwelled within them—in a matter of moments. Fire was a man-made peril, but an even greater danger came from the sea itself, from waves made monstrous by a raging wind.

Tranquil Sea had heard horrifying stories of the great *tai-foos*, the big winds that killed thousands upon thousands, but for the first thirteen years of her life Aberdeen had been spared. Yes, there had been storms. Ferocious ones, she thought. But they were nothing, the adults told her, mere sighs compared with the huffs and puffs of a true typhoon.

Her family believed that Tranquil Sea herself was the reason Aberdeen had been so blessed. Her birth, on May 1, coincided with the birthday celebration for Tin Hau, the Motherly Empress of Heaven and Goddess of the Sea. In honor of their patron goddess, fishermen decorated their junks with flowers and lanterns, and then, in bright-colored flotillas, they journeyed to her many seaside temples to pay homage. There, amid sounding gongs and prancing paper dragons, they lighted firecrackers and joss sticks and made lavish offerings of symbolic money, pink dumplings, and sweet fruit.

It was while her father, uncles, and grandfather were honoring Tin Hau at her temple in Joss House Bay that Tranquil Sea was born. And that, her family decided, cast a magical spell on the wind and the waves of Aberdeen.

But the magical spell came to a catastrophic end six weeks after Tranquil Sea's thirteenth birthday. Was the magic always destined to be shattered? she would wonder forever. Or had she caused its ruin herself by displeasing Tin Hau? Had she permitted fantasies of the forbidden life on land to dance too long in her mind before banishing them to their shadows?

Tranquil Sea's entire family perished before her eyes. The boats that only moments before had seemed so safe simply disintegrated. She was certain that her own death would soon follow. She had lived on water all her life, but she could not swim. Swimming would have been quite futile, anyway, against the rage of waves. She clung to a plank of teak, all that remained of *Pearl Moon*, a scrap of wood as foolishly defiant as she; and even though her heart was torn apart by the violence around her and the devastating loss of everyone she had ever known and loved, she could not let go. She could not will her own death.

It would happen soon enough. In the storm-tossed moments until she joined her loved ones beneath the sea, she would honor their memory by remembering them, by grieving for them, by keeping them alive within her for as long as she could.

She awakened on the beach at dawn. The sky was gold and the air was still and the sea was emerald glass. Last night's scene of death seemed a mirage, a terrifying phantom of her imagination, a harsh and horrifying warning to a mind that had strayed too far into fanciful longings for forbidden worlds.

But as her gaze lifted from the kelp-strewn sand to the harbor that had been her home, she saw the truth with brutal clarity: last night had been neither mirage, nor phantom, nor warning. It was real. The place on the emerald sea that had been her home, her entire universe, had simply vanished. No junks bobbed languidly on its smooth green surface. No sampans sped jauntily from one cluster of boats to the next. Everything was gone without a trace, swallowed whole.

When, eventually, she drew her gaze from the place where once there had been such happiness, her eyes beheld a virtual miracle. In the distance, across the harbor, she saw boats, entire islands of them. Somehow they had survived, as had the floating restaurants, and many of the gleaming varnished yachts were also unscathed. Sampans darted in and out, and from this distance their hectic activity seemed almost normal; but in truth, on this day after so much death, their frenzied bustling was merely a symbol of the frantic search for loved ones lost at sea.

Tranquil Sea knew no one in that part of the harbor. But, undoubtedly, her father had friends there. Perhaps the boy she was destined to marry lived there. Even though she did not yet know his name, it was quite possible that the arrangements had already been made between the fathers.

She was alive, perhaps he was alive. Despite the devastation, the certainties of her life could go on. And even if there was no fiancé awaiting her, the people on those faraway boats would welcome her, an orphan from the monstrous storm. She needed only to begin walking along the shore and she would be rescued, returned to the scents of fish and sea and teak and smoke . . . and to the certainties of tradition . . . and to the ever-present threat of another typhoon.

No. The protest came from every cell in her body and from the thousand weeping places in her shattered heart. She could not return. She *would* not. She had been spared a gasping death, and more: she had been flung onto land, that forbidden place which the whispers deep within her had always insisted was where she truly belonged.

This was her destiny, where she was meant to be, where she would begin again.

Her slender legs knew all the rhythms of the sea, its soft sighs and lazy yawns, its treacherous lurches and hazardous heaves. In thirteen years her steps had never faltered. Ballerina graceful, she could leap from the bow of *Pearl Moon* to the bow of the next junk and the next, anticipating every pitch and sigh, dancing, twirling, soaring across the waves.

But it was with great difficulty that Tranquil Sea walked on land. The sand was so unyielding, so different from the fluid buoyancy of the sea. She staggered, her catlike balance gone, and there was such dizziness. This was the land sickness about which her father and uncles complained, yet another reason to disdain life on shore.

This will pass, she told her swirling head as she stumbled from the hardness of the sandy beach to the even greater hardness of Fu Lam Road. It *must.* I cannot return to the sea. I have to walk to the other side of the island, no matter how far it is, and find the dress shop on Queen's Road West. That is my destiny now. That is where I belong.

Fu Lam Road was littered with palm fronds and wooden debris from the decimated shanties of Aberdeen. It was cluttered, as well, with traffic. People from the north side of the island had come to see the devastation for themselves, and there were trucks, the same ones that came every day, searching for what was left of yesterday's catch. The trucks represented the greatest truth about a life dependent on the whims of nature: there was little time to mourn the past, because today was already here and today needed to be survived.

As Tranquil Sea made her way through Aberdeen she drew little notice. Her crumpled black tunic and trousers were still damp from the sea, and she wore no shoes, and her waist-length black hair was wind-tangled and sea-snarled, and her pretty face was ravaged by her near drowning and her overwhelming loss. But those around her were damp as well, and their losses, too, were great, and they, too, had nearly drowned.

It wasn't until she was beyond Aberdeen, on the road that wove a winding path through the mountains of dragons, that the barefoot waif, so clearly of the sea, began to attract curious stares from passersby. Some merely slowed to see the face that belonged to the slim body with the staggering gait, but others called out to her that she was going in the wrong direction.

Finally, when the words came from a man who had stopped his truck beside her, and had a kindly face that reminded her of her drowned grandfather, she answered defiantly, "No, I'm not going in the wrong direction! I'm on my way to Queen's Road West."

"Do you know how far away that is?"

"It doesn't matter!"

"Where is your family?"

"Gone . . . except for my aunt. She has a dress shop on Queen's Road West. That's why I'm going there. To find her."

The kindly face greeted her with skepticism, but after a moment he said, "Let me give you a ride, then. I happen to be driving right by Queen's Road West."

She had not imagined getting into any type of vehicle until her land sickness was conquered, but to the man who looked like her grandfather, she said "Thank you" and with wobbling legs climbed into the cab of his truck.

The dizziness was with her still, and it came more quickly,

more terrifyingly, because the speed of the truck was as foreign to her as the land. So it was through a whirling blur, an ever-spinning kaleidoscope, that she beheld for the first time the splendor of the world beyond the emerald mountains: the gigantic towers of glass gleaming ebony and gold beneath the summer sun, the fleet of freighters rocking gently on the green-and-silver waters of Victoria Harbour, the astounding crush of cars and buses and humanity.

The typhoon that in a single breath had taken away her entire world seemed not to have even touched the northern side of Hong Kong Island. It was a usual Wednesday here. Goods were being traded and vast fortunes were being made.

When they reached Central, the whirling kaleidoscope stood still for a moment, as if it were important that she see clearly the girls who strolled beneath the skyscrapers. Only slightly older than she, they walked in small groups, laughing and talking. They wore stylish dark silk suits, and their shining black hair was shoulder length, and their strides were purposeful yet buoyant, confident—and so steady.

I will become one of them, she vowed. One day I, too, will be able to dance on the land with my head held high.

"This is Queen's Road West," the truck driver said, breaking the silence that had traveled with them since Aberdeen. "Do you know where your aunt's shop is?"

"Not exactly, but I'll recognize it when I see it." With that, because the truck had stopped in traffic—and because the kindly face seemed skeptical again—she hurriedly thanked him, opened the door, and landed with a dizzying jolt on the unyielding pavement.

Tranquil Sea knew precisely how she would recognize the dress shop. She would see the distinctive patterns of beads and sequins created by her mother and grandmother. A drowning wave of sadness swept through her at the memory of the nimble fingers of the loved ones who had so patiently taught her their craft and with whom there had been such happy times spent sewing together. Now they were gone, and she was in this forbidden place about which she had dreamed, and if only, please, *please*, she could undo everything that had happened by undreaming those dishonorable dreams . . .

She closed her eyes, and felt the sway of her slender body, moving still as if at sea, and prayed desperately that when she opened them again she would awaken from this nightmare. She would be on the deck of *Pearl Moon*, and her mother would be calling to her that it was time to begin the day's work, and with such joy she would scamper inside, not even glancing toward shore and vowing never more to dream of the world beyond the dragons.

But when she opened her eyes she was in the new world still, and despite all the spinning strangeness, there was something hauntingly familiar about this alien place, something oddly welcoming. As she wandered from shop to shop, amid glossy bolts of satin and silk, her eyes squinted against the shining brilliance and she was reminded of sunrise on the sea, the almost blinding glitter of golden rays on shimmering emerald.

The fabric shops that lined Queen's Road West were quite small. Their brightly colored wares overflowed onto the street like exuberant rainbows. The best of what each shop had to offer was placed at the very front. It was in this place of honor that she came upon her own designs. The creations of her loved ones were displayed as well, slightly farther back, and that caused another flooding wave of sadness. She staggered past her own designs to theirs, gently caressing them as her eyes at last filled with tears.

When Tranquil Sea informed the truck driver that she was going to Queen's Road West to find her aunt, the only surviving member of her family, it was the first lie she had ever told.

But her words were more prophecy than falsehood. Vivian Jong, the proprietress of the dress shop, became her family.

It was because of Vivian that Tranquil Sea truly survived, that she was allowed to grieve and then be able to go on. Vivian was a sprightly sixty-five, widowed for almost forty years, childless, wealthy, joyfully independent, and eccentrically liberated. Hers was one of the most successful dress shops in Hong Kong, and her seamstresses not only enjoyed a pleasant working environment—in a city well known for its sweatshops—but excellent wages as well.

Vivian Jong's belief in fairness in the workplace was just the beginning of her revolutionary ideas. A woman could be every bit as successful as a man, she asserted. Even a Chinese woman, and even in British-ruled Hong Kong. Despite the constraints placed on Chinese women by centuries of tradition, in Hong Kong there was extraordinary freedom. The laissez-faire capitalism that flourished here was both gender-blind and race-blind.

A Chinese woman could establish a major international house of fashion, Vivian told the girl who had become the child she had always wanted. Of course, that Chinese woman needed to be especially smart, endlessly diligent, and passionately committed to her dream. And because Hong Kong was a British Crown Colony, not only did she need a proper Englishwoman's name, but she must have flawless mastery of the Queen's English as well.

Tranquil Sea became Juliana Kwan, and the grateful orphan of the sea soon became the keeper of Vivian Jong's daring dream. Juliana wanted to pursue their dream right away so that it could be achieved—in all its splendor—while Vivian was alive to savor it.

"No, Juliana," Vivian said softly, in Cantonese, to the girl who had only just begun to learn the necessary English. "It will be many years before you are truly ready. You must be patient. But it will happen. You will make it happen. You have a magical gift that cannot be denied. One day Pearl Moon will be the most desired label in the world."

"Pearl Moon?" Juliana echoed, frowning, torn between the woman she had come to love on land and those she had loved and lost at sea. "I thought the label would be Vivian Jong."

"Thank you, my dear." Vivian's eyes sparkled with love—and with wisdom. "But it must be Pearl Moon. We both know that."

They were on the veranda of Vivian's house, a charming Victorian on Mount Cameron Road in the green hills overlooking Happy Valley. The balmy air was fragrant with the perfumes of plumeria and jasmine, and the sky was brilliantly clear, without the hazy veil that sometimes blurred the horizon to the north. On this crystal-clear day, as they spoke of faraway dreams, the towering black mountains of the People's Republic of China seemed close enough to touch.

As she stared at the ominous darkness of those mountains, a troubled frown touched Vivian's youthful face. "Someday, Juliana, you will need a full British passport."

"British?" Juliana repeated with surprise. Almost from birth, she had heard about the British. They were evil barbarians, immoral pirates who had poisoned her ancestors with opium—"foreign mud"—and then lured them into an unfair and bloody war. The Chinese fought valiantly for their land, but they were vastly outmatched by the military might of the British Empire, and at the end of the devastating war, Hong Kong had been seized by the British as imperial booty. From her parents, Tranquil Sea had learned of the ancient hatred toward the *gweilos*, the "pale ghosts" who had stolen from the Celestial Empire the most valuable deep-water harbor between Shanghai and Singapore. From Vivian, Juliana Kwan had learned a more contemporary truth, and a more practical one: to succeed in modern-day Hong Kong one needed to play by British rules. That made sense. But to *become* British? "No . . . I couldn't."

"But you must." Vivian drew her worried gaze from the black mountains of China and smiled gently at Juliana. "You'll only be fifty in 1997. That may sound old to you today, my little love, but it's not. You will be young enough to move Pearl Moon to England, to begin again there, if you must."

The history lessons taught in the floating city of junks in Aberdeen Harbour had focused bitterly on the First Opium War. It was as a consequence of that war, in the 1842 Treaty of Nanking, that Hong Kong Island and the villages of fishing junks nestled in its harbors were ceded to the British. Tranquil Sea had never been told about the Second Opium War, which came eighteen years later, following which Kowloon Peninsula became a possession of the British Empire; nor did she know that on July 1, 1898, England had agreed to lease from China, for a period of ninety-nine years, the land known as the New Territories.

"Nineteen ninety-seven?" Juliana asked. "What happens then?"

"The British lease expires and the sovereignty of Hong Kong reverts to China."

"But . . . isn't that what we want?"

"I don't know, my darling. Perhaps not. It's impossible to know how things will be in the future." Vivian could not foretell the future, but she had vivid memories of the past. In 1949, when China fell to communism, a tide of refugees had flooded Hong Kong. And now, as scholars, authors, and artists were beginning to come under the harsh scrutiny of Chairman Mao and his followers, the numbers seeking asylum were increasing anew. Vivian looked at the gifted young artist who sat beside her and repeated quietly, "Someday, Juliana, to be safe, you will need a British passport."

CHAPTER 2

Victoria Peak
Hong Kong Island
April 1965

O
ne month before Juliana's eighteenth birthday and nearly
five years after the typhoon that had changed her life
forever, something happened that changed her life once
again—and again forever.

It wasn't a natural disaster this time, the violent whimsy of an
enraged goddess, but it came without warning, without omen,
and like the typhoon that had transformed her from a child of the
sea to a young woman of the land, it felt like destiny.

She had believed, when the winds shattered the magical spell
that had been cast over Aberdeen, that there would be no more
magic for her. But there was, magic and tragedy woven together,
embroidered like threads of silk in the tapestry of her life.

It was the second of April, almost twilight. Juliana had just
delivered an evening gown to a magistrate's wife on Old Peak
Road. She had come to the Peak in Vivian's chauffeured car, but
she had sent the driver home, wanting to linger at the summit as
the golden light of day faded into moonlit darkness.

Two narrow roads encircled Victoria Peak, creating a magnificent promenade through a lush forest of fan palms, banyans, and

camphor trees. Birds serenaded, and cicadas hummed, and drag-onflies darted in the foreground of Hong Kong's most breathtak-ing views. If one strolled the length of the Hong Kong Trail, one would find vistas of the entire island, including Aberdeen Har-bour and its floating city of junks. Juliana came to the Peak often, but she never journeyed to the southern side to view from the heights the place that had once been her home. Her life in Ab-erdeen was now a faraway and almost dreamlike memory. She had never returned. She doubted that she ever would.

Tonight, as always, she walked only along Lugard Road, on the northern side, stopping when she reached her favorite vantage point. The view was straight down, at once dizzying and spectacu-lar. She was high above even the most presumptuous of Hong Kong's skyscrapers, suspended in air, and as she peered down at the jewel-bright glitter of the lights below, her hands curled tightly around the sturdy wrought-iron guardrail along the trail's edge.

That was where Garrett Whitaker found her. The springtime sun was long gone, as was the pink-and-lavender sunset. The trail was faintly illuminated by the glow from the city below, but were it not for the silver light of the crescent moon, he wouldn't have seen her until he was so close that she would surely have heard his approach.

As it was, Garrett stopped a short distance away, surprised by the discovery that he was not alone and even more surprised by the realization that although he had come here for solitude, his privacy seemed undisturbed by her presence. Indeed, it was as though this exquisite woman haloed by moonlight was supposed to be here . . . waiting for him.

The sheer craziness of the thought almost made Garrett turn away in disgust—and concern. He was well acquainted with mad-ness. Over the past few months he had seen the insanity of war taint the minds of those around him. But, until this moment, he believed he had been able to remain distant from it, emotionally detached as always.

Garrett's ability to remain aloof was a trait—a flaw?—that had been with him all his life. It had merely been honed to perfection at the Naval Academy. He had other traits that made him an outstanding officer as well: integrity, self-discipline, calmness under fire. His nerves and heart were made of steel, but there were gentle places, too, for his family.

Because of their father's hard work, Garrett and Blake Whitaker had been born into great wealth. Neither Garrett nor his older brother had needed to enroll in the Naval Academy, or to become pilots who would go to war if the nation called. They could have attended Harvard or Yale, and they most assuredly could have avoided the conflict in Southeast Asia. But the Whitaker boys had a deep sense of patriotism. The freedoms that had enabled their dirt-poor father to achieve financial security for his family were freedoms for which they were willing to give their lives.

Blake and Garrett were both stationed in the Gulf of Tonkin, but on different aircraft carriers. Both flew combat missions over North Vietnam. Both were constantly tested by the madness of war. And both saw friends shot from the sky.

Garrett was able to talk to Blake only occasionally, but he knew without doubt that his older brother was not going mad. And neither was he.

The crazy idea that somehow he was destined to be here, now, with this breathtakingly lovely Chinese woman had nothing to do with war, but rather with Hong Kong itself, this mystical place where even he had become enchanted with the notion that the events of one's life were controlled by luck and winds and gods and dragons.

He was supposed to be here.

And she was supposed to be here.

And because this was Hong Kong, the man who had always imposed such tight control on his destiny—and on his heart—relinquished both to the gentle bidding of the silver moon. It was precisely at that moment, when Garrett yielded all the steel within

3 3

him to whatever the moon had in store, that Juliana turned to him, enticed by something she could not name, but that she had no wish to defy.

"I'm Garrett," he said softly as he moved toward her. With each step he saw her more clearly, the shining black shoulder-length hair caressed by the evening breeze, the dark eyes glittering far brighter than all the lights below, the full lips that parted slightly in wonder and in welcome.

More than once in the past five years Juliana had wondered why she worked so tirelessly to learn English, to speak it so flaw-lessly and with such regal elegance that anyone who heard it would believe she had been raised on a grand manor in England, not in a crowded city of fishing boats.

Now she knew why.

He was why.

"I'm Juliana."

What now? Garrett wondered, his mind disciplined as always, scripting, controlling, impatient and restless. Do I ask her if she feels it, too? Do I tell her that the Garrett Whitaker I have known for twenty-four years has never believed in love, much less in love at first sight, but that the man who is here with her now is falling in love . . . already has?

As he gazed at her lovely face and saw her serene joy, Garrett realized he didn't need to tell her anything. She already knew. And as to what would happen next? It would happen. If he be-lieved in the magic of Hong Kong, in the mystical mandates of the moon and the wind and the stars . . .

It was then that the wind intervened, as if in reply, a sudden whisper that made her moonlit black-silk hair dance and her slender silk-clad body shiver.

"You're cold," he said gently. I kept you waiting, didn't I? While I was lingering on the other side, looking down at Aberdeen Har-bour, you were here, despite the chill and the darkness, waiting for me. "Have dinner with me, Juliana. I'm staying at the Peninsula. We'll dine at Gaddi's. I've already made reservations, for myself, but I'm sure—"

Garrett's words were stopped as she shivered again and a shadow of fear touched her lovely face. Was he mad after all? Had he imagined an enchantment that existed only through his moon-crazed eyes? Was she trembling with fright because she had heard about the unquenchable lust of American sailors on leave from the war being waged such a short distance from this exotic paradise?

"Juliana?"

"The Peninsula?" she echoed softly, her mind a swirl of surprise and worry.

He was wearing the uniform of an American naval officer, and from what Juliana had heard virtually all visiting military men, both officer and enlisted, stayed on Hong Kong Island, in Wanchai mostly, with its all-night bars and easy sex for an easy price. But this naval officer was staying at Hong Kong's grandest hotel, located on Kowloon Peninsula, an eight-minute ferry ride across Victoria Harbour.

Juliana had not been on the water for five years and had privately decided that she never would be again. She would live her entire life on Hong Kong Island *and* she would realize the dream of Pearl Moon. She would design clothes for the wealthy women who lived in Hong Kong but who traveled extensively. If her designs were good, her name would travel with them and eventually others would come to Hong Kong to have their wardrobes designed. She would accomplish the dream without ever leaving the island, without ever again experiencing the terror of a gasping, suffocating death.

"We can go somewhere else, Juliana. Anywhere you want."

His gently spoken words drew her eyes to his, and it was then, as she looked up at the man who wanted her to cross the water with him, that Juliana knew the truth: this tall, dark stranger—

whose green eyes gleamed with inner fire—was the most important dream of all.

"The Peninsula is fine, Garrett. That's where I want to go."

By the time they took the Peak Tram down the mountainside and walked from Garden Road to the Star Ferry terminal, the breeze that had been a chilly caress had become a bitterly cold wind. Garrett draped his jacket over her delicate shoulders, and his arm cloaked her, too, but still, when Juliana saw the silver-tipped waves beckoning from the harbor, she trembled.

"I'm afraid of the water," she confessed. "I can't swim and—"

She stopped, realizing with a surprising yet confident certainty that she shouldn't tell him the truth about her past.

"And?"

"And it's a foolish fear, isn't it, for someone who lives on an island?"

"We don't have to go across, Juliana," Garrett said with a gentleness that had been born just for her. "But if we do, I promise that you'll be safe. I'm a very good swimmer, and I would never let anything happen to you, not ever."

When Juliana spoke again, her voice was soft, and yet strong. "I do want to go to Kowloon, Garrett. Tonight . . . with you."

The windblown roughness of Victoria Harbour wasn't dangerous. If it were, the ferries wouldn't be running. Indeed, Juliana thought as they crossed the gangplank, there was once a time when she regarded waves such as these with pure joy. True, such exuberant rocking could have caused mishaps with fire, but those blazing tragedies were rare, and frolicking waves were common, and on nights like this she had danced like a ballerina, leaping from rocking bow to rocking bow, meeting the surges, anticipating the valleys, in a graceful pas de deux with the sea.

Over the past five years she had become accustomed to the

motionlessness of land. The unyielding hardness that had once made her dancing sea legs stagger felt secure to her now—and safe. As she boarded the swaying ferryboat Juliana wondered if the nimble sea nymph she once had been would return, a familiar and happy memory.

But it didn't. Her legs were instantly unsteady and the pitching of the ferry felt hostile to her, as if the boat were trying to pull away from her, shunning the touch of her feet as she had so defiantly shunned forever the sea. Was Tin Hau, Goddess of the Sea, angered still by her betrayal?

If it hadn't been for Garrett, Juliana would have fallen. But the grace with which his longs legs conquered the earth stayed with him when he went to sea. His balance didn't falter, nor did his hold of her, and even when they were seated, he held her still, balancing her fear with his confidence, just as his strong, steady legs had found safe footing for them both.

"So beautiful," he murmured as the ferry departed the pier and began its short journey across the harbor to Tsim Sha Tsui on Kowloon.

Garrett was looking at her as he spoke, but the tenderness of his voice suddenly made Juliana so shy that when she lifted her eyes, she sought the view instead of him. It was a familiar scene, the nighttime skyline of Hong Kong from Victoria Harbour, but until now Juliana had known it only from photographs. Now, as she truly witnessed its dazzling splendor, she agreed, "It is beautiful."

Garrett smiled at her shy and lovely profile and waited until she turned to him. And when at last Juliana answered the silent call of his heart, he repeated softly, "So very beautiful."

As soon as they reached the Peninsula's peach-and-gold lobby, Juliana placed a call to Vivian. Her words were simple—she was with a naval pilot she'd met at the Peak—but they were so eloquently embellished by her obvious joy that Vivian's worries were promptly allayed. Since her fifteenth birthday, Juliana had been desired. But she had always viewed men warily, resolutely spurning their advances, interested only in her designs and in her dreams.

But now, because of an American pilot, Juliana had not only cast off her wariness, but she had conquered a fear that Vivian had begun to believe would be unconquerable. Still, to be sure, she repeated, "You're at the Peninsula, Juliana?"

"Yes. And it's every bit as magnificent as you've always told me," Juliana said quietly, remembering all the times when the harbor was as smooth as glass and Vivian suggested that they travel to the "Pen" for its famous high tea. "Garrett and I are going to have dinner here and . . ."

Juliana didn't know what would come next. She knew only that it was impossible that she would ever choose to leave him.

"You're safe with him," Vivian said, a statement not a question, because the joy in Juliana's voice had already given her the answer.

"Yes."

"Then I won't worry about you."

Gaddi's was one of Hong Kong's most celebrated restaurants. Royalty dined here, as did presidents and playwrights, movie stars and shipping moguls, and powerful taipans with their elegant tai tais.

Crystal chandeliers from Paris sparkled overhead, and at their feet lay ankle-deep Tai Ping carpets, and nearby was the priceless coromandel screen, circa 1670, from the Emperor's Summer Palace in Beijing, and in front of them, served on the finest of porcelain, was stunningly presented French cuisine.

But Juliana and Garrett were virtually unaware of their lavish surroundings. They were lost in the wonder of their love, not wanting to take their eyes from each other, not even for a second. Both sensed how precious each moment was, how fleeting, how rare.

It was a magical world of desire and dreams, of soft words and softer smiles, of truth and of lies.

Garrett told Juliana no lies, neither in the words he spoke nor in the messages of love sent by his dark green eyes. Her lovely eyes bravely mirrored his love, but there was very little truth in what she told him.

Juliana did not know what compelled her to lie to Garrett. It wasn't shame about who she was, nor was it worry that if he knew of her humble beginnings he would cease to care. But something she could not name, and yet had to obey, commanded her to deceive him.

Garrett believed that all Juliana's words were true. It would never have occurred to him that on this evening, when their hearts were joined by the greatest truth of all, the woman he loved would tell him lies.

"My parents died shortly after I was born," Juliana said. "They had gone sailing and there was a sudden storm and they both drowned."

"No wonder you're afraid of the water."

"I'm not afraid, not anymore, not with you." The intensity of his eyes in response to her soft confession made her tremble with an unfamiliar yet powerful longing. After a moment of confusion, she resumed the make-believe story of the sea orphan of wealthy parents who had been raised by her even wealthier aunt and had been educated in the excellent schools founded by the British in Hong Kong to ensure impeccable education for their own children.

When she spoke about Vivian, the truth at last, Juliana's voice filled with loving pride. "She's a thoroughly modern woman, far ahead of her time. Her dress shop is enormously successful and she's made another fortune by investing in Hong Kong's premier trading companies."

"Are you planning to follow in her footsteps?"

"I hope to. Not in the stock market, but in the world of design. One day, Aunt Vivian and I will have our own house of fashion." Juliana smiled softly. "We've already given it a name."

"What name?" Garrett asked gently of the glowing eyes that shone with dreams.

"Pearl Moon," Juliana said. "We're going to call it Pearl Moon."

"Can you stay with me tonight, Juliana?" Garrett asked at the end of the gourmet meal they had scarcely touched. "Will you?"

"Yes." Tonight, tomorrow, for as long as you want me.

Tranquil Sea, the daughter of a poor fisherman, had become Juliana Kwan, the surrogate niece of one of Hong Kong's most independent and visionary women. Her clothes were elegant, her hair stylish, her speech regal and refined. She looked modern, sophisticated, savvy, but in truth she knew almost nothing of the intimacies shared between women and men.

She had heard about the Chinese girls, many much younger than she, who sold their bodies to the American GIs who came to Hong Kong for "R and R." Such girls were viewed by the community with arch disdain—and there was greater scorn for those who simply gave their bodies away, without even money to show for their shame.

But the servicemen who frequented bars like the Den in Wanchai were high on drugs and drink and lust. Surely the girls who worked there didn't feel about their sailors the way she felt about Garrett . . . or did they?

Did they tremble with wanting?

Did they need desperately to breathe the same air that he breathed, to be as close to him as possible for as long as possible?

Did they know with absolute certainty that their hearts would break when they said good-bye?

Did they begrudge each swiftly passing moment, despite the magic, because far too soon the memories of magic would be all that were left?

No, Juliana decided. They couldn't possibly feel what she felt. Not day after day, night after night, a new man every time.

"Juliana? What is it? You look so sad."

"I was missing you."

"I've missed you all my life, Juliana." His voice was soft—and solemn—with love. "Now that I've found you, I won't ever let you go."

It is the first lie he has told me. But, Juliana realized, he doesn't know it's a lie. He believes that we have forever.

She wanted to believe his words, and she believed with all her heart that if it were possible for them to be together always, Garrett would make it happen. But she could not conquer the ominous pulse that beat deep within her, relentlessly ticking away. Each tick seemed to signal a small death, each passing moment a tiny piece of a brilliant dream that had glittered briefly and then died.

Juliana sensed the disciplined strength and resolute will of the man who had already changed her life forever. But still she thought, Even you, Garrett, even you cannot change destiny.

When they were alone in his room, he gently cupped her face and said, "You've never made love, have you?"

"There's never been anyone . . . I've never wanted to before."

"We don't have to make love now, Juliana, not until you're ready. There's no hurry."

"You have to return to Vietnam."

"Yes," he answered solemnly. "But I'll come back to you, my love, whenever I can. And when my tour of duty is over—"

"Make love to me now, Garrett," Juliana interjected with soft urgency. There is a reason to hurry. We don't have forever. I don't know why. I only know that it's a truth more powerful even than our love.

Garrett Whitaker had made love before, emotionally detached yet masterful forays into pleasure, but loving Juliana bore no resemblance to anything he had ever experienced. She was delicate and fragile, yet her passion was as strong as his, her desire as fearless and unashamed, and she awakened within him a gentleness he had never known before, an exquisite tenderness that existed for her alone and for their magical love.

In the morning, a suitcase arrived for Juliana. It was filled with beautiful clothes, satins and silks carefully folded by Vivian, to be worn by Juliana for the man she loved.

"From my aunt."

"She *is* modern. I'd like to meet her."

"You will."

But Garrett never met Vivian. When Juliana called to thank her for the clothes and to suggest that they all meet for tea at the Pen, Vivian lovingly declined—as if she, too, believed that the next six days were all the time the young lovers were ever to have, six days in which to create memories of love to last a lifetime.

"I'll write to you," he promised before he left. "And I'll be back as soon as I can. Please don't cry, Juliana," he whispered, tenderly kissing her tears as he fought his own. "I *will* be back."

No, you won't, she thought with a certainty that terrified her.

Juliana's anguished confidence that she would never see Garrett again was offset, a little, by her equally confident belief that although he was returning to war, he was not about to die.

"I love you, Juliana."

"I love you, too, Garrett—always."

CHAPTER 3

When Garrett and Juliana left their magical world of love, each found a tragedy awaiting them. For Juliana, the massive heart attack suffered by Vivian during her absence was grim proof that her love for Garrett was as forbidden—and as dangerous—as her girlhood dreams of life on land. For Garrett, the death of his older brother in a fireball above the jungles of Vietnam meant blinding rage and a wish for revenge that verged on madness.

But it did not mean that his love for Juliana was wrong.

Nonetheless, Blake's death took Garrett away from her.

On his way home to Dallas, during a refueling stop in Tokyo, he placed a phone call to the house overlooking Happy Valley. As soon as he identified himself, an obviously hostile housekeeper told him what had happened to Vivian. She was convalescing now, the woman conceded, feeling much better now that Juliana was at her bedside, where she *should* have been from the beginning—instead of with him.

Garrett knew that no messages had been left for Juliana at the Peninsula. Vivian had known where Juliana was and had chosen not to send for her. Garrett might have tried to deflect the house-keeper's fury with those truths, but he didn't. Neither did he attempt to reach Juliana at the hospital. Now was not the time to share his tragedy with her, and if Juliana heard his voice she would know something terribly sad had befallen him as well.

He would call her from Dallas.

Dallas . . . it was so very far away from Hong Kong. The glaring Texas sun was so hot and so bright that it threatened to burn from his memory the delicate images of Juliana and their love, and his parents' grief was so deep, their hatred of all that was Asian so intense, that his week in paradise seemed more illusory than real.

Only five days had passed since he had kissed her farewell tears, but still, as Garrett placed the call to her from Dallas, Juliana seemed almost a phantom to him, floating, ethereal, an impossible gossamer dream. Then he heard the silk that was her voice, and even though it was soft and far away, journeying into the vastness of space before reaching him, she was real, his memories were real, and with her love she gently balmed the raw and weeping wounds of his heart.

Juliana's gentle love had undoubtedly healed Vivian as well. She was home already, stronger every day, but, Garrett knew, it was far too soon for Juliana to leave her. And, he knew, it was also far too soon for his parents to welcome Juliana into their home. They would hate her on sight, an irrational hatred born of grief. They already hated Hong Kong. For four tormented days following Blake's death, when they hadn't known where Garrett was, or how to reach him, to their shattered hearts it felt as if they had lost both sons.

Douglas and Pauline Whitaker had expected Garrett to sense that Blake had died, and Garrett would have expected it as well. It seemed impossible that his brother's heart could stop beating without a sympathetic response from his own. But he had felt not a falter, not a stumble, neither had he heard even the softest whisper of despair. He had been so lost in the magic of Juliana, so consumed by their joyous love that the silent scream of his brother's dying heart had gone unheard—and for that Garrett felt great guilt.

Blake Whitaker had been the heir and Garrett had been the spare. On his return from Vietnam, Blake had planned to work with Douglas, learning to manage the vast empire of companies that had begun with Texas oil but had long since been diversified. That was what the heir planned to do, wanted to do—and the spare?

Garrett had always been the more restless, and the more reckless, and of the two he was also the more patriotic. He would fly for the navy until he became its top gun; and after, because he was committed to public service but far too impatient to be a politician, he would go to the Pentagon, a commander to whom the commander in chief would turn for sage advice.

Of the two Whitaker boys, Garrett had always seemed the one destined for greatness—or for disaster. But the disaster had befallen Blake, the more careful one, and now the only greatness Garrett could achieve was a private one, a greatness of character, the devotion and loyalty of a son to his parents. The restless son, the reckless one, now became the responsible one.

"I'll return to Hong Kong as soon as I can, Juliana," he promised softly. "For now, for a while, I need to be here, helping my parents with their sadness and learning about my father's businesses."

Garrett didn't speak aloud his plan to try to convince his father to expand several of his companies to Hong Kong. From his week in Hong Kong, he had no doubt that the potential for growth there was virtually boundless. But Garrett knew as well that all the compelling business reasons in the world might not persuade Douglas Whitaker to invest in Asia, not now, perhaps not ever, just as his parents might never accept his love for Juliana.

But they would have to—because Garrett Whitaker was willing to give up every dream, every restless urge to soar among the clouds . . . but he would not give up the dream of Juliana.

"You can't ever return to Hong Kong, Garrett."

"What? Juliana—" He stopped abruptly because the second half of her devastating pronouncement was just arriving.

"And I can't ever leave."

"We're going to spend our lives together," Garrett countered forcefully, wanting his words to reach her swiftly, without lingering in the vast, dark space that lay between them. "I'm going to return to Hong Kong, Juliana, just as soon as I possibly can."

"*No*, Garrett, you cannot. You *must* not. Don't you see?"

"All I know, Juliana, all I see, is that I love you."

"And I love you! But look what harm our love has already caused those we love. Your brother, my aunt."

"You can't believe that our love had anything to do with what happened to them . . . ?"

"But I do, Garrett," Juliana answered softly, and in the solemnity of her quiet words Garrett heard centuries of Chinese tradition: the abiding belief in the preordained mandates of the heavens and the stars, and the serene and nondefiant acceptance of that celestial destiny. "Even when we were together, I sensed that the little time we had was all that was ever meant to be."

"You're feeling guilty that your aunt needed you and you weren't there for her. I feel the same guilt about Blake. I was so lost in our love that I didn't even sense the moment of his death. But that's because our love is so strong, Juliana, so powerful and so right. I'm coming to Hong Kong."

"No, Garrett!" she cried. "Please promise me that you won't—not ever."

"*I love you, Juliana.*"

"And I love you! I will never love anyone else. But please, *please*, promise me that you won't return."

"How can I promise you that?"

"Because," she answered softly, "you have told me that you love me. If you really do, then you will make that promise to me."

Women had tried to test Garrett's commitment to them before, issuing silly ultimatums, forcing him to reveal his true indifference, then raging at him for it, and then relenting, pleading for another chance. But Juliana, the only woman he would ever love, was not testing him. She knew his love for her. She knew he would never impose his will on her, never compel her to live a life of fear.

"I promise, Juliana. I won't come to Hong Kong, nor will I try to change your mind. But I will always love you, all my life, only you."

"And I will love you, Garrett, only you."

"I'll wait for you, Juliana, and when it feels safe for you to live our love, I'll be here."

"It won't ever feel safe, not ever. Please don't wait for me, Garrett. Make that promise to me, too."

Garrett Whitaker had known Elizabeth Parish all her life. Their parents had been friends forever, and with the birth of their children, the bonds became even closer. The Parishes loved Blake and Garrett Whitaker as if the boys were their own, and to the Whitakers, Beth Parish was the beloved daughter they would never have.

The moment Beth focused her young eyes beyond the world of her parents, she fixed them on Garrett. As a little girl, she followed him like a shadow, her admiration wide-eyed and unconcealed, his amusement at her obvious idolatry as fond and gentle as a brother's.

It was Blake who made the discovery that seemingly overnight the coltish Beth had become a willowy beauty. She should have been infatuated with Blake, Garrett thought, the crown prince and the lovely princess. It was a union the Whitakers and Parishes would have embraced with pure joy.

But Beth was always interested only in Garrett. To her, he was perfect, a true Prince Charming, and even though Garrett knew that such an assessment was far from accurate, he cared enough about Beth to conceal from her his not-so-charming aspects. He was her friend only, never her boyfriend, never even her date. Beth believed with absolute certainty that one day she and Garrett would marry. In the meantime, however, she dated and laughed and learned, and in the meantime their friendship flourished.

Beth saved every letter Garrett wrote her from the Naval Academy, from flight school, and even from Vietnam. Garrett kept each of Beth's many letters only until the next one arrived, rereading it more than once in the interim, and although he received letters from a number of women during his tour in Vietnam, Beth's were the only ones he ever answered. If a little emotion spilled into his words, a little anger or frustration or sadness, it was all right to reveal such vulnerability to Beth.

Garrett did not understand, not really, not until Juliana, that Beth was in love with him. And in the weeks following his return to Dallas, after Juliana had said good-bye to their love forever, he realized that he loved Beth as well. It wasn't the all-consuming love he felt for Juliana, of course, the once-in-a-lifetime passion that shut out the world. But it was love, Garrett knew that now, and it had history and common bonds and great respect and caring.

Garrett had made a solemn promise to Juliana that he would never ask from destiny more than the week of paradise they had already been granted. He made an equally solemn vow to himself that Beth, who had so joyously agreed to be his wife, would never suspect that there had once been a woman named Juliana.

Garrett and Beth were married two months after his return to Dallas. The wedding seemed rushed to outsiders, but to the hearts that were struggling so hard to find a glimmer of hope following the death of a beloved son, it came just in time. The marriage of Garrett and Beth promised rebirth, stability, and the continuity of family and tradition.

He needs me. The thought came with such power that it could not be denied.

Garrett needed her. His heart was calling to her. It wasn't merely her own heart, overflowing with emotion as she cradled his two-day-old daughter in her arms.

Juliana had felt the new life inside her even before Garrett left Hong Kong. He had left with her the most precious of all gifts of love, and now, as she held their daughter, she realized how sustaining that gift had been. All this time she'd had part of him alive within her, and he'd had only memories.

But now, for some reason, the memories of their love weren't enough. Garrett needed her, and unlike Juliana, he had no part of her to cradle close to his heart.

What consequences will there be if I call him? Juliana silently demanded of the fates. Who will be harmed? What tragedy will result?

None, please, she prayed. It's just a phone call and he needs me so much. Grant me this, *please.*

It was almost midnight. Garrett was pulling into the drive of his home for the first time in nearly forty-eight hours. The doctors had told him that he needed sleep and then banished him from the neonatal intensive-care unit until eight o'clock the following morning.

He would be alone in the Highland Park mansion. His parents were with the Parishes, staying with them, because Robert and Iris Parish needed them more than he.

The phone began ringing just as Garrett opened the front door. As he moved swiftly to answer it, his heart raced with fear and he fought to control a rising sense of panic.

Something has happened, he thought. They said she was stable, but she senses that I've abandoned her. She knows my voice, and now she knows it's gone, and . . . "Hello?"

"Garrett?"

"Juliana," he whispered, hoarse with the need she had sensed and with the emotion which he had held so tightly in check. *"Juliana."*

When he could speak, Garrett told Juliana about his marriage seven months before. He had loved Beth, he explained softly. It was a different love from theirs, but a good and gentle one.

Beth became pregnant on their wedding night and the next seven months were happy ones as they shared together the joyous promise of the little life she carried. It seemed as if the tragedy of Blake's death was behind them, and they were all beginning to heal, but two days earlier, on the morning of New Year's Eve, Beth had started to bleed, a torrent of crimson that quickly stole her consciousness—and eventually her life.

The baby girl was delivered just before Beth died. She was two months premature, tiny and fragile, and it seemed unlikely that she could possibly survive. But she had, and with each passing second her chances of survival were enhanced, and tonight the doctors had pronounced her to be so stable that he had dared to come home.

Tears filled Juliana's heart as she heard Garrett's anguish, but she filled her voice with soft confidence as she said, "She *will* survive, Garrett. Your daughter will survive. She'll have your courage and your goodness and your strength. Please tell me everything about her—her name, and the exact time when she was born, and what she looks like."

"Her name is Allison," Garrett began, his voice touched with a father's loving pride despite his immense sadness and loss. "She was born at nine in the morning on the thirty-first. She's tiny—so very tiny—but she's a fighter. And," he added quietly, "I'm very sure that she will grow up to look like Beth."

"Who was very lovely . . ."

"Yes. She was very lovely, Juliana, and young and happy and—" Emotion stopped his voice.

Eventually, at Juliana's gentle urging, he spoke again, and they talked, for a very long time, about Beth, and Allison, and the happy news that Vivian was as good as new.

Juliana confessed that it was only because she sensed his need that she had made the forbidden call. Garrett knew without her saying it that nothing had changed; and now, at last, he believed as strongly as Juliana that six days of love was all that they were ever meant to have. He couldn't return to Juliana, not now, not ever. He owed far more than that to the lovely young woman who had lost her life giving birth to his daughter, and to Beth's parents, and he especially owed to the infant girl who was fighting so valiantly to survive the unwavering belief that she was the child of a great and enduring love.

Garrett would never return to Hong Kong, and Juliana would never leave. He knew now, without question, the truth that Juliana had already known nine months before.

Neither wanted to say good-bye. Both knew that this time their farewell would truly be forever. During the lingering silences between their quiet words, Juliana made an emotional decision.

"Allison looks like Beth, Garrett, but your other daughter

looks like you." It was true, although Juliana alone knew it. The doctor who had come to the house above Happy Valley believed that the baby he delivered was pure Chinese. He didn't notice that her eyes were dark jade not midnight black, or that her skin was more alabaster than gold, nor did he see in her small perfect features the gifts of her father, his strength and pride and courage and will.

The stunned whisper that traveled back through space was hoarse with anguish—and soft with hope. "My other daughter, Juliana?"

"She was born at ten fifty-five on the night of the first," Juliana said, astonished still by the coincidence. "With the time difference between Hong Kong and Dallas, that means that she was born just five minutes before Allison. They're sisters, Garrett, born as if they were twins."

"And she's fine, Juliana? *You're* fine?"

"Yes," Juliana assured him. Hers had been a labor of pure love. "We're both just fine."

"Good," he said, his voice quiet with relief. "What's her name?"

Juliana answered first in Cantonese. "It means Daughter of Greatest Love."

"Daughter of Greatest Love," Garrett echoed softly as he thought about the daughters, the sisters, the almost twins. The firstborn's name was Daughter of Greatest Love, and that was who she truly was, but the other, Allison, would believe it could have been her name as well, that there could never have been for either Garrett or Beth a stronger or more committed love.

"That's her private name," Juliana said. "To the world she'll be Maylene. Is that all right with you, Garrett? It's neither Chinese nor American, but a little of both, as she is. And unique, as she is."

"It's a beautiful name, Juliana."

"She's beautiful."

"I want to take care of her, Juliana. I want to take care of both of you." Garrett didn't add the rest—"the only way I can." The fact that money was all he could ever offer the woman he loved and the daughter he would never see made his heart scream with pain.

It was then, at last, that Juliana understood the reason she had been compelled to lie to him the night they met: so that he wouldn't worry about her, so that their lives could go on separately, with no ties except the invisible ones of the heart. She had told him that she was wealthy. It hadn't been true then, but it was now. Following her heart attack, Vivian had a will drawn up leaving everything to her. "We need nothing, Garrett. I told you about Vivian's fortunes. Maylene will never want for anything."

Except a father. The thought plunged into his heart like a jagged-edged knife. "What will you tell her about me?"

"About us," Juliana amended softly. "I will tell her that we loved each other very much, a love to last a lifetime, and that we were planning to spend our lives together, loving her, but . . ."

"But what?" he asked gently.

"But that you were killed before you could return to Hong Kong. This is what I will need to tell her, Garrett, because our very bright little girl is going to begin wondering about you long before she's old enough to understand the truth. I hate the lie, but I think it's necessary. Don't you?"

Yes, he thought as the knife twisted ever deeper. "Tell her this truth, though, Juliana—tell her I would have loved her with all my heart."

"I will," Juliana promised. Then, quite suddenly, she felt danger. It was as if destiny, impatient with this forbidden phone call that should have lasted minutes but had gone on for hours, was about to issue a harsh punishment for her brazen defiance. Urgently she implored, "Please let us go, Garrett. Please promise me that you will never try to find out about us."

"Oh, Juliana, no. I'll want to know about you, that you're happy and safe. I'll worry about you."

"*Please*, Garrett. We'll be happy and safe, I promise. But we must say good-bye. We *must*."

"Juliana . . ."

"I have to go now." Juliana heard the desperation in her own voice, calmed it, and said softly, "I will love you always, Garrett, *always*, and in loving Maylene I will love Allison as well."

"And I will love Maylene . . . and you . . . always."

Long after the phone call ended, Juliana felt the menace still. She cradled Maylene against her, gently kissing the soft black silken hair on her small lovely head as she spoke silent words of reassurance to herself. It's going to be all right. Just one final phone call. There will be no tragic consequences. The tragedies are over, they *have* to be, there have already been far too many.

For one week it seemed that her prayers had been answered. They were all out of danger. She and Garrett could live their separate lives, loving each other still and loving their precious daughters.

But on the eighth day, perversely, because eight was supposed to be a lucky number, tragedy struck anew, and Juliana Kwan's life was changed once again . . . and once again, forever.

PART TWO

CHAPTER 4

Trade Winds Hotel
Central District, Hong Kong Island
Sunday, June 6, 1993

"How does it feel to be back in Hong Kong?"

Maylene wasn't surprised by the question, or that James Drake had waited until now to ask it. Their gourmet dinner was over, and the vintage champagne, more golden bubbles with every elegant course, had worked its magic on her pain—and its menace on her defenses.

James wanted a truthful answer, and it would take her fatigued and floating mind a few moments to fashion one, but there was no rush. No one was waiting for them to relinquish their candlelit table with its spectacular view. They were in the very private dining room of James's penthouse, on the hotel's fifty-third floor. Their meal had come from DuMaurier's, the Trade Winds's French restaurant and one of Hong Kong's finest.

As Maylene pondered James's question, her eyes traveled to the view outside. Tonight Victoria Harbour was a smooth black mirror, a vast reflecting pool from which twinkled the galaxy of lights that haloed its shores. It was a sight of breathtaking beauty; but, like everything in Hong Kong, the emotions it evoked in her were bittersweet.

Maylene had been away from Hong Kong for nine years, and during the twenty hours since her return, she had tried to remain sharply focused on the reason she was here. But it was impossible. The past was all around her. From her office in Drake Towers, she saw Victoria Peak, and from her apartment on the Trade Winds's forty-eighth floor, she could watch the Star ferries crossing the harbor to Kowloon. Her perch was so high, in fact, her magnificent view so commanding, that she could even see the Peninsula Hotel . . . where she had been conceived.

The first time Maylene had seen again the famous blue-green silhouette, she was swept by rushes of anger—and of anguish— that were far more powerful than she had expected them to be. She had subdued her renegade emotions with a stern reminder: she would be viewing the Peninsula often, and at a range close enough to see clearly its guardian lions, because just one block east on Salisbury Road lay the Jade Palace construction site.

The Jade Palace . . . the reason Maylene Kwan had finally returned to Hong Kong. An architect, Maylene had joined Titchfield & Sterling's London office only weeks before the letter from James Drake arrived. Titchfield & Sterling wasn't the only architectural firm to receive the solicitation, of course. The call for sketches from one of the world's premier developers had been sent to all the top firms. As was typical of James Drake, he knew precisely what he wanted his Hong Kong hotel to be: a work of art, a magnificent sculpture that celebrated the spirit of Hong Kong, the unique harmony of East and West.

There was no doubt that the thirty-eight-year-old real-estate mogul would be deluged with sketches. Designing for James Drake was an architect's dream. True, he expected excellence, *demanded* it, but it was that expectation, coupled with his unrelenting commitment to quality, which assured that, in the end, every one of James Drake's buildings was a masterpiece of both structure and style.

Titchfield & Sterling's senior partners strongly encouraged

any of their architects with even a passing knowledge of Hong Kong to submit ideas. The more submitted, they reasoned, the greater the likelihood of coming up with something that James Drake would want.

For Maylene, sketching a building that symbolized Hong Kong was simply a matter of putting on paper an image that had danced in her mind for years. It wouldn't be what James Drake wanted, of course, because it was far from a portrait of harmony. It was instead a reflection of her own experiences in Hong Kong, an intensely personal statement about the agony of being split in two and yet yearning to be whole; of loving half of oneself, *trying* to, while loathing the other half, and then reversing the process; of fragile roots divided at their delicate tips, uncertain where to seek a home, and yet desperate to know where they truly belonged.

That was Maylene Kwan's vision of Hong Kong—and of the Jade Palace. She knew its discord, but was quite oblivious to its grace. She was unable to see in her sketches her own sense of wonder, her brave attempts at peaceful reconciliation between the two disparate parts. As a result, when the man who had asked for harmony and celebration, not discord and torment, requested that she fly to Hong Kong to discuss further details with him, Maylene flatly refused. James Drake's interest in her design was idle curiosity at best, she decided, and if he was as besotted with Hong Kong as his letter implied, he might merely be planning to harangue her for her heresy.

Besides, Maylene believed that her design for the Jade Palace could never actually be built. It was, after all, an illusion. At first glance, the building would look purely Chinese, but before one's eyes, its British legacies would suddenly appear, and in another moment the two distinct architectural styles would magically blend into one. The visual illusion was challenging to explain, difficult to sketch, and surely impossible to translate into a towering structure of glass, marble, and steel.

But James Drake's interest in her extraordinary design was far from idle curiosity, and finally, after many long-distance conversations, he told her that he was coming to London to meet with her. It wasn't until he was actually en route from Kai Tak to Heathrow that Maylene learned from a member of her firm that the journey to England was as emotionally difficult for James as a casual trip to Hong Kong would have been for her.

Four years earlier, just days before they were to move to Hong Kong, his pregnant wife, Gweneth, had died in a tragic accident, a gas explosion in their country home in Wales. After recovering from wounds that he himself had incurred in the inferno, James moved to Hong Kong anyway, escaped there. In four years he had not returned to London . . . not until he was forced to by the architect who stubbornly refused to travel to Hong Kong and whose vision of the Jade Palace was, astonishingly, so very close to his own.

That night in London, during dinner at Claridge's, James Drake told Maylene Kwan that he was going to build *her* Jade Palace. And, he added, even though it was abundantly clear that she was reluctant to return, he needed her on site, in Hong Kong, during what was bound to be the complicated construction of her remarkable design.

And, that night, Maylene agreed to come.

And now she was here, and James was asking her how it felt to be back, and even though she had already lied to him, successfully she believed, Maylene knew that it was a difficult—and risky—endeavor.

Drawing her gaze from the reflected glitter of Victoria Harbour, she met eyes the color of steel and said truthfully, "Pleasure and pain."

James greeted the candid confession with a faint smile and appraising eyes. The beautiful, gifted, complicated woman who sat before him was so very like the extraordinary building she had designed: a portrait of harmony and conflict, one moment Asian, the next British, the next a rare and intoxicating blend of both. Maylene had told him that her father was British, an aristocrat who died before her birth, and that her Chinese mother, from whom she had been estranged for years, lived in Hong Kong still. James had concluded that there was truth in what she told him, but that there were lies as well.

James had no idea why Maylene had felt it necessary to lie to him, but he was in no position to question her. He had, after all, lied to her about the most important truth of his life.

"Pleasure and pain," he echoed softly. "Would you care to elaborate?"

No, Maylene thought as she left his dangerously inquisitive eyes. Her own fell to her empty champagne flute, then to his, nearly full and draped casually by his elegant hand.

It was an elegant hand, and a lethal one. James's childhood in Hong Kong had instilled in him an interest in the martial arts. He was a black belt now, quite capable of committing swift, silent murder with his bare hands. He would never perform such a deadly act, of course, because, above all, James Drake was a master of his emotions.

The lethal hand draped with such controlled power around the delicate crystal was like the man himself: elegant grace cloaking fiery rage. Maylene understood his rage, and she knew, too, its futility. His wife's death had been a freak accident. No one was to blame. Nonetheless the dark fury within him hungered for revenge. And, it seemed, since Gweneth Drake's executioner had no human face, James blamed himself, tore himself apart instead.

"I don't think I'll elaborate tonight, James," she answered finally. "It's much too long a story."

"I'm not going anywhere."

"But I am." Maylene smiled as she rose to her feet. "You expect me to begin work bright and early tomorrow morning, don't you?"

"You know I do." James smiled in reply, relenting easily, respecting her wish to drop the topic of her bittersweet memories of Hong Kong. Standing, too, he said, "Oh, I forgot to tell you. I found a photographer."

"The one I suggested in London?"

"No, someone else. It was sheer luck. When I was in San Francisco last month, I happened to see a book she'd done. I've got a copy in the living room for you, something to look at if jet lag keeps you awake. I hope you'll agree her work is remarkable."

"I'm sure I will."

As they walked toward the living room Maylene was swept with sudden hope.

Maybe I can do this, she thought. Maybe sometime in the next seven months I will be able to confront my anguished and angry ghosts . . . and even find the courage to see my mother. And if I need help, *strength*? Perhaps I can talk to James, who knows about rage and who, already, I trust far more than I've ever trusted any man.

Maylene did trust James. On that night in London, after telling him yes, she would come to Hong Kong, she and James had talked, quietly, honestly, for hours. They had even talked, quietly and honestly, about love. When Maylene shared with him her confident belief that she would never fall in love, James replied that he, too, had once felt that way—and with matching confidence. But then he met Gweneth, and it had happened, swiftly, deeply, and forever. It would never happen again, he added solemnly, nor did he even want it to.

As Maylene listened to James speak of his love for Gweneth, she realized that this man, who had known physical intimacy with a woman he loved, would not have the slightest interest in casual liaisons of pleasure. Most beautiful women would have greeted the realization that stunningly sensual James Drake was not going to seduce them into his bed with petulant disbelief.

But not Maylene. She knew all too well the chilling truths about herself, the iciness that lay beneath the sultry surface of her rare and exotic beauty. From childhood she had known that she would never be more to any man than merely a trophy, a unique prize to be claimed, sampled, but not loved. It was not until she was a woman, however, that Maylene had learned the rest: what a terribly disappointing trophy she was.

No man had ever wanted Maylene Kwan for more than a night—and no man ever would. Her fascinating face and enticing body made heated promises of lush passion and extravagant pleasure. But it took her lovers almost no time to discover that the provocative package was merely a facade. Inside, the ravishing alabaster beauty was pure ice, awkward, uncertain, and inept.

But James Drake would never learn those disappointing truths about her. For that, Maylene felt grateful, and strangely safe, and it made her trust him all the more.

It was then, when they reached the living room, that the man she believed she could trust handed her *Lone Star Serenade*. It took Maylene a moment to comprehend what she was holding, and a moment more to recover from the staggering blow. But she did recover, because Maylene Kwan was accustomed to emotional assaults that came from nowhere. She had spent her life being stared at by complete strangers, people who were at first intrigued by her unusual beauty and then disdainful of it. She had become a talented actress, smiling when her heart was breaking, laughing when all she wanted to do was cry.

Maylene couldn't smile now, not yet, nor could she even look up at the man who had, perhaps, betrayed her fragile trust. Her eyes were riveted on the cover of the book and the name of the photographer emblazoned in teal blue: Allison Parish Whitaker. And, after a moment, suddenly powerless to prevent the actions of her own hands, she felt herself turning the book over, to the color picture on the back.

Maylene had seen a photograph of her father, on the day she discovered all the lies, but she had never seen her sister, until now. . . .

She was golden! Her honey-colored hair shined brightly, as if caressed by its own private moon, and her face was radiant, too, glowing from the inner warmth of love. The little sister of bewitchingly beautiful Maylene Kwan was neither sultry nor glamorous, but there was a wholesome loveliness, a beguiling, wide-eyed innocence.

Allison Parish Whitaker was an heiress, a beloved and cherished princess, but sunglasses, not a tiara, crowned her shimmering golden head, and at her ivory throat, in lieu of diamonds, were the carelessly tangled straps of her light meter and camera. Her cheekbones were undeniably aristocratic, her nose delicate, and her lips, generous and full, curled softly into a smile of welcome.

And what of Allison's eyes? Did she, like Maylene, possess colorful proof of an inheritance from their green-eyed father? Yes—except that the eyes of the illegitimate daughter, the half-breed infant whom Garrett Whitaker had not wanted, were the darkest of jade, black-shadowed and filled with tormenting secrets . . . while the golden daughter viewed the world through a green that was as bright and clear as treasured emeralds. And, like flawless gems whose worth was unquestioned, the remarkable eyes of the daughter who was loved were unshadowed, fearless, and shining with dreams.

"Maylene?"

James's voice was soft, but it shattered the silence like thunder. Before lifting her eyes to him, Maylene set the book on the nearby teak-and-crystal table, releasing it quickly, as if it were on fire and her fingers were being mercilessly seared.

Then, as she prepared to meet the gaze of the man she had believed she could trust, and wondered anew if James had betrayed her after all, so soon and with such cruelty. Maylene had no doubt that James Drake could be cruel. He would only have to permit a tiny portion of the rage that lived within him to rise to the surface.

How well Maylene knew the cruelty born of rage. For that horrible time between her discovery of the truth and the day, nine years ago, when she left Hong Kong, she had allowed such cruelty to surface. Allowed it? Yes, sometimes, *yes.*

In the beginning, of course, her hurtful words had come of their own volition—and without warning. They simply flowed from her wounded heart on a rushing river of pain. Then, in the beginning, her lack of control—and even the words themselves— were understandable. She was only thirteen, after all, and her entire world had been shattered, and she hurt *so much.* But there were other times, far too many to forgive, when Maylene *could* have held the unkind words deep inside, *could* have kept the screams of pain to herself. But she hadn't. Instead, and so willfully, she had lashed out at the mother she loved.

For the first thirteen years of her life, all that dwelled in Maylene's young heart was a most gentle and generous love. She *knew* about cruelty, of course. She had long been its victim, the target of endless taunts from classmates. It seemed unimaginable that she, of all people, would ever intentionally hurt anyone. But on that day when her world changed forever, there it was—*cruelty*—alive and thriving within her.

Maylene wanted desperately to believe that she had been visited by an evil spirit. It seemed logical that such a sinister phantom would choose for its home a young heart, innocent and screaming with pain—and it was so very tempting to hope that it was something quite distinct from her, an unwelcome guest who, one day, could be compelled to leave.

But Maylene would not permit herself the luxury of believing that the cruelty didn't truly belong to her. Even at thirteen, she was far too responsible to shift the blame. No, this unkindness, this calculated hurtfulness, was part of her, an inheritance, no doubt, from her cruel and heartless father. It had been there all along, in hiding, and now both she—and her mother—knew the truth about the evil that lurked in the dark shadows of Maylene's soul.

Maylene left Hong Kong believing that she had caused irreparable harm to her relationship with the mother she loved. From the moment she arrived in London, as if in penance for the uncontrolled outbursts that had destroyed so much, she imposed rigid discipline on every aspect of her life. She dressed impeccably, the height of fashion, and her long black hair was worn tightly restrained, with never a silken thread out of place. Her grooming was immaculate, and her provocative body was slim and fit, and her work was precise, meticulous, flawless.

And what about her emotions? What happened, in London, when the pain within became too great to endure? Did she, at those times, permit harsh and hurtful words to escape her lips? No. Not once. Not ever. She kept the pain inside. And the cruelty? It was kept inside, too, directed inwardly only . . . precisely where it belonged.

For the past nine years Maylene had lived a life of rigid control, as perfect as she could possibly be. No one had been observing her impeccable behavior, of course. No one *cared*. And yet, perhaps, there had been a purpose to her penance—hidden, until recently, even from her. During the past few weeks, as she prepared to return to Hong Kong, a dangerous—and joyous— thought had begun to dance in her mind. Perhaps, somehow, she would find the courage to see Juliana again, to ask of her beloved mother that she forgive the unforgivable. And if that faraway day ever came, she would offer Juliana a brave reassurance: I'm *better* now, Mother. My anger—and my anguish—are under control.

But were they? Even before she saw Allison's photograph, the emotions of being back in Hong Kong were far more powerful than Maylene had imagined they would be. And now? Now, as the worry that James might have betrayed her triggered memories of the ancient betrayal that had shattered her world, she felt terrifying whispers of rage.

I'm under control, she told herself. *I have to be.*

She looked up then, to the man who had his own private black belt in discipline and control. She knew that James was quite capable of making his gray eyes as hard and unreadable as granite—but their message now was crystal clear. He was concerned about her, that was all. There wasn't the slightest shadow of treachery.

What James had told her was the truth. He had discovered the book quite by chance. His decision to choose Allison Parish Whitaker as the photographer for the Jade Palace was all just an incredible coincidence—simply, horribly, an accident of fate . . . like the simple yet horrible accident that had killed his wife.

Tear this accident apart for me, James! Take your lethal, elegant hands and strangle it to death!

"Maylene?" The soft question became a quiet command. "Tell me what's wrong."

Somehow the talented actress within her found a way to make her eyes flash with indignation as she demanded, "This Allison Whitaker, she's an American, isn't she?"

"Yes." Watching her very carefully, James added, "And, as you've doubtless deduced from the title of the book, she's a Texan—another Texan."

"There wasn't a single British or Chinese photographer capable of taking pictures of Hong Kong?"

"For what I want she's the best. Just as you are. Just as Sam Coulter is."

With these last words came an unmistakable reminder. She and James had disagreed, too, about his choice of Sam Coulter to build the hotel. But, in the end, Maylene had been compelled to concede that James was right. The man who had built Le Bijou on L'ile des Arcs-en-ciel was indeed the best choice for the Jade Palace. Both hotels were architectural dreams that could vanish with the bright light of day if not constructed with meticulous care. Maylene was not happy that she was going to have to rely on a man from Texas to make her extraordinary vision become an extraordinary reality, but she accepted it. She had even promised James that in three days, when she met the Texan with whom she would work so closely for the next seven months, she was going to be unbelievably charming to him.

And when she met her little sister? When she was face-to-face with the daughter who had been loved not abandoned?

The question filled her with such fear that she blurted out, "Please find another photographer, James!"

"Tell me why, Maylene," he replied calmly, intrigued and mystified by the turbulence in her beautiful jade-green eyes.

"You *know* why! The Jade Palace is a symbol of Hong Kong, re-member? As much as possible everyone involved should be either British or Chinese."

"With very few exceptions everyone is."

"Not Sam Coulter. Not Tyler Vaughn."

"Sam Coulter and Tyler Vaughn worked together on Le Bi-jou," James said, patiently reiterating information that she knew very well. "I readily admit that always before I've relied on Hong Kong–owned trading companies. But, as you know, Grand Prix was the supplier for Le Bijou and Sam specifically requested that Tyler be involved. It's best for the Jade Palace, Maylene. Tyler Vaughn's reputation for on-time delivery of top-quality materials is impeccable. And there's something else you don't know about him, something I haven't told you."

"That he used to be a race-car driver? I know that, James, but I don't consider the willingness to risk one's life by driving a car as fast as possible a terribly impressive credential."

"What you don't know about Tyler, Maylene, is that he has a very deep commitment to Hong Kong. In 1989, after what happened that June in Beijing, thousands of people left the territory. Businesses pulled out, tourism plummeted—"

"I know that, James," she interjected softly. She knew all about the fear and chaos in Hong Kong after Tiananmen Square. She had been in London then, worrying about the mother with whom she had severed all contact years before. Juliana Kwan had become quite famous during those intervening years, an internationally acclaimed fashion designer. She was one of the lucky ones, able to emigrate if she chose, her lucrative business more than welcome in any number of countries. But Juliana had always vowed never to leave Hong Kong, and she didn't, not even during that unstable time after Tiananmen. Juliana Kwan and Pearl Moon were still here, in this small corner of the planet where no distances were great—except for the vast distances of the heart. "So Tyler Vaughn didn't join the throngs who left in the summer of eighty-nine."

"Actually, that was when he arrived. He'd made the decision to expand Grand Prix to Hong Kong before Tiananmen and he didn't revoke it despite the fact that at the time it seemed a very risky commitment to keep."

"We've already established that he's a risk taker, and now that the scare has passed and Hong Kong is booming once again, he's profited immensely." Maylene knew that her flip reply was unfair to Tyler Vaughn, that she was casually discounting the integrity of the man who had honored a commitment from which many others might have—indeed, *had*—simply walked away. But she was making no concessions to James right now—especially since he himself had so casually discounted her concerns about Allison. "You really don't care about my opinions at all, do you, James? All your promises about how this would be a collaborative effort were just rhetoric, weren't they?"

The muscles in James's jaw rippled, but his voice remained absolutely calm. "This *is* a collaboration, Maylene, but please don't forget that I'm the one paying the bills. That fact gives me ultimate responsibility—and liability—for the project, and it also gives me the final word on every decision. I care very much about your opinions," he said softly. Then, even more softly, he added, "But what I'm really interested in is your real reason for objecting so strenuously to Allison Whitaker."

"I *told* you my real reason, and you obviously *don't* care." Her shrug was dismissive—and a little defeated. "It's late, James, and I'm really very tired. I'll see you in the morning. Thank you for dinner."

She took only two strides toward the door before she was stopped. She hadn't even sensed his movement, but suddenly he was there, standing in front of her, his lethal hands wrapped around her upper arms.

James Drake's touch was like his voice, deceptively soft, velvet over steel. The lean fingers that encircled her flesh were gentle—but imprisoning—and they were warm, proof positive of the fires of rage that were so carefully banked deep within.

James knew how tough Maylene was, how determined and controlled. He saw that determination now in her jade-green eyes, and something else—surprising flickers of fear.

This was not the way James wanted to learn her secrets. Releasing his gentle yet imprisoning grip, he said softly, "I'm sorry."

"No, *I'm* sorry, James," she whispered, so grateful that he wasn't going to push. "I'm not sure what's wrong with me."

James doubted very much that that was true. But, smiling, he suggested, "Why don't we chalk it up to jet lag?"

"And to too much champagne?"

"And to the pleasure and pain of returning to Hong Kong."

Maylene knew that there was a fourth conspirator as well. Every month, with the reliability of the moon, a sense of hopelessness descended on her, stealing her control, swirling her emotions, and making her feel more raw, more precarious, than usual. It was, she supposed, nature's way of making certain that she was achingly aware of the womb that would never bear children of love.

"Friends?" James asked softly, and when she nodded assent, he queried, "And collaborators?"

"Meaning?"

"Meaning that I value your opinions—although I have the final say."

Maylene smiled at last. "Aha."

"And meaning that even though it's my money, I want the Jade Palace to be ours."

"Thank you."

"You're welcome. And most of all meaning that I need to be able to trust you to put the hotel ahead of whatever personal feelings you might have."

"Are we talking about professionalism, Mr. Drake?"

"We are indeed, Miss Kwan."

"You're suggesting that I have to be nice to *all* the Americans?"

The gentle teasing stopped then.

"It's more than a suggestion, Maylene," James said solemnly. "Will you?"

James should have asked "Can you?" not "Will you?" but still Maylene told him yes. And, as she stood before the man who had such surprising faith in her, Maylene allowed herself a magnificent fantasy.

Everything was within her control. It was simply a matter of choice. If she wanted to, if she chose, she could be authentically gracious to Allison and Sam. With the fantasy came an extraordinary feeling: the wonderful way it would feel to be truly free of her anger, her anguish—and her fear.

CHAPTER 5

Sam Coulter's 8:00 A.M. rendezvous with James Drake had been arranged before Sam left his ranch in San Antonio. They would meet in the Trade Winds's lobby, walk to Drake Towers, and since neither man routinely ate breakfast, they would talk over coffee in James's office.

Although it was only 7:45, Sam was already in the lobby, more than ready for the day to begin. Today, and the ten that would follow until the ground breaking, were necessary, but Sam was eager to be done with them and to actually begin work on what would be by far the greatest challenge of his career.

From the beginning, even though it cost him jobs, Sam Coulter had always been very selective about the buildings he agreed to build. To his way of thinking, any man-made creation that was to be permanently etched on the face of the planet had to be worthy of claiming space that might otherwise have been filled by nature. As a result of such a philosophy, Sam's early projects were challenges that no other builders would touch. Now he was every developer's first choice.

Sam thrived on challenge. The more complicated the project, the better. The outcome was never in doubt . . . until now.

The problems posed by the Jade Palace eclipsed all that had come before. The remarkable structure had the potential to be a monumental triumph—or a monumental disaster. Everything had to be done exactly right.

As his experienced eyes now appraised the lobby of James Drake's other Hong Kong hotel, Sam realized that what James had promised him was true: no expense would be spared. He would be given the best of whatever raw materials he needed to make the Jade Palace a masterpiece. James would do his part. The rest was up to Sam.

The decor in the Trade Winds's lobby was as expensive, tasteful, and elegantly sophisticated as the craftsmanship in the structure itself. The snow-white marble floors were adorned with plush carpets, intricately designed, undoubtedly antique. Sprinkled throughout were conversation areas, ensembles of brocade chairs in rust and gold surrounding gleaming mahogany coffee tables, discreetly arranged to create a feeling of absolute privacy. Perched atop black marble pedestals stood mammoth porcelain vases, priceless remembrances of ancient dynasties that were filled with bountiful bouquets of orchids, plumeria, bauhinias, and birds of paradise. Scenes from China's mythology, carved in jade, were displayed on the marble walls, and overhead, casting shimmering prisms of light, hung massive crystal chandeliers.

It was the lobby of a hotel, but it felt like the intimate sitting room of a king.

And who was seated in this grand sitting room? The Trade Winds boasted a truly international clientele. Despite the diversity of their nations of origin, however, the men and women sent a surprisingly uniform message of power and success—and a deep and abiding passion for ever more of each. Their clothes were haute couture, their demeanor regally calm, their refined voices quiet and subdued.

But, Sam knew, these people were making deals worth billions.

Sam had heard about the frenetic pace of Hong Kong, where fortunes could be made or lost overnight, and where, as the clock ticked relentlessly toward the uncertainties of 1997, each swiftly passing second became ever more important. There were still vast fortunes to be made in Hong Kong, and glorious dreams to be achieved, and fiery passions to be fulfilled.

Sam had expected to *see* the frenzy, but he liked the regal calm far better. So this was the way high-stakes games were played in Hong Kong. Good. *Wonderful.* Sam Coulter had always loved poker. And no matter what cards he was holding, he always won.

Quite suddenly a player appeared who clearly did not know the rules. He was American, Sam decided. Young, harried, late for a meeting and perhaps unprepared, he was jogging across a centuries-old carpet accustomed to far more stately strides. The man was making a beeline for the hotel's revolving front door . . . and the most direct route to his destination ran straight through Sam.

Sam felt sympathy for the man whose desperation was so obvious. In another setting he might even have offered quiet counsel. But at this moment he feared that anything that hindered the man's progress toward the hotel door would only fuel his panic.

So Sam did the only thing he could do. He stepped out of the way, clearing the path, avoiding a possible collision—and creating one.

Sam caught her as she was twisting down. Her grip on her briefcase had already been released in reflexive anticipation of what seemed an inevitable—and inevitably hard—landing on the snowy marble. But the harsh landing never happened. Sam averted it.

As he righted her the expression that greeted him was one of dark fury—and it held all the breathtaking beauty and splendor of a tropical storm.

"I'm very sorry," Sam offered swiftly. "It was entirely my fault. I wasn't looking."

She seemed startled by his apology. Then, with the world-changing dazzle of the sun appearing from behind a cloud, she smiled. The ferocious storm became a vague memory and there was new splendor, brilliant now, sparkling, and breathtaking still.

"It wasn't really your fault," she said, startling him anew with her accent—the Queen's English, spoken as if she were a royal princess. "I saw what happened. He was on a collision course with you." As her head tilted thoughtfully, the incandescent light from the chandeliers caressed her lustrous ebony hair, creating the magnificent illusion of rainbows at midnight. "I'd decided that you weren't going to move, that he was going to have to go around you."

"He needed all the help he could get."

She nodded, and Sam saw an enchanting softness, an unmistakable touch of sympathy, as if she felt authentic compassion for the man's plight. Had she, too, known the feeling of being hopelessly out of place and yet desperate to belong?

"Still," she countered quietly, "you *could* blame him for forcing you to step back."

"It was my step," Sam said simply. "I'm responsible for it, and I'm very sorry that it affected you."

"No harm done."

She started to bend to retrieve her briefcase, but Sam swooped faster. He noticed then the very high heels she wore, and the delicate ankles so precariously perched, and he recalled that she had been twisting when he caught her.

"Are you hurt?" he asked softly when he returned to her eyes.

"No, I'm fine. Thank you."

They should have parted then, the incident over, but for several heartbeats their eyes lingered, hers surprised and yet inviting, and his, concealing their own surprise, but not their interest.

Then suddenly the spell was broken, as if each remembered that this was Hong Kong, where every second counted. There was work to be done, vast fortunes to be made.

And glorious dreams to be achieved, Sam thought as her high heels clicked a carefully measured tattoo toward the revolving door and beyond. *And fiery passions to be fulfilled.*

Then she was gone, but not forgotten, an intriguing portrait of contrasts. Who *was* she? he wondered. A high-fashion model with a briefcase? A Chinese princess raised in England, or a British one raised here? And were the eyes that darkened with fury one instant and dazzled with sunshine the next *really* the deepest shade of green?

James appeared precisely at eight o'clock.

"How was your flight?" he asked as he and Sam began the six-block walk to Drake Towers.

"On time and uneventful."

"Tyler met you?"

Sam nodded. "We stopped by the construction site on the way here. Quite a location. It's hard to imagine a better view."

"I don't think there is one. You saw the trailer, I assume. That will be your on-site office. It should already be equipped with everything you'll need, but if it isn't, let me know. There's an office for you in the Towers as well. You'll need it for meetings over the next ten days, but it's yours as long as it's useful to you."

"Thanks. What's on the agenda for today? I know I'm seeing Tyler at three. What about the foreman?"

"Chan Peng. At one. He and his crew are the best in Hong Kong. They did both the Trade Winds and Drake Towers for me, as well as two condominiums in Stanley and six apartment complexes in the New Territories. Peng doesn't have a degree in engineering, in fact no formal education at all, but other builders have told me that his instincts are pure gold. He won't offer his input, however, unless you ask."

"That's good to know. I will definitely ask." They had walked less than a block along Chater Road, but already James Drake was living up to his reputation. During the coming week, Sam would be meeting with the myriad of people involved in the Jade Palace. Each meeting was important, but aside from Sam, there were three people whose contributions would determine the project's ultimate success or failure: the taipan whose trading company would supply the finest quality custom-crafted building materials, the foreman who would oversee and orchestrate the efforts of the large crew, and, of course, the architect. James had scheduled appointments with two of those three for this afternoon. Even before asking, Sam was confident that he would be seeing the architect this morning. "And the meeting with the architect? Will that be today?"

"Yes. You'll see her this morning, from nine until eleven-thirty, after which I thought the three of us would go to lunch."

Her? The word halted almost everything except Sam's long, graceful strides. He had seen all the sketches, of course, as well as the all-important blueprints for the superstructure itself, the skeleton of steel over which the jade, alabaster, and gold flesh would be contoured to create the stunning illusion. The additional blueprints, the detailed diagrams of the interior, would be prepared while the building was under construction.

Everything Sam had seen had borne the same identifying information: Titchfield & Sterling, Ltd., Grosvenor Square, London, England. And below that: M. Kwan, Architect.

He assumed that he would be meeting a Michael Kwan, or a Mark or a Martin, and Sam Coulter had great expectations of Mr. M. Kwan. The brash architect who had so shamelessly put an almost impossible concept to paper had damned well better have some thoughts about how to transform his two dimensions into three, and, more importantly, he'd better be prepared to work. Sam expected him on-site, tromping through the mud that was inevitable during Hong Kong's impending rainy season and fearlessly standing on rain-slick steel girders high above the earth as, together, they tried to reconcile what Mr. Kwan had so brazenly sketched with what was possible given the laws of physics and gravity.

And couldn't a *Ms.* Kwan do all of that just as well? an inner voice demanded, chiding him for what had all the appearances of full-blown male chauvinism. Yes, of course she could, depending on what kind of woman she was.

She would be an intrepid climber of slippery steel, Sam assured himself. James Drake would not have hired anyone less than the best, the most experienced. . . .

"This is Maylene."

"We've met," Sam said quietly. "We bumped into each other earlier in the lobby of the hotel."

He had wanted to see her again. In fact, in the minutes between the time she vanished and James arrived, he decided that he would. Even if the concierge wouldn't reveal the name of the Asian-British model-businesswoman, he would surely agree to relay a message to her.

But now she was here, as startled as he, and although her lovely mouth attempted a gracious smile, Sam saw storm clouds in her dark green eyes. *Ms.* M. Kwan wasn't happy to see him. Well, he wasn't exactly thrilled about seeing her, either.

Sam knew with absolute certainty that she was not a veteran of tromping through mud and climbing steel girders. Yes, admittedly, stiletto heels and designer silk suits could be exchanged for work clothes. But experience was not so easily donned. She was young, under thirty. How many of her designs had actually been built? No matter the number, it wouldn't be nearly enough.

Sam needed a colleague, a peer, someone who brought a wealth of experience to complement his own. It wasn't a frivolous wish. It was absolutely essential if there was to be any hope of pulling off the building coup of the decade.

But James had given him this glowering novice, and it made no sense. James Drake was likened to the great producers of Hollywood, a man who assembled the best talent, provided them with an almost limitless budget, and then watched a blockbuster be born.

James was the producer of the Jade Palace, and Sam was the director, and Maylene Kwan? She was the gifted writer who had created a script of truly lyrical beauty and had presented Sam with a challenge as difficult as making a motion picture from a poem—and who was going to be no help whatsoever. Indeed, like a first-time writer passionately wedded to her words, she was likely to be a hindrance. She might not understand the need for flexibility, the necessary willingness to make changes here and there no matter how magnificent the original.

James Drake's instincts were supposed to be impeccable, his vision flawless. But this time, it seemed, the perfect vision was dramatically, perhaps fatally, blurred.

What could have caused such a clouding of vision, of judgment? It didn't take Sam long to find the answer. She was standing right in front of him, this exotic woman who was an ever-changing portrait of contrasts, storm and dazzle, Chinese and British, alabaster skin and jade-green eyes.

James and Maylene were lovers. The intimacy between them was obvious, even now, as they exchanged glances in a secret language that excluded Sam. Elegantly austere James Drake seemed unbewitchable, but clearly he had fallen under Maylene's enchanting spell. As a token of his love—or at least of his passion—he had given her the Jade Palace, a half-billion-dollar trifle. Then, as gift wrapping, he had given her Sam Coulter, the man who would rescue them both from their folly.

And if he failed? It would be a career disaster for Sam, a huge write-off for James—and for Maylene? She would emerge un-scathed. Architecturally her concept was brilliant. She had de-pended on those far more experienced than she to determine if her concept could become reality. They, not she, had been wrong, and it would be Sam Coulter who would be held most responsible.

And would he accept the responsibility? Maylene already knew that he would. This morning, at the hotel, she had learned that Sam Coulter always assumed full responsibility for every step he took, no matter if that step had been taken to avert a calamity caused by someone else.

He could still walk away from the Jade Palace. He could tell James that on careful reconsideration he had decided that the risk–reward ratio was simply far too high. There would be a few moments of awkwardness, perhaps even anger, and then it would be over. He could leave Hong Kong this afternoon.

But . . . he liked Hong Kong. He was already captivated by the intensity that churned beneath its regal calm.

And . . . he had accepted the offer to build the Jade Palace be-cause he had enough arrogance to believe that if any builder on earth could make its remarkable illusion work, it was he.

And . . . he couldn't leave Hong Kong anyway. Garrett Whitaker had asked him to keep an eye on his daughter, and he had promised that he would, and in all these years Garrett had never collected on the favor Sam owed him. Keeping an eye on Allison Parish Whitaker was quite trivial compared with what Sam owed her father: *everything*—his life, his hope, his dreams.

Sam wasn't sure why Maylene was glowering at him, but he leveled his dark blue eyes at her challenging jade-green ones, smiled, and suggested softly, "So, Maylene, shall we get to work?"

When Maylene seemed surprised, not relieved, by his sugges-tion, it occurred to Sam that perhaps she'd been trying to drive him away, intentionally hoping to provoke him into packing his bags and leaving Hong Kong. Suddenly the Jade Palace seemed an almost inconsequential challenge in comparison with the Jade Princess. Sam's smile became genuine. He liked challenges. He *thrived* on them.

James withdrew then—leaving Maylene alone with the tall, dark stranger from Texas . . . and with her own rising sense of panic.

Sam Coulter had *tricked* her. He was supposed to have been a caricature of a cowboy, easily—and instantly—identifiable by his battered boots, ragged jeans, rumpled tan suede jacket, silver belt buckle embedded with turquoise, and, of course, his Stetson. He was not supposed to have been wearing an impeccably tailored charcoal-gray suit, nor should his head have been covered only by thick, sensually curling dark brown hair.

His accent should have betrayed him, too, a lazy, insolent, ugly twang; but although clearly American in his speech, his southern drawl had been so soft—or so hidden—that she hadn't even detected it.

And, the greatest trickery, *treachery*, of all: he was not supposed to have made her feel what she felt when his strong hands so effortlessly broke her fall and his seductive dark blue eyes appraised her with such unconcealed interest. Maylene had no name for those feelings. They were totally unfamiliar to her, warm and wondrous—and completely, and so dangerously, in his control.

It was she who was supposed to have been in control, working with the Texan because she had to, because the Jade Palace meant so very much to her and she needed him to make it happen. Maylene had planned to be impeccably polite, civil and refined, all the while fortifying herself inside with icy contempt and arch disdain.

And now?

Now the sexy blue eyes were glinting at her, interested, amused, and invoking rushes of heat within her that were at once thrilling and terrifying.

"Please have a seat," Maylene offered.

"In a moment. I think I'll wander around your office first and admire the photographs of all the buildings you've designed." Sam's tall, sleek body didn't wander, only his eyes did, feigning surprise as they surveyed the barren walls. "Oh, I see that there aren't any."

"I left them in London. The cost of transporting them all would have been immense. I take it you brought yours with you, Mr. Coulter?"

"No, Ms. Kwan. But, then, I didn't really need to, did I?" His gaze returned to her. "Is this your first major project? Be honest."

His expression told her quite clearly that he wasn't going to let her be anything else. "Yes."

"Ain't love grand?"

"I beg your pardon?"

"Let's face it, your only credential for this project is that your lover happens to be paying for it."

"James and I aren't—" Her lush lips closed abruptly.

"You and James aren't what, Maylene?" Sam asked with soft surprise and intense interest. "Aren't lovers?"

"That's hardly any of your business."

"But it is. My business is building buildings. Anything that pertains to the success—or failure—of that endeavor is my concern. The Jade Palace may be a lark for you, but for me it's a very serious undertaking."

"As it is for me. I'm an architect. This is my career." *This is all I have, all I ever will have.* "James and I met *after* he chose my design for his hotel. We have immense respect for each other, but our relationship is professional—as it should be."

Do you have a lover? a wholly unprofessional voice wanted to know. Clamping down on the enticing query, Sam said, "Let me tell you about my usual professional relationship with an architect, okay? We work very closely. Each of us brings to the project a spirit of cooperation—and, of course, our energy and expertise."

Glancing at the sheaves of blueprints strewn around the office, Sam decided that Maylene Kwan had ample energy, and her impassioned response to his suggestion that, for her, the Jade Palace was merely a lark had convinced him that the hotel was terribly important to her as well. But wanting it to succeed simply wasn't enough.

"I admit that I have very little experience," Maylene confessed softly. "But before leaving London, I showed the blueprints to several top architects and structural engineers."

Sam arched a slightly skeptical eyebrow. "Do you remember what they said?"

She had the right to bristle, and she did, but after a moment she issued a sedate challenge. "I wrote everything down."

"I'd be very interested in seeing what you have."

Maylene turned to a file cabinet, removed a manila folder, and handed it to him. "I'd meant to type my notes, but I haven't had a chance."

Sam opened the thick file and scanned the top handwritten sheet. Her writing was eminently legible and remarkably unadorned, and her words showed a precise and appropriately focused grasp of what was going to be so difficult about the Jade Palace. He was, begrudgingly, impressed.

"Do you mind if I just take a look at these now?"

"No, please go ahead. I . . . if there's something you don't understand . . . can't read . . . "

Sam smiled. "I'll feel free to ask. Meanwhile, please have the others come back in. I don't want to impede progress and I assure you they won't bother me."

"The others?"

"The people who are assisting you with the drafting." It

seemed an unnecessary clarification, but it only caused uncertainty, a fragile vulnerability that evoked in Sam the astonishing urge to protect her from harm. Clarifying further, with a gentleness that surprised them both, he said, "There are three computers in this office, Maylene."

"I'm using all of them."

"No one's helping you?"

Maylene shrugged softly. "Several local firms have offered their help, but so far I think I'll be able to do everything myself."

"Would you like a cigarette?"

Sam's question ended an hour of concentrated silence, he studying her meticulous notes, she working at one of her three computers.

Good, Maylene thought as his question registered. At last he was behaving according to type. A Marlboro man. Now, perhaps, she could feel a little disdain—and, if so, then surely she would be able to control the effect he had on her, *wouldn't* she?

Turning from the computer screen to him, she answered, "No." Then, smiling prettily, she added. "Thank you."

"Do you mind if I smoke?"

Her smile was pretty still, her voice soft as she said, "Yes, I do."

She was on the moral high ground here, she believed. As she waited for Sam to light up despite her objection, to reveal his true cowboy boorishness, she felt surprising disappointment at the impending triumph. Some foolish—yet defiantly hopeful—part of her did not want to bid farewell to the warm, wondrous, dangerous feelings he evoked.

But there was to be no farewell. Once again Sam Coulter tricked her. With a nonchalant shrug, he returned to his reading, without a cigarette.

They didn't speak again until it was almost time to meet James for lunch.

"I'd like to spend some time at the construction site with you, Maylene."

"Oh, yes, of course."

"How is tomorrow afternoon, say about three?"

Maylene consulted her desk calendar. "Three's fine. Should James be there, too?" *Shouldn't* he be?

Amusement glittered in the seductive blue eyes at her obvious hesitancy in being alone with him. "I can't imagine why."

CHAPTER 6

The Jade Palace
Salisbury Road, Kowloon Peninsula
Thursday, June 10, 1993

A s Maylene approached the trailer that would serve as Sam Coulter's on-site office, she felt a disconcerting mix of annoyance and apprehension.

The annoyance was fully justified, of course. She knew that Sam and James had already walked the property, and although she might have been flattered that Sam was bothering to repeat the process with her, as if he valued her input, she knew it wasn't true. He just wanted her on his turf, in his lair, to make further disparaging remarks about her lack of expertise.

And the apprehension she felt? It was, she feared, actually eagerness in disguise. Some brave, wild, dangerous part of her wanted to see him again, to be caressed anew by his dark blue eyes and to feel once more the wondrously warm—and strangely joyous— sensations discovered by him.

The trailer door was ajar, so without knocking, Maylene walked in—and beheld the strong, lean silhouette of a cowboy. Admittedly, he wasn't wearing a hat, nor did she see one, and his denim work shirt was open at the collar, not cinched with a string tie, and the oval belt buckle he wore was brass not silver and without stones of any kind. But his jeans were well-worn, and as her eyes traveled down his long legs, they came upon badly battered boots.

Sam was gazing out the window at Victoria Harbour. His body was absolutely still, yet absolutely powerful, and his face seemed carved in stone, proud, hard, uncompromising. He was a portrait of arrogance, and a portrait, too, of a loner, a maverick, a man who cared only about his horses, his cigarettes, his range . . . the kind of man who would abandon his daughter without a backward glance.

A man worthy of nothing but contempt.

Before speaking, Maylene drew a calming breath, inhaling the scent of cigarette smoke as she did.

"Mamas, don't let your babies grow up to be cowboys."

Sam had been thinking about her, gentle thoughts, and because of those thoughts he heard more softness than disdain in the familiar country-western lyric enchantingly spoken in her elegant English. It was only when he turned that he realized her words were very far from a gentle tease.

Smiling, wishing he had a Stetson to tip, he drawled slowly, "Well, howdy, Miss Maylene, ma'am. Mighty fine day, ain't it?"

His dark blue eyes perused her with a laziness as slow and sexy as his drawl. Yesterday her suit had been flame, and today she wore navy trimmed in white, but like yesterday she looked as if she had just stepped off the runways of Paris. The straight skirt would severely limit her strides, but she wasn't going to be leaping like a gazelle anyway. Today's heels seemed even higher than yesterday's model.

"I assume you brought your work clothes with you. Feel free to change in the other room."

"These are my work clothes."

The cigarette that smoldered in Sam's left hand went slowly to his mouth and stayed there, casually imprisoned by his lips as its curls of smoke narrowed the seductive blue eyes that appraised her with unconcealed interest.

He's a cowboy! Maylene urgently reminded the giddy warmth that glowed within. He's a cowboy Pied Piper, beckoning to sensations I've never known, luring them to the surface and compelling them to follow wherever he chooses. He's arrogant, chauvinistic, despicable.

But *so* sexy, the renegade sensations purred. Even the way he smokes is sexy.

The way he smokes? her mind scoffed. With the thought came a semblance of control and softly hissed words. "I hope you don't die of lung cancer before the hotel is completed."

Sam grinned, stamped out the cigarette, and queried, "Really? You care?"

"Just about the hotel. So, are we going to walk around the site?"

The earth was parched, thirsty for the summer rains that had yet to come. The ruts left by tractors used to level the ground were rock-hard and unyielding. Maylene teetered, but she did not stumble, a feat accomplished through sheer will.

Sam had spent much of the previous night worrying about how he and Maylene were going to work together. It was so necessary that they be able to focus without distraction on the hotel. Peripheral issues, such as their personal feelings for each other, did not belong in the workplace. But it would help if those feelings, good or bad, were clearly defined.

We don't like each other. Fine. We're grown-up professionals, so let's proceed with the task at hand.

Or . . . we're attracted to each other. Fine. We're consenting adults, so let's do something about that attraction after hours.

But Sam Coulter's feelings for Maylene Kwan were not clearly defined. They were ever changing, as mercurial as she, one moment stormy, the next dazzling, and the remarkable jade-green eyes, welcoming one moment, warning the next, seemed just as conflicted.

For the next seven months he and Maylene needed to be architect and builder, united in their commitment to this most challenging goal. But how? After a sleepless night Sam still had no answer, and he would have greeted the optimistic suggestion that it would happen of its own accord, as early as today, with great skepticism.

But it *did* happen today. Amid the dust of the parched earth beneath the blazing hot June sun, Sam and Maylene talked with quiet excitement about the Jade Palace. It was as if they could both see it, majestic and magnificent, glistening alabaster and gold and jade beneath the brilliant azure sky. As they discussed the logistical problems her design would present, Maylene's intelligent eyes were thoughtful, analytical, and so clear of shadows that the lustrous jade shimmered bright emerald.

It had happened. They *were* architect and builder, unafraid of exchanging differing views because they were so bonded by their deep passion for the project itself. But, Sam realized, even as architect and builder, there were layers, undercurrents, *other* passions, that would make this professional relationship more wonderful—and more dangerous—than any he'd ever had before.

They walked through the grand entrance that only they could see, but which each saw so clearly, and in the place where the lobby would be, they could hear the splashing fountains and sense the exquisite harmony of fragrances of tea roses from England and gardenias from China.

After discussing the treasures of art that would be displayed on the green marble walls, and the jade and bronze statues that would grace the white marble floors, they journeyed beyond the lobby to the harbor. When they reached the water's edge, they looked back, as if marveling at the magnificent illusion—and the magnificent reality—of the Jade Palace itself.

Eventually their eyes met. But there was such intimacy in the dark blue, such desire, such wishes for passion that the woman of ice knew she could never meet, that Maylene's response was fueled by fear—and by bitter disappointment for them both.

"Is there anything else you wanted to discuss, Cowboy?" she asked sharply.

"About the hotel? No, I think that just about covers it for now . . . Jade."

Her voice was sharp and edgy, and his was caressing and gentle, but "Jade" seemed to be a knife itself, plunging into her fragile heart and spilling anguish—and anger—into her beautiful green eyes.

"You really are a bastard, aren't you? A rednecked Texan complete with all the prejudices."

Many an angry woman had called Sam Coulter a bastard. It wasn't technically accurate, but as a description of his behavior it had on numerous occasions been quite apt. But the son of an alcoholic rodeo cowboy had never before been accused of being prejudiced, not against anyone, not ever.

It bothered him—a lot.

"I think you'd better spell out what you mean." His voice was dangerously quiet. "Real slow, ma'am. We rednecks have a reputation for being pretty stupid."

"You've been prejudiced against me since the moment we met."

Sam's dark blue eyes sent an explicit and intimate reminder of when and how they had met. Only when he was certain that her memory had traveled to the Trade Winds's lobby, where there had been, at the very least, an instant and powerful chemistry, did he say, very softly, "Hardly."

"I meant in the office," Maylene countered swiftly. "When you realized that I was the architect."

For the past hour Sam and Maylene had been able to quietly discuss the problems inherent in the creation of the Jade Palace, and what could be done to overcome them. Working together with care, with shared passion, and with intelligent, thoughtful calm when obstacles loomed ahead, they could make her extraordinary vision come to life.

Sam realized then, with a jolt, that there was something else he wanted, something far more extraordinary than the Jade Palace. If it were possible, if it could be done, he wanted a relationship with this complicated woman—an important relationship: meaningful, emotional, and committed. For Sam, who had never before wanted more than the ordinary with a woman, it was a stunning realization.

The hotel designed by Maylene Kwan was extraordinary, as was the fantasy that danced now in Sam's mind. And, he mused, like the Jade Palace, the idea of a relationship with Maylene was, perhaps, an impossible illusion—and, as with her hotel, if careful attention wasn't paid to every detail, if everything wasn't done exactly right, the result would be disastrous.

Maylene's accusation now was, of course, far more than detail. It was the foundation itself.

"Your belief that I'm prejudiced against you is something we need to talk about," Sam said quietly. "Please tell me, specifically, in what ways you believe that to be true."

"My age."

"Which is what?"

"I'll be twenty-eight on January first, the day after the Palace opens." She lifted a defiant chin. "How old are you?"

"Thirty-six." Sam didn't need to elaborate that—in their business—eight years translated into a vast difference. Nor did he. "I have no problem with your age, Maylene, although I fully admit that when I first saw you I was concerned about your experience— or lack thereof. But I'm getting over that. Next prejudice, please."

"My sex."

"If I were a card-carrying redneck I suppose I would indeed have a little trouble with that. And I confess that until yesterday morning I believed I would be meeting a 'Michael' not a 'Maylene' Kwan." The lazy half smile that was devastating proof of his innate sexuality touched his lips. "But I'm really a nineties kind of guy. I think I'm going to be able to adjust to that surprise without difficulty. So, there, I'm not prejudiced against you after all."

Sam hoped for a smile in return, but Maylene's expression was grave still, and sad, and almost ashamed.

"What, Maylene? Tell me."

"My race."

"Your race?" It was a gasp, released as if he'd been struck. "You think I'm prejudiced against you because you're Chinese?"

"Half Chinese," she corrected harshly, punishingly.

The punishment, Sam realized, was directed toward herself not toward him. He ached for her pain and cursed himself for having unwittingly caused it. Did she truly believe that "Jade" had been intended as a taunt, a merciless reminder that the indisputable proof of her mixed—and apparently shameful—parentage glittered in her beautiful dark green eyes?

His face grew solemn, his eyes gentle, and when he spoke his deep voice held an even deeper tenderness. "Believe me, Maylene, I am not prejudiced against you because of your race. Look at me, please. It's really terribly important that you believe that."

Her long inky-black lashes were downcast in shame, but at the tenderness in his voice they lifted, and when they did Sam saw what looked like hope. Fragile, delicate hope.

"Although I fully recognize that you might not have meant it in an entirely positive way, to me 'Cowboy' is a term of endearment." His gentle tease caused the faintest glimmer of a smile on her lovely lips and a tiny—and yet oh-so-brilliant—sparkle of bright green in her dark jade eyes. "When I called you 'Jade' I meant it as a compliment. We're building the Jade Palace, after all, and it's my understanding that jade is highly prized."

He stopped abruptly, worried that once again his words might unwittingly cause pain. He knew that jade was greatly valued by the Chinese. Said to contain mystical powers against evil, it was considered a symbol of wealth, of beauty, and of virtue. But Maylene was only half Chinese, and clearly ashamed of her mixed heritage. Did that mean that she excluded herself from the beliefs and traditions of those whose blood was pure?

But Maylene smiled then, rescuing him, rescuing them both, and admitted, "Yes, jade is highly prized."

"I knew it was the right nickname for you," Sam offered, his voice soft, calm, even though his heart thundered with relief. Maylene's belief that he was prejudiced against her because of her race was an enormous obstacle; and they had gotten beyond it—*together*. He wanted to talk about her, to learn more about what caused the shadows and the storms, but he sensed it was far too soon.

Instead he smiled . . . and she smiled . . . and this time, when Maylene felt quivers of panic at the intimacy, rather than bristling—and yet needing to look away—she smiled still as she left his eyes and turned toward Victoria Harbour. Sam followed suit, and for a while they marveled in silence at the bustle of one of the world's busiest ports.

The harbor was a cauldron of activity. Ancient junks crossed the wakes of ultramodern hydrofoils, sampans darted amid container ships and cargo freighters, and walla-wallas and Star ferries provided passage between Hong Kong Island and Kowloon. There was a warship, too, floating languidly atop the choppy green waters, and in the distance a mahogany-hulled sloop skimmed across the white-tipped waves. Once, the journey from peninsula to island could only be made by boat. But now a constant flow of gleaming gold-and-silver Rolls-Royces streamed through a car tunnel beneath the sea, and through its own submerged conduits, the Mass Transit Railway sped its passengers as well. Overhead, a flock of helicopters shuttled those who preferred to be transported high in the shimmering air.

"Oh!" Maylene exclaimed, turning toward him.

"What's wrong?"

"Just as I was leaving to come over here, Mrs. Leong, James's administrative assistant, asked me to give you a message."

"Is it too late to give it to me now?"

"No, but . . . I just can't believe I forgot." Maylene's memory was usually precisely ordered and unfailingly reliable. But not today. Within moments of leaving Drake Towers, Mrs. Leong's message had been forgotten, Maylene's mind wholly consumed by the prospect of seeing Sam.

"Well," Sam assured with a smile. "You've remembered now. So tell me."

"She was able to reach Golden Eight. He and James will be here at six this evening."

"Golden Eight?"

"The *feng shui* master." When her clarification didn't seem to make any more sense to Sam than Golden Eight's name, Maylene concluded, "I guess you didn't even know the meeting was in the works. I assumed it was something you and James had discussed."

"No."

Sam had no idea what she was talking about, and it was quite obvious that he should have. During the past few months, while building a cliff-top resort in Bermuda, he had, by fax and by phone, made the necessary preconstruction preparations for the Jade Palace. In the process, during telephone conversations with Tyler and James, he had gleaned a few facts about construction in Hong Kong.

The impending turnover of sovereignty to the People's Republic of China had escalated rather than diminished Hong Kong's building boom. As a provision of the Joint Declaration, the government in Beijing agreed to honor all existing land leases for at least fifty years. It seemed prudent, however, to have the buildings completed and fully operational before 1997.

A six-day workweek was de rigueur in all businesses in Hong Kong, and construction crews would work a seven-day week without complaint. The summer months provided long hours of precious daylight, and every second was used—when it could be. The downside was the weather. The summer monsoon, the prevailing wind from the sea, brought drenching rains and sometimes even raging typhoons. There might be days or even weeks when construction had to be suspended.

Sam knew these facts about building in Hong Kong before his arrival, and in the past two days he had learned something else. All buildings under construction, even those that climbed seventy stories into the azure sky, were enmeshed in skeins of bamboo and draped with bright green netting. Although the bamboo scaffolding appeared delicate and precarious, he was assured that it was very strong—and that the construction workers of Hong Kong had the balance of trapeze artists.

Now, Sam realized, he was going to learn something else about building here.

"I'm lost," he confessed. "It's obvious that I should know who a *feng shui* master is, but I don't. Will you tell me?"

"Yes, of course, I'd be happy to." Maylene's words were gracious, but a soft frown touched her face, and when she spoke there was uncertainty in her voice. "The Chinese believe that nature is a living creature with whom man should attempt to live in harmony."

Sam suddenly understood her uncertainty. *Feng shui* obviously involved ancient Chinese beliefs, the exotic mysticism of the Orient, and Maylene was worried that he would think it foolish. Quietly, truthfully, he said, "I guess I believe that, too."

Maylene smiled wryly. "You may not believe that the natural cosmos is populated by gods and ghosts and spirits and dragons."

"But maybe I should," Sam offered gently. His reading in anticipation of his trip to Hong Kong had been purely technical and extremely focused: how one could abide by the laws of optics and gravity and yet accomplish the Jade Palace's magnificent illusion.

Now, because of Maylene, he wanted to know everything about Hong Kong. "Please tell me all about *feng shui.*"

"Okay. Well, let's see. It means, literally, 'wind and water,' and its purpose is to place man in the most harmonious relationship possible with the spiritual world. Such harmony is considered the best hope for good fortune, good luck. The *feng shui* master offers advice on how to deflect evil spirits and woo good ones."

"What kind of advice?"

"Depending on how confident he is, all sorts of things—wedding dates, business ventures, what horses to bet on at Happy Valley. Mostly, though, his suggestions are quite practical, aimed at putting things in proper physical alignment with roaming spirits. For example, having a view of water is a good *feng shui.* If one doesn't have a view, one needs to create one. That's why there are so many aquariums in Hong Kong."

Sam smiled, interested, encouraging. "What else?"

"Well, because spirits can only move in straight lines, they can be kept out of buildings by installing the doors at a slant, or by putting in revolving ones."

"So *feng shui* is quite important in construction."

"Yes. Very."

"You'd better tell me more."

Maylene's whirlwind architectural tour of Hong Kong—based on the decrees of *feng shui*—started with the Regent, the harborside hotel located less than a quarter of a mile from where they stood. Since both the Regent and the Jade Palace were on Kowloon Peninsula, she began by explaining how the peninsula got its name.

"In the late thirteenth century, the last emperor of the Sung dynasty fled here in an attempt to escape the Mongols. When he saw the peninsula's eight hills, each of which he believed to be the home of a dragon, he wanted to name his own new home 'Eight Dragons' in their honor. He was just a boy, and had forgotten that emperors, too, were dragons. Once reminded, he changed the name to Kowloon, 'Nine Dragons.' Dragons are revered creatures in Chinese mythology, and are generally regarded as good, not evil. Still, one definitely tries not to provoke them. In fact, great efforts are often expended specifically to please them. Which brings us to the Regent. The *feng shui* consultant strongly advised that the dragons of Kowloon not be forgotten." Maylene smiled. "Which is why the walls of the Regent's lobby are all glass, so that the dragons can see their way to the harbor to bathe."

The windows of Maylene Kwan's Jade Palace were to be tinted a lustrous jade—except for the lobby atrium. There, the glass would be crystal clear. Now Sam knew why. "Did Golden Eight make a similar suggestion for the Palace?"

"No. The atrium glass was clear on the original sketches." Maylene shrugged. "I have no problem with the dragons wandering through our lobby, do you?"

Sam smiled. "None at all. They're more than welcome. Does Golden Eight have any concerns about the hotel?"

"Not really. In fact, he thinks the alignments are very propitious. I'm sure James just wants you to meet him because he'll be dropping by from time to time to make certain everything still feels right."

Having finished with the special considerations of building in Kowloon, Maylene gestured across Victoria Harbour, toward the skyscrapers of Hong Kong Island, and beginning with the controversial Hong Kong and Shanghai Bank, she asked. "What do you think of Hong Kong's heavily fortified twenty-first-century space station?"

"I like it. Do you?"

"Very much."

"Was it a *feng shui* nightmare?"

"Not really. The suspended escalators had to be installed slightly askew, but that was easy. The only real problem came with Stephen and Stitt, the two bronze lions. They'd guarded the previous incarnation of the bank, and when it was time for them to be moved to their new location, it had to be done just so—at four o'clock on a Sunday morning, using two cranes, lifting them simultaneously so as to engender no jealousy in either beast."

"I saw them yesterday. They seemed quite content with their new home."

Maylene nodded. "And the bank itself has enjoyed good fortune."

"What about the Bank of China?" Sam asked as his gaze shifted to the building that, until very recently, had been Asia's tallest structure. Designed by I. M. Pei, its long lines sent messages of confidence and style.

"The bank itself is flourishing, but they had to pull out all stops to ensure its good luck. Even though the segmental increments are suppose to resemble bamboo shoots, propelling themselves ever higher with each successive growth, there was a great deal of concern about the sharpness of the angles. Which is why, on August eighth, 1988, the luckiest day of the century, they held an elaborate topping-out ceremony."

"Here's a wild guess—there's something lucky about the number eight."

Maylene smiled. "In Cantonese, 'eight' is a homonym for 'prosperity.' "

"Hence Golden Eight."

"A nickname given to him by satisfied customers."

"He has lots of customers?"

"All the good *feng shui* men do. Courting luck is a favorite Chinese pastime—maybe even an obsession—so those proficient in *feng shui* are consulted by everyone, from the most humble amah to the most powerful taipan. Well," she amended, "not *the* most powerful taipan." She pointed to Victoria Peak. At its very summit stood a pristine white building, its windows gleaming bright copper in the afternoon sun. "That's Peak Castle, home to Sir Geoffrey Lloyd-Ashton, owner of Hong Kong's largest trading company. Sir Geoffrey apparently regards *feng shui* as pure nonsense."

"Because?"

"Because every *feng shui* expert in the territory believes that Peak Castle is blinding the mountain's dragon."

"And Sir Geoffrey doesn't care?"

"I gather he doesn't. In fact, he supposedly rather likes the fact that Hong Kong's unofficial name for his castle is Dragon's Eyes."

"Has his defiance of *feng shui* brought him bad luck?"

"Not yet." Maylene shrugged. "By all accounts, his life is quite perfect, as is, according to James, the interior of the castle."

"Is James a frequent guest?"

"I think so. Lady Lloyd-Ashton and James's wife—" she stopped abruptly, and frowned.

"I know about James's wife, Maylene," Sam said quietly. "At the time of her death, I was working with an architect who knew James very well. She knew Lady Lloyd-Ashton?"

"Gweneth Drake and Eve—Lady Lloyd-Ashton—were girlhood friends in England. James speaks very fondly of Eve. I imagine he could arrange for you to see the inside of the castle if you wanted."

"I'd like to see it. How about you? Or have you seen it already in photographs?"

"Peak Castle's never appeared in *Architectural Digest* and never will. Dragon's Eyes is for Sir Geoffrey's eyes only—and for those of his invited guests."

"That makes me want to see it all the more, and a lot less likely to ask James to arrange a tour." Sam smiled, and she smiled, and after a moment he asked, "Speaking of photography, do you happen to know when Allison Whitaker is scheduled to arrive?"

Of course I know, Maylene thought, stunned—and suddenly fearful. Somehow keeping the smile in her eyes, she replied, "Sunday night."

"Do you know if James plans to meet her plane?"

"We both plan to." Smiling still, she asked, "Do you know her?"

"No, we've never met. But I know her father. I spoke with him shortly before leaving Texas and he mentioned that Allison would be over here as well."

Maylene nodded, as if that information were of passing interest only, then, as casually as possible, she turned to the ever-interesting activity of Victoria Harbour. As she stared, unseeing, at the drama of boats and waves, her thoughts screamed. You know my father? Did he ask you to keep an eye on Allison, the daughter he loves, to protect her from the dark secrets that lurk here? Or does Garrett Whitaker have any memory of Hong Kong at all?

Sam could only see Maylene's profile now, but he saw clearly that, quite suddenly, her beautiful eyes had iced over, denying him access. Sam had been counting on the expressive green to guide him on his journey to her heart. He knew that the voyage would be a perilous one, ever challenging and unpredictable, but he had expected to be able to see his way.

But now he knew, and he shouldn't have been surprised, that this complicated woman would not be so easily read. When her heart was in greatest jeopardy—and in greatest need—she would simply close off, just as he did.

Sam Coulter was a builder of great buildings, a master at his craft, an expert sculptor of steel and stone. Such towering structures were, however, all that he created. He most assuredly did not build relationships, not enduring ones. He had sexual liaisons, of course, brief forays into pleasure. Very little building was required for such encounters, very little preamble necessary at all.

Except for his buildings, what Sam Coulter did mostly was destroy.

And now, with this complicated woman, for the first time ever, he wanted to build. There were no blueprints for love in his life . . . and as Sam saw the jade-green ice that was brilliant proof of Maylene's own deep pain, he wondered if he would end up destroying them both.

Maylene left, precipitously, citing an appointment in Drake Towers. After she was gone, Sam searched the hard earth until he found two perfect prints of her shoes in the dust. After measuring them carefully, he returned to the trailer and placed a call to San Antonio.

Forty-five minutes later, when the fax machine on his desk came to life, Sam assumed it would be in follow-up to his request. But the fax wasn't from Texas. It came instead from just across Victoria Harbour.

In her clear, no-nonsense handwriting, she wrote:

Cowboy,

No sooner said than done! You *will* get your look into the Dragon's Eyes. James just told me that we've all been invited to a dinner party at Peak Castle a week from Saturday.

J

Sam was pleased at the prospect of spending an evening exploring the controversial landmark, but that pleasure paled in comparison with how he felt about the way Maylene had signed the fax.

J, short for Jade. Somehow she wasn't quite bold enough to write all four letters of his term of endearment, but she was accepting it, wanting it . . . and the master builder who knew so very little about building relationships of the heart nonetheless saw the *J* for what it was: the small yet monumental cornerstone of what could be the most extraordinary creation of his life.

Later that night, just before 11:00 P.M., Eve, Lady Lloyd-Ashton, stood before a window in Peak Castle's master suite and watched the taillights of her husband's forest-green Bentley disappear down Mount Austin Road. As soon as the lights vanished from sight, she turned away.

Too quickly, she realized as the sudden twisting motion triggered sharp stabs of pain. Eve paused, breath held, until the piercing pain and its aftershocks subsided. Then she resumed her journey toward the telephone, removing a piece of paper from the pocket of her robe as she did. The green silk robe was a Pearl Moon design, and in her pocket was the home telephone number of its talented designer—and her friend—Juliana Kwan.

Eve had never called Juliana at home before. All of the many previous calls she had placed had always been to the Pearl Moon boutique, brief impersonal conversations to schedule fittings. But now, because Eve had been worrying about her friend, and because she had personal news to share, she dialed the unfamiliar number in Happy Valley.

Juliana answered on the first ring, her soft voice at once apprehensive and hopeful.

"It's only me, Juliana," Eve greeted with gentle apology. "You haven't heard from her?"

"Oh, Eve, hello. No, I haven't heard."

"She's only been back in Hong Kong for five days," Eve reminded quietly. "She's undoubtedly terribly preoccupied with the hotel. She'll call."

"She hasn't for nine years."

"No, but now she's returned to Hong Kong, she's *chosen* to, and for a long time you believed that she never would. That's hopeful, isn't it?"

"I've permitted myself to believe that it is," Juliana admitted. "I've even let myself believe it might mean that she's forgiven me . . . us . . . and that she finally understands that she was loved."

"You could call her, Juliana. You could tell her everything all over again. I know you think she remembers clearly what you told her, but maybe she doesn't."

A soft, wistful smile touched Juliana's lips. How she wished it was all simply a failure to communicate, a mother–daughter misunderstanding that could be magically resolved by speaking words now that had somehow been overlooked all those years before. But Juliana knew that there were no missing words. On the day when she'd been forced to tell her devastated thirteen-year-old daughter that her father hadn't died after all, Juliana told Maylene every important truth; and she had repeated those truths *so many times* over the next five years.

There was no doubt that Maylene heard her words. Indeed, her bright daughter memorized them all, playing them back, verbatim, with her own interpretation.

That's not *love*, Mother! He *used* you and *abandoned* me. Don't you get it? Don't blame it on fate, some romanticized notion of star-crossed destiny! He *chose* not to be with us. He betrayed us, and all these years, you've betrayed me by pretending that he was dead—and that he was wonderful. I wish he *were* dead, Mother, and I can tell you he's *not* wonderful, or loving, or honorable. He was a sailor interested in sex, nothing more, and I'm the bastard child who's a living symbol of that shame! You try living in this place with green eyes and white skin and features that aren't pure. People *stare*, Mother. They taunt and they tease. But do you know how I've survived their contempt? By believing I was different from the other half-breeds of Wanchai, a child of love not lust. But I'm not, Mother, because everything you've ever told me was a *lie*.

"Juliana?"

"I'm sure she hasn't forgotten anything."

"But she's older now, more mature."

"Maylene has always been mature," Juliana countered quietly, remembering the little girl who, to protect her mother, had lovingly concealed her own immense torment. "I need to let her come to me, Eve, if she wants to. She's returned to Hong Kong because of the Jade Palace, to create something magnificent in the place where she was so unhappy. I don't want to interfere. It wouldn't be fair."

Eve drew a steadying breath, and then was forced to wait as new screams of pain echoed throughout her body. When she finally spoke again her soft, elegant voice gave no clue to the silent battle that she was waging still. "I'm going to meet her, Juliana."

"You are?" Juliana whispered. "When?"

"A week from Saturday. Geoffrey wants to have a dinner party in celebration of the ground breaking of the Jade Palace."

"And Maylene is going to be there?"

"James said that she would be."

"You didn't tell James that she's my daughter."

"Of course not. I promised that I'd never tell anyone, Juliana, and you know I wouldn't break that promise."

"I know." Juliana's voice filled with fondness for her friend, the compassionate woman who had such a gift for seeing into the hearts of others—and yet seemed quite blind to the generous gifts of her own. "I'm glad you'll be meeting her, Eve."

"Would you like to be here that night, Eve? I could ask Geoffrey—"

"No," Juliana interjected softly. "Thank you for offering, Eve, but Maylene needs to come to me, if she wants to. After all this time we can't see each other by chance . . . or by surprise."

CHAPTER 7

The midnight moon filtered through a veil of clouds, casting the sea in battered silver and the sand in faded bone. The March breeze was cool and crisp, and he was running, and the waves were crashing. Still, he heard the distant sound, a faint thunder exploding in the night.

But it wasn't thunder, and even though he had no idea what it was, had no way of knowing that it was a sound that would signal the end of his dreams, he turned and began running back toward the house . . . and as he did the sky before him glowed a brilliant orange, illuminated by the inferno below.

He ran harder, his heart bursting, and now the night air resonated with the screams of sirens. It doesn't matter, he told himself. Even if the house is on fire, there's no one there. She's in London, sleeping peacefully, lost in blissful dreams of love.

But his attempts to reassure himself were strangely futile, as if he already knew, as if he heard now in the loving voice that had bid him good night a message he hadn't heard before: she was going to join him tonight, after all. She missed him too much to stay away, and although her pregnancy made her tired, the boundless joy of carrying their baby gave her more than enough energy to make the long drive to Wales.

Her car was there, mercilessly illuminated by the inferno that had once been their seaside home. The firefighters tried to prevent his journey into the flames. But he was far too powerful for them, his love for her stronger than any other force on earth.

His gasping lungs inhaled fire and smoke, but he ran ever deeper into the blaze, lured by her frantic voice. "Help me, James! Please help me!" He could see her silhouette through the mist of smoke and flames, a shadow on fire, and somehow he could even see his son within her womb, calling to him, too, counting on his father to save him from a fiery death. . . .

James awakened gasping, as breathless as he'd been on that long-ago night. His lungs inhaled pure air now, not fire and smoke, but he was suffocating nonetheless, consumed by harsh, searing pain. It was a dream, the only one he ever had, a nightmare that survived even the brightest light of day, because, except for the very end, it was all true, an indelible memory of his desperate effort to save his wife and unborn son.

Gweneth hadn't screamed for him, nor had his baby. Both had died instantly, never awakening from their dreams, never knowing the terror of the smoky blaze. There was nothing James could have done to save them, nothing anyone could have done.

James had almost died, too, amid the fire and smoke, and had it not been for the sinister revelation about that night, he might have simply allowed his injuries to kill him.

"It wasn't an accident, James, not a simple explosion caused by a leakage of gas. There was a bomb. Gweneth was murdered." The quiet yet thundering words came from a friend, a classmate from Cambridge who was now with Scotland Yard, and who had come to the ICU to personally give James the devastating news.

The ashes of the country home in Wales had yielded few clues. There was no doubt, however, that the murderer was a "professional," a hired assassin. The plastic explosive that had been used was the state-of-the-art weapon of a terrorist, and the sabotage itself had been so discreet that a less sophisticated investigation might never have uncovered the truth. Indeed, because the saboteur had obviously been so assiduous in his efforts to hide all traces of his treachery, Scotland Yard decided to let him assume that he had succeeded. For the moment, and perhaps for as long as the case was open, neither the press nor the murderer would learn that Gweneth Drake's death had been ruled anything other than a tragic accident.

James spent long hours searching his mind for possible suspects. *He* had been the intended victim, of course. It was he who should have been in that bed—alone. His lovely wife had had no enemies. Nor, until then, had he. There were business rivals, fierce competitors for the most valuable properties on earth, but that the quest for land could become deadly seemed beyond imagination—until, quite obviously, it had. Since James was expanding his real-estate empire to the Pacific Rim, and especially to Hong Kong, it was most likely that his mortal enemy was there, a land developer who was willing to commit murder to protect the domain that James was about to invade.

The doctors had believed that James Drake would not survive. He had neither the will to compel his seared lungs to heal, nor the physical reserves to fight the pain of his badly burned flesh. Following the visit from his friend from Scotland Yard, however, his recovery was nothing short of miraculous.

The day after leaving the hospital, James flew to Hong Kong and embarked on a construction program that was far more ambitious, far more *aggressive*, than any he would have considered had Gweneth been alive. Then, much of his time would have been devoted to his wife and son. But now every second of his life was devoted to a single purpose: finding—and then killing—the man who had stolen his dreams. And how would James lure the monster from the shadows? By systematically invading and conquering the killer's precious domain.

James Drake became Hong Kong's wealthiest and most highly respected developer. He flaunted his dominance, building ever more magnificent structures, capturing the best land and the most lucrative contracts. It had been four years and still his murderous enemy, the thief of dreams, had not been provoked. Yes, often, the competition was fierce, and sometimes ruthless, but there had never been even the softest whisper of danger.

James waited, a caged beast ravenous for a chance at his prey, his hunger mounting with each passing day of captivity. Four years—and nothing, except immense success, meaningless without Gweneth, and nightmares, and a blazing fire of rage that burned ever more intensely the longer it was held within.

Now, after four years, he was at last building the Jade Palace—for Gweneth, because of Gweneth. She had always insisted that the idea for the magnificent hotel was *theirs*, conceived at precisely the same instant, but in James's memory, it was hers, and it was definitely she who had chosen the name. They had been in complete accord on the project itself: there needed to be an enduring symbol of Hong Kong, the enchanted place that James had loved since boyhood and that after only a few weeks Gweneth had come to love as well.

Hong Kong ... it had saved his heart, his spirit, his very soul—and had given him the most extraordinary gift of all, the ability to love. Because of Hong Kong, James Drake had become a far better man than he was ever meant to be.

Had he been raised in England, an only child on his family's vast estate, James had little doubt that he would have become as cold and remote as his parents. Theirs was a marriage of pedigree only, and although both parents felt a sense of satisfaction—and perhaps relief—that their loveless union had so swiftly produced the requisite male heir, his mother obviously believed that her responsibilities toward that son ended with his birth, and his father's only lingering role was one of harsh discipline.

But James spent his boyhood in Hong Kong, not England. His home itself, the stately mansion on Old Peak Road, was filled with great wealth, but was quite barren of true riches, of emotion and of love. Yet just beyond the mansion's immense stone-gray walls lay a world of brilliant color and boundless treasures, and it was there where the boy was truly raised, and nurtured—and saved. James learned to speak fluent Cantonese, and in the tropical air alive with gods and ghosts and spirits and dragons, he felt strangely safe, and the people of Hong Kong became the only family that mattered.

And the heart that, from birth, had been destined to be as cold as ice? It filled with warmth instead—and with affection and gratitude—to the people and place that had rescued him. Despite that warmth, however, James did not believe that he would ever fall in love. It seemed impossible that the chilling influences of his parents could be so wholly denied.

But James Drake did fall in love, and it was with great joy that he anticipated returning to Hong Kong to share its splendor with his wife and son—and to build the Jade Palace in loving tribute to the people to whom he felt he owed his happiness.

Had Gweneth been alive, the Jade Palace would have been his first project in Hong Kong. Indeed, the letter that was to solicit sketches from the world's premier architects had been drafted, with Gweneth's enthusiastic and talented help, just days before her death, and copies were scheduled to be mailed the moment they reached Hong Kong.

No letters had been mailed, of course. And in this new Hong Kong, where even the most brilliant memories were now shadowed by the lurking menace of Gweneth's murderer—and where each day might be the one in which James would fight to the death with that killer—the once joyous dream had been indefinitely postponed.

But James could not forget Gweneth's words: "You must build the Jade Palace, darling, you *must*. And long before 1997, too. If the world truly understands what a rare treasure Hong Kong is, perhaps its future will be more secure." Nor could he forget his own solemn commitment to his boyhood home. Still, as he mailed the letter he and Gweneth had drafted four years before, James truly believed that their dream would never be realized, and as he waited for replies he sent silent apologies to his beloved wife. I can't do it, my love. Not without you. We agreed it had to be perfect, remember? I don't have the heart to make that happen. You were my heart . . . and you are gone.

The proposal submitted by Maylene Kwan truly stunned him. It did not, of course, conform to what he and Gweneth had envisioned, a joyful celebration of the harmonious marriage of East and West. There was celebration in Maylene's design, but there was conflict as well—a vision, James realized, that was far more authentic than what he and Gweneth had planned. Hong Kong's origins were, after all, rooted in conflict, and throughout its history there had been struggles. Maylene's vision was historically more accurate—and, emotionally, it was remarkably close to what James himself felt about Hong Kong since losing Gweneth: torment, and yet reverence still . . . wonder at its mystical majesty despite his own anguish.

And if this authentic portrait of conflict amid harmony seemed too harsh? The effect would be softened by the hotel's lush and fragrant gardens, and the art treasures housed within . . . and by the photographs of Hong Kong as seen through the rose-colored lenses of Allison Parish Whitaker.

It was 5:00 A.M. In fifteen hours the photographer whose rosy optimism was so obvious from her pictures and which flowed so joyfully from her soft, lovely voice would be arriving in Hong Kong. Indeed, at this precise moment, as James Drake was leaving his bed to spend what remained of the night perfecting the swift, lethal moves of his body, Allison Whitaker was in San Francisco, just boarding United's overwater DC-10.

For almost twenty-eight years Garrett Whitaker had kept his solemn promise to Juliana. Despite the relentless urgings of his heart, he had never once attempted to find out about the woman he would always love and the daughter he would never see.

But now, moments after Allison's call from San Francisco, an excited report that the flight was scheduled to depart on time and she would be boarding soon, Garrett reached for the phone.

He wasn't breaking the vow, not really. Even if the operator in Hong Kong provided him with phone numbers for Juliana and Maylene, he wasn't going to call. He just needed to know if they were there. Garrett wanted to know *much* more than that, of course: that their lives were happy, filled with love and joy—and that they knew he loved them still, always.

As he dialed the overseas number his mind traveled through time to his final conversation with Juliana. He allowed the memory to surface, believing he would have many minutes to cherish it. But just seconds after dialing, there was ringing, and then a clear, pleasant voice, and he was forced swiftly back to the present. Twenty-eight years had passed. Things had changed. Phone calls to the other side of the planet were routine, and voices no longer lingered forever in the vastness of space. Except for her British accent, the directory-assistance operator in modern-day Hong Kong could have been in Dallas.

"I have no residential listing for Juliana Kwan," she said with polite apology. "There are many J. Kwans, however. Do you happen to have her address?"

Twenty-eight years had passed. Things had changed. Juliana was probably—undoubtedly—married, and Vivian Jong was probably no longer alive, and the house in which she and Juliana had lived in Happy Valley was probably a high-rise condominium complex, and . . .

"There's a business listing for Juliana Kwan," the operator offered into the silence that lingered because of emotion not technology. "Is the Juliana Kwan you're trying to reach the fashion designer?"

"Yes," Garrett said softly. "Yes, she is."

"Shall I give you that listing?"

"Yes. Please."

The operator's voice vanished, replaced by a recording of the number, and that was just as well, because the emotion that accompanied his joyous thoughts would have made further words quite impossible.

Juliana is alive.

And she is living her dream.

It was a very long time before Garrett trusted his voice enough even to think about placing the second call to directory assistance in Hong Kong. Would he find a home phone number for his daughter? Or a business listing, perhaps? Was she a designer, too? Had mother and daughter realized Vivian's dream together?

But Garrett never placed the second call. As he imagined the conversation with the operator he was flooded with an emotion so drowning that he could not speak.

He had spent the past twenty-eight years loving the daughter he would never see, missing her, wishing for her happiness. She lived in his heart as the Daughter of Greatest Love, and even though he knew the other unique and beautiful name Juliana had given her, he did not know how Juliana spelled Maylene.

PART THREE

CHAPTER 8

Kai Tak International Airport
Kowloon Peninsula
Sunday, June 13, 1993

"Twenty minutes until touchdown," the United Airlines pilot announced. He'd made a few announcements during the long transpacific flight, but until now there hadn't been a great deal to say. Now, however, he became quite animated. "For those of you who've never been to Hong Kong before, don't worry, I *do* know where I'm going. The reason it will seem as if I'm heading for a spot beside a fleet of ships and between a cluster of skyscrapers is because that's exactly where I *am* going. So, just relax and enjoy!"

It was like landing in a treasure chest of jewels, Allison decided. Brilliant against the black sky, and in every color of the rainbow, the lights of Hong Kong greeted her. As the jet swooped ever closer to earth, some of the lights came into lovely, exotic focus, and even though she couldn't read the brightly glowing neon, the graceful Chinese characters sent a clear and glorious reminder of the grand adventure that lay ahead.

She felt like Dorothy, beholding for the first time the dazzling brilliance of the Emerald City. Hong Kong was *beyond* the Emerald City, though, far more than simply a shimmering green. There were rubies here, and diamonds, sapphires, amethyst, and jade. And unlike the Land of Oz, the glittering jewel-bright Crown Colony was very, very real.

When the jet came to a stop at a remote spot on the tarmac, the lights that had seemed so bright and so close were suddenly faraway. As Allison and her fellow passengers traveled by bus to the main terminal, their journey amid the towering silhouettes of jumbo jets was one of shadows. She was amazed by the number of mammoth planes that cluttered the darkened runways. Parked at seemingly random angles, they loomed overhead like a great herd of slumbering dinosaurs. The effect was quite eerie, at once ancient and modern. The prehistoric-looking monsters were, in fact, symbols of what Kai Tak truly was—one of the busiest airports on earth.

Then the dinosaurs were gone, as were the shadows, and Allison was in the brightly lighted terminal experiencing firsthand the gracious efficiency for which Hong Kong was so renowned. Although it took her less than five minutes to clear immigration, her luggage was already waiting for her, spinning slowly on one of the many shining stainless-steel carousels.

Exit Door Four, she reminded herself as she gathered her suitcases. That was the door through which James had told her to exit baggage claim. Both his careful instructions and her careful memorization were quite unnecessary. The door that led to the waiting hotel limousines was well marked in both English and Chinese.

Allison paused for a moment before guiding her baggage cart through the door. She had already glimpsed the Emerald City. Now she was about to meet Oz himself, the wizard whose elegant and quietly impassioned voice had coaxed her from her cocoon. James Drake believed in her talent, needed it, needed *her*, and because of his confidence Allison had become convinced that she had wings . . . and could fly.

Oz was an *illusion,* Allison sternly cautioned her suddenly pounding heart. Merely a phantom of smoke and mirrors.

Maylene stood beside the gold-tone Rolls-Royce limousine, watching the door through which Allison would appear. Her heart had been racing all day, and during the drive from the Trade Winds to Kai Tak, every cell in her body had begun to tremble.

Help me, James, she had implored silently during the drive.

But James hadn't sensed her unspoken plea, nor had he noticed the anxiety in her jade-green eyes. He was far away, oblivious to her torment, perhaps lost in his own, or maybe simply preoccupied with problems that had arisen with the resort he was building near Australia's Great Barrier Reef.

Maylene had to rely on herself, to find her own control over her swirling emotions. But she hadn't found it yet, and in another moment she would be face-to-face with her little sister.

Most of those emerging through Exit Door Four had quite obviously been to Hong Kong before. Their calm expressions sent the confident message that they knew precisely what to expect: a gracious welcome by the on-site representative of their hotel followed immediately by the arrival of their prearranged Rolls, Daimler, or Bentley. On this Sunday night most travelers were businesspeople, eager to get to their hotels, to bed, to recover fully from jet lag before the high-powered meetings that would begin in the morning.

Suddenly, amid the stream of confident faces came an uncertain one. She wasn't quite sure where to look, or what her luminous emerald eyes would see, but the green seemed enthusiastic nonetheless, and totally unafraid. The cotton dress she wore was hopelessly rumpled from the long flight, and her shoulder-length hair, although obviously combed, somehow seemed mussed as well. But there was a freshness about her, a glowing radiance, an aura that was pure gold.

As Maylene's perfect silk-stockinged legs teetered atop high fashion's highest heels, her heart teetered on the edge of disaster. What if something deep within suddenly compelled her to lunge, to attack, to destroy? What if some vicious impulse she could neither detect nor control forced the sharp fingernails that now dug so mercilessly into her own flesh to find a new, deep, *bloody* home in Allison's long ivory neck?

I won't let it happen, Maylene told her trembling heart. I cannot, *will* not, permit the cruelty within me to surface ever again, no matter how much I hurt inside. Somehow I'll sense the impulses in time, and I'll stop them. . . .

It was then that the emerald eyes found her, a soft, searching, hopeful gaze—and despite her vow, Maylene suddenly felt herself moving, propelled by something entirely beyond her control. But even as she was experiencing a rush of terror, Maylene realized the astonishing truth. She was *gliding*, not *lunging*, floating gracefully toward Allison as if pulled by a powerful magnet from deep within the golden girl.

"Allison? Hello, I'm"—*your sister, your sister!*—"Maylene Kwan."

"Oh," Allison whispered, her remarkable eyes glowing with what looked like wonder. "You're the architect. It's so nice of you to take the time to meet me. James has told me how brilliant you are."

As Allison spoke, her soft voice seemed to fill with admiration, as if she were proud of Maylene for being so gifted, and not the least bit resentful, just authentically happy that such talented people existed on the planet and that she was lucky enough to meet one of them.

For a few stunned moments Maylene simply stared, unable to speak. Here she was: her sister. Wholesome, rumpled . . . and *lovely*. And, Maylene realized, so gloriously unafraid. It was as if Allison had nothing to hide, no shameful secrets, no private torments.

Of course she has nothing to hide! an inner voice suddenly reminded. Allison was chosen, remember? She was *chosen*, and you were *abandoned*. She was *loved*, and you were *hurt*. You should hate her, hate her, *hate* her.

But, Maylene's heart whispered.

But *what?*

But how can I blame her for being chosen over me? If I'd been my father and I'd seen this golden creature, I would have chosen her, too.

"James is also here," Maylene murmured finally, gesturing toward the Rolls into which Allison's luggage was already being loaded. "He got a call just as we pulled up. There's a problem with a resort he's building in Australia. We can get into the car if you like, it won't bother him, or we can wait here until he's finished."

"It's fine to wait here." Allison smiled. "The air is so warm, so *tropical.*"

In truth, the night air was hot and humid, barely a breath and a promise away from rain. Maylene liked the sultry warmth, and had always felt a little cold in England, but summertime visitors to Hong Kong often found the steaminess quite smothering.

Softly, somehow needing to know, Maylene asked, "Do you really like the heat, Allison, or are you just being polite?"

"I really like it." Allison's lovely smile became a lovely frown as she added, "It's going to make my hair curl, though. I guess that's okay for now, it got a little limp on the plane, but . . . but I'm babbling, aren't I?"

Allison shrugged, a gesture that tilted her head and caused Maylene to focus more closely on the golden hair—and with that focus came the discovery that there was, after all, something false about the sister who seemed too good to be true. Allison's hair color wasn't natural, it couldn't be, because on closer inspection there wasn't just moonlight, there was fire as well. The illusion rivaled what Maylene hoped to accomplish with the Jade Palace. At first glance Allison's hair was pure gold, the next moment a brilliant red, and then a perfect harmony of each.

The color couldn't be real, natural . . . but it *was*. It was simply too extraordinary to be anything else. But how, Maylene wondered, had nature achieved such a magnificent blend? Was it a mix of separate strands of flames and moonbeams? Or did each shining silken thread contain within itself the remarkable ability to be at once red and gold?

Another uncertain tilt of Allison's head drew Maylene from her silent musings to her sister's questioning eyes. At a loss for words, Maylene's gaze fell to a thick paperback book wedged into Allison's purse.

Maylene couldn't see the title, but the book's thickness, coupled with glimpses of red lettering on white, led to an educated guess. "You're reading *Noble House*?"

"All the way across the ocean." With a frown, Allison added hastily, "My suitcases are filled with nonfiction books about Hong Kong, but I'd never read *Noble House*, so I thought . . ."

"It's a good book," Maylene reassured. Then, because it was suddenly very important that her sister like the place that had been her home, she asked, "Are you enjoying it?"

"Yes. Very much. May I ask you something, though? It's probably a foolish question, but . . ."

"Ask," Maylene urged.

"Well, it wouldn't be correct to refer to James as a *taipan*, would it? I mean, from what I've read, even though taipan means 'leader' in Cantonese, it's generally used to refer to the head of a trading company."

"That's right, although in terms of power and influence in Hong Kong, what James has rivals that of any taipan." Maylene smiled. "You're reading very carefully, aren't you?"

"Yes, well, I want to know—"

Allison stopped then, because, suddenly, there he was.

Oz himself.

But *not* Oz, because James Drake was no illusion. Or was he? Allison saw no mirrors, but there was most definitely smoke, smoldering sensually in his intense gray eyes.

His hair was the color of midnight and it framed a face that was at once elegant and harsh, and as strikingly intense—and as compellingly sensual—as his eyes. He was shadow and stone, Allison decided. And passion and power . . . and now he was standing beside Maylene, where he belonged, his darkly stylish handsomeness complementing perfectly her exotic beauty.

"This is James," Maylene announced softly to the pink-flushed face of her sister. "Our fearless taipan."

James heard the surprising gentleness in Maylene's voice, but still he gave her a look that sent a solemn reminder of her promise to be nice to the girl from Texas.

"She's reading *Noble House*, James! And we were just discussing the appropriate use of *taipan*." Maylene left his stern and now somewhat skeptical gray eyes and returned to her sister's glowing emerald ones. "Whether it's absolutely correct or not, Allison, James *is* a taipan. In fact, the only discernible difference between him and the *Noble House* taipans of thirty years ago is that the job now is *much* tougher. In addition to the fact that 1997 is only four years away, the advent of car phones, fax machines, and pagers has made everything far more immediate—and relentless. *Our* fearless taipan, however, never lets the pressure get to him."

James might have arched a bemused eyebrow at Maylene's teasing yet obviously admiring words, but his attention was suddenly—and wholly—captured by Allison . . . her melodic laugh and sparkling green eyes and the golden-red hair that curled exuberantly in the humid night air.

"Hello, Allison," he greeted softly. "Welcome to Hong Kong."

"Hello, James. Thank you. I'm very glad to be here."

Urged by him, by the voice that had been so convincing over the telephone, Allison had come to Hong Kong. She had left the safe haven of her family's love determined to discover her wings, and then to fly. Her heart was flying now, *soaring*, carrying her mind to dizzying heights. The safe cocoon was a faraway memory—as was the ease with which she had spoken to the elegant voice when it had been an ocean away.

Now she stood before him, her heart fluttering furiously, proof positive of her wings, as her mind searched frantically for words to say. Would the sensual yet austere wizard be interested in hearing that from the night-black sky Hong Kong seemed to her a treasure trove of jewels? Or that the shadowy silhouettes of 747s looked to her like dinosaurs? Or that she loved the tropical steaminess that a more sophisticated woman, mindful of her stylish hair, would view as a distinct nuisance?

Allison dismissed all those observations as hopelessly naive, and she didn't have the courage to speak aloud the most important observation of all: that in the silver smoke of his taipan eyes she saw something more than the solemn responsibility he bore, something deep, something dark . . . something that, to her, looked very much like pain.

Allison didn't say a word. She only smiled. And James smiled in reply, a surprised, tender smile that made her want to sing, and dance—and cry.

CHAPTER 9

I
t was usually in the purview of one of the Trade Winds's
white-uniformed bellmen to show a new guest to her apartment and to describe in meticulous detail the many services
offered by the hotel. But tonight the bellman had been excused.
Tonight, for Allison Whitaker, the hotel's owner had chosen to
assume those duties himself.

Allison knew from her reading that all of Hong Kong's five-
star hotels placed a premium on service. But as she listened to
James Drake's succinct recounting of amenities available in his
hotel, she decided that it was the Trade Winds that set the gold
standard of luxury by which all Hong Kong's other hotels were
judged.

In addition to a staff dedicated to anticipating every conceivable
need—even before the guest did—most services were available
around the clock. Clothes were pressed or laundered twenty-four
hours a day; rooms were cleaned at the precise time specified by the
guest; and every floor had several butlers, who, within minutes of a
request, would appear with hot tea, buttered scones, baskets of dim
sum, or newspapers from around the world.

In-room dining was offered by all of the hotel's restaurants. If one was in the mood for French cuisine, one ordered from DuMaurier's, and the Blue Lantern was famous for its sweet and colorful Cantonese, and there was hot and spicy Szechuan from the Wild Ginger, and for traditional British fare, one needed only to select from the menu provided by Elliott's. The hotel's entire fourth floor was dedicated to fitness—a complete Eden Health Spa, a running track, and an indoor pool—and on the thirtieth floor, a beautifully landscaped outdoor pool overlooked Victoria Harbour.

Guests of the hotel's residential apartments enjoyed additional services. The kitchens were kept fully stocked with staples, as well as the finest in wine, liquor, and champagne, and since few business visitors to Hong Kong had time to shop for groceries, a preprinted shopping list, with selections for every imaginable taste, was supplied. Within two hours of giving the list to one of the butlers, or faxing it to the concierge, the desired items would arrive.

"This is wonderful," Allison whispered over and over as James showed her the apartment and casually chronicled the luxuries of life at the Trade Winds. She wished for more imaginative words to say, but silently rejected every other breathless superlative that came to mind as even more hopelessly wide-eyed and naive.

In desperation, she decided to seek help from the beautiful, sophisticated woman who was so obviously at ease with James. Maylene had been silent for a while, as James had assumed the role of gracious host, and now, as Allison looked toward her, she saw that a dramatic transformation had taken place. Maylene Kwan no longer appeared at ease. Indeed, Allison decided, she seemed tense, anxious—and quite troubled.

Allison wanted to help. It was an impulse that was as instinctive to her, as much a part of who she was, as her brilliant emerald eyes. She smiled at Maylene, a gently questioning smile to which there was absolutely no response. Maylene's troubled green eyes were unseeing . . . even though, Allison realized, they seemed to be staring right *at her.*

After a confused moment Allison returned her attention to James. But before she murmured yet another breathless *wonderful,* his pager sounded, not for the first time. It was a muted beep, but an insistent one, and even though his expression didn't reveal concern as he read the displayed message, Allison sensed his sudden restlessness.

His words, spoken with soft apology and unhurried calm, confirmed what she had sensed.

"I'm going to have to answer this fairly soon," he said. "But first I want to show you your office and darkroom."

"My office and darkroom?"

James smiled at her surprise. "Follow me."

He led the way to the apartment's second bedroom suite, an impeccably decorated room to which had been added a mahogany desk, two four-drawer file cabinets, a typewriter, a computer, and a fax machine.

"The file cabinets lock and are also fireproof," James explained. "Theft has never been a problem in the hotel, but you might want to keep a duplicate set of negatives in a safe-deposit box downstairs in any case."

Allison couldn't imagine anyone wanting to steal her photographs, but the expression on his face eloquently communicated a rather remarkable fact: James Drake believed her photographs of Hong Kong would be as valuable as the most precious of gems.

"The bath seemed the logical place for the darkroom," James continued. "I'm told that it's fully stocked and state-of-the-art, but if there's anything else you need, please let me know. The man who set it up is the photographer who'll be converting your photographs into murals for the hotel, so he has a vested interest in being certain that the negatives are the best quality possible."

"Thank you," Allison murmured, at once elated and terrified by his confidence in her talent. Yes, she had taken lovely—and loving—portraits of her native Texas, and yes, they looked quite beautiful bound together in *Lone Star Serenade*. But could she really do justice to this exotic place that was so enchantingly foreign to her? And would flaws easily hidden in book-sized photographs be glaringly revealed when enlarged to murals? Would she disappoint the man who clearly expected so very much of her? *Too* much?

Suddenly and overwhelmingly Allison Parish Whitaker felt like an impostor. What was she *doing* here? What had possessed her to embark on this grand adventure? She was wearing sensible low-heeled taupe pumps, not ruby-red slippers, but perhaps it was time to tap her heels together anyway. That, coupled with the silent mantra *There's no place like home*, would surely transport her back to the lavender-and-cream bedroom in Dallas where she belonged, surrounded by magazines about weddings and brides.

But Allison did not tap the heels of her sensible shoes together, nor did her heart allow the sensible mantra. Instead, she bravely met the gaze of the man who expected so very much of her, and when she did, her fluttering heart soared ever higher, carried to the lofty heights by an astonishing truth: this is where I belong, *this* is home.

The wizard was not an illusion, and the only smoke was in the color of his eyes, and there wasn't a mirror in sight. Then, quite suddenly, there *was* a mirror, as the message in his sensuous eyes seemed to become an identical reflection of her own.

Yes, Allison, the glittering silver was telling her. This is where you belong. *This* is your home.

Even before James's pager sounded again, shattering the moment, Allison's mind was already shattering the mirror. James belonged with *Maylene*, not with *her*. In this rarefied air where she had soared, where oxygen was in such short supply, she had merely become momentarily confused.

"I guess I'd better deal with this," James said as he silenced his pager. "I'm sorry I won't be able to stay for tea. Maylene will tell you anything I've forgotten about the hotel." He looked to Maylene, not for confirmation of her willingness, but to ask a question. It was a moment before he posed it, however, a moment during which, with the silent power of his smoky silver stare, he compelled Maylene's distracted jade-green eyes to meet his. "And will you also give Allison directions to the Towers?"

"Yes," Maylene murmured. "Of course."

"Good." James returned to Allison. "I'll see you in the morning, Allison. Sleep well."

Then James was gone, and Maylene and Allison were alone, seated on a couch in the living room, the hotel's traditional welcoming pot of hot green tea steaming on the table before them. Maylene knew that James expected her to be the gracious hostess now, sipping tea and chatting animatedly with Allison. But how could she chat at all when her mind swirled with desperate thoughts?

Maylene had permitted herself to believe that the actual moment of first seeing her sister would be the most emotional—and the most dangerous. If she could just survive—control—that moment, she promised herself, all the ones that followed would be easier.

But it wasn't true. Her heart raced faster than ever now, fueled by ancient fears she knew all too well and by foolish longings she dared not name. The foolish longings were powerful, and quite bold. They had actually compelled her to search for some physical proof of sisterhood with the golden girl . . . a search that came to a crushing halt when the ancient fears issued a punishing reminder: there are no bonds of any consequence between wicked Number One Daughter and lovely Number Two Daughter, *nor would Allison want there to be.*

Remembering that harsh reminder now gave Maylene the control she needed to look at Allison, and when she did, she met brilliant emerald eyes that were as different from her own dark jade as good was from evil. Brilliant—and uncertain.

"Please don't feel that you have to stay, Maylene."

There. See? She doesn't want you here. She's *dismissing* you. And you should seize this perfect opportunity to leave. If you don't . . . who knows what will happen? Who knows what cruel— or what foolish—words you might speak?

I'm just going to speak *polite* words, Maylene told herself. Polite lies. "I guess you've noticed how distracted I've been? Please don't take it personally, Allison. My mind keeps wandering to a problem I'm having with the blueprint for the hotel lobby. I'd like to stay for tea . . . if that's all right with you."

Allison smiled. "Yes, of course. I'd like that."

For a while their conversation flowed, carried by Allison on a soft, rushing river of enthusiasm. She raved about the drama of the landing at Kai Tak, and the jewel-bright glitter of Hong Kong's famous skyline, and the bountiful luxuries of the Trade Winds, and how terribly nice it was of James to have put the darkroom in her apartment, how very thoughtful, how *wonderful* actually . . .

It was then, in the midst of a gush of words about James, that Allison faltered. Her cheeks flushed bright pink and her glowing eyes fluttered away. But only for a moment. As if she had given herself a mental shake, she looked up again and offered quietly, "I guess I don't need to tell you how wonderful James is."

She thinks that James and I are lovers, Maylene realized. And . . . she herself is obviously quite dazzled by James.

For any woman to be dazzled by James Drake was not a surprise. His elegant sensuality was compelling enough, and there was even more: the inner core of fire, which, despite how tautly it was controlled, smoldered with promises of breathtaking passion.

But what surprised Maylene, what truly amazed her, was Allison. She was obviously attracted to James, yet neither her expression nor her voice held a trace of envy. Nor, Maylene realized, did Allison seem to harbor even a whisper of doubt that she and James were intimate. It was as if it made perfect sense to Allison that a man like James would choose as his lover a woman like Maylene . . . as if Maylene were truly deserving of such love.

But Maylene Kwan was *not* deserving of such love, and she could prove it right now. Yes, Allison, she could confess. I do indeed know how wonderful James is. I know the look of raw desire in his silver eyes when he allows his passion to flame—just for me—and I know, too, the feel of his lethal, elegant hands as they caress my silken skin.

And if she spoke such words? Would Allison see them for what they were, cruel lies from a most unworthy heart?

No, Maylene decided. Her sister's flawless emerald eyes would not see the evil. The lovely green seemed quite blind to such darkness of the soul.

"James and I are good friends, Allison," Maylene said finally. "But we're not lovers."

Allison frowned, and then asked softly, "Is he married?"

"No."

As Maylene saw brave, delicate sparkles of hope dance in Allison's eyes, she felt a powerful wish to protect. It was an almost forgotten emotion, in hiding for fifteen years and badly rusted by countless tears spilled deep within. But, for the first thirteen years of her life, such loving protectiveness had been Maylene's constant companion. Every day of her young life she had concealed from her beloved mother the truth of her own sadness. She had wanted no unhappy shadows cast on the private world of love in which she and Juliana dwelled, nor on the bright, shining memory of the father who would have been with them, protecting them both, had he not died.

Now the daughter who was the true beneficiary of that father's protective love was sitting before her, hopeful, vulnerable, and ready to trust—and it was not too late for Maylene to prove her own cruelty. With just a few words she could set a vicious trap for her sister's hopeful heart—and end forever the foolish longings of her own. James is obviously attracted to you, Allison. I'm his friend, after all, I can tell. All you need to do is offer yourself to him. . . .

But Maylene set no trap. Instead she shared with her sister the truth about James Drake. Such a revelation was not a betrayal of James, Maylene decided. Gweneth Drake's tragic death was hardly a secret. Sam knew, after all, as did Sir Geoffrey and Lady Lloyd-Ashton. For that matter, everyone in Hong Kong who had met Gweneth during her Christmastime visit knew, as did anyone in England who happened to read newspapers or watch television at the time of her death.

"James *was* married," she began quietly. "Four years ago his wife, who was pregnant with their unborn son, was killed in an explosion at their country home in Wales. It was an accident, something faulty in the gas lines."

"Oh, no," Allison whispered, her delicate hopefulness swiftly replaced by sadness. "Was James there?"

"He was running on the beach when he heard the explosion." Maylene had learned that detail from James. What she said next had been told to her by Titchfield & Sterling's senior partner. "Even though there was no hope of saving Gweneth, when James reached the house he went inside—and almost died as well." Maylene paused, then offered a firm but gentle warning. "James is married to his work, Allison. He isn't involved with anyone, nor does he want to be—especially not now."

"Because of the Jade Palace?"

Maylene nodded. "It was Gweneth's idea. He's building it because of her, because of a promise he made to her."

Silence fell then, and for many moments the sisters were lost in their own private thoughts. Eventually, Allison reached for the teapot, to pour them each a little more tea, and when she did, Maylene's attention focused on the silver bracelet. She had noticed it earlier, and assumed it to be simply a piece of jewelry, but now she saw the engraved crimson caduceus.

"Is that a medical-alert bracelet?"

"Yes." Allison shrugged. "I guess I'm so accustomed to being around people who know I wear it that I forget about it."

"Are you okay?"

Allison smiled. "As long as I don't get a blood transfusion, I'm perfectly fine. I have a severe allergic reaction when I'm given other people's blood."

"That's something that can be detected in advance, isn't it?"

"Yes, usually, but not in my case. With the routine cross-matching techniques used in blood banks, everything looks fine, completely compatible—even though it's not. My hematologist in Dallas has devised a complicated set of tests that will detect the incompatibility, but it hardly matters. In ten years of testing, he hasn't found a single unit that would work."

"So what if you needed blood now?"

"I couldn't get it," Allison said simply, without drama, despite the simple, dramatic truth that a blood transfusion would very likely be fatal. She had survived—barely—the transfusion she had received, but her immune system was fully sensitized now, heavily armed against any future invasion. The response next time would be more swift, more powerful than the last. She smiled a brave, lovely smile. "I just have to believe that I'll never need another transfusion."

"You won't." Maylene's voice was soft, as if she were a sister, as if she were allowed to care. "That must have been very frightening for you."

"For me, yes, but mostly for my father. He was with me when

the reaction happened, and I remember his terror. I wanted to tell him not to worry, and how much I loved him and my grandparents, and—" Allison stopped abruptly as she remembered another truth of her life that Maylene didn't know. "My family is my father and grandparents. My mother died when I was born."

Allison's lovely face, saddened still by the loss of the mother she had never known, triggered long-ago memories for Maylene—how very much she had loved the father who she believed had died, how terribly much she had missed him, how perfect she believed everything would have been if only he were alive.

She had something in common with her golden sister after all. Both had spent long hours imagining how their lives would be if only the missing parent was with them. For Maylene, such imagining had been pure fantasy, shattered forever at age thirteen. And for Allison? Her mother *had* died, that was real, and surely, had Beth Whitaker lived, she would have loved her daughter with all her heart.

Now, speaking to her own long-ago fantasy, and the bond the sisters once had shared, Maylene whispered, "I'm sorry, Allison."

The phone trilled then, midway between Allison's quiet "Thank you," a melodic intrusion that, for Maylene, caused great anguish.

It was Garrett Whitaker, the father Maylene had loved, and missed, so desperately . . . the father whose face had filled with terror when he feared that he was watching his beloved daughter die. He was calling Allison now, to make certain that she had arrived in Hong Kong—and was happy and safe.

What a loving father! The thought came to Maylene without warning, and with excruciating pain. What if that loving father had ever called *her*—just once!—to see if she was happy and safe? And what if he had been there—just once—to pick up the pieces of her shattered heart whenever someone had called her a half-breed child of a whore?

"Yes, Dad." Allison laughed softly. "I'm here, safe and sound. Everything's just fine . . . Yes, I was met at the airport, by both James Drake and Maylene Kwan. She's the architect for the Jade Palace, and she's here with me now, visiting and drinking tea . . . Dad? . . . Oh, good, for a moment I thought we might have lost the connection."

Garrett Whitaker seemed to have recovered quickly from the shock of learning that his daughters were together, sipping tea. *Of course* he recovered quickly, Maylene realized. For almost twenty-eight years he's held the confident belief that there's nothing to worry about, no lurking ghosts that could ever come back to haunt him.

But right now, if she chose, Maylene could set Garrett Whitaker straight. She merely had to take the receiver from her sister's silver-braceleted hand and hiss softly, Hello, Daddy, it's me, the daughter you abandoned. Surprised that I know all about you? Well, I do. Your clever coercion of my mother only lasted thirteen years. No, she didn't betray you. She never would. She pretended that you were a dead hero, just as you told her to. I discovered the lies myself. I know the truth about you, Daddy. You're no hero . . . except to Allison . . . at least you *were* her hero . . . until now.

But Maylene didn't reach for the phone. Instead, she walked to the wall of windows, stared at the glittering brilliance outside, and thought about her father's voice.

What did it sound like now, as it softened with love for Allison?

And what about Garrett Whitaker's heart? Did any part of it, even the tiniest corner, ever wonder about the daughter he had left behind? Did any part of it, even the tiniest corner, ever *care*?

Because she had a visitor, Allison's conversation was politely brief. It ended with a promise that she would call often and with wishes of love for her grandparents. As soon as Maylene heard the receiver being replaced in its cradle, she summoned every ounce of actress that lived within her. She believed that Allison's radiant eyes were quite incapable of seeing the darkness that dwelled within her soul . . . but Maylene was not nearly so confident of her lovely sister's blindness to pain. She had to escape before Allison saw how troubled she was, how frantic, how desperate.

As she turned from the bright lights of Hong Kong to the bright eyes of her sister, Maylene said, "I think I'd better go now, Allison. That blueprint problem is beckoning to me again. I think I'd better just go deal with it."

They walked together to the door, and in another moment she would be on her way to the sanctuary of her own apartment. Sanctuary? a voice taunted. You mean the place with the spectacular view of the Peninsula Hotel?

Yes, that place . . . any place . . . I just need to get away—now.

But when Allison opened the door, there, in the doorway, stood Sam Coulter.

After exchanging warm hellos with Allison, Sam left the smiling emerald eyes, and to the haunted jade-green ones he greeted softly, "Hello, Maylene."

"Hello, Sam." Maylene's gaze fell away swiftly from his. It had to. Sam Coulter wasn't blind to her dark secrets and hidden shames. He seemed to see shadows when no one else could. Speaking to the tall, lean, cowboy body that blocked her escape, she said, "I was just leaving."

Sam didn't budge. "I'll walk you home, Maylene. I just wanted to say a brief hello to Allison."

"Hello, Sam," Allison repeated dutifully. Then, with a smile, she added, "Good-bye, Sam."

Maylene's apartment was on the same floor as Allison's, just down the hall, and normally, from where she was standing, she could have easily seen her apartment door. But not now. It was hidden behind Sam. But it was there, calling to her, urging her to make a mad dash.

No, she told herself. I must walk sedately down the hall with him, eyes forward, voice cheerful. And I must begin that walk *now*. Except . . . "Oh, Allison, I forgot to give you directions to Drake Towers."

"Do I really need them, Maylene? According to my maps, I go out the front door, turn left, and walk along Chater Road for six blocks."

"That's really all there is to it," Sam said. "What time are you meeting with James?"

"At ten."

Sam frowned. "Maylene and I are meeting with Tyler at the construction site at nine."

"Meaning you won't be able to escort me?" Allison teased. "Sam, no matter what my father may have told you, I am really quite capable of walking six blocks, *especially* in a straight line!"

"Really?"

"Yes!" The teasing vanished then and she said quietly, "You're in Hong Kong to build a magnificent hotel, Sam, not to be either a bodyguard or a baby-sitter. Please."

"Okay," Sam agreed. "But if you need anything, Allison, I'm here."

CHAPTER 10

"Invite me in for a drink, Maylene."

Sam's voice was soft, as if he actually cared for her, and the dark blue eyes that caressed her seemed to care as well, and she was so vulnerable, so hurting, so needy. What if Sam really did care? she wondered. What if she *could* confess to him the anguished secrets of her heart?

Get *over* it! an inner voice chided. Sam Coulter couldn't care less about your wounded heart. His interest is a little more superficial than that. He likes your body. He hasn't yet guessed the disappointing truth of the iciness that lurks just beneath the sultry steam. But invite him in anyway, pathetic Number One Daughter. Get him to tell you about Garrett Whitaker. Maybe you'll learning something terrible about the father who abandoned you.

"Jade?"

"Please come in, Cowboy."

Maylene offered him alcohol from the expensively stocked bar, but Sam wanted only Perrier—and answers. She seemed so fragile to him, and he saw such conflicting messages in her beautiful eyes, wanting his help . . . while at the same time warning him away.

"How are you?"

"Fine," she lied. "Good."

"I think something's bothering you."

Maylene answered with a noncommittal shrug, and Sam decided not to push but to wait, to linger over his Perrier forever if need be.

Maylene broke the silence almost immediately, but not with a confession. She was playing the role of hostess, it seemed, making polite conversation with her guest. The dark shadows had been banished from her eyes and the jade green was now shimmering so brightly that its very brilliance blocked all access to the intriguing depths.

"What was it that Allison's father told you about her?"

"I beg your pardon?"

"She said, 'No matter what my father told you about me.' I wondered what that was."

"Only that she'd be here and hadn't done much traveling on her own. For the record, he didn't ask me to be either a bodyguard or a baby-sitter. Why?"

"No reason." Maylene took a slow sip of her own Perrier. "Do you know him very well?"

"Who? Garrett Whitaker? No, not really." Sam paused, then added solemnly, "Just one important fact—that he was willing to risk his own life to save the life of an eighteen-year-old kid he didn't even know."

Maylene realized she wasn't going to learn anything damning about her father, *au contraire*, but she wanted to hear the story anyway, because it was obvious that the eighteen-year-old whose life had been saved was Sam.

"How?" she asked softly. "What happened?"

"I was working on one of Whitaker Oil's offshore rigs in the Gulf of Mexico. A storm hit and we capsized. The Coast Guard helicopters showed up fairly quickly and picked up most of the crew, but the combination of nightfall, gale-force winds, and heavy seas forced them to abandon the rescue effort before it was complete. We didn't now for certain that they weren't coming back, but it was an easy guess." Sam shrugged, as he had shrugged then, but his face was grave as he remembered the sheer terror of the others. He'd felt contempt not compassion for their fright, and if he could have escaped to an isolated spot on the sinking rig, that's exactly what he would have done. But there were no isolated spots. They were all congregated in the only place that wasn't already submerged, and even though most of them were older than he, they looked to him for strength—and Sam told them lies. Someone will come, he promised, his voice an island of calm in the raging sea of fear. No one guessed the truth—that his reassuring calm was merely cool indifference to his own death and to theirs. "When I heard the chopper, I thought I was just imagining things. But it was real, a Whitaker Oil helicopter coming to rescue us."

"He rescued all of you?"

"Eventually, but it took two trips. One of us had to stay behind."

Sam hesitated, wondering if Maylene would assume that it was he who had remained on the sinking rig, or that he, like the others, had pushed and scrambled, grabbing frantically at the rope harness that was lowered from the hovering helicopter. For a wondrous moment the shimmering jade-green eyes gave him access to her heart. She knew he had let the others go first. But, Sam realized, she didn't know why. She was imagining a nobility that didn't exist.

"No one was waiting for me," he explained quietly. "The others had parents, family, girlfriends. Some even had wives and children.

It didn't really matter whether I got off that rig—at least that's what I thought. Just before they left, someone shouted down to me that Mr. Whitaker would be back. Until then, I hadn't even known that he was the one who'd come to get us."

"But you knew him."

"No, I only knew of him. I'd never met him, and he knew absolutely nothing about me."

"Except that you were a hero."

"No, Jade," Sam said softly. "I was just somebody who didn't really care."

Like you? he wondered. Is there something so destructive deep within you that in the same situation you wouldn't care, either, wouldn't believe it mattered whether you lived or died, might even view your death with a sense of relief?

"Did you believe he was going to come back for you?" *The way I believed, all those years, even though my mother told me he never would?*

"I don't remember even thinking about it. It seemed impossible that he could even if he wanted to."

"Were you frightened?"

"No." Sam hesitated, debating whether to tell her about the times in his life when he *had* been frightened. When he was three, listening to his parents, their screaming voices slurred by alcohol. He hadn't understood the meaning of his mother's words—"You *raped* me, remember?"—but he understood very well their hatred for each other, and that somehow he was the reason for it. Or when he was four, and his mother vanished forever, leaving him alone to face his father's brutality. Or later, when he knew what rape meant and that he was a child of violence not of love. Or as a teenager, when he was finally so strong that his father stopped trying to kill him—and Sam realized that was something he was now going to have to do himself.

Sam Coulter was quite capable of such self-destruction, of

course. His father's savage blood flowed, *seethed*, in his own veins. But unlike his father, Sam never permitted the violence to spill over onto anyone else. He wasn't so kind, however, to himself. He drank, and smoked, and used drugs; and when his grades threatened to be good, when it looked as if with very little effort he could actually become a success, he disappeared from school for weeks on end.

Somehow, despite the free rein he had given the destructive forces within him, Sam survived to age eighteen. His life changed dramatically then, but the demons lived within him still, tightly controlled now, but not silent. That was why he smoked, as a concession to them, proof positive that despite outward appearances, he still knew full well that it was his destiny to destroy himself.

Someday Sam would tell Maylene those truths. But not now. Not before she knew, without his ever having to tell her, that his violence would never touch her, that she would be safe with him—always.

"What did you do while you waited for Garrett Whitaker to return?" Maylene asked. *Did you dream, as I did, of happiness, of love, of knowing at last where you truly belonged?*

"There was a case of beer and a carton of cigarettes. I figured I had just about enough time to finish both before the rig sank." His voice was as harsh, as desolate, as the man he had been on that stormy night. But it softened as he said, "But Garrett Whitaker came back, even though he shouldn't have. He's the hero, Maylene. He should never have risked his life to save mine."

"But he did. Why?"

"It was his oil rig, and I was one of his crew, and he felt a solemn responsibility to me."

To a stranger . . . but not to his own daughter. "That night changed your life, didn't it? He changed your life?"

"Yes. He had absolutely nothing to gain—and everything to

lose—by rescuing me. I decided the least I could do was try to turn my life into one that was worth saving."

"Did he help you?"

"You mean money for college? He offered, but I didn't accept. He'd already helped me in the most important way."

"But the two of you remained close over the years?"

"Not really. We've run into each other from time to time. Our politics are the same, as are our favorite charities."

"You really believe he's a hero."

"Yes. Don't you?"

For you, yes, and for the golden daughter he loves, but . . .

As Maylene had listened to Sam's story the shadows had returned to her eyes, and the gifted actress had forgotten to hide them, and now, to Sam, she seemed fragile again, and so very vulnerable.

"Tell me about the heroes in your life, Jade," he urged softly. "Or better yet, tell me about the most important—the most life-changing—moment."

My heroes were my parents, Maylene thought. *Until I learned that he wasn't really dead and that she'd been deceiving me all those years. And the most life-changing moment? That day, when I discovered all the lies.*

"Maylene?" Sam asked gently, fighting the frustration he felt as he watched the beautiful jade-green eyes begin to ice over. He had opened his veins for her, not a crimson rush of every truth, but far more than he'd ever shared before. And in return? She was withdrawing from him, shutting him out.

"I'd have to think about it," she answered dismissively. "I'm not sure there really have been any heroes, or, for that matter, any life-changing moments."

"Okay, Jade. You think about it." *And I'll think about the fact that trying to care about you is undoubtedly the most self-destructive thing I've done in my entire self-destructive life.*

CHAPTER 11

I'm really quite capable of walking six blocks! Allison had teased with a soft laugh and sparkling eyes.

And now, as she began that six-block walk, her eyes sparkled anew and her entire being tingled with an energy that seemed as boundless as the treasures to be discovered in Hong Kong.

She had slept deeply, awakening wonderfully refreshed and eager. She asked the laundry to press the blue-and-white cotton dress she planned to wear, and when it returned thirty minutes later, crisp and wrinkle free, she set about deciding what shoes to wear, what belt, what jewelry.

Most of the space in the two suitcases that had traveled with Allison from Dallas had been devoted to street maps, guidebooks, lenses, and filters. She'd packed just enough clothes to last until Wednesday, when the rest would arrive, and even though she'd tossed in only a small selection of color-coordinated accessories, it seemed to take forever to choose between white and blue for her feet, and between blue and red for her waist, and between pearl and gold for her neck and ears.

Then came the issue of her hair. She'd packed gold barrettes, bobby pins, and rubber bands, but they were functional only, worn privately when she wanted to keep her hair from falling into her eyes, when she was reading, writing, or in the darkroom developing film. She toyed briefly with the idea of trying to *style* her hair, a dramatic sweep off her face, perhaps, or even something truly sophisticated like Maylene's sleek chignon. But she abandoned the idea without so much as touching a golden-red strand. It was hopeless. The instant she walked into the balmy sea-kissed air, any smoothness she'd managed to achieve would give way to riotous tendrils and renegade curls.

Hopeless, she thought as she walked in that warm air now and felt the curls begin to dance. Hopeless and foolish and . . . James is married to his work, and to the memory of his wife, and if ever he were to become involved again, it would be with a woman like Maylene. For now, though, the Jade Palace—his promise to Gweneth—is his only passion.

And I will put every ounce of this extraordinary energy I feel into taking the best photographs I can, Allison vowed. For James, perhaps to make him smile.

The sidewalk along Chater Road was a briskly flowing river of purposeful humanity. The road itself, however, was a sluggish—and remarkably silent—flow of cars, taxis, limousines, buses, and trolleys. Allison heard the heavy breathing of engines, and the occasional cheerful jingle of a trolley bell, but, amazingly, not the expected blare of horns. Four hundred and eighteen cars per mile of roadway made Hong Kong's traffic the most congested on earth. But there was such *civility* to this traffic. Even the taxi drivers wore pristine white gloves, and it all seemed so polite, as if everyone were on their way to high tea.

As Allison flowed with the river of humanity she looked up at the skyscrapers overhead. Their tinted windows glistened pink, indigo, silver, and gold, and the glass towers themselves fairly shimmered, their sharp, stylish edges blurred by invisible waves of heat from the blazing summer sun. She would capture this shimmering brilliance on film, she decided, but not in the usual way. Each building would be photographed as a reflection off another, a tower of gold mirrored on silver, or pink on indigo, or even gold on gold. . . .

When she neared Murray Road, Allison stopped envisioning the pictures she would take and focused her eyes and her thoughts on the destination that lay ahead—Drake Towers, shining ebony and silver against the azure sky, its stylish lines elegant and austere.

Just like the man who owned it.

Allison was surrounded by towering monoliths of steel and stone, and now one was in graceful motion, walking toward her . . . to meet her. The suit he wore was as black as his hair, but even from this distance, and despite the sweltering day, James Drake looked cool, like a midnight shadow.

There was heat, though, in his eyes—not reflected brilliance from the sun, but the glitter of molten silver from fires deep within. He was, Allison decided, a silver-eyed panther, sensual, powerful, predatory. Of all the portraits of Hong Kong, his would be the most magnificent.

The silver eyes found her then, and seemed to gleam with quiet satisfaction as they smiled their welcome. Murray Road still separated them, and it would be a few minutes more, because the pedestrian traffic light now glowed with the bright red symbol of a halted man.

As Allison waited at curb's edge she thought more about a portrait of James Drake. It would, she realized, be quite impossible. One could never truly capture his passion, his power, his pain . . . it was then that Allison's thoughts took an unsettling turn. Hong Kong's silver-eyed panther already *was* captured. Yes, the graceful power of his strides and the proud confidence of his carriage sent the undeniable message that he was master of his domain. But there was something in his eyes, something *more* than his immense sadness over the death of his wife. It was as if he were a caged beast, pacing, prowling, searching, *hungry*.

That anyone or anything could cage James Drake seemed a ridiculous notion. Allison let it go just as the pedestrian light became green, its symbol now walking. Every fluttering cell in her body wanted to close the gap between herself and James as quickly as possible. But the woman who had spent her life trying not to die, to stay safe and alive for those she loved, paused dutifully to look for oncoming traffic before venturing off the curb.

There was none, so she took a buoyant step into the street, toward James, smiling at him as she did. And then, in a flash, Allison saw what no one, except a few firefighters in Wales, had ever seen: fear in his fearless panther eyes.

"Allison! Watch out!"

A horn blared then, a rare strident sound created by the white-gloved hand of the Daimler's startled chauffeur. Instinctively, Allison stepped back to the curb, and as she did, the stately hulk of the heather-green limousine rolled by, only inches away.

She knew immediately what had happened, her almost fatal mistake. This was British Hong Kong. Here, as in England, one drove on the left-hand side of the street. Here, as in England, when you wanted to check that it was safe to cross the street, you looked to the right, not the left, for oncoming traffic.

It was a foolish mistake, unequivocal proof that although Dorothy wasn't in Kansas anymore, she'd brought her naïveté with her to Oz. Had the Daimler been traveling faster, her foolish mistake might have been a tragic one. As it was, she was fine, safe, no harm done, except to her pride—and to her silly hope that she might appear even a little worldly, a little womanly, to James.

He was beside her now, and the fear, if it had ever truly existed, was replaced by concern. "Are you all right?"

"I'm fine!" she assured him as they crossed Murray Road. "I feel like an idiot, of course."

"Don't. It's a natural mistake."

"Well . . . thank you."

Once they safely reached the curb, as if she'd managed the entire six-block walk without incident, James greeted softly, "Good morning, Allison."

"Good morning, James."

"Did you sleep well?"

Allison looked up at eyes darkly shadowed by their own lack of sleep. What made James Drake so sleepless? she wondered. Nightmares? Worries about his empire? Relentless nocturnal pacing within his invisible cage?

Now the darkly shadowed eyes were looking concerned, so delayed was her reply. Allison's well-rested eyes sparkled as she answered, "Yes, thank you. Unbelievably well."

The decor of James Drake's penthouse office was like the man himself, stark yet elegant, a place of sleek sophistication designed in somber shades of shadow and stone. The solitary spot of color stood on his slate desk, a small amber statue of a T'ang dynasty horse.

The floor-to-ceiling windows were tinted silver on the outside, Allison knew, but they looked crystal clear from within, affording absolute privacy while at the same time providing a spectacular view of the world below. Most of the world *was* below. Only the Bank of China and Central Plaza stretched higher into the bright blue sky.

"I had hoped to spend this morning showing you Hong Kong, but I'm afraid I must leave for Sydney within the hour."

"Oh, yes, of course. I hadn't really expected . . . From what I've read there are excellent tours. I'd planned to spend the next few days taking some of those, to get an overview first, then I'll start wandering on my own."

"My administrative assistant, Mrs. Leong, will arrange the tours for you, and when you're ready to begin your wandering, a car and driver will be made available for your use at all times."

"I won't need the car and driver, James. I'll get to know Hong Kong much better if I use public transportation. Besides, unless I'm going to the New Territories or across the island, I imagine most of my travels will be by ferry or by foot."

James hesitated several moments before answering, and when at last he spoke there was not a trace of condescension in his voice, not the slightest indication that he believed he was conversing with a naive or foolish girl. Instead, amazingly, his voice seemed to belong to a man who cared very much for the woman to whom he was speaking.

"Please be careful, Allison."

"I will be," she promised softly.

As she met his eyes Allison saw something new, something that matched the voice . . . a deeper gentleness . . . a brighter silver . . . something that to her fluttering heart looked almost like longing, like *desire*. Then it was gone, quicksilver hardening to stone, and surely it had been an illusion, a mirage created by the intense heat that blazed within him.

"Good," James said finally, his voice a little harsh, a little parched, as if he, too, had been in the desert in Allison's astonishing mirage.

"How long will you be in Australia?"

"Until Saturday afternoon. There's a party that night, a celebration of the Jade Palace, to which, of course, you're invited."

"How nice. Where will it be held?"

"Let me show you." James led the way from the wall of windows overlooking Victoria Harbour across the vast expanse of shining black granite to the southwest corner of his office. Gesturing to the building that was perched atop Victoria Peak like a lustrous crown of snow-white pearls, he said, "There. Peak Castle."

"Is it a hotel?"

"No. It's a private residence, the home of Sir Geoffrey Lloyd-Ashton and his wife, Eve. You'll like her, Allison. I'm pleased that you'll be meeting her so soon."

Eve? she echoed silently as she heard the fondness in his voice. Who was Eve? And what was her relationship to James?

Allison didn't ask James about Eve, nor did she ask either James or the very helpful Mrs. Leong about appropriate attire for the evening at Peak Castle. It would be a black-tie affair, extremely formal, silk tuxedos and satin gowns. Remarkably, Allison already owned the gown she would wear. It would be arriving Wednesday, a part of her "Hong Kong wardrobe"—an improbable collection of shorts, sundresses, and evening gowns. The latter, along with an assortment of cocktail dresses, were from her trousseau, glamorous clothes she would have worn had she become Mrs. Stephen Gentry.

The gown she would wear to the party at Peak Castle was her favorite. That she owned it at all was surprising. She'd insisted on buying it despite the polite but firm objections of both grandmothers—a foreshadowing, perhaps, of even greater defiance to come. Iris Parish and Pauline Whitaker liked the gown, of course. Who wouldn't? The floor-length ivory *peau de soie*, adorned with intricate swirls of iridescent sequins, was the perfect dress for the eve of a fairy-tale wedding. It sent a lovely message of innocence, of purity, and there was even more: every luminous sequin contained its own tiny rainbow.

Allison and her grandmothers discovered the gown of rainbows in the designer boutique at Neiman Marcus. The Pearl Moon label was unfamiliar to them, but the saleswoman knew a little about it. "The designer is from Hong Kong. I can't remember her name, but she's a she, which is undoubtedly why her designs are so *very* romantic. Pearl Moon has been a sensation in Europe for several years now, and in just the short time that the designs have been marketed in the States, the sales have been phenomenal."

Had Pearl Moon been from Dallas, or New York, or even Timbuktu, Allison's grandmothers would have embraced the stunning gown without the slightest hesitation. But because it was from Asia, from Hong Kong, they balked, and the granddaughter who always tried so hard to please was uncharacteristically defiant. This gown, she insisted, this romantic creation that shimmered with the pastel promises of an infinity of rainbows, was what she would wear on the eve of her wedding.

On that day in Neiman Marcus it seemed beyond imagination that neither the wedding nor the gala planned for the evening before would ever happen. But six weeks later, as Allison packed her wardrobe for Hong Kong, she decided the lovely gown would be perfect for another event—the grand opening of James Drake's Jade Palace on New Year's Eve.

Now she would wear the gown even sooner, which meant that she would need another one for New Year's Eve. There were others in her trousseau, though nothing nearly so romantic. But, Allison mused, she was in Hong Kong now, in the land of Pearl Moon. She would find a Pearl Moon boutique, and if the gown she sought didn't already exist, perhaps she could meet with the designer and arrange to have something made—something in jade-green silk, something very special to wear in celebration of that very special night.

CHAPTER 12

Peak Castle
Victoria Peak
Saturday, June 19, 1993

Cynthia Andrews had as much ambition as any taipan. But it wasn't vast wealth she sought, or even immense power. What Cynthia wanted, quite simply, was fame. The beautiful and talented BBC reporter had enjoyed minor fame in London, but her stories were always local, and she wanted international scope, and her lifelong contempt for the monarchy made what passed for "news" in England—the never-ending saga of the lives and loves of the royals—quite distasteful to her.

Nineteen ninety-two had been Queen Elizabeth II's self-proclaimed "*annus horribilus*," the year during which she had watched the marriages of her children crumble and her favorite castle go up in smoke, and it had been the final straw for Cynthia as well. She wanted to report real news, *serious* news, and there was plenty of both in Hong Kong. Although the transfer of sovereignty to the People's Republic of China was still four years away, important daily dramas were already being played out as Hong Kong's governor began the dangerous dance of democracy with the government in Beijing. The BBC did not want to lose Cynthia Andrews, but she threatened defection to CNN unless she was not only transferred to Hong Kong but also given the opportunity to cover Governor Patten's ongoing waltz with China.

Cynthia's professional demands were met, and once settled in Hong Kong in mid-April, she discovered an unexpected—but entirely welcome—dividend of her move. Tyler Vaughn was in Hong Kong.

Two years earlier, while in Monte Carlo to cover the visit of the Princess of Wales, Cynthia had been near the finish line when Tyler won Monaco's famous Grand Prix. For the Formula One race-car driver turned shipping tycoon, the race had been a grudge match against the course that four years before had almost cost him his life. Cynthia had been close enough to see clearly his reaction to his remarkable victory. More solemn than jubilant, and not the least bit surprised, the warrior who had successfully vanquished his ancient enemy was already far away, his piercing blue eyes searching the horizon for new worlds to conquer.

Cynthia hadn't met Tyler in Monaco. But she privately vowed that should the opportunity ever arise, she would find a way to compel him to focus his restless energy on her, at least for a while. Tyler's victory in Monte Carlo marked the end of his racing career, but he was as nomadic now as he'd been during his years on the Formula One circuit. He roamed from port to port, overseeing his shipping empire from homes he owned around the world. Because of the Jade Palace, however, his restless wandering would come to a temporary halt. Until the hotel opened, he would live in Hong Kong, in a suite at the Regent, and he would personally assure that the custom-crafted building materials and treasures of art that were off-loaded from his ships matched precisely what had been ordered.

Shortly after her arrival in Hong Kong, Cynthia began to plan when and how she and Tyler would meet. As impatient as she was, she realized that it probably wouldn't happen until August. Beginning that month she would be adding a "Newsmaker Interview" segment to her Friday-night newscast. What better guest than the thirty-six-year-old owner of Grand Prix, the trading company that in just four years had become second in prestige only to Lloyd-Ashton's?

And sometime, either on the air or after, Cynthia would ask the man with a known passion for things fast and dangerous what he found to satisfy that passion now that his livelihood depended on the slow journeys of mammoth ships rather than the breakneck speed of race cars. And then, with her most provocative smile, Cynthia would offer him a wholly satisfying outlet for that passion.

But Cynthia hadn't been compelled to wait until August to meet Tyler Vaughn. In the middle of May, before she ever called to arrange the interview, they met at Happy Valley Racetrack. At the invitation of one of the Jockey Club's stewards, both were enjoying the day of horse racing from the luxury of a private box.

Cynthia's affair with Tyler was barely a month old . . . and already she sensed his restlessness. But she was philosophical. Their liaison was based on pure lust, without the slightest pretext of love, and it was as sultry, as steamy, as Hong Kong's weather in June. For as long as the pleasure lasted, she would savor it.

Tonight, because of Tyler, she would have the particularly delicious pleasure of being among the elite few attending the gala in the rarefied air atop Victoria Peak. Cynthia would never know if Tyler had been planning to ask her to go with him. When she spotted the invitation addressed to him—and guest—she had essentially invited herself. The gilt-edged invitation was itself a collector's item. It bore the golden imprint of Sir Geoffrey Lloyd-Ashton's personal chop, his name, in Chinese characters, hand-carved in stone, as unique and distinctive as a fingerprint.

In response to her purring plea, an amused Tyler gave her the chopped invitation as a souvenir, and now he was giving her this evening with Hong Kong's crème de la crème—billionaires only, and the governor. The journalist within her would be hard at work, of course, because to the wealthy and powerful dining this evening at Peak Castle, the future of capitalist Hong Kong was of paramount importance.

"No interviewing," Tyler warned, reading her thoughts as he slowed his Lamborghini to a gentle stop.

Just before her door was opened by a white-uniformed valet, Cynthia smiled innocently and asked, "Interviewing? *Moi?*"

"I mean it, Cyn."

"I know, and I won't. Just listening will be enough."

Cynthia Andrews did not believe in fairy tales. But, she mused, if one were going to create a fairy-tale castle, Peak Castle would be it. Even the two flights of white marble steps leading to its main entrance added to the mystique. During the steep ascent, eyes were necessarily drawn heavenward, toward the pristine white edifice framed by the pink-and-lavender splendor of the summer sky and crowned on this June evening by a rare sight, the dazzling alignment of Venus and the crescent moon.

Had the all-powerful Sir Geoffrey Lloyd-Ashton personally arranged with the gods for the romantic conjunction of planet and moon? A gift for his wife, perhaps, the woman he cherished above all his other treasures?

Cynthia had believed that when she left England she was leaving royalty behind. But here she was, ascending the marble steps of Peak Castle, the home of Hong Kong's very own royal couple. Sir Geoffrey's claim to the crown of Hong Kong was quite legitimate, of course. As the territory's wealthiest and most powerful citizen, Hong Kong was, arguably, his own private kingdom.

And Eve? The woman who twice a week—never more, never less—deigned to leave her castle in the clouds to wander among her admiring subjects? Lady Lloyd-Ashton's only apparent claim to fame was her blue eyed, sable-haired, ethereal beauty—and the fact that armed with that powerful weapon, she had accomplished what a legion of other women had attempted and failed: she had charmed the charmer. Only twenty-six at the time, sixteen years younger than the dashing taipan, Eve had nonetheless managed to seduce Hong Kong's master seducer into marriage.

By all accounts, after seven years of marriage, Sir Geoffrey was still completely bewitched. Lady Lloyd-Ashton was cherished by her handsome husband, and Sir Geoffrey was adored by his beautiful wife, and they were, without question, Hong Kong's perfect fairy-tale couple.

Cynthia refused to acknowledge that the aching emotion she felt might possibly be envy, and by the time she and Tyler reached the top of the stairs, it was safely repackaged as pure contempt—just in time to meet face-to-face the woman who was apparently so enamored of the regal lifestyle that she fancied herself a princess.

"You must be feeling terribly confident," Cynthia greeted. Her voice was pure silk, and her lips were smiling, but the violet eyes that studied Eve were intent, as if Cynthia were inspecting an alabaster statue not a human being. "You are, after all, one of the few untarnished princesses left in the British Empire. That's quite an accomplishment these days. Don't you agree, Tyler?"

Tyler could not agree that the woman standing before him was confident of anything—even though she should have been. Her beauty was breathtaking. Tall and slender, everything about her suggested centuries of impeccable breeding. Her innate riches were so bountiful, in fact, that one of her most glorious attributes had been all but discarded. The lustrous sable-brown hair, which might have spilled in luxuriant cascades down her back, was cut very short, rendering it merely a stylish frame for the exquisite face . . . with its startlingly blue eyes.

They were sapphire, Tyler decided. And haunting. *And so very haunted.*

"I'm sorry," he said quietly, answering Cynthia's question but speaking to Eve, not leaving the stricken sapphire and apologizing for whatever had caused such pain. "I have absolutely no idea what you're talking about."

"Lady Lloyd-Ashton is known as the Princess of Peak Castle," Cynthia explained. "But, to her credit, unlike so many of Great Britain's other modern princesses, she is untainted by even a whisper of scandal."

Tyler did not want to leave Eve's eyes. He believed that her bewilderment—and even her pain—had lessened just a little in response to his silent apology.

But Cynthia had to be stopped. And Tyler's chilling look did stop her—cold. Even as the color was still draining from Cynthia's beautiful cheeks, Tyler returned to Eve. Smiling, he said softly, "Good evening, Lady Lloyd-Ashton."

For a wondrous moment Eve's haunted blue eyes bid adieu to all their ghosts, and hope—and gratitude—fairly shimmered. "Good evening, Mr. Vaughn."

It was then that Sir Geoffrey Lloyd-Ashton appeared. Extending a warm hand and with an equally warm smile, he greeted, "Hello, Tyler. Delighted that you could join us for this celebration."

Tyler was compelled to draw his gaze from Eve, but his words, spoken to her husband, were also for her. "So am I."

"And Miss Andrews," Geoffrey continued. "Hong Kong's star reporter. Welcome to Peak Castle. You must allow me to introduce you around. I'm sure there are people here you'd like to meet."

Cynthia cast a defiant glance at Tyler, smiled demurely at Hong Kong's most powerful—and so handsome—taipan, and replied, "Indeed there are, Sir Geoffrey."

For a fleeting moment Tyler wondered if Geoffrey was going to offer his tuxedoed arm to Cynthia, stepping in front of Eve as he did, without ever even acknowledging that she was there. But before whisking Cynthia away, Geoffrey turned his full attention to his wife, and when he did, his expression was one of unconcealed tenderness.

"You look ravishing tonight, my love," he said, his voice intimate, his eyes caressing. It was obvious that Sir Geoffrey Lloyd-Ashton would have been quite content to gaze for hours at his beautiful wife. But after only a few moments he smiled disarmingly and returned to Cynthia. "Miss Andrews? Shall we go?"

Tyler didn't watch as Cynthia and Geoffrey descended the gold-banistered staircase to the castle's great room. Instead, he looked at Eve. The ghosts had returned to her eyes, haunting them with sadness. Tyler smiled at her, but, it seemed, the phantoms had so clouded her vision that she could not see.

Tyler decided that he would try to reach her with words. But, before he uttered a syllable, and with a single blink of long sable lashes, the sapphire eyes were focused again, and brilliantly clear. More guests were arriving and Lady Lloyd-Ashton had to be the most gracious of hostesses . . . of princesses.

James, Allison, Sam, and Maylene had originally planned to travel together to Peak Castle in one of the hotel's Silver Cloud limousines. The plan began to unravel at 4:00 P.M., when Maylene made the decision to borrow James's Jaguar and drive herself, and at six, James himself realized that he had several more overseas calls to make. He informed the bell captain that only Sam and Allison would be leaving the hotel at 6:45 and that he would need another car later on.

James knew that dinner would not be served until nine. Eve had told him that he needn't arrive until then, needn't bother with the two hours of preliminary social banter. But because of Eve, who was hostessing this party in honor of his hotel, James arrived at 7:30.

Because of Eve . . . and because of Allison.

James hadn't seen Allison since Monday, but while in Australia, an image of glowing pink cheeks and radiant emerald eyes had shyly—yet so boldly—danced in his mind, even during the most sacrosanct of times: when he was supposed to be wholly focused on solving the construction problems at the resort . . . and when he was alone, thinking about Gweneth.

James wanted to spend time with Allison, *needed* to. Surely, when confronted with the real woman, not the enchanting fantasy, his impossible feelings for her would promptly disappear.

He found her on one of the castle's many marbled terraces. She was standing very still, staring down at the city. A rainbow of colors, reflected from the lights below, glittered off her golden-red head, and there were more rainbows shimmering off the evening gown she wore. James couldn't see her face, but he could imagine her lovely expression—and he forced himself to confront the truth: the only thing that was truly impossible was his fantasy that his feelings for her could so easily vanish.

Softly, so softly, he posed a question more to his own heart than to hers, "Are you feeling guilty?"

At the sound of his voice, Allison felt soaring happiness, so glad that he was here and that he had bothered to find her. During the days since she had last seen him, she had made a brave promise to herself. She knew that she could wait forever for clever, sophisticated words to pop into her mind. So, she had vowed, the next time she saw James Drake, she would just *talk* to him, to speak as she always had, with forthright and unadorned candor. And if her honest words sounded hopelessly naive? Then so be it. That was who she was.

As she turned to James, Allison's fluttering heart took flight. Venus and the crescent moon were behind him, casting his face in dark shadows, but she could see his silver panther eyes, glinting with his inner heat.

Talk to him, she told herself. Honest words, beginning *now*.

"Very guilty," she confessed softly. "How did you know?"

"The first time we spoke, when I said I hoped you could be

here this soon, you mentioned a wedding this weekend that you were planning to attend."

"I'd forgotten I told you that."

"Were you supposed to be a bridesmaid?"

"No." The soft shake of her head sent bursts of moonlit fire into the summer night. "I was supposed to be the bride."

"Allison . . . I'm very sorry."

"Thank you, James, but it's really okay. It wasn't destined to be what a marriage should be." *What your marriage was.*

"Still," James reminded quietly, "you're feeling guilty."

"Not about that." As her head tilted thoughtfully at the admission that she felt no remorse about her precipitously canceled wedding, the soft curls that haloed her face became dancing moonbeams . . . and then dancing flames . . . and then a magnificent pas de deux of each. "I was thinking about my family, my grandparents especially. For emotional reasons, they didn't want me to come to Hong Kong. I know they hoped I'd arrive, hate it, and take the first flight back to Dallas."

"But you're still here."

"Yes."

"You don't hate Hong Kong."

"Oh, no," Allison answered softly, bravely keeping faith with the promise she had made to her heart. "I love it."

Sam knew the exact moment when Maylene arrived at Peak Castle. He had been watching for her, worrying about her, wondering why she had made the decision to come alone. But when he saw her appear at the top of the white marble staircase, Sam chided himself for his concern.

She had wanted to make a grand entrance, that was all. And indeed she did. All eyes were riveted on the golden vision, and an awed silence greeted her as she made her slow, regal descent. She wasn't wearing a crown, nor did she need one. Her lustrous black hair, swirled luxuriantly atop her head, glittered as if laced with diamonds.

The unwritten, but understood, attire for this evening's gala at Peak Castle was quite formal—black tuxedos and long silken gowns. But to this black-tie affair, Maylene Kwan wore pants. Her outfit was elegant, expensive, unmistakably Chanel. Shimmering folds of gold lamé draped provocatively around her perfect torso before flaring into loose, flowing trousers.

Sam was about to be the first to look away from the golden goddess, but then he saw her eyes, the deep shadows of pain, and he knew the truth. This was how Maylene survived in a world in which she perceived only hostility and contempt. She took the offensive, drawing attention to how different she was, accentuating—celebrating—her uniqueness.

It wasn't truly a celebration, Sam knew. Maylene hated being on display, but she believed she had no choice. She was an exotic creature, and people would stare no matter what she did, but by giving them a reason to stare, she maintained a little dignity, a small shred of control.

Sam didn't turn away. He watched, restless and aching, while Maylene slowly walked the gauntlet of Hong Kong's rich and famous. As soon as she'd met everyone she needed to meet, he rescued her.

"I need a private moment with my architect," he explained before whisking her away.

After guiding her out the nearest door, onto a terrace fragrant with plumeria, he said softly, "You made it."

"Of course!"

Her tone was brusque, brittle, the wounds of her heart raw and weeping.

"I'm not them, Maylene. I'm your friend. I want to be."

His words confused her, or perhaps it was his gentleness.

"Was there something you wanted to discuss, Sam? A problem with my design for the hotel?"

"No." Sam smiled. "Sentimental journey?"

"I beg your pardon?"

"I wondered where you were, why you drove yourself instead of coming with us. I was worried about you."

A dangerous, foolish part of her wanted to confess everything to him. Yes, it had been a sentimental journey. First, she drove past the apartment where she and Juliana had lived during those joyous years, when there had been such love, and in the years that followed, when there had been only the hurt and the lies. Then she drove to Mount Cameron Road, where, from a short distance away, she viewed the charming Victorian house that overlooked Happy Valley—Vivian Jong's home, the place where her mother had lived when she and Garrett Whitaker met and where Maylene herself had been born. Her mother lived there now, again, as she'd always vowed she would. Juliana Kwan's recent purchase of the expensive property was proof that she was lost still in romantic memories of her imagined love.

There was only one thing that was real about the "love" between Garrett Whitaker and Juliana Kwan—their child, the daughter from two worlds . . . neither of which wanted to claim her.

"Jade?"

"I was just in the mood for a drive." She found a radiant smile then, a beautiful mask, and asked, "What do you think of the castle, Cowboy?"

"Magnificent."

"But you're frowning."

"I guess it all seems a little presumptuous."

"To establish oneself as king of the mountain?"

"Yes. Or," Sam added softly, "to believe that you actually have the right to blind a dragon."

"Do you know about *feng shui*, Allison?"

Sir Geoffrey Lloyd-Ashton's question came between the fifth and sixth courses of the eight-course meal, a Cantonese feast prepared by one of Hong Kong's master chefs. The forty dinner guests were seated, at tables of eight each, in the castle's banquet hall. Reproductions of Florentine frescoes adorned the walls, and massive Venetian-glass chandeliers glittered overhead, and in each of the room's four corners stood a marble statue sculpted by Donatello.

And at the round hand-carved mahogany table, where the evening's honored guests were seated with their host and hostess, the dinner conversation flowed as freely as the rice wine. Geoffrey was an expert storyteller, but he was equally adept at coaxing others to tell their stories, welcoming each tale, however modest, with great interest.

Now his interest was focused on Allison, Hong Kong's newest visitor.

"I've read about *feng shui*," she replied. "And from the tours I've taken, I've learned a little more. But, Sir Geoffrey, I'd like to hear your definition."

Geoffrey laughed appreciatively at her finesse in tossing the question back to him, and after a moment the master raconteur graciously complied. He gave an expansive, accurate, and entertaining description of the four-thousand-year-old science of "water and wind," finishing with, "In Hong Kong, one must never forget the dragons. This is a hilly place, and there's a dragon living in every one. I imagine, Allison, that during the tour of Victoria Peak you heard a bit about Peak Castle? That it stands in brazen defiance of the decrees of *feng shui*? That, in fact, it blocks the view of one of Hong Kong's most celebrated dragons?"

Allison answered with a lovely smile framed by pinkened cheeks. "Yes, that was mentioned."

Sir Geoffrey Lloyd-Ashton seemed more amused than concerned that his unrepentant mockery of the mandates of *feng shui* was still a topic among tour guides ten years after the castle had been completed—and it was obvious that he had no qualms whatsoever about any adverse consequences that might befall his home.

"Water isn't a big problem up here, over eighteen hundred feet above sea level," he explained. "And if the wind ever tried to blow the castle off Victoria Peak, it would have to take a substantial part of the mountain with it. So, Allison, I do hope you'll feel comfortable coming to visit us."

"I will, Sir Geoffrey. Thank you."

Allison might have assured him that she knew about the prohibition of cameras within the castle walls, but Geoffrey's interest had already shifted elsewhere.

"What about you, Maylene?" he asked. "Do you believe in *feng shui*?"

There wasn't the slightest edge in Geoffrey's voice, and it was a perfectly logical question to pose to the Hong Kong native who was also the architect of its most grand hotel, and earlier, when he had offered lavish toasts to everyone at the table, Geoffrey's words of praise for Maylene had been quite lyrical.

But still, to Sam Coulter, the polite question felt like a taunt. And, Sam knew, that was precisely how it felt to Maylene. She was seated beside him. He sensed her stiffen beneath the flowing gold.

But the dazzling actress made a dazzling recovery. With a coy smile, she teased lightly, "I *half* believe in it, Sir Geoffrey."

If Geoffrey's question had been posed as a test to see if Maylene was sensitive about her impure blood, perhaps even ashamed of it, she had passed with flying colors. In fact, her sparkling jade-green eyes sent the radiant message that her mixed heritage afforded her the luxury of enjoying only the best of each culture, embracing the traditions she liked and simply ignoring the rest.

The test—if there had been one—was now over. Or was it? Sam wondered. The woman draped in gold beside him obviously didn't know. Geoffrey's smiling eyes were appraising her still, and Sam could sense her steeling herself for more questions, preparing herself to dazzle no matter how much she hurt inside.

But Sam Coulter did not want Maylene Kwan to hurt— not ever.

With a slow, easy smile followed by a slow, easy drawl, he said, "I may be a newcomer to Hong Kong, Sir Geoffrey, and I may be a cowboy, but it just so happens that I believe in *feng shui*."

Sam's words had the hoped-for result, drawing Geoffrey's attention from Maylene to him. Not the least bit disconcerted, their gracious host offered approvingly, "Good for you, Sam. And more to the point, good for the Jade Palace. Hopefully, your belief will help bring even more good fortune to this all-important project."

"Even more?" Allison asked.

It was James who answered. "I assume that Geoffrey is referring to you, Allison, and to Maylene and Sam and Tyler."

"Quite right, James," Geoffrey agreed. "And also, of course, to you. But there *is* even more. I don't know if it's *feng shui*, or terrific joss, or merely the thinning of the ozone layer, but the Royal Observatory is just about to issue a prediction that the summer rains are still at least a month away—probably longer."

"You mean no rain until late July?" Cynthia asked with a frown. "That would be very unusual, wouldn't it?"

"Very," Geoffrey affirmed. "But every year the seasons seem to shift a little more. Even the typhoons are appearing later and later into the fall. A dry summer would be good for you, wouldn't it, Sam?"

"I'd be a very happy man if I could pour the hotel's foundation into rock-hard earth."

"And how about you, Allison? I would assume that dry weather's easier for taking photographs."

"Yes, although I can always find rainy-day projects. But if the air would stay just the way it is a little longer, that would be wonderful."

"The way it is? You mean unbelievably humid?"

Allison blushed slightly at Cynthia's shocked query. "It *is* because of the humidity, I suppose, because of all the water in the air. But the effect is remarkable. Brilliantly clear—and yet shimmering. Magical." Her blush deepened. "Anyway, it photographs very well. I hadn't planned to begin taking pictures this soon, but I had to see."

"You hadn't planned to take pictures this soon?" Cynthia repeated with surprise. Putting off till tomorrow what could be done today wasn't the way of Hong Kong—it *couldn't* be.

Allison shrugged. "I'd intended to spend more time just wandering around and getting acquainted."

"Wandering? By foot?"

"By foot, by ferry, by train . . . and soon, I hope, by air." Allison looked at James. "Mrs. Leong said that she would arrange for me to borrow one of your planes. I hope that's all right."

"Of course. My planes and my pilots are entirely at your disposal."

"Thank you." After a heartbeat's hesitation, Allison added softly, "I won't need a pilot, though, not until I'm actually ready to take pictures. I'm going to fly a few reconnaissance missions on my own first."

"You're a pilot, Allison?" The question was Eve's, her first words of the entire meal. In response to Allison's nod, she elaborated, "That's very impressive. Don't you agree?"

Eve's question was directed to James, but her voice was so quiet that he didn't seem to hear. In truth, James was far away, lost in an image of the future that, he hoped, would never come to pass. It was an image of courage, of a mission entirely different from soaring over Hong Kong in search of its most dazzling views. James Drake didn't know that Garrett Whitaker was a pilot during the war, or that he had once risked his life to pluck Sam

Coulter from a sinking oil rig in a raging sea. But nonetheless he had no difficulty envisioning Garrett Whitaker's lovely daughter flying daring rescue missions of her own, transporting desperate refugees away from the devastation of a ravaged Hong Kong.

"I'm afraid I haven't exactly impressed James with my ability to walk," Allison murmured finally, answering Eve's question herself. "So I imagine he's not too sure about my ability to fly."

"What's wrong with the way you walk, Allison?" Sam teased. "Too Texan?"

"Too American. Too accustomed to cars traveling on the right-hand side of the street." To James, whose silver eyes were once again entirely focused on the present, on *her*, Allison said, "Since I last saw you, I've mastered crossing streets."

The silver glittered slightly, a private smile, just for her. "I didn't doubt for a moment that you would."

"Are you planning to drive in Hong Kong, Allison?" Cynthia asked.

"Drive? I—"

"No," Maylene interjected emphatically. Then, more softly, she explained, "I really don't think you should, Allison. Even for those accustomed to driving on the left side of the road, it's tricky, nerve-racking, and even dangerous."

"I agree," Geoffrey concurred. "And there's no need, is there? You have the entire fleet of Trade Winds limousines at your disposal."

Cynthia's violet eyes had widened during the exchange, and now they flashed. "Are you going to stand for this, Allison? If you were a man—a *male* Texan, like Sam—this conversation would not be happening. I, for one, believe that if you can fly in Hong Kong's crowded airspace, you can certainly manage its crowded roadways. In fact, I'm confident of it." Cynthia tilted her head toward James. "What about you, James? We all know that Maylene drove your car here tonight. You'd trust Allison to do the same, wouldn't you?"

It had nothing to do with trust, of course, and James happened to agree with Maylene and Geoffrey that there was simply no point to Allison's driving in Hong Kong. But as he looked from Cynthia's challenging violet eyes to Allison's uncertain emerald ones, he realized that she still felt embarrassed about her misstep in Murray Road—and that it was important to her that he believed her capable of navigating the most congested traffic on earth.

Smiling at the lovely emerald, he said softly, "I absolutely trust you to drive my car, Allison." That was all he needed to say. With his words, her uncertainty magically vanished. But selfishly, wanting to see more magic—a radiant sparkle—James added, "In fact, I'd like to be a passenger when you do."

"Oh! I'd like that, too."

"It's a date, then. We'll make it a celebration. In December, when your photographs are being made into murals for the hotel, you can drive me across the island and we'll have dinner in Aberdeen, on one of the floating restaurants."

"You can hold him to that, Allison," Geoffrey said. "It's a gentleman's promise and you have a table full of witnesses. In the meantime, since we can't hear about your driving adventure until December, tell us more about your plans to fly above Hong Kong. Do these reconnaissance missions need to be solo flights?"

That would be best, of course, so she could concentrate fully, but . . . "Would you like to accompany me, Sir Geoffrey? I'd be delighted, and I could certainly use a guide."

"Thank you, Allison. That's a very tempting offer. But, actually, I wasn't thinking about myself." Geoffrey looked then at his beautiful wife, his eyes filling with cherishing tenderness as he did. "You'd enjoy soaring above Hong Kong with Allison, wouldn't you, my love?"

"Yes," Eve answered swiftly, because she had to, because it was the gracious reply. And Lady Lloyd-Ashton even smiled. "Yes, I would enjoy it, very much."

After a moment Geoffrey's caressing gaze left his princess and returned to Allison. "Unfortunately, though, she won't be able to. My beloved Eve has a terror of flying. We discovered her fear when we flew here to be married. She's never flown since, and I would never want her to."

"But being up here, at Peak Castle, *feels* like flying," Allison countered softly. Looking from her host to her hostess, she said, "The invitation is always open. And if we do go, and you get even the least bit frightened, I promise I'll land right away."

"That's terribly generous of you, Allison," Geoffrey said. "But why don't the two of you just do your flying from the castle? The moment the weather changes, why don't you join Eve here for lunch?"

"That would be lovely," Allison murmured to Geoffrey, then once again turned to Eve.

"I'll look forward to it, Allison," Eve said, her words this time far more than merely a gracious reply. Indeed, Eve was sorry that their luncheon was at least a month away, perhaps longer. But Geoffrey had spoken: she and Allison would get together when rain clouds shrouded Hong Kong . . . and not before.

"What an evening!" Cynthia raved as she and Tyler walked toward the main entrance of the Wisteria Gardens condominium on Arbuthnot Road. "I loved every minute of it. Didn't you?"

The question was far from rhetorical, and when Cynthia heard his answer—and the ominous quiet in his tone—she knew at once that he had neither forgotten nor forgiven.

"Not every minute, Cynthia."

"I suppose I shouldn't have made an issue about Allison driving, but—"

"You know I'm not referring to that."

Cynthia did know, of course, and now her violet eyes flashed with defiance. "I can't believe you're still annoyed! I said nothing to Lady Lloyd-Ashton that wasn't absolute fact. And, quite frankly, I thought she'd be *flattered*. She knows she's the Princess of Peak Castle, Tyler. That's what she *wants*."

Was it really what Eve wanted? Tyler wondered. Was the life she was living everything she had hoped? It seemed fairy-tale perfect and yet . . .

"Her only purpose in life is decorative," Cynthia embellished, pressing her advantage as the harsh lines of his face were gentled slightly by some unspoken thought. "She spends one morning a week as a volunteer at Children's Hospital, but that's undoubtedly just for show, and beyond that *nothing*!"

The harshness returned to Tyler's face then and Cynthia saw the cold fury in his ice-blue eyes.

"You're not coming upstairs with me, are you?"

"No."

Cynthia felt her own fury that he had so obviously been enchanted by the faux princess, but there was absolutely nothing to be gained by further provoking Tyler Vaughn. Instead, she consoled herself with the memory of a tête-à-tête she'd had with Sir Geoffrey. They should meet sometime for drinks, he had said. The pretext of the proposed rendezvous had been her work, a chance for her to learn about Hong Kong from its most powerful citizen, but there had been a subtext, too, in the taipan's dark seductive eyes. Sir Geoffrey might treasure his princess, but the meager offerings of Eve's pale, thin body were clearly not enough to satisfy him.

"I guess this is good-bye, then, isn't it, Tyler?"

CHAPTER 13

Dragon's Eyes
Sunday, June 19, 1993

It was nearly 2:00 A.M. The princess was alone in the castle. The other half of Hong Kong's fairy-tale couple had gone to spend what remained of the night with one of his mistresses.

Geoffrey would be gentle with his mistress, Eve supposed. His sexual violence had already been spent—on her.

Even before the evening began, Eve had known that no matter what she did, no matter how perfectly she maintained the facade, this night would end with brutal passion. Evenings like this always did. Geoffrey loved putting his princess on display, showing the world the exquisite treasure that belonged to him—and then, what he loved most of all, reminding Eve of that possession.

Geoffrey had played with her this evening, as he often did in public, trapping her in a game that only he could win. No one else ever knew of their private games. And Eve alone knew the darkness of the desire that others saw glittering in Sir Geoffrey Lloyd-Ashton's cherishing eyes.

Tonight, during dinner, in front of witnesses and with caressing tenderness, Geoffrey had asked her if she would like to go flying with Allison. Eve *had* to say yes, politeness demanded it, even though she knew that Geoffrey would never permit it—especially not with someone as lovely and sympathetic as Allison.

Did Geoffrey really believe that she would share her private shame with Allison—with anyone? Eve wondered. Did he really imagine that she would ever involve anyone in what was destined to be a futile attempt at escape?

No, of course he didn't. The man who virtually owned Hong Kong, and who had made his wife so famous that her every move was watched by over five million pairs of admiring eyes, was not the least bit worried that Eve would ever try to flee. He merely enjoyed tormenting her with the fantasy—that was all.

Geoffrey enjoyed tormenting her in front of witnesses, that private game, and he enjoyed tormenting her still, when they were quite alone.

Tonight, once all their guests had left the castle, his dark eyes gleaming with conquest, he had asked, "Are you terribly disappointed not to be able to go flying with Allison, my princess?"

"No," Eve had whispered, just as his lips crushed hers.

And no, no, *no!* her delicate body had pleaded as, with bruising violence, Geoffrey had claimed his most prized possession.

But Eve had scarcely heard her body's frantic plea. As always, the moment Geoffrey touched her, her mind had floated far away. And now, in the aftermath of his violent passion, her wounded flesh cried still—and was still unheard.

Eve was thinking about the young woman who had been so blind to her own beauty, and so desperate to be loved, that she had been blinded to the greatest truth of all: that it was her beautiful shell—and nothing else—that Sir Geoffrey Lloyd-Ashton had wanted. . . .

Eve knew the story of her conception. As a little girl she was never allowed to forget it, as if it were her fault, as if she had chosen to become the despised symbol of her mother's betrayal . . . as if she had asked to be born. The man who would become her stepfather was a barkeep. His pub, the White Horse Tavern, was located in a seaside village near Weymouth. Her mother was a barmaid there, and her biological father, a local longshoreman, was a regular customer who liked the ale and enjoyed even more flirting with the saucy bar wench whenever she and her lover were feuding.

The sultry barmaid's affair with the sexy dockworker had the desired results: rage, jealousy, reconciliation, and marriage. And it had an undesired one: pregnancy. For perverse and punishing reasons, both Eve's mother and stepfather wanted her to be born.

In the end, it was Eve who was punished most by their decision. Even her name was a punishment, the temptress from Eden, the wayward creature who had lured all men to sin. Her stepfather loathed her. He saw his enemy in her small face and, even before she understood the words, harangued her for her ugliness. Her mother hated her as well, revising history in a way that cast her father as a villainous seducer, even though it was she who had done the seducing.

Eve spent most of her childhood wishing she were dead. She believed without question that she was unspeakably ugly and wholly unworthy of being loved. Eve never looked at herself, but even if she had, and even though it was there from the very beginning, she would not have seen her exquisite beauty. She would only have seen what everyone else saw, an image that made her an object of ridicule outside her home as well as within: a hunched and painfully thin creature whose heart-stopping blue eyes were desperately sad, desperately fearful . . . desperate.

"Get away from the edge! Please! You might fall!"

The frantic voice came from behind her, from a human being, and it was as compelling in its wish that she be safe as were the calls of the sea that implored her to jump.

Eve came often to this grassy spot on the limestone cliff high above the English Channel. It was a remote corner of a vast estate, but the paths she followed from the village were known only to herself and the deer. Never before had she encountered another soul.

But now, on this summer day that marked the beginning of her fifteenth year on earth, a day that she had decided would be her last, she had been discovered. Even now it wasn't too late. She still could jump. True, the concern in the voice was so embracing that it felt as if she was being held, as if someone cared enough to stop her from plunging to her death.

But it was just a voice, and surely its elegant and lovely owner would have neither the courage nor the inclination to dash to the cliff's edge. Except that now, above the shouts of the sea that were urging her to jump—*quickly!*—Eve heard the fall of rapidly approaching footsteps. Instead of jumping, she turned—and beheld the outstretched arms of Lady Gweneth St. John.

There were times, for fun, for show, when Gweneth Frances St. John rode sidesaddle. She had an extravagant outfit for such occasions, a lavish reminder of Regency England: green velvet, with ruffles and lace, and a hat to match, jauntily perched and gracefully garnished with a long curving plume. There were other times, for less frivolous show, when she rode astride. Then, as she competed for blue satin ribbons and gleaming gold trophies, she wore a thoroughly modern riding habit. But today, for galloping through the meadows above the sea, Lady Gweneth St. John wore jeans, a bright pink T-shirt, and scuffed riding boots.

Given her attire, she might have been the daughter of a stable hand. But Eve knew without question, and without resentment, that this girl, almost exactly her own age, was highborn. There was such grace about her, such graciousness.

"Please come to me," Gweneth said, stopping her own charge toward the cliff's edge not because of fear for her own safety but because of what she saw in the remarkable blue eyes. The girl had been planning to jump. Gweneth was suddenly quite certain of that. If she kept moving closer, narrowing the distance between them, might that suddenly compel her to take the lethal leap? "Please?"

Eve had come to this cliff, intending to jump, many times. Always before, she had been stopped by the sheer beauty that surrounded her. She would become enchanted by the grandeur of azure sky and sapphire sea, escaping from herself entirely, and she would decide to go on, for no reason other than the chance to marvel yet again at nature's glorious tableau.

The splendor of sky and sea was there again today, but Eve hadn't seen it. She had been focused within, on darkness, on despair. But now her eyes saw a splendor she had never seen before: the boundless generosity of a human heart.

She moved toward Gweneth with the first graceful step of her life, and for that amazing moment her hunched body straightened, as if all this time she had been a forgotten marionette and now some gentle being in the heavens was pulling invisible strings and giving her life at last.

"You scared me," Gweneth whispered with relief when Eve was safely away from the edge. "Maybe this isn't true for you, but when I stand near a ledge like that—especially if I look down—I get a little dizzy, a little confused, and I fear that I might fall . . . or even jump . . . and it terrifies me."

"I come here often," Eve explained, wondering if Gweneth had guessed that in another lonely heartbeat she would have jumped. Reassuringly, she added, "I'm used to standing near the edge, but today, I admit, I was feeling that dizziness."

"But you're all right now."

"Yes I am. Thank you."

It seemed unlikely that they would become friends, the barmaid's symbol of faithlessness and the beloved daughter of an earl. But they did, and it wasn't a one-sided friendship, Eve needy and taking, Gweneth giving and strong.

The moment they met was not only the neediest in Eve's life, but it was the neediest in Gweneth's as well. To that point, Gweneth's life had been blissfully unblemished, untouched by sadness and cloaked in love. Everyone proclaimed her to be a rock, always willing to offer sympathy, comfort, and surprisingly sage advice. But it was easy to be a rock when one's life was as solid as stone. Until her father's body was crushed beneath his favorite polo pony, Gweneth's strength had never been tested. The earl had survived, and was already home, but weak. Gweneth's entire family, including her father, turned to her for strength.

Now Lady Gweneth St. John needed her own rock, someone to whom she could confess the fears she had to hide from her family.

Eve was that rock.

By summer's end, when the earl was fully recovered and Gweneth left for West Heath, the two girls were best friends. Gweneth had generous wishes for her new friend: that Eve would believe in herself, her gifts, her worthiness. The aristocratic girl who had been cherished from birth possessed boundless confidence. She tried, without success, to give some of hers to the friend who had none, *less* than none. "You should apply to college, Eve. With your grades you would easily win a scholarship. You could become a doctor, or a nurse, or a social worker, some career in which you could put your compassion to best advantage."

But Eve had different ambitions, and although they seemed very modest to Gweneth, to Eve they were enormous, far beyond anything the teenage girl who had almost hurled herself into the sea could ever have dreamed. After graduation from secondary school she left forever the home that had been a source of such irreparable damage to her sense of self. She found a tiny flat in London, worked as a teller in the Bank of London and Hong Kong, and devoted her free time to visiting children in a nearby hospital. At last she was at peace, living outside herself, helping wherever she could, finding quiet joy in the splendor of a rose, a sunset, the radiant innocence of a young child's smile.

Eve did not truly feel part of the world. She believed herself to be invisible, an appreciative observer, immensely grateful for the simple privilege of being allowed to watch. She watched with great pride her gifted, confident, vivacious friend. Gweneth excelled at Cambridge, taking a first in English literature, and then, because of her stylish, clever way with words, she launched a successful freelance career writing articles for magazines.

Gweneth was in Milan, covering the fall collections for British *Vogue*, on that fateful day when Sir Geoffrey Lloyd-Ashton strode into the Bank of London and Hong Kong. The taipan of Hong Kong's premier trading company was in England on business, the acquisition of three more ships for his fleet. The negotiations for the freighters had gone exceedingly well, and as he was on his way to the races at Ascot, and since luck seemed to be with him, he decided to withdraw a little extra cash from his account.

At first he was only vaguely aware of the young woman in the teller's cage, an awareness that, for Geoffrey, was far from pleasant. He was a connoisseur of beauty, and from what he could see, she was quite wretched. Her thick sable-brown hair was long and unrestrained, virtually concealing her face, and her clothes were hopelessly unstylish, and her thin body was hunched, as if she were attempting to become smaller, perhaps disappear entirely, and as her pale hands counted out his money, Geoffrey noticed with disgust that her nails had been chewed to the quick.

But then she spoke, to thank him for using the bank, and even though her accent was miserably common, the rich, soft tones of the voice itself were hauntingly familiar. He stared at her then, willing the curtain of sable to part, and when it did, Sir Geoffrey Lloyd-Ashton saw a ghost: *Rosalind*, the only woman he had ever really wanted . . . and the only one who had ever dared to defy him.

Rosalind had been dead for sixteen years, and to Geoffrey, that death had been the most brazen—and unforgivable—defiance of all. She had dared to die before he had the chance to punish her for leaving him.

But now, here was her twin, and Geoffrey felt himself being drawn to Eve as powerfully as he had been drawn to Rosalind. With work, this wretched creature could become an exact incarnation.

In fact, Geoffrey mused, she could be even *better*. Indeed, perhaps, she already was. Eve was so meek, so insecure, so delightfully submissive. Such subservience was what Geoffrey had always wished for in Rosalind—what Rosalind would have become if only he had been given more time to break her.

But this woman already was broken. She merely needed to be taught to walk and speak and dress as Rosalind had—like a princess—and her sable-brown mane, Rosalind's exact shade, could be cut short to reveal the exquisite face . . . and this time she would not get away.

Eve fell in love with him, of course. She was twenty-six and painfully shy and lonely, and Geoffrey was forty-two and confident and dashing, and although it seemed impossible that a man like Sir Geoffrey Lloyd-Ashton could fall in love with her, he claimed that he had.

Within two weeks Eve was in Hong Kong, in the suite at the Mandarin Oriental hotel where she would live during her improbable metamorphosis from diffident bank teller to stylish mistress of Peak Castle. Eve had no idea how to make such a transformation, but Geoffrey did. He personally oversaw her diction and posture, and once her accent and carriage were suitably aristocratic, he brought in experts to whom he gave specific instructions regarding clothes, makeup, and hair.

Eve was a model pupil, so grateful to be loved, so eager to please. Geoffrey had lovingly promised to make her into "his fair lady," and Eve, an innocent yet willing accomplice to that creation—and to her own destruction—was absolutely unaware that her fiancé's true intent was far more Svengali than Pygmalion.

On their wedding night, after Eve had changed into the ivory silk negligee he had chosen for her, Geoffrey made her stand before the mirror in their bedroom.

"Look at yourself, my beauty. Look at your face. You're a princess now. People will be watching you. This is the way you must always look."

Eve followed Geoffrey's command, just as she had so carefully followed the instructions given to her by the makeup specialist and hairstylist Geoffrey had found. She knew the way Geoffrey wanted her to look, and precisely how to make it happen. She looked like that now, and on this night, as Eve gazed at her own image in the mirror, she expected to see something new, something wonderful. But even on this night, when she stood beside the man who claimed to love her, she saw only what she had always seen: despair. Indeed, to Eve, her sadness was more obvious than ever. Deprived of its concealing sable-brown curtain, her face was fully exposed, its gaunt and haunted features mercilessly unveiled.

Eve saw neither beauty nor happiness. But Geoffrey was pleased with her looks—and that was what mattered.

It was then that her new husband issued another command.

"Undress for me, Eve. No, don't turn away. I want to watch you." Once again she obeyed, and when she stood naked before him, a hopeful and terrified virgin, his eyes raked over her painfully thin white body as he issued a soft warning. "Don't ever gain any weight, Eve. Not an ounce."

Eve and Geoffrey never made love, not even on the first night. They had sex—at least he did—and Sir Geoffrey Lloyd-Ashton was rarely gentle when he claimed his princess. Geoffrey's fierce passion caused great damage to Eve's delicate flesh, even when he took her between the satin sheets of their canopied bed. And there were other times, when his desire would not wait, that he crushed her against the hard surfaces of his castle, the cold marble floors, the jagged-rock fireplaces, the ornate banisters carved in gold. Her alabaster skin bore large bruises after that, lingering gravestones of his violent love.

Geoffrey desired her. Of that there was no doubt. But the darkness of his desire both bewildered and terrified her—as did the way his personality seemed to change the moment they became man and wife. Gone was the warm, charming, loving man who had courted her. Oh, he existed still—in public, always, and in private when it suited him. But there was another Sir Geoffrey Lloyd-Ashton, for her eyes only, and that man was very cold, and his dark eyes mocked, and . . .

And Eve blamed herself. She tried to please him—oh, how she tried—and in bed, and in the eyes of Hong Kong, Geoffrey's princess seemed to succeed. But the facade of perfection wasn't enough. Geoffrey was obviously terribly disappointed with her. And why not? He had undoubtedly discovered the same truth that had been hammered into her brain—and carved into her heart—from the moment of her birth: she was worthless . . . and totally unworthy of being loved.

But it was Eve who was yet to discover the truth, and when she did, it was the most devastating discovery of all. . . .

"I say, Eve, Nigel and I think you're a terribly good sport."

The words came from Beatrice, wife to Nigel Lloyd-Ashton, Geoffrey's cousin. The couple was visiting from Gibraltar, where

Nigel oversaw Lloyd-Ashton Trading Company's Mediterranean operations. On this spring day, Eve and Beatrice were at the Museum of Tea Ware in Flagstaff House. They had spent the past fifteen minutes admiring a tea set from China's Jiangsu Province.

"Good sport, Beatrice?"

Beatrice frowned. "Oh dear. Nigel warned me not to mention this to you, but it seemed such an impossible coincidence that you could look so precisely like her. We assumed that Geoffrey must have shown you her picture, and that you offered to style your hair exactly like hers, and wear the same sort of clothes, and . . . oh dear." Her frown deepened. "You know nothing about Rosalind, do you?"

"No." *Except that sometimes, when his eyes are dark with passion—and with conquest—Geoffrey calls me his rose.* "Beatrice, please tell me."

"It was so long ago. It hardly matters anymore."

"Please."

Beatrice sighed dramatically. "Well, I've come this far, haven't I? Really put my foot into it this time. All right, then. It really *doesn't* matter, Eve. Even though your looks are virtually identical, your personalities aren't alike at all—and it's obvious from Geoffrey's devotion to you that he vastly prefers your reticence to Rosalind's wildness. Oh, she was an untamed one, all right, spirited, like a Thoroughbred. She was highborn, of course. In fact, she absolutely insisted that the man who had raised her wasn't truly her father. She was descended from royalty, she said, the love child of some minor European monarch or other, a displaced princess, a modern-day Anastasia. Nigel and I weren't ever sure that we really believed that claim, but Geoffrey did. And even if her behavior wasn't always quite as *subdued* as a princess should be, it was, at all times, absolutely imperious. We all forgave her, of course, because she was so extraordinary, a whirling dervish who swept everyone in her path right along with her."

"Including Geoffrey." *Geoffrey was in love with the wild, enchanting, confident princess.*

"Yes. Oh, theirs was a volatile—and passionate—relationship, have no doubt of that, but we all knew that they were right for each other." Beatrice shook her head. "But, even after they were engaged, Rosalind's flare for the dramatic didn't wane. A month before they were to wed, she told Geoffrey that she was leaving him, that she'd fallen in love with someone else." Beatrice paused, tugged thoughtfully at her lower lip, and finally admitted, "Geoffrey doesn't actually know that I know that, that *anyone* does. We—four couples who'd been friends since college—were at the Lloyd-Ashton summer home in Scotland at the time. Everyone was outside, except for Geoffrey and Rosalind—and me. I was resting, and their room was right next door, and I overheard their row. I'm certain that, had she lived, they would have gotten back together, but . . ."

"She died?"

Beatrice nodded solemnly. "That day, just moments later. She rushed out of the house, got into her car, and started to speed away. She was looking behind her, to make certain that Geoffrey was in hot pursuit, I suppose. She didn't see the truck that was coming up the drive. I shouted to her from the window, and Geoffrey and the others shouted, too, but Rosalind didn't hear our warnings. She was killed instantly, before our eyes. She was only twenty-six." After a significant pause Beatrice forged ahead with the obvious. "Extraordinary, isn't it? That's the exact age that you were when you and Geoffrey met. He must have believed he was seeing a ghost. It's all really quite uncanny, Eve. In your looks, in your remarkable beauty, you and Rosalind could have been twins."

Remarkable beauty. Of all the devastating words Beatrice Lloyd-Ashton had uttered, those were the ones that haunted Eve the most. From birth, she had believed herself to be wretchedly ugly. She had spent her life trying to become invisible, to shield her face and body from ridicule. She had always felt detached from her physical being, and yet oddly protective of it.

But now it was that outer shell that had betrayed her—by being beautiful after all, by possessing a beauty that she could not see . . . but that had beckoned to Geoffrey.

Eve believed that she understood everything then, that she was desired—and punished—because of her resemblance to the wild and defiant Rosalind. But Eve was wrong. Rosalind was all but forgotten. Geoffrey's dark desire was now for Eve alone. He wanted to possess her wholly, to conquer and control; but in a way that was far more infuriating to him even than the petulance of Rosalind, Eve defied his possession. She had a core of privacy that would not be owned, and that made Geoffrey want to possess her all the more—and to hurt the despicable wretch whom he had transformed into a princess . . . but who dared to defy him with her regal serenity.

There was one truth of which Eve was absolutely certain—and absolutely correct. Geoffrey would never let her go. And unlike Rosalind, who, save for a tragic accident, could have fled to freedom, Eve could never escape. She was, quite literally, a captive in a tropical paradise.

Lady Lloyd-Ashton could not simply vanish among the people of Hong Kong. Her beautiful face was too well known. And even though Kai Tak airport was one of the busiest on earth, with daily flights to virtually every major city on the planet, Eve could not board any of them. Her passport was locked in a vault in Geoffrey's office, and if she applied for a replacement, the news would travel swiftly to him, as all news about her invariably did.

The only country with which Hong Kong shared a border was China. The eighteen-mile national boundary was twined with barbed-wire fences and patrolled by heavily armed soldiers. Admittedly, the wire and border guards were intended to keep refugees from escaping Communist China, not from fleeing capitalist Hong Kong, but Eve would be detained nonetheless.

Eve could neither fly away nor run away, and there was little hope of escape, either, in the shark-infested waters of the South China Sea. She was physically trapped, and she had come full circle, returning to the isolation and despair of her childhood. Indeed, despite the grandeur of her new home, the perch atop Victoria Peak was hauntingly reminiscent of the seaside cliff where she had stood so often as a girl. From any of a hundred places on the grounds of Peak Castle, Lady Lloyd-Ashton could take a single lethal step.

But she never would. Eve had learned other lessons from her childhood. She had learned to float far away from her pain, to find quiet joy in the splendor of the world around her. And that, not death, would be her escape.

The natural splendor of Hong Kong was virtually boundless, and for Eve, there were even other joys. From the very beginning, because he wanted his princess to be admired, Geoffrey had supported her wish to work as a volunteer at Children's Hospital. And, of course, there was Gweneth. She was a world away, yet her lively letters and phone calls kept her close. "I'm getting married, Eve, can you believe it? He and I are both positively stunned. He's a confirmed bachelor and you *know* my feelings about my career. But now we're getting married, and we're even talking about having a house full of children. Can you come to the wedding? I need a matron of honor and I want you to meet James and I want to meet Geoffrey at last."

Eve didn't attend Gweneth's wedding. Geoffrey didn't want to go, nor would be permit Eve to leave Hong Kong without him. Eve doubted that she would ever see her friend again, but then there was another phone call and more joyous news: James and Gweneth were coming for a visit. And if Gweneth liked Hong Kong—"Which I *will*, Eve, because James loves it so!"—the move was going to be a permanent one.

The Drakes visited Hong Kong for two weeks during the Christmas holidays. For Eve, every second of that time was filled with hope. As always, Geoffrey was dazzlingly charming—and loving—in public, but magically, during those two weeks his charm didn't vanish the moment they were alone. He was wonderful to her, and he seemed as genuinely happy as she that James and Gweneth would become part of their lives.

While Geoffrey graciously introduced James to the power brokers of Hong Kong, Gweneth and Eve wandered the festively decorated streets. They laughed, and chatted, and explored, and shopped. Despite Hong Kong's worldwide reputation as *the* shopper's paradise, Eve knew very little about its bountiful offerings. Her clothes arrived at Peak Castle by chauffeured limousines, a never-ending—and unsolicited—array from Hong Kong's top fashion designers, each competing for the coveted award: to become Lady Lloyd-Ashton's exclusive designer. Geoffrey chose the outfits he wanted her to wear and returned the rest.

And as for odds and ends for the castle? Trinkets that would add her personal signature to her new home? Geoffrey greeted her first few attempts with such cold contempt for her taste that Eve had long since stopped making even the smallest purchases.

But somehow Gweneth Drake knew all about where to shop in Hong Kong. Never questioning Eve's lack of experience, she simply led the way.

"Before leaving London, I made an appointment with Juliana Kwan herself," Gweneth explained as they crossed Des Voeux Road and made their way to the Landmark. "She has boutiques in Kowloon as well, at the Regent and in Ocean Terminal, but this is where *she* is. Have you really never heard of her, Eve? Or of Pearl Moon? Her designs would look absolutely smashing on you."

The designs that Gweneth wanted for herself were maternity clothes. She would be five months along when she and James moved to Hong Kong, definitely showing—and definitely in need of stylish yet comfortable mother-to-be outfits for the tropics.

And she would have them, Juliana Kwan promised. They would be ready on her return.

But Gweneth Drake never returned to Hong Kong. One week before that joyously anticipated day, she died in an explosion in their country home in Wales. Eve learned of the tragedy from Geoffrey. The moment the grim news reached the Teletype machine at *The Standard*, Geoffrey was notified. He drove to Peak Castle immediately, his unexpected midday arrival home filling Eve with fear even before he spoke. Always before, such a surprise visit meant that he wanted her, wanted suddenly and urgently to possess—and to hurt.

The sad news Geoffrey gave Eve on that rainy day in early March hurt her terribly, but Geoffrey himself was very gentle. And three weeks later, when a grave and gravely wounded James Drake arrived in Hong Kong, it was Geoffrey who vowed that they would help Gweneth's bereaved husband any way they could.

But James resisted their overtures. The harsh lines of his solemn face sent a clear warning to stay away, and he resolutely refused to talk about Gweneth or his pain.

Eve helped James the only way he would permit her to: without his knowledge. She went to Juliana Kwan's boutique, to make certain that a call to James's office, a polite reminder that his wife's maternity clothes were ready, wouldn't inadvertently be made.

Eve was greeted by Juliana, a welcoming smile that swiftly faded to concern as Juliana saw Eve's sadness.

"Come in here," Juliana urged softly, guiding Eve into one of the boutique's private fitting salons. When they were alone, she asked gently, "What's wrong?"

"Gweneth . . . died."

Gweneth Drake died, but she left with Eve the indelible memory of her generous heart. And because of Gweneth, Eve suddenly had two friends in Hong Kong: Juliana and James. No matter how distant James was, how unwilling to discuss his pain, his eyes always softened for his beloved wife's best friend, and Eve and James both knew that they would be bonded forever by their immense love for Gweneth.

Eve's friendship with Juliana began as her friendship with Gweneth had, at a time of great need. And, as in that friendship, the need was surprisingly reciprocal. Both Eve and Juliana had sadnesses buried deep in their hearts. They shared Eve's grief about Gweneth, and her worries about James, and, eventually, Juliana shared with Eve her sadness about the daughter she had lost. And even though Eve never revealed the most grim truths of her marriage, she confessed to Juliana that despite the facade she maintained, her marriage to Geoffrey was not quite as perfect as all of Hong Kong believed it to be.

Juliana Kwan had never sent a trunk of gowns to Peak Castle, refusing on principle to participate in such a contest. But because of Gweneth Drake, Juliana became Lady Lloyd-Ashton's exclusive designer. The day after she and Eve had visited Pearl Moon, to arrange for her maternity clothes, Gweneth returned to the boutique with another request: a gown—"soft, romantic, and hopeful"—for her friend, a gift that Gweneth planned to give Eve on her return to Hong Kong.

When Eve showed Geoffrey the gown that Juliana had made for her at Gweneth's request, his eyes darkened with pleasure. He had, he realized, been selecting the wrong clothes for Eve. He had chosen outfits like Rosalind had worn, bold and vibrant and sleek, but Juliana Kwan's romantic designs were far better, creations of pure hope—for the princess who had no hope.

Geoffrey loved commanding Eve to undress before him. She

always took such reverent care not to damage the clothes that Juliana had made, as if by carefully preserving the romantic garments she could preserve the romance—and the hope—as well.

The sapphire silk gown that Eve had worn to the party in celebration of the Jade Palace lay on the chaise longue in the master suite. It was quite unharmed, a witness to the night's fierce passion, but not its victim. As Eve rose from the bed to return the gown to its hanger, her body screamed with pain.

As always, Eve ignored the cries. She no longer felt protective of her body. Indeed, it was now a completely separate thing—and a hated one. Her body had betrayed her, after all, by possessing a beauty that she could not see. And all the bruises on her alabaster flesh, and all the screams of physical pain, were quite trivial when compared with the screams and bruises of her heart.

Quite suddenly, and quite startlingly, Eve's thoughts returned to memories of tonight's brutal passion. *Why?* With the answer came a memory of gentleness, not violence, and she saw anew the image to which her mind had floated while Geoffrey had ravaged her. Usually such images were merely flows of color, soft pastels, dancing, swirling, free; and on the rare occasions when she envisioned actual shapes, she saw portraits of nature—a sunset, a flower, the moon, the stars.

But tonight the image had been of a man. It was a remembered image, a wondrous memory. Eve knew his reputation, of course, his passion for fast cars and faster women. And yet . . . there had been no restlessness in the blue eyes that had gazed at hers. They had seemed content to linger, and they seemed to be telling her that he could see beyond the exquisite shell, into the deepest shadows of her heart, and that he understood her pain—and that he cared.

CHAPTER 14

Causeway Bay Children's Hospital
Monday, June 21, 1993

"Lady Lloyd-Ashton?"
The voice belonged to one of the nurses on Ward Three, and as Eve turned to answer she cringed inwardly at how tentative the voice was, how deferential. For seven years Eve had spent every Monday morning on this ward. It was she who felt humbled by the experience, grateful for the opportunity to help if she could, and admiring of the nurses and doctors. But because of who she was—who she was married to—she was treated differently from the other volunteers.

Eve smiled at the nurse. "Yes?"

"Lily Kai was admitted over the weekend. She's doing well now, and will be going home this afternoon, but . . . she knows that Monday is your day and asked me to tell you that she's here. I know that your time today is nearly up, but she's been in radiology all morning and has only just returned. If you don't have time, I can tell her—"

"Of course I have time."

The nurse smiled at last. "Oh, good. She's in her usual room."

As Eve walked toward Lily's room she thought about the

brave little girl. They had met almost precisely a year ago, two days before Lily's fourth birthday. . . .

"*No, no, no! Please!*" The cry was soft, desperate, and frightened, and without a thought Eve rushed into the room—and encountered a trembling and tearful little girl and a gentle but slightly frustrated nurse . . . who became overtly anxious at the sight of Eve.

"Lady Lloyd-Ashton!"

"I'm sorry," Eve apologized. "I heard her cry and . . . is there anything I can do to help?"

"I don't think so. No. But thank you." With a sigh the nurse explained, "Her intravenous has come out, and she really needs to be getting her medications. Her parents always make a point of being here whenever there are needle sticks, but this was unexpected. I'm just about to ring one of them at work."

"I'm *trying* to be brave." Lily looked at Eve, her glistening dark eyes both beseeching and earnest. "But it *hurts*. They always tell me it doesn't, but it *does!*"

"I'm sure it does," Eve said softly, kneeling then, so that she was eye level with the girl. "Hello, Lily. My name is Eve."

"Have you ever had an IV?"

"No," Eve admitted. Then, with a smile, she suggested, "Why don't I have one right now?"

Lily's eyes widened—as did those of the nurse—but it was Lily who asked the obvious. "Why?"

"Well, that way I can see how much it hurts and maybe together we can think of a way to make it hurt less."

"How?"

Eve drew a soft breath, then offered the only thing she could: the truth. She was an expert on pain, after all, and even though she had perfected the technique since her marriage to Geoffrey, even as a little girl, younger than Lily, when the verbal harangues of her parents became too great, her mind had simply floated away. "Why don't I tell you what I do when something hurts me? First of all, I admit that it hurts. Then, in my mind, in my imagination, I go far away from the hurt. I think of something that I like, something that makes me happy."

It took the nurse—who was usually far and away the best venipuncturist on the ward—several attempts to get the needle into one of the delicate lavender veins on Eve's hand. Throughout the process Eve smiled reassurances to the nurse as she spoke to Lily.

"It does hurt, doesn't it? Now, help me find a happy thought." Eve didn't have Lily's full attention. The young eyes were focused intently on Eve's hand, frowning, worrying. "Lily? Help me find a happy thought. Tell me something you love to do."

"Fly my kite."

"With your parents?" When Lily nodded, Eve said, "Tell me where you go to fly your kite, and exactly what it looks like, what color and shape, and what the sky is like as you look up at it. . . ."

Eve had never flown a kite, but Lily's description of hers—a pink-and-blue butterfly with a long silver tail—was so vivid that Eve promptly forgot the sharp yet oddly aching pain in her hand. Eve was a master at ignoring pain, of course. Was it pure folly—and totally unfair—to imagine that such a visualization technique might actually work for a frightened four-year-old child?

In fact, Eve's technique probably didn't work for Lily. As the nurse inserted the intravenous needle into a vein on Lily's small hand—a slick feat accomplished on the first try—Lily's eyes glistened anew, and her lips trembled, and the fingers of her free hand dug deep into Eve's palm. And as Eve gently reminded that yes, it did hurt, Lily whispered softly, "Ow, ow, *ow*."

But this time Lily didn't pull away, and as she listened to Eve quietly describe the grandeur of a butterfly kite soaring into a sapphire-blue sky, Lily's fear did seem to float somewhere . . . to Eve, to the gentle sapphire eyes that were smiling at her.

That night, Sir Geoffrey Lloyd-Ashton and his princess had attended a black-tie gala at Government House. Privately, Geoffrey was quite displeased with the deep purple bruises that marred the pristine whiteness of Eve's hand, as if he alone had the right to violate his wife's delicate flesh, to inflict pain and cause visible damage. But, at the gala, Geoffrey displayed Eve's bruises proudly, tiny badges of his beloved princess's courageous compassion.

Geoffrey's displeasure with the skin-deep legacy of that day at the hospital would have paled into insignificance had he realized the more far-reaching consequences, the beginning of the very special relationship between Eve and the little Chinese girl. Lady Lloyd-Ashton always requested of even the most casual of acquaintances that they call her Eve. At Children's Hospital, Lily Kai alone, too young to understand matters of propriety, honored Eve's request. Indeed, Lily was one of the few people in Hong Kong who addressed Her Ladyship with such informality.

Eve learned from the nurses that Lily's medical problem was an atrial septal defect, a congenital heart anomaly which, ultimately, would require surgical repair. The doctors wanted to let Lily grow as much as possible before the open-heart surgery, hoping to defer the procedure until she was six or seven. But during the past few months, blood-flow studies—as well as more frequent respiratory infections—had forced their hand, and Lily's operation had been tentatively scheduled for December.

Now Lily was in the hospital again, and even though the nurse had said that she was fine, going home today, Eve's chest tightened with worry as she neared Lily's room. In February, Lily had been admitted with pneumonia. She had been so weak, so pale, her small lips tinged with blue . . . frail, and yet brave, as always. Eve would never forget how Lily looked then, lying in her bed, connected to an assortment of plastic tubes, absolutely motionless, almost lifeless. . . .

Lily Kai wasn't lifeless today. She sat on the edge of her hospital bed, her legs dangling over the side, and when she caught sight of Eve, her small face lighted with happiness.

"Eve!"

"Hello, Lily." Eve breathed at last, a breath of relief and joy. When she reached her little friend, she sat down beside her on the bed. "How are you?"

"Fine." Lily shrugged. "I have a cough, but it's not bad."

"Good. I'm glad." As Eve watched, a transformation took place. The ever-brave Lily started to crumble. Her head bent, casting a curtain of fine black silk across her pretty face. Then her delicate hands started twisting together, and then her legs began to move, swinging nervously against the bed. "Lily? What's the matter?"

"My operation."

Had the surgery date been moved up? Eve wondered. Or was the bright little girl who had always talked so matter-of-factly about the "hole in her heart" and the surgery that would correct it finally beginning to truly understand the seriousness of that prospect? "What about your operation, Lily?"

Lily's legs answered first, moving even faster. "I was just wondering . . ."

Wondering if you might die? Eve's own heart died more than a little at the thought. Hiding her fear, she smiled and encouraged, "What were you wondering, Lily?"

"Could you . . . if you . . ." Lily stopped, and Eve wasn't certain that she would continue, nor did she guess where the halting words had been trying to go. Then they came, on a brave rush. "I know that if you were here on that day, if I talked to you right before I went to sleep, everything would be fine!"

"Oh, Lily," Eve whispered. "Of course I'll be here that day."

The silky black head lifted then. "You will?"

"Yes, I will. I'll see you just before you go to sleep, and I'll be right here when you wake up."

"But my operation isn't until December. Will you still be in Hong Kong then?"

"Of course I will be. I live in Hong Kong. Did you think I was going to move away?"

To Eve's utter amazement, Lily Kai nodded.

"I'm not going anywhere, Lily. And I'll be right here, with you, on the day of your surgery."

"You promise?"

"I promise."

The Excelsior Hotel's second-floor restaurant afforded an excellent view across Gloucester Road to the Causeway Bay Typhoon Shelter. In the foreground, at harbor's edge, stood the Noonday Gun, immortalized in song by Noël Coward, but already a legend in Hong Kong long before the famous lyrics.

The polished brass Hotchkiss gleamed brightly beneath the midday sun, a glittering symbol of Hong Kong's colorful past. In the middle of the last century, Jardine Matheson, the newly formed colony's premier trading company, established the practice of firing twenty-one-gun salutes every time one of its clippers arrived safely in port. The colonial governor, incensed that such ceremonial pomp was being extended to a merchant vessel, especially one undoubtedly loaded with opium, ordered Jardine's taipan to cease the unseemly practice immediately. Moreover, in punishment, he proclaimed Jardine Matheson to be the colony's official timekeeper. Every day, precisely at noon, they would be responsible for announcing the time by firing a single shot.

The century-old tradition continued still. The original cannon had been replaced in 1901 by the Hotchkiss, and midnight on New Year's Eve had been added to the list of permissible times for firing, but it was still Jardine Matheson that provided Hong Kong with its daily noonday boom.

It was almost noon now. A man in a white uniform loaded the gun as interested tourists congregated nearby. Juliana sat across Gloucester Road, in the Excelsior's restaurant, sipping tea as she waited for Eve. It would be another half hour, at least, before Eve arrived, and Juliana knew she might well be late. Her friend never left the hospital early, and sometimes there was a lonely or frightened child who needed her to stay even longer.

The Noonday Gun fired then, an event that Juliana witnessed rather than heard. The cannonlike blast was muted by the typhoon-proof glass, but she saw the puff of white smoke, a perfect fleecy cloud, so pure, so pristine—and that, even as she watched, vanished swiftly, cast asunder by the breeze from the bay.

For most Hong Kong residents, the Noonday Gun signaled the future, a booming reminder that there were only so many days left until 1997, and that in this place of so many glittering treasures, time was rapidly becoming the most precious one of all. Like a starter's gun, the noontime blast urged all who heard it to race forward, to capture dreams before they vanished like smoke in the wind.

But to Juliana, who saw only the vanishing white cloud, today's explosion triggered memories of the past, where once there had been dreams, so pristine and so pure, but that had vanished before her eyes. . . .

Eight days after Juliana had defied destiny by calling Garrett, because he needed her so desperately, the fates meted out their revenge for her impertinence. Vivian suffered a second heart attack, this time fatal. Even as Juliana tried to deal with the enormity of the loss and with her own immense guilt, there was more devastation to come. Despite the fact that Vivian Jong's success had come long after her husband's death, and with money she had earned herself, the family of the husband who had been dead for over forty years laid claim to her entire fortune.

Everything was rightfully theirs, the relatives maintained. *Nothing* should go to the young woman who had no blood ties whatsoever to either Vivian or her husband.

Juliana Kwan was a gold digger, they said, pure and simple. Not so pure, they amended swiftly. She had just given birth to an infant with dark green eyes, shameful proof of the type of woman she truly was. And there was more damning evidence. Juliana had been with her lover, not at Vivian's bedside, nine months before, and coincident with her eventual appearance, the controversial will had been drawn up. Clearly the opportunistic and immoral waif had taken advantage of the frail and dying woman, pretending to care for her while convincing her to defy centuries of Chinese tradition by bequeathing her worldly goods to an outsider rather than to her family.

Since Vivian Jong's fortune was substantial, the family she hadn't seen for decades pursued it with a vengeance. They retained the services of Miles Burton, a high-priced and highly regarded British barrister, and they implored him to see that the matter was resolved quickly—*before* the lunar new year began.

By ancient Chinese tradition, the start of the new year—the first day of the first moon after the sun entered the constellation of Aquarius—was a time of rebirth and new beginning. One greeted it with a clean slate: crisp new clothes, a brightly scrubbed house, and a sparklingly clear conscience. All debts were to be repaid before the new year began, all quarrels and disputes resolved.

During the weeklong festival itself, Hong Kong would be a brilliant bouquet of the symbolic flowers of prosperity; and celebrants would feast on sugarcoated melon seeds, chocolate coins, candied fruits, and lotus stalks; and bright red *lai see* envelopes filled with lucky money would be lavished on family, colleagues, and friends; and everywhere one would see or hear the familiar invocation *Kung Hei Fat Choy*—Rejoice and grow rich!

In the weeks leading up to the celebration, the people of Hong Kong sought to ensure prosperity for the coming year by soliciting the support of Tsao Kwan, the Kitchen God. Since the kitchen was the center of family life, that was where Tsao Kwan lived. His presence there was commemorated with a special shrine, a monument that could be as simple as his name, written in gold characters and emblazoned on red paper, or as elaborate as a figurine made of porcelain or jade.

It was the Kitchen God's duty to observe his family carefully, to note their behavior and their deeds, and to prepare a dossier on them to present to the Jade Emperor in heaven. Because an unfavorable report from the Kitchen God could result in a new year filled with bad luck, and a glowing one could cause lavish prosperity, great effort was expended to ensure that his words would be very good indeed.

The Kitchen God's seven-day journey to heaven commenced on the twenty-fourth day of the twelfth moon. Prior to his departure, offerings were placed at his shrine, sweets, usually, in hope of encouraging him to say sweet things. Cane sugar was placed at his feet, or even on his lips, and sometimes his impending journey was fortified with opium as well, to blur—and yet make pleasant—the memories of his family.

The Kitchen God's presence in Vivian Jong's house overlooking Happy Valley was commemorated with a delicate porcelain figurine. Year round, at his shrine, Vivian placed fresh, fragrant flowers, and as the new year approached she burned perfumed joss sticks and filled vases with symbolic flowers of prosperity and luck. But she never smeared his porcelain lips with sugar. "He knows we've been good," she explained to Juliana. "He knows how much love there is in this family."

Juliana didn't break the tradition established by Vivian, nor did she forget it. Somehow, despite her grief, she created beautiful bouquets of peach blossoms, jonquils, and chrysanthemums.

Juliana would never know if the flowers were enough. When the Kitchen God was only halfway to heaven, the magistrate made his ruling. Vivian Jong's will was null and void. Everything was to go to her deceased husband's relatives.

"Miss Kwan."

Juliana recognized the voice at once. It belonged to Miles Burton, the man whose convincing portrait of her as an unscrupulous seductress had caused the magistrate to rule against her. Because of the clever barrister, at a time when Hong Kong was about to celebrate its most joyous festival, its time of family and feasting and friends, she and her family, her beloved infant daughter, had no home, no money, no food.

The magistrate's ruling was only ten minutes old, but already Juliana was staggering along Harcourt Road, her legs as wobbly now as when the child of the sea had walked for the first time on land. She was in foreign territory once again, dizzy and off balance, and now the man whose clever words had been as devastating as the long-ago typhoon was calling to her.

Juliana clutched her month-old baby daughter even closer to her and kept walking. But moments later Miles Burton was in front of her, blocking her path, looming above her as ominously as the black mountains of China.

"I am not your enemy, Miss Kwan. The magistrates of Hong Kong are legally obliged to follow the principles of common law. They have no choice. Even if you had been represented by the best barrister in the colony—even if you had been represented by me—Vivian Jong's family would have won."

"But it's not what Vivian wanted." Juliana narrowed her eyes. "You know that, don't you?"

"Perhaps I do. Which is why, Juliana, I want to offer my help."

Juliana was so stunned by his offer of help that she didn't notice that he had addressed her by her first name—or that his voice had been seductively silky when he had.

"Never," she hissed softly. "Never will I accept your help."

Never, never, *never*. The vow echoed in her starving brain, a defiant mantra even as her feet betrayed her. She was walking toward his office on Wyndham Street, and even though it had been almost four weeks, her balance was unsteady still—unsteady now because of starvation.

February had been unseasonably cold and relentlessly damp. It was truly amazing that the young mother had lasted so long in the elements. She had managed to make a little money by selling the few garments she'd been allowed to take with her. The amount she received for her dresses was trivial compared with their worth, but it was enough to buy warm clothes and blankets for Maylene.

They slept outside, finding shelter in alleyways between buildings and sometimes in Victoria Park, and by day Juliana searched for work. But no one wanted as an employee a new mother whose main concern was so obviously for the tiny baby she held with such loving care. What attention would she pay to her job? they wondered. And when it came right down to it, would she even be able to relinquish the grasp of her child, to free her hands to do the work for which she was being paid?

Sweatshops were for those willing to work endless hours in cramped conditions without complaint. Many saw in Juliana's determined eyes that she was potentially such an employee. If it weren't for the child, they would have hired her in an instant. But as it was, no one offered her a job, nothing at all, not in four weeks of constant searching.

It had been a very long time since Juliana had been warm, and even longer since she had eaten. But it wasn't for herself that she made the journey to Miles Burton's law office on Wyndham Street. It was for Maylene.

For four weeks, Juliana had managed to keep her precious daughter warm and fed and dry. Despite the fact that she ate nothing herself, there was still rich, nutritious milk for Maylene. The extra pounds she'd carried during her pregnancy were efficiently converted to food for her baby, and when those pounds were gone, her body found ways to make food still, scavenging from its own tissues. Every cell in Juliana's body gave of itself, all it could, for her daughter. But, very soon, there would be nothing left to give.

For Maylene, for the very survival of her Daughter of Greatest Love, Juliana needed the help of Miles Burton.

"Miss Kwan. You've come."

"Yes."

"You've lost weight. You are very thin."

He seemed to be appraising her, as if trying to decide whether he found her more alluring plump and lush or gaunt and thin. Juliana felt his intimate inspection and fought a sudden quiver of panic.

"This is the weight I prefer, Mr. Burton. I've worked hard to lose the extra pounds I gained during my pregnancy."

"So there's no point in offering you scones and tea?"

"None." Juliana gave a soft shake of her head for emphasis, a gentle gesture that caused waves of dizziness. She needed to eat again, and she would for Maylene, but there were words to say now, quickly, before her starving, floating mind forgot what she had so carefully rehearsed. "I'm here to accept your offer of help. I would like to borrow some money."

"Borrow?"

"Yes. I would pay it back, of course, with interest, and if my business does well, I would be prepared to share some of its profits with you."

"What business, Juliana?"

"I wish to resume my career as a dressmaker. I'm hoping that some of Vivian's clients will be willing to have me design their clothes." Juliana hadn't approached any of Vivian's clients yet, of course, hadn't stood beneath the porticoes of their expensive homes rain-drenched and starving. The elegant women of Hong Kong had to be approached properly, through formal letters of inquiry written in perfect script on fine linen, and before beginning her own business, Juliana needed an address and a telephone number and fabric and sequins and needles and thread.

Miles Burton smiled, and his dark eyes seemed amused, and Juliana's heart, already galloping from starvation, raced with hope. He thought her plan foolish, perhaps, but he *was* going to help.

"I'm afraid you misunderstood my offer. I'm not interested in an investment opportunity, Juliana. I'm interested in a mistress."

It wasn't an indecent proposal, not in Hong Kong in 1966. Wealthy Englishmen frequently had Chinese mistresses. It was socially acceptable, entirely correct, an arrangement that worked quite well for all concerned—the man, his mistress, and even the aristocratic wife whose marriage was based on pedigree rather than passion.

"It would only be for nine months," the barrister elaborated. "After that I'm returning to England, permanently. Until then, however, and for four months after I leave, I will provide you with a comfortable two-bedroom flat, and food and clothing. And, so long as it doesn't interfere with your availability to me and the costs are reasonable, I'll help you with your business."

Juliana's racing heart stopped beating, and her starving mind shrieked its defiant mantra, and in another moment she would die.

But she could not die. She needed to live for Maylene, to make nourishing milk for her baby.

Juliana Kwan was in a foreign land once again, but she understood with brilliant clarity the language Miles Burton was speaking.

He was asking her to sell her soul.

"Are these terms acceptable to you, Juliana?"

No! Never! her mind cried.

Yes, her heart answered, beating again, almost calmly now, resigned to its fate. Yes, for my daughter, I will sell my soul.

A moment later Juliana heard herself answer his question, her voice as calm and as confident as her heart. "Not entirely."

"Oh?" he asked, with mild interest. This was expected. The mistress always countered with *her* terms, the jewels she wanted, the gowns she would need, the weekly pampering at Hong Kong's finest salons. "What else would you like?"

"A full British passport for my daughter."

"Just for her? Not for yourself as well?"

"No, just for her." Even then Juliana knew that she would never leave Hong Kong. It was her home, where she had fallen in love. . . .

She couldn't think about Garrett, not now. She couldn't remind herself that if he had any idea of her plight, he would, in an instant, send her a fortune. She had merely to pick up the phone and call.

But she never would, never could, because what price would the fates demand if she did? Maylene's life? Allison's?

The two-bedroom apartment was luxurious, and she and Maylene were safe and warm, and Juliana told herself that she was very lucky. Miles Burton didn't hurt her. His sexual tastes were neither perverted nor cruel. He even scheduled his visits when Maylene was asleep.

It was all terribly civilized.

But . . . her body had been a gift of love to Garrett, only to him, always, and after he left, it belonged to their precious daughter, to nurture her, to cradle and protect. No one else should ever have known its intimate secrets and its gentle gifts.

Juliana tried to convince herself that what she sold Hong

Kong's most brilliant barrister was no different from what she sold its wealthiest women. To him she sold her body, and to them her talent, and both were business transactions, no more, no less. But every time she went to bed with him, she lost a little more of herself, her hope, her spirit, her soul.

She didn't hate him. How could she? He had saved her daughter's life. The price she'd had to pay was very great . . . and it was very small . . . because Maylene was everything.

Finally, although to her heart it felt like an eternity, the nine months passed. On the eve of his departure for England, Miles Burton gave her the agreed-upon British passport for Maylene. He reminded her, too, of the other promise he had made. She and Maylene could remain in the apartment for four more months.

Juliana didn't accept the offer. Her small business was doing well enough for them to survive, and although it would have meant four more months of income undiminished by housing expenses, she was desperate to move with her daughter to a place of their own, however modest, a private world of love untainted by remembrance of what she had done.

Long before she was old enough to make a conscious memory, Maylene knew all about her mother. It was a knowledge of the senses, a magnificent tapestry of sight and sound, and taste and scent and touch, a soft, rich weave of magic and of love.

"I love you, May-May," was a constant chorus, and when Maylene was old enough to ask about her father, the first words from Juliana's lips were, "He loves you, too."

"Where is he?"

"In heaven. We can't see him, my love, but he's with us, always, loving us, protecting us, smiling at us."

Maylene wanted to know all about her father, and she loved

hearing her mother talk about him, because her mother's beautiful face lighted with such happiness whenever she did.

Juliana told Maylene all the truths she could: where and when they met, and how much they loved each other, and how very much he would have loved his little girl. And so that he could be as real to Maylene as possible, Juliana told her daughter Garrett's name.

The rest of her words were lies. Garrett Whitaker was British, she said, and even though he'd had to return to England shortly after they met, he was on his way back to Hong Kong, to be with them forever, when he died.

Maylene knew all the romantic places of her parents' love; and when she and Juliana went to Victoria Peak, to that special place on the Hong Kong Trail, or when they rode the Star ferries to Kowloon, Maylene felt his presence, just as Juliana did; and when she and her mother strolled together along the streets of Hong Kong, and Juliana held her hand, Maylene believed that her other hand was held as well, by her father.

As Maylene grew older she needed her father's invisible presence even more. She was living proof of his love, but the wondrous gifts he had given her were ridiculed by her classmates. Her eyes were jade green, and she was tall, and her skin was alabaster instead of gold. There was a soft curl to her long black hair as well, and her features were stunning, yes, but different, wrong, *impure.* To her classmates, it was obvious: Maylene Kwan's mother was a whore and her father had been a sailor, drunken, probably, and seeking nothing more than an evening's pleasure.

The taunts pierced Maylene's young heart, but her anguish was less for herself than for the parents whose wondrous love was being so horribly degraded. At first, she valiantly countered the taunts, "He was British and he *loved* us!" But that only shifted the slurs against her mother from sailor's whore to Englishman's mistress. And, Maylene learned, it didn't change who *she* was, nothing did. Her blood was impure, and that seemed to give everyone the right to stare at her and mock her and try to make her feel ashamed.

Maylene had no friends, but that didn't matter. She had her mother, and she knew the truth: she was the Daughter of Greatest Love.

Maylene became a gifted actress, hiding her pain from everyone, including, *especially*, from the mother she loved so very much.

"You lied to me!" *Fortune* magazine shook in Maylene's trembling hands. "This is him, isn't it? This is my father."

At Maylene's words, Juliana glanced briefly from her teenage daughter's ravaged face to the photograph Maylene displayed. It was Garrett, thirteen years older than the man she had known, but so handsome still, and so beloved. At any other time Juliana's heart would have soared with pure joy to see his face again, but not now, not when for Maylene the visage was an anguished symbol of betrayal.

"Yes," Juliana answered softly. "He's your father. May-May, let me explain—"

"There's no need! It's all here in the article. He was a navy pilot in Vietnam, one of the thousands of sailors who came to Hong Kong in search of whores."

"*No.* It wasn't like that at all."

"Really? I think it was *exactly* like that . . . exactly like what everyone's been saying all along."

"Everyone? What do you mean?"

"*Everyone*, Mother. I'm an outcast, a hated half-breed, didn't you know?" Maylene saw her mother's startled eyes and pleaded, "You have no idea how hated I am, do you? Of course not. *Your* blood is pure, and your features are perfect, and your eyes aren't green."

"Oh, my darling," Juliana whispered with soft despair. "You're so beautiful, May-May. You look like your father, remember?"

"I don't *want* to look like my father, not anymore! Don't you see, Mother? I *hate* the way I look!"

"Oh, May-May. I love you so much, and so does he, and you have friends—"

"I *don't* have friends. I've only pretended that I do, so you wouldn't worry about me. Do you want to know what I do after school? I swim until I can't swim anymore and then I go to bookstores. I read about other places—anywhere but Hong Kong—and I look at pictures in magazines and dream about getting away from here. That's how I discovered this article about my supposedly dead father. Oh, I wish he *were* dead!"

"No, you don't. Please, my love, let me tell you the truth."

"The truth, Mother?" Maylene echoed with disbelief. "How would I know?"

"Please," Juliana repeated softly. "Please let me explain."

Maylene seemed fearful of learning any more truths, but finally she nodded, a resigned gesture that made Juliana's weeping heart weep even more. It was as if Maylene's willingness to hear the truth was more self-destructive than hopeful, as if it would give her more reasons to hate herself, rather than ones that would set her free.

Juliana didn't tell her daughter about Vivian's will, or their cold and rainy February of homelessness in Hong Kong, or about Miles Burton. She told Maylene only the events before that time: her deep and forever love for Garrett Whitaker; her ominous certainty from the very beginning that six days were all they were ever to have; the tragedies that had befallen Blake and Vivian while she and Garrett had lived their love; the reason for his marriage to Beth; Allison's birth and Beth's death; Garrett's offer to support them and her refusal of same; and finally the death of Vivian Jong just eight days after her final, forbidden call to him.

"You believe it was destiny for you to spend your lives apart?"

"Yes, I do."

"That's delusional, Mother, a romanticized notion of star-crossed lovers. It wasn't *destiny* that kept you apart, it was *choice*. He chose not to be with you—with us!—because for him there was never any love at all."

"That's not true."

"Of course it is. Maybe you don't even know. Maybe you've convinced yourself that your version is the truth. But it's not. I wish I'd never been born! Couldn't you have *done* something?"

"Maylene, *no*. I've loved you with all my heart from the moment I knew you were alive inside me. Do you know when that was, my darling? Just hours after you were conceived, before your father even left Hong Kong."

"Oh, Mother, do you hear yourself? That's impossible. It's just another delusion. *This* is the truth—I'm a half-breed child of lust."

"No, my May-May, you're a precious child of love, the Daughter of Greatest Love, and someday, my darling, you will understand. Someday, when you fall in love—"

"I will *never* fall in love. And I can assure you that no one will ever fall in love with me." Even then, at age thirteen, Maylene Kwan knew her own destiny. Eurasians were desired, yes, as mistresses, as exotic trophies, but they were not considered worthy of love. As children of lust, they were renowned for their artful sensuality and, like their mothers, for their willingness to please. That was the reality for Eurasians in Hong Kong. And in the other places of the world? In the faraway lands about which she had read? Was there, somewhere, a place where people wouldn't stare, a place where, perhaps, she might even belong? "I need to get away from here, away from Hong Kong—forever!"

"Oh, May-May," Juliana whispered to the thirteen-year-old daughter who was so very much like the girl Tranquil Sea had been at exactly that age, torn between two worlds, not certain where she belonged, but searching . . . dreaming.

When Juliana left her own home at thirteen, there had been,

for her, no other choice. The life she had known at sea was gone, ravaged without a trace. Maylene believed that her life, the private world of love in which she dwelled with her mother, was totally shattered as well. But it *isn't*, Juliana thought. I'm still here, loving you, and I can't let you go, my May-May, not now, not yet, not when you are so young—and so devastated.

Juliana Kwan's lies had caused such anguish, and yet it was with another lie that she began the new life with her daughter. "Vivian left a trust fund for you. It will be yours when you're eighteen, by which time it should be quite substantial. She also arranged for you to have a full British passport. So, my darling, when you're eighteen, if you still want to, you can leave Hong Kong. Until then I will try to convince you how loved you truly are, by both your father and me, and even if you don't believe my words, perhaps you will remember them . . . and someday, perhaps, you will understand—and forgive."

Maylene remembered Juliana's words. During the five years before she left for England, she played them back perfectly, with her own angry and anguished interpretation of her parents' "love." The hurtful words flowed from a heart that was so deeply wounded that sometimes it needed to scream its immense pain, to *share* it, and even though Maylene's taunts made Juliana ache with sadness, she would have gladly endured them forever if they had helped Maylene. But, Juliana knew, her sensitive daughter only hated herself all the more for her own cruelty.

By the time Maylene left, Juliana recognized that it was for the best. Her beloved daughter needed to get away both from Hong Kong and from her. Juliana prayed that Maylene would find happiness in her new home. She would, at least, be able to live quite comfortably. For the past five years Juliana had worked tirelessly to make truthful the lie she had told about the trust fund. As a result, the once make-believe inheritance had become worth a small fortune.

Then the Daughter of Greatest Love was gone, perhaps forever, and Juliana, who for the past eighteen years had cared only about her child, filled the immense void with a dream that had mattered once, long ago, before there was love. The dream had been Vivian's, but Juliana had been its keeper, and over the next nine, lonely years the success of Pearl Moon surpassed even their wildest imaginings.

It was the change in sound, from the hum of animated conversation to hushed whispers of awareness, that drew Juliana from her memories. The hushed whispers announced the arrival of Lady Lloyd-Ashton.

"I'm sorry I'm late," Eve said as she joined Juliana. "There was a little girl who needed to talk."

Juliana smiled softly. She had just now been remembering a little girl who had been mercilessly teased by her classmates, and had needed desperately to talk, but who, to protect her mother, had hidden her own sadness. That brave, loving little girl was now a grown woman. Had Maylene found anyone with whom she could share her secret pain? Juliana wondered. Oh, how she hoped so.

Eve saw the hope and the worry on Juliana's face. Gently, truthfully, she said, "As you imagined it would be, I think it's somewhat difficult for Maylene to be back in Hong Kong. But, Juliana, there's no doubt that while she's here she'll be working with people who respect and care about her very much."

"Really? Do you mean James Drake?"

"James, yes, of course. But all of them, really, everyone involved with the Jade Palace." Eve considered for a moment, then added, "Especially the builder, Sam Coulter. I get the impression that he cares very deeply."

"And does Maylene feel the same way about him?"

"I think so, but . . . it's a little hard to tell."

"Because she's such a good actress."

"Yes," Eve agreed quietly. "She is."

"Did she look well, Eve? Healthy?"

Eve smiled. "Healthy—and extraordinarily beautiful. Her arrival caused quite a sensation." Eve tilted her head thoughtfully and then gently answered Juliana's unasked question. "She wasn't wearing one of your designs, Juliana, but she would have known not to. Maylene may have been away for nine years, but she knows there are unwritten protocols in Hong Kong. I'm sure she checked and was told that any designer label was acceptable at Peak Castle—except Pearl Moon."

It was one of Geoffrey's well-known mandates: in the presence of his princess no one else was to wear Juliana Kwan's designs. Pearl Moon was Eve's signature label. The mandate didn't hurt Juliana's business, of course. Lady Lloyd-Ashton's appearances at Hong Kong's black-tie galas were as carefully rationed as her twice-weekly forays from the castle. There was ample opportunity for the other glamorous women of Hong Kong to display their Pearl Moon best.

"People are still adhering to that?"

"Absolutely, and you know that Maylene would have known to check." Eve smiled. "Allison Whitaker, however—"

Eve's words were stopped by the sudden clatter of porcelain on porcelain as Juliana's teacup hit the side of its saucer, spilling its contents onto the pink linen tablecloth.

"How careless of me," Juliana murmured, somehow finding words.

A busboy appeared instantly and began to repair what was only a minor mishap. In moments, almost too quickly, the tablecloth was replaced, and even though nothing had been broken, hot tea steamed from a fresh teacup.

"Are you all right?" Eve asked.

"Yes, of course." Juliana might have blamed the spill on the once delicate fingers that now gave eloquent testimony to her years of intricate needlework. Her joints ached sometimes, and they were always slightly swollen, but both Juliana and Eve knew that the fingers were very far from clumsy. They could dance still, creating enchantments of magic on shimmering silk. Smiling, praying that some of her daughter's ability to act had been inherited from her, Juliana said, "I was just paying more attention to you than to the saucer. You were saying something about someone named Allison?"

"Allison Whitaker. She's the photographer James has commissioned for the murals for the Jade Palace. She wore one of your gowns to the party, the rainbow sequins on ivory silk. It looked very lovely on her, as if you'd made it especially for her."

In loving Maylene, I will love Allison, too. Were both beloved daughters really in Hong Kong? Yes, Juliana knew it was true, because although it happened very quickly, she was quite certain that the trembling that had tumbled her teacup had begun just an instant *before* Eve spoke Allison's name.

Still, more to keep the conversation going than because she needed further proof, she said, "I designed the rainbow-sequined gown for Neiman Marcus. Allison Whitaker must be an American."

"She is, from Texas, like Sam. He's from San Antonio and she's from Dallas, but apparently he knows Allison's father."

How glad Juliana was that she had never told her friend Garrett's name, or the name of his other daughter, or even that they lived in Dallas. She trusted Eve without question, of course, but once before she had made the devastating mistake of revealing the name of the man she loved.

"Is it because of Sam that Allison's doing the photographs for the Jade Palace? Did he recommend her to James?" *Did Garrett ask him to?*

"No. It's just coincidence. James discovered Allison's work himself, quite by chance."

Coincidence. Chance. The words echoed in Juliana's mind still, hours after she and Eve had parted. Neither she nor Garrett had conspired to bring their daughters together. Neither had defied the fates. And yet, unbelievably, Allison and Maylene were both in Hong Kong, united by the Jade Palace, the structure that would forever celebrate the improbable marriage of East and West.

This was a new destiny, Juliana decided. She knew not where it would lead, but only that she must not intervene. Somehow she must keep her heart from making dangerous, forbidden wishes. Juliana knew the wishes were there, of course, wondrous dreams, but she dared not allow them to dance and twirl, not even for a moment.

It was safe, though, to think about the daughters that destiny had already brought together. Would Allison's presence make it all the more difficult for Maylene to be back in Hong Kong? Or, by some magic, would the sisters become friends?

Juliana hoped, and she worried. But never, not once, did she fear that Maylene would reveal the truth to Allison. No matter how her lovely daughter's sensitive heart cried with pain, Juliana knew that this time Maylene would keep all her anguish deep inside.

Oh, my beloved May-May.

PART FOUR

CHAPTER 15

The Jade Palace
Thursday, July 8, 1993

"Hello."

A welcoming smile embellished Sam's greeting to Maylene as she walked into his office at the construction site. He hadn't seen her since the party at Peak Castle. There had been no need to see her, no professional one, that is. The excavation of earth did not require the input of the architect. For that matter, neither did what was to begin today: the pouring of concrete around the top-grade steel beams, setting them for eternity, a foundation that would ensure the Jade Palace's survival despite whatever natural or political disasters might occur.

Maylene didn't need to be here today, not professionally, but Sam had asked her to come. He had assured her that nothing was wrong, but still the first words from her lips, after softly echoing his hello, were words of worry.

"Is there a problem?"

"No. I thought you should see the progress we've made."

"Oh. Yes. Thank you." Maylene walked to the window, and although she already knew the answer—from James, from the view from her apartment, and from the skies that still shimmered brightly with unspilled drops of rain—she asked, "You're ahead of schedule, aren't you?"

"Way ahead. Just like you."

"I'm just trying to keep up with your pace."

"It will be a long time before I need the blueprints you sent me yesterday," Sam said gently, worried about her. "So, Maylene, other than working around the clock, how have you been?"

"Fine," she lied, not looking at him, her eyes fixed on the massive hole in the parched earth.

In truth Maylene had never felt more conflicted, more tormented, more torn. She had returned to Hong Kong with the hope that she would find the courage to see her mother again—once the Jade Palace was built, and triumphant—and that prospect was perilous enough.

But now there were other dangerous journeys to make.

Sometimes, when she awakened in the middle of the night, confused by unremembered dreams, she felt an almost overwhelming impulse to scamper down the hall in her nightgown and robe for a late-night chat with her sister.

And sometimes, something very powerful and very deep whispered to her to find the cowboy, to see if he was awake, and restless, and lonely, too.

For years Maylene had feared the hurtful words she might blurt out when her heart screamed with pain. But now, even more terrifying, were the desperate ones that might flow, unbidden, from the heart that yearned for love.

You're my sister, Allison, my sister! I know it's hard to believe. You're so golden, and I'm so tarnished, and if you don't want to have anything to do with me, *believe me* I'll understand. But . . . I just wanted you to know that I'm proud of you, so very proud.

Hello, Cowboy. It's me. I wondered if you'd like to hear more about the dragons of Hong Kong? You seemed so interested that day as we stood at harbor's edge. Interested in the dragons—and in me. I know I looked away from your caressing eyes. The intimacy scared me. But . . . I feel braver now.

Maylene no longer questioned her ability to prevent her screams of pain from escaping her lips. But because she could not trust herself to contain the desperate wishes of her lonely heart, she had carefully avoided both the radiant emerald eyes and the seductive blue ones.

Early this morning, however, and quite by chance, she and Allison had met. Maylene was on her way to Drake Towers and Allison, her eyes bright with anticipation, was off to Blake Pier to observe one of Hong Kong's most graceful rituals, the ancient art of tai chi, practiced at dawn by elderly Chinese in the grassy parks and at water's edge.

Their conversation had been eager but awkward, rushes of words followed by sudden silence. They talked of the weather: how wonderful it was for the Jade Palace, how busy they both were because of it, how there weren't nearly enough hours in the day. It was as if they were both finding excuses—or perhaps apologies—for not having gotten together. And then, just before going their separate ways on Chater Road, Maylene suddenly saw brave determination in Allison's eyes, and in another moment, perhaps, Allison might have suggested that despite their frantically busy lives, they should get together after all.

Maylene would never know. Just as her heart was bravely and determinedly promising that she would say yes to whatever Allison had in mind, strident warnings crushed the hopeful promise. You *know* what you'll talk about, don't you? Allison's loving father, of course, or perhaps her happy childhood. And maybe Allison will share with you her hopeful philosophy of life, her resolute belief that one should be kind *always*, never vicious, never cruel. . . .

Before Allison could speak, Maylene announced brusquely that she needed to go, to get some ideas on paper before a breakfast meeting with James. The sisters parted then, but Maylene had been reliving their chance encounter still, hours later, when Sam called with his mysterious request that she come to his office at the site.

Now she was here, and she felt both desire and fear, as if she knew that Sam Coutler was at once the key to the very survival of her heart . . . and the most certain path to its total destruction.

Maylene took a soft breath, not knowing until she did which would win, desire or fear, but as she inhaled the familiar scent, fear triumphed.

Turning from the parched earth to Sam, she glowered at the cigarette in his hand. "You obviously don't care about your own lungs, but what about mine? There is a great deal of very convincing scientific data concerning the damage caused by secondhand smoke."

Even before the dangers were widely known, Sam had always made a point of keeping his smoke away from others. His compulsion to destroy, after all, was entirely personal. He had no desire to impose on anyone else the damage he was systematically causing the delicate structures within his lungs.

Had he not been so captivated by her, so intrigued by the play of emotion in her beautiful eyes, he would have stubbed out the cigarette the instant she appeared. But he had been captivated, and despite the increasing warmth on his fingers, a warning that the cigarette was burning low, it had been forgotten. His attention had been wholly focused on another warmth: a soft, bright glow in the lustrous jade. He'd been permitted only a fleeting glimpse before she crossed to the window to gaze outside.

Now her magnificent eyes were back, glaring—and yet fearful?—the warm glow replaced by shimmering green ice.

"I'll make you a deal, Jade," he said softly. "If you give up one of your self-destructive habits, I'll quit smoking today—forever."

Maylene stopped her defiant echo—"One of *my* self-destructive habits?"—because she knew all too well that she had them, and it was quite obvious that Sam Coulter knew it, too.

"You don't even need to tell me which one you plan to abandon," he drawled slowly, easily, as if not the least bit concerned about the cigarette ember that was beginning to touch his skin. "It would be nice, however, if I were to derive some secondhand benefit, just as you will if I stop smoking."

"Secondhand benefit?" Maylene echoed, aloud this time, and hurriedly, because it was quite obvious that Sam wasn't going to extinguish the cigarette until they had made a deal.

"I'd like to see more smiles from you than glowers. So, if you would give up whatever it is that makes you glower at me, even when I'm not smoking, I'd appreciate it."

With any other man, Maylene would have lifted her chin and taunted, "You think it's something self-destructive in *me* that makes me glower at *you*? Isn't that a bit arrogant? Don't you think it's possible that the reason I glower at you is because of you?" But Maylene couldn't ask those defiant questions, of course, because Sam Coulter was absolutely right: she glowered at him because something deep within her wondered how it would feel to be touched by him, to be *loved* by him—but she was far too afraid to permit herself to find out.

There wasn't a flicker of worry in the seductive blue eyes, but surely his flesh was beginning to burn. . . .

"Okay!" she exclaimed. "I agree."

Still Sam Coulter did not stub out his cigarette. Instead, slowly, calmly, he commanded, "Smile . . . please."

Maylene obeyed, a wobbly smile that became relieved and then quite radiant when, at last, he extinguished the cigarette.

"Much better," Sam said softly.

As he spoke his eyes remained on her, not even casting a curious glance to the place on his finger that had burned. He could look at it later, for the rest of his life. There would be a scar, he knew, a permanent reminder of the day when, for her, he had taken from his own demons of destruction their only vice. Sam felt their fury already, and their promise: they would not be denied. They would find other ways to cause mischief. Indeed, even now, they were racing from his lungs to his heart, to lie in wait for the destruction that would come as a result of his caring about Maylene Kwan.

"I got you a—" Sam's sentence was interrupted by the sudden appearance of Chan Peng.

The foreman of the Jade Palace was flanked by his two sons, who were also members of the crew. Less than an hour before, the father had looked just like his sons—tan, wiry, virtually indestructible. But now he seemed frail, perishable, and there was an eerie green pallor beneath the bronze.

As the sons settled their father in a chair, Sam and Maylene moved toward him.

"Peng?" Sam asked. "What happened?"

"I don't know." The bent head gave a bewildered shake. "It must be food poisoning."

Sam wanted to call an ambulance, but Chan Peng resolutely refused. His sons could take him home and his wife had herbs for all known ailments.

Sam didn't argue very long with the frail father before turning to the sons. "If he doesn't get better very soon, he needs to see a doctor."

"He will," the eldest son said solemnly as he helped his father to his feet.

Before leaving, a faint hint of Chan Peng's familiar wry smile touched his pale green face. "Are you going to be able to manage without me, Sam?"

Sam returned the smile. "Just barely. I think, however, that even I can supervise the pouring of concrete. I'll need you back though, Peng, for the tough stuff."

"I'll be back," he vowed.

After the ill father was gently escorted away by his two healthy sons, Maylene said, "I guess I'd better be going. You have concrete to pour."

"It's still being mixed. Besides, you can't leave until I tell you the real reason I lured you over here."

"The real reason?"

"I got you a present. It's not a big deal," he assured softly as he saw her sudden worry. "In fact, it's really more necessity than present, something you'll have to have once I start needing you all the time."

Needing you all the time. Sam was speaking professionally, the builder's need for his architect, but the gentleness of his tone conveyed layers of meaning that went far beyond the demands of the Jade Palace. As Sam watched her reaction he saw shimmering hope, as if she wanted him to need her in all ways . . . and then, suddenly, he saw despair, as if Maylene believed that she was destined to disappoint.

Sam blocked the impulse to tell her that she would never disappoint him, never could, with the reminder of the private vow he had made: in this most important creation of his life, he had to build slowly, carefully, lest he frighten her away.

Smiling gently, he retrieved her present from the floor behind his desk. "I got the box in Hong Kong, but the contents are from San Antonio."

As Sam handed her the bright red cardboard box, Maylene asked softly, "You've been reading about Chinese customs, haven't you, Cowboy?"

"Yes, ma'am," he affirmed, relieved that she seemed pleased, not offended, that he'd bothered to learn about Chinese gift giving, even though she was only half Chinese. "My books tell me that gifts should be wrapped in red, because that symbolizes happiness and luck."

"Yes . . . thank you."

"You're welcome. My books also tell me that although it's customary for the gift recipient not to open the present in front of the gift giver, thus saving face all around in case of a disaster, it's also acceptable for the giver to request that it be opened in his presence if he so chooses. Is that right?"

"You're a good reader."

"So, Jade, please open them now."

"Them?"

The worry was returning to her eyes, anxiety about what he was giving her and uncertainty about his watching her reaction. Sam gave her elaborate hints in advance. "A matched set, hand-tooled, custom-made, and absolutely essential for tromping around in the mud, assuming the monsoonal rains ever come, and a must-wear, too, for climbing up on steel girders. Beginning about September, you and I are going to be doing that all the time, day after day, until the Jade Palace is everything we want it to be. So . . . open."

They were cowboy boots, of course. Tan-colored, like his, but unscuffed, as his had been many years ago.

"They're beautiful, Sam."

"More importantly, they're functional. And, hopefully, they're also the right size. I took the liberty of measuring your footprints the first day you were here."

"You did?"

"I did. There are socks in there as well, specially designed to ensure the comfort that cowboys—and cowgirls—have come to expect."

"You think I have the makings of a cowgirl?"

"Sure," Sam answered softly. *You can be my cowgirl anytime.* "If you want to be."

For a wondrous moment her luminous jade-green eyes shimmered bright emerald and she said, as softly as he, "Yes, I definitely want to be."

When Tyler first saw her from his office, he wondered if she was an illusion, his imagination come to life. During the past few weeks he had stood often at this picture window, staring across Victoria Harbour and heavenward, toward Peak Castle, thinking about her, worrying about her, hoping for her sake that her marriage was wonderful—yet fearing that it was not.

Based on what data? he had demanded of himself a thousand times. No husband could have been more attentive than Sir Geoffrey. It was obvious to everyone how much he loved his wife, *treasured* her. Then why, when Eve believed that no one was looking, when she believed herself to be quite invisible, had Tyler seen such haunted sadness?

Tyler had hoped, and he had worried, and he wondered if he would ever see her again. And now Lady Lloyd-Ashton was here, far away from her castle, standing at harbor's edge as she watched the activity at Grand Prix's loading docks. On this July afternoon, *Le Mans*, the newest addition to Tyler's fleet of oceangoing freighters, was being unloaded. With surprising delicacy and ease, massive cranes plucked from its hold the cargo of green, red, and orange containers, each the size of a railroad car.

Eve was in no danger. Indeed, she was not even on Grand Prix property, but adjacent to it, on the picturesque harborside esplanade. The lantern-lined walkway originated at the Star Ferry Pier and ended almost two miles east at Grand Prix shipyards in Hung Hom Bay. Along the way, one passed notable Hong Kong landmarks: the Victoria Clock Tower, followed by the elaborately tiled—and elaborately controversial—Cultural Centre, then the Jade Palace construction site, the Regent Hotel, the New World Shopping Centre, and finally the Tsim Sha Tsui East Ferry Pier.

The waterside promenade was very popular, its harbor views beyond compare, and at either end of the day, it was often quite crowded. In the coolness of dawn, it was a hub of exercise, the slow-motion gracefulness of tai chi practiced by locals a sublime counterpoint to the fast-paced jogging of fitness-addicted foreigners. Indeed, early-morning jogging among its business guests was so predictable that the Regent's white-gloved doormen greeted the exercisers with towels on their return. In the evening, beginning at twilight, the lamplit esplanade belonged to lovers, for leisurely romantic strolls in the warm summer air.

In the heat of the day, however, the walkway was usually quite empty, and regardless of the hour—except for Tyler, who lived at the Regent and walked to work—almost no one journeyed to its farthest and most industrial reaches.

But on this hot July afternoon, Lady Lloyd-Ashton was here, all alone, far away from prying eyes—except his.

Since the second week of her marriage, no matter how bruised her body or how aching her heart, on Mondays and Thursdays the Princess of Peak Castle appeared in public. Twice weekly was the proper amount of exposure, Geoffrey had decided, the appropriate balance between regal mystique and noblesse oblige.

Sometimes Eve merely wandered, visiting temples and shrines and museums, but often she had a specific itinerary, provided by Geoffrey:

Go to the Jade Market, Eve. Buy a trinket, something small, but be very sure that it's real. I don't want you embarrassing me.

You're meeting the governor's wife for luncheon at Pierrot at one. Don't be late, and if the subject of schooling comes up, yours was entirely at home, with a governess.

Dr. Kingsley will see you at three. I want you back on birth-control pills. You'll just have to find a way to cope with the headaches.

Eve was grateful that Geoffrey's mandate was for only two days away from the castle. Except for her volunteer work at the hospital and her appointments at Pearl Moon, she anticipated such days with a sense of dread. The people of Hong Kong were wonderful to her, of course, welcoming and gracious, but she hated being on display and lived in perpetual fear of committing a social faux pas that would annoy her husband.

There was no doubt that Geoffrey would learn of such a social misstep. Over five million pairs of interested and admiring eyes watched Lady Lloyd-Ashton's every move. Sightings were reported to the local papers and published in minute detail in the society columns. Early on, Sir Geoffrey had decreed that every article and all photographs of his princess were to be submitted to him, for his approval, in advance of publication. It was a rather profound infringement on the freedom of the Hong Kong press. But when the territory's most powerful man issued an edict, even the journalists complied.

On her days away from Peak Castle, Eve found sanctuary at the hospital, and with Juliana at Pearl Moon, and today she had wandered here, to this remote place at harbor's edge . . . and it, too, felt to Eve like a safe haven.

"Lady Lloyd-Ashton."

Eve turned. "Mr. Vaughn."

"Are you thinking about stowing away?" It was a gentle tease, but it caused confusion, as if she had once actually imagined such a daring escape, but now had almost forgotten that brave, long-ago dream. More softly, and no longer teasing, he asked, "Do you come here often, Lady Lloyd-Ashton?"

"No, never before. I had lunch today at the Peninsula, and then I stopped by the construction site, and then . . . I just kept walking." It sounded like a casual impulse, but it hadn't felt that way at all. Something very deep had compelled her to journey here. And, Eve knew, it wasn't the long-forgotten fantasy of stowing away. It was something far more dangerous . . . and far more wondrous. As she met his gentle, dangerous, wondrous gaze she said softly, "Please call me Eve."

"And I'm Tyler. Is Eve short for Evangeline?"

"No, just Eve." Her brilliant blue eyes filled with hope. "I like Evangeline, though."

"So do I. It seems right for you."

"Thank you," she answered softly.

Once again his words had caused confusion, as if even though the idea of being called Evangeline filled her sapphire eyes with hope, it was quite impossible for her to imagine ever being anyone but Eve.

"You're not working at the hospital today?"

"No. I'm only there on Monday mornings."

Remembering Cynthia's petulant remark that Lady Lloyd-Ashton's volunteer work at the hospital was merely for show—and not believing it—Tyler offered, "You enjoy working there, don't you?"

"Oh, yes." All confusion magically vanished and the remarkable sapphire lighted with happiness. "I'd work there every day if—" Eve stopped abruptly.

If what? Tyler wondered. If your days weren't filled with more important things, like teas and luncheons with Hong Kong's other tai tais?

No, he decided as he looked at her glowing eyes. The luminous blue told him with eloquent clarity that few—if any—engagements were more important to Eve than her mornings at the hospital.

If what, then? If Geoffrey *let* you? It was an extraordinary thought, and it was followed by an even more astonishing one: If you were my wife, Evangeline, and if I knew that something made your eyes glow with such happiness, I would move heaven and earth to give it to you.

My wife. Until this moment that two-word phrase had not existed in Tyler Vaughn's personal dictionary. But now, with her, because of her, it did. Very softly, with more gentleness than he had ever spoken before, he asked, "If what, Eve?"

Perhaps it was the softness of his voice, the *intimacy*, or perhaps she somehow read his extraordinary—and forbidden—thought. Tyler didn't know. He knew only that, quite suddenly, Eve looked away, toward the harbor, its waters molten gold in the long rays of the afternoon sun.

She *had* to look away, because . . . because, quite suddenly, she had desperately wanted to confess to him all the painful—and shameful—truths.

And what if she did? she wondered. What if she admitted to Tyler that Geoffrey had only wanted her because she resembled a beautiful—and defiant—ghost? And that he had never known, or cared, about her heart? What would happen then?

Nothing, Eve told herself. Nothing *can* happen . . . because Geoffrey will never let me go.

"It's late," she said softly to the dappled gold. Too late for me, for us. Leaving the glittering waves, but not quite meeting his glittering eyes, she said, "I'd better go. It was nice seeing you again, Tyler."

"It was nice seeing you, too, Eve."

Eve turned from him then, leaving Tyler to watch as she began the journey that would take her back to her castle . . . and to the man who, perhaps, did not truly care about her happiness.

Her lovely head was held high, and her posture was perfect, tall and straight and regal. But she seemed weighted, her fragile body fighting with all its strength to keep from being crushed.

"Evangeline."

It was a soft whisper on the afternoon breeze, and like a tropical zephyr, it shimmered with heat.

For a breath-held moment everything stopped, the golden waves, the balmy breeze, his thundering heart. Then, at last, she turned. Tyler saw it as if in slow motion, frame by magnificent frame, the ballerina's graceful twirl . . . the courageous blossoming of a delicate flower beneath the warm caresses of a golden sun.

"Come sailing with me."

How can I? she wondered. How can I not? "When?"

"Whenever you want," Tyler said, walking toward her, crossing the line into the forbidden, unwilling not to. "Today, tomorrow, the next day. Whenever you want."

As Tyler saw the emotion in her eyes, the drama of hope and despair, he realized he had seen something similar at Peak Castle, during dinner, when Geoffrey said how much Eve would love to go flying with Allison—but couldn't.

"You're not afraid of flying, are you?"

"No."

"He just doesn't want you to."

"No, he doesn't."

"Come sailing with me, Evangeline. We'll fly over the waves."

CHAPTER 16

Pearl Moon
The Landmark
Thursday, July 15, 1993

"**P**lease be careful, Eve."

"Thanks to you, Juliana, no one will recognize me." Eve smiled her gratitude then looked down again at the outfit she wore.

It was the perfect disguise: pure tourist. Its vivid brightness was so typical of what visitors to Hong Kong wore in the tropical heat that instead of drawing attention, Eve would simply blend into the crowd. The peacock-blue T-shirt Juliana had purchased from a street vendor featured a junk, its sails unfurled, with HONG KONG emblazoned in fuchsia in both English and Chinese. Juliana had made walking shorts, in matching fuchsia, and to hide her friend's familiar face she'd bought a broad-brimmed hat and large sunglasses.

A purple-striped beach bag completed the ensemble. Eve's Lady Lloyd-Ashton attire was inside, as was a large purse. At the end of the afternoon, before returning to Peak Castle, the brightly clad tourist would walk into the ladies' room in the lobby of the Hilton on Garden Road, just a block from the Peak Tram, and moments later the well-known image of subdued elegance would emerge.

"No one will recognize me, Juliana," Eve repeated. "No one will even notice me."

"I wasn't worrying about that."

Eve's expression became thoughtful. "You don't need to worry about Tyler. When I'm with him, I'm . . ." She faltered then, lost in a wholly unfamiliar and totally wondrous sensation, feeling it and yet unable to name it.

"Safe?" Juliana offered softly.

"Yes," Eve replied with quiet amazement. "Safe."

Juliana smiled as her memory journeyed to a faraway time, when "safe" was what she had felt, amid other wondrous feelings, with Garrett. Now, just as Vivian had said to her on that long-ago evening, she said to Eve, "I won't worry about you, then."

Tyler Vaughn's *Seven Seas* was moored in Causeway Bay, in one of the slips in the typhoon shelter allotted to the Royal Hong Kong Yacht Club. The brightly varnished mahogany sloop bobbed in gentle welcome as Eve arrived.

And then there was the greatest gentleness of all. . . .

"Hello," he greeted softly. "I'm so glad you could make it."

"So am I," Eve replied, a little disbelieving still.

She had phoned him on Monday afternoon, using Juliana's private line at Pearl Moon, to make plans for today, but until this morning she hadn't known if Geoffrey would have his own agenda for her on this Thursday away from the castle.

He hadn't, and Eve had been floating ever since. But, she realized, she hadn't truly breathed until now . . . and now she felt breathless again as tender blue eyes searched for hers in the dark shadow cast by the hat and behind the enormous sunglasses.

"Let's get out of here," Tyler said, wanting to see her and knowing it was far too risky for her to shed even the tiniest part of her disguise until they were safely away from port.

They sailed east out of Victoria Harbour, beyond North Point and Junk Island and Cape Collision and Joss House Bay, finally reaching the South China Sea, blue-green beneath the azure sky.

Eve's hat came off first, and she smiled as the warm sea breeze ran its gentle fingers through her hair. Then, although the summer sun shone brightly, she took off her sunglasses, because he wore none, because they both wanted to see the other's eyes.

"Tell me everything about yourself, Eve, from the moment you were born."

Eve bravely obeyed his soft command. She told him the shameful truths of her childhood, and about the lonely, never-loved little girl whose despair had driven her to the limestone cliffs of Weymouth, and that she would have leapt to her death had it not been for Lady Gweneth St. John—and Eve felt safe, ever safer, as Tyler embraced even her most anguished confessions with tenderness and concern. A wistful smile touched her lips as she spoke of what had become of her after that day on the cliffs, her friendship with Gweneth, her bold move to London, and the solitary peace that she had found there.

Then the smile faded, and she stopped speaking, as if her story was finished . . . as if the story of Eve had ended in London, seven years ago.

"You met Geoffrey in London?" Tyler asked finally.

"Yes. At the bank. I told you how I looked then—hunched over and unstylish, with my long hair mostly concealing my face and my fingernails chewed to the quick. . . ."

Tyler smiled gently. Eve had made such a point of telling him how she had looked then, wanting him to know who she truly was. But Tyler already knew. From the first moment at Peak Castle, he had seen the real Eve, the shy and uncertain woman who was haunted by sadness, and who, despite her striking beauty, wished to be invisible . . . and whose most extraordinary beauty of all lived within her lovely heart.

"You told me," he said softly. And now, Tyler feared, Eve was going to tell him something that he didn't want to hear: that Geoffrey had seen the loveliness of her heart and fallen in love with it. Somehow that didn't sound like Sir Geoffrey Lloyd-Ashton, nor did the expression in Eve's blue eyes suggest that Geoffrey had done what Tyler wished he could have been there to do—to create with his arms a loving sanctuary for her hunched body and to kiss with exquisite tenderness all the mercilessly bitten flesh of her fingertips. "What happened?"

"Despite the way I looked, Geoffrey was able to see my un-canny resemblance to a woman named Rosalind, a woman who died a month before she and Geoffrey were to have wed. The re-semblance was only skin deep, of course. She was elegant and re-fined—an aristocrat, perhaps even a royal. With work, however, with a complete makeover . . ."

"You became Rosalind."

It was the greatest shame of all, that she had been so desperate to be loved, so blind to the truth. But now, to the man who had so gently embraced every other shameful confession, Eve said, "Yes. I became Rosalind."

Eve had just admitted to him that she had permitted Geoffrey to re-create her in another woman's image, and the expression on her lovely face told him that she accepted all the blame, that she had been a willing accomplice in that ultimate destruction of self, and it was obvious that she was going to offer no apology for what she had done.

But, so gently, Tyler asked, "You didn't know about her, did you?" *You had no idea what Geoffrey was doing to you . . . to Eve?*

Her eyes filled with gratitude that, somehow, he knew. "No," she said quietly. "I didn't know. Not until much later." *Much too late.* Eve shrugged softly, and then smiled. "I like the way I speak now. When I hear myself, my accent and my words, I hear Gweneth. And my posture is much healthier."

"And your hair?"

"I prefer it long." Eve shrugged again, then smiled again, and said, "Now tell me about you, Tyler. Everything from the moment you were born."

She isn't going to speak of her marriage, Tyler realized. But, he thought, what more is there to tell? For the past seven years she has been Lady Lloyd-Ashton—just as Rosalind would have been— a picture-perfect princess, *but not Eve.*

The story of Eve had indeed ended seven years before . . . except that lovely Eve dwelled inside still, uncertain and shy—and longing still for the mane of sable hair that would conceal her beautiful face and permit her once again to be invisible.

But I have found you, Eve. I know that you are there, and that you are so very lovely, and . . . Tyler wanted to say those words now, but it was far too soon, and she was waiting to hear about him, wanting to learn about him as he had learned about her.

As Tyler began the story of his own life, he wondered if Eve expected to hear about a man born to wealth and leisure, who raced expensive cars as a lark, an escape from boredom, and whose trading company had been inherited. He guessed, correctly, that she would be pleased to discover that his beginnings had been as humble as hers.

"I was born restless, and with a compulsion to fix things. My parents had too little love, too many children, and not enough money. For a very long time, because I was too young to know any better, I actually tried to fix the love part. When I realized that was impossible, I did what I could about the money. I quit school, got a job as a mechanic in a gas station, and contributed everything I made to the family coffers. The extra income didn't help. It merely provided additional fuel for the fighting and ultimately was squandered. Eventually, I couldn't stand watching anymore. I left home, hitchhiked across the country, and found work as a mechanic at a speedway. After a couple of years I convinced someone to let me race."

"And you won everything there was to win."

Tyler smiled. It was almost true. He had set records that no one was ever going to touch. "I won a lot of races."

"But you don't race anymore, do you?"

"No."

"I'm glad you've stopped," Eve whispered. "It seems so terribly dangerous."

Most of the women Tyler had known—*all* of them, in fact—had been thrilled by his racing. They always wanted to be on the sidelines when he raced, to watch the lethal speed, the thunderous power, the unpredictable drama. Tyler had often wondered if they anticipated with equal pleasure the drama of a fiery crash or the triumphant glory of a win.

But now, here was Eve, and even though he no longer raced, she worried still about the past, about the terrible things that might have happened to him.

"It's really not that dangerous," he assured gently. "Not if you're confident and decisive."

"But . . . what if someone crashed in front of you?"

"If you're good, you can usually drive around—or through— a crash." A wry smile touched his lips. "Of course, sometimes such actions have major consequences. In my case, the consequence was Grand Prix Shipping."

"Really? What happened?"

"I was racing at Monte Carlo, and was in the lead, but there were cars in front of me, ones that I was lapping. A rookie driver lost control. To avoid hitting him, I had to go off a fairly steep part of the course."

"And if you hadn't made that decision?"

"He would have been killed, and I would have been fine—except that I never could have lived with myself."

"Were you badly injured?"

"I had a few broken bones," Tyler admitted, underplaying the injuries that had almost cost him his life. "I also had a hospital room in Marseilles overlooking the port and endless hours to watch the activity on the loading docks. And guess what? The more I watched, the more I saw things that needed to be fixed. One small Mediterranean fleet was particularly inefficient. To keep my mind busy, I thought about the changes I would make if it were mine. The idea became so appealing that I did a little research. Not surprisingly, the company was in deep financial trouble."

"So you bought it?"

"Eventually. No banker in his right mind would finance a race-car driver with no business experience, so I ended up making a private deal with the owners, a promise to pay them out of the profits I made. Fortunately, there were profits."

Eve smiled at the understatement. Grand Prix was a stunning success. Under Tyler's guidance the small Mediterranean fleet had become a major global shipper.

After a moment her smile faded and she repeated softly, "I'm so glad you don't race anymore."

"What do you wish for, Eve?"

They had been sailing for five hours, flying across the aquamarine waves, enveloped by the caressing warmth of the summer day—and by the even warmer caresses that came from deep within. They were west of Lantau Island, but soon they would have to come about . . . so that she would have ample time to become Geoffrey's princess once again before returning to Peak Castle.

Now Tyler was asking what she wished for, and as he saw her surprise he realized that no one had ever before asked Eve what *she* wanted . . . and that the woman whose sense of self had been battered from the moment of her birth had never before made wishes on her own. "Don't think about it, just tell me, whatever comes to mind."

"I wish that Gweneth were alive."

"I wish that, too," Tyler replied gently.

They sailed in silence for many heartbeats before Tyler spoke again.

"Tell me more wishes, Eve."

Tyler Vaughn was enough of an idealist to believe that, given an infinite list of wishes, most human beings would, eventually, articulate ones for the planet as a whole—health, happiness, and peace for all its creatures, great and small. But except for specific wishes for happiness for Juliana and James, and for a little girl named Lily, that was where Eve's list began.

When at last she finished, her eyes aglow with visions of universal peace and joy, Tyler urged, "Now tell me a personal wish, something just for you, something selfish, if you possibly can."

It seemed, for a while, as if Eve would be incapable of finding such a wish. But finally, encouraged by his tender smile and emboldened by his loving eyes, she whispered, "I wish we could sail like this forever."

That was his wish, too. Because now Tyler knew the truth: there had been purpose to his restlessness. He had been searching, his heart had been, and he hadn't even known it . . . but now she was found, and for the first time in his restless life, Tyler Vaughn felt peace.

"We can, Evangeline," he said quietly, his blue eyes solemn—and joyous—with love. "We can sail until your hair is as long as you want it to be. We can leave right now."

Eve drew a soft breath, astonished by her own words—the truth of them, the boldness of her confession—and by his. It was a dream. On this glorious day, when the sky was the color of her eyes, and the sea breeze caressed her skin like whispered kisses, and the aquamarine waves were trimmed in gold, she was living a dream. Wondrous, glorious . . . but impossible.

Eve knew the dream could not be, but still, on this day, even as she softly shook her head no, there was a joyous yes, as if the hair that was being tossed and swirled by the caressing wind was already long and free.

Impossible.

Tyler saw the dream in her brilliant sapphire eyes—and then, too swiftly, he saw it fade. Eve had seen the dream, and for several wondrous moments the glowing blue had bravely told Tyler that she wanted it as much as he.

But the glow had faded, and now her clouded eyes were downcast, staring intently at the pale hands knotted tightly in her lap.

"I shouldn't have said that."

"Yes, you should have," Tyler countered, his voice soft—and strong. "It's what I want, too. I love—"

Eve looked up suddenly, stopping his words of love . . . and almost stopping his heart. Her blue eyes had not lighted anew at his tender admission of love. Instead they were haunted, fearful, and this time, when she shook her head, there was no wondrous illusion of long sable strands dancing in the wind . . . and now she was turning away from him, toward the glittering golden horizon to which they would never sail.

For most of this enchanted afternoon, she had been Eve . . . and when Tyler had seen the dream of her love in her eyes, she had become Evangeline. But now she was Lady Lloyd-Ashton again, Rosalind again, imprisoned in that life and unable to see beyond it.

Her lovely blue eyes were blind to so much, Tyler thought. To the inconsequential beauty of her flesh and the extraordinary beauty of her heart . . . and now the sapphire was blind, too, to the possibility of their dream.

Tyler knew that obstacles lay in the path to their future. There was Geoffrey, of course, but even Hong Kong's most powerful taipan was easily overcome, as all obstacles could be, once Eve truly believed in his love. But that would take time. Since birth, Eve had been told that she was nothing, less than nothing, and totally unworthy of being loved. And Geoffrey, the only man who had ever claimed to want her, had betrayed her.

It would take time for Eve to believe in his love, Tyler knew—because first, Eve needed to believe in herself. And until she could truly see her worthiness? Until she was no longer blind? Tyler would be her eyes. Eve would see her loveliness through him, as he saw her . . . if she would let him.

Moments earlier, for the first time in his restless life, Tyler Vaughn had felt peace. And now, despite his many near-fatal flirtations with death, for the first time ever Tyler felt fear.

And it was the greatest fear of all.

The fear of living his life without Eve.

As he drew a soft breath even the balmy sea breeze felt cold. "Why don't we just take day sails, then?" he asked softly. "We'll sail whenever you want, whenever you are free." *And someday, my Eve, my Evangeline, when you trust my love, we will sail forever.*

Tyler wondered if she had heard him. But she had—because, at his gentle words, she stiffened, as if she, too, had felt a sudden icy breeze.

Free? The word pierced her very soul. She would never be free, and she should end this torment now. . . .

"Evangeline? Will you sail again with me?"

It was as if, unbelievably, she heard fear in his gentle voice, as if he was afraid that she would say no, as if he was uncertain of her love.

Eve had to turn to him then, and to the loving and worried blue eyes she had to whisper softly, "Yes, I will sail with you . . . whenever I can."

CHAPTER 17

Trade Winds Hotel
Tuesday, July 20, 1993

"It's Allison Whitaker, Mrs. Leong. I just got your message."
The message to phone James Drake's administrative assistant had been given to the hotel operator at 11:00 A.M., and the red message light in Allison's apartment had been flashing ever since. She had returned to her apartment at two, but had been so focused on getting ready for her meeting with James that it wasn't until now, almost 3:30, that she noticed the blinking light.

"Oh, Miss Whitaker, good. I'm so sorry to say Mr. Drake won't be able to meet with you at four today after all."

"Oh. Well, that's fine. It doesn't really matter," Allison murmured. "As I told you when I called to schedule, it wasn't an emergency. I just wanted to show him some of the photographs I've taken. If I drop them by the office sometime, perhaps you could let me know if he thinks they're all right?" *Or not all right.*

Penelope Leong waited politely for Allison to finish, then said, "Mr. Drake wondered if you would be free to have dinner with him tonight."

"Yes, of course, but he doesn't have to do that."

"Naturally," Mrs. Leong replied, her voice eloquently communicating the fact that James Drake didn't have to do anything, ever, unless he chose to. "He hoped that it would be convenient for you if he arrived at your apartment at seven, to look at the photographs, followed by dinner at the Blue Lantern at eight."

"These are wonderful, Allison," James said, not for the first time, as he slowly made his way through the small stack of photographs she had decided to show him.

"Thank you," she answered, not for the first time, at last embellishing, "I just wanted to be sure I was on the right track."

The panther eyes that had been intently focused on her photographs now turned their entire attention to her, the full force of their glinting steel.

"You are, Allison," he said softly. "These are truly magnificent."

James Drake had just told her that her photographs were magnificent, but now his intense gaze seemed to be saying something else: that now, as he looked at her, not her photographs, he was beholding something quite magnificent still. Allison couldn't see her own glowing emerald eyes, or the curls of fire and moonlight that danced around her face, or the soft womanly smile that touched her lips. She knew only of the heart that fluttered, as always, when she was with him, and of the rush of heat that filled her cheeks.

"You've only looked at a few. Maybe the rest are disasters."

James smiled. "I doubt that."

But to allay Allison's worry, and because he felt an extraordinary—and impossible—urge to tenderly touch her lovely face with his lethal hands, James left her eyes and returned to the photographs that were dazzling proof of the hopeful vision of the glowing green.

The photographs were familiar images of Hong Kong, yet

quite unique. Imaginative—and sensual, James decided. A feast for the senses.

The intoxicating fragrances of incense, perfumed joss sticks, and salty sea air drifted from the satiny paper; and one could almost taste the sweetness of *nor mai chi*—coconut snowball dim sum—and the delicate flavor of jasmine tea; and hear the sharp *click-click* of mah-jongg tiles in the back alleys of Kowloon and the music of a thousand songbirds in the market on Hong Lok Street; and touch the bounty of wares sold in the Lanes, the shining silks, the soapstone chops, the carved jade dragons.

And in every photograph one saw the magic of Hong Kong, the fascinating cosmopolis of contrasts, where golden eagles shared the azure sky with jumbo jets, and where ancient Buddhist temples nestled beside towering skyscrapers, and where fortune hunters and fortune-tellers alike found a myriad of ways to thrive.

Allison's photographs captured—and celebrated—the intriguing contrasts. In one, taken in Mah Wa Lane, a shopkeeper made swift calculations with his abacus, while the next, taken just blocks away, revealed the ultra-high-tech inner sanctum of the Hang Seng Stock Exchange. There, in a vast room that most closely resembled "mission control," impeccably dressed and politely silent men and women sat at rows of computers as they calmly launched Hong Kong into a prosperous future.

Next came a portrait of a Hakka woman lovingly tending her precious acre of farmland in the New Territories, while across the waters on Hong Kong Island, stable hands cared for prized racehorses in the high-rise, air-conditioned stables adjacent to Happy Valley Racetrack. A short distance away, in Statue Square, Allison had spotted a flag bearing Hong Kong's coat of arms. The warrior's shield, etched with images of nineteenth-century trading ships, was held equally by a lion and a dragon, and a second lion, wearing a crown, clutched in its paw a gleaming pearl. The flag, which so clearly symbolized Britain's dominion over "The Pearl of the Orient," now flew in the shadow of the Bank of China—and it was on the wall of that towering skyscraper that Allison found her next subject: a small, eight-sided mirror strategically placed to deflect evil spirits.

The second-to-last photograph that Allison had selected to show James was a cheerful collage of Star ferries, a visual image that artfully embraced both the spirit and energy of Victoria Harbour.

"This is very nice."

"Probably too whimsical for the hotel," Allison said. "But once I discovered the names, I couldn't resist. I had to find a way of memorializing them all."

"You've lost me."

It was a surprising confession for a man like James to make, but he seemed quite untroubled by it. Indeed, the eyes that met hers didn't seem to mind at all being lost with her.

"The ferryboats," she murmured finally. "Their names . . . it seemed so charming."

She was lost now, too, in the smoky promises of his silver eyes. Lost . . . and somehow found.

James lingered far longer than he should have in the enchantment of Allison Whitaker. He had returned to Hong Kong with a single purpose, to find and destroy the man who had stolen his dreams. For the past four years his lethal hands had been waiting restlessly for the chance to kill—not to love—and his heart had been solely—and solemnly—committed as well to its deadly revenge. But now, at this moment, the heart that had hungered so long for the death of a monster ached with a different kind of longing entirely.

James forced himself to break the enchanting spell. Looking again at the photograph, he silently read the names emblazoned in gold on the green bows of the famous ferries. Charming names, as Allison had said, all ending with *Star: Twinkling, Morning, Silver, Meridien, Day, Shining, Northern, Lone, Golden,* and *Celestial.*

When he finished reading, James said quietly, almost to himself, "I'd forgotten about the names."

He had known them once, of course. As a boy, he had known all the names, as if they were friends, and each of the ten boats had even had its own personality, ten more spirits alive in the tropical air. Once, riding the Star ferries across the green-and-silver waves of Victoria Harbour had been pure joy. But in this Hong Kong tainted by the lurking menace of a mortal enemy, it had merely become another form of transportation.

Since Gweneth's murder, James's vision of the Hong Kong he loved had been darkly veiled, shadowed by a smoky mist from his own fiery rage. But now, here was Allison, seeing its splendor with brilliant clarity, reminding him of the wonders that had saved a young boy from the cold and empty life to which he had been destined from birth.

Were the spirits of Hong Kong conspiring to save him yet again? Using Allison as an innocent accomplice, were they attempting to lure him from his loneliness and his rage? James could not deny that it would be wonderful to see Hong Kong anew through sparkling emerald eyes.

Wonderful . . . but impossible.

The elegant hands that were trained to kill, were *eager* to kill, gently set aside the collage of Star ferries, revealing the final picture Allison had wanted him to see. And when he did, James stared at it in stunned silence, his body completely still even as his mind swirled.

How did she know? No one, not even Gweneth, had ever known. It was something he had been planning to share with Gweneth on their return to Hong Kong, a joy that he had been saving.

Moments before, James's mind had idly toyed with thoughts of friendly and determined spirits colluding with an innocent Allison to cast soft glimmers of light into the darkness of his heart. It had been a fanciful notion, appealingly mystical . . . but something that James did not truly believe.

But now, confronted with this photograph, James was left with an awesome truth. Allison was acting alone, without any spiritual conspirators whatsoever. It was her lovely heart—her joyful magic—that was so valiantly attempting to cast its golden light into the blackness of his.

Allison saw with alarm the dark frown that suddenly shadowed his face, and in the stillness of his silence, she felt an even greater darkness. What had she done? She had believed that James would like this photograph and had saved it for last because it was her favorite.

"The view seemed so unique to me," she began haltingly. "So different from the other views of the city and harbor."

"More dragon's eye than bird's eye?"

"Yes," Allison answered softly. "You've been there, haven't you?"

"On Po Shan Road in the Mid Levels? The rocky ledge near the first switchback? Yes, I've been there, but not since I was a boy." James paused, still a little stunned, still staring at the photograph. His voice was solemn with remembrance. "I used to spend hours on that ledge. From age eight, I was sent to boarding school in Scotland. I didn't want to go, to leave Hong Kong, but it's a centuries' old tradition for young male aristocrats to be educated at cold, spartan, disciplinarian schools."

But not *your* son, Allison thought as she heard the soft edges of fury in his voice. You would never have sent your own son away.

"The ledge on Po Shan Road was always my last stop before returning to school. I would memorize the view, vowing to hold it in my mind until I came back." James looked at her then, his eyes intent and gleaming, as he confessed with soft amazement, "Somehow, Allison Whitaker, you discovered my favorite place in all of Hong Kong."

At the Blue Lantern, secluded in a private corner illuminated by candlelight and city glow, Allison found herself in the extraordinary position of having James Drake's undivided attention. His calls were all being held, he told her when she observed that his pager had been silent, and not once did his mind seem to wander to the responsibilities of his vast empire of buildings and land.

Allison was center stage, all by herself, precisely where James wanted her to be. And as for the script for this command performance? James wanted to hear the story of her life, in whatever words she chose. Keeping the promise she had made to speak only honest words to James, however foolish or naive, Allison told him everything he wanted to know. Boldly and without apology, she described the undazzling life she had lived, safe and protected in her cocoon of love.

"When did you discover your gift for photography?"

Allison didn't even attempt to amend *gift* to *aptitude*. She knew James wouldn't let her. "When I was ten, the year I developed rheumatic fever."

James searched his well-read memory. "Rheumatic fever? You were living in Dallas at the time?"

"Yes, and it was considered very unusual. Because of the routine treatment of strep throats with penicillin, rheumatic fever has become rare in the United States. I had a sore throat, but . . ."

"You didn't complain about it," James finished softly. "You didn't want to worry your family."

"It wasn't really that bad." As Allison shrugged, ripples of reflected candlelight shimmered off her golden-red curls. "Of course, by not telling them, I ended up causing far more worry."

Allison had already told James about the fragile infant who had almost died at birth and about the eighteen-year-old whose reaction to a blood transfusion had nearly been fatal as well. For a delicate butterfly raised in a protective cocoon, Allison's quiet life had been visited by a surprising amount of unwanted drama. James guessed that he was about to hear about even more.

"You didn't have a mild case of rheumatic fever, did you?"

"I didn't develop any neurologic complications whatsoever." Allison's voice held a defiant note of pride. Then, with a wry and lovely smile, she added, "But I did manage to have both arthritis and carditis."

"Which meant staying in bed?"

"Yes, for almost eight months."

"That must have been difficult." James smiled. "But I imagine that you were a model patient."

"I suppose so. I understood how necessary it was, and for the first few months I was so weak that all I wanted to do was sleep anyway. After that, as I became stronger, I spent the days reading and playing board games with my family. Finally, the doctors said I could go for short walks around our property. That was when my father bought me a camera. I loved it immediately, and it was wonderful, creative, distracting therapy. I forgot all about how much I was missing, the horses I wasn't riding, the hopscotch I might never play again."

"But eventually you did ride again, didn't you? And play hopscotch and learn to fly airplanes." *And become engaged to be married.*

"Yes, all of those things."

"Are you all right now? No long-term consequences?"

"I'm fine." The hand that wore the silver-and-crimson bracelet gave a graceful wave. "My joints get a little creaky sometimes, when I'm in one position for too long or when I overdo."

"Like when you spend all day every day walking around Hong Kong?"

Candlelight danced in Allison's shimmering emerald eyes. But the true glow, the dazzling golden radiance that lighted the brilliant green, came from within. "Maybe it would be a problem if I were anywhere but Hong Kong. But here, with the tropical warmth, it's been very easy."

"And your heart?"

Allison's heart was, in fact, far stronger than she had ever imagined. It had been fluttering all day in anticipation of seeing James, and when the moment finally arrived, it had soared to even greater heights, at once dizzying and glorious. The beats of her soaring heart were rapid but amazingly strong . . . especially given the intimacy with which it was being examined.

Allison's heart had been subjected to intimate probes before. To make certain that there were no untoward sequellae from her rheumatic carditis, tiny plastic catheters had thoroughly explored all four chambers, searching for flaws and finding none. Those medical findings had been terribly important to Allison, but they paled in comparison with what she herself had discovered because of James: joy, pure, and tingling, and overflowing from a fountain of happiness deep within.

"My heart's perfectly fine," she answered at last. "No evidence of valvular damage whatsoever."

"Do you expect your fiancé to materialize at any moment?"

"No," Allison replied swiftly, startled. Then, laughing softly, she asked, "Did you ask that because we were on the subject of my heart?"

"I guess so."

"He's not going to materialize, James, and neither my heart nor I want him to."

"Are you sure, Allison?" James asked gently as a frown shadowed her lovely face. "You look uncertain."

"Not about that." Her teeth tugged briefly at her lower lip.

Then, decisively, keeping her promise of candor, she said, "James, there's something I feel you should know."

As James realized what was troubling her he felt a mixture of regret and relief. She needed to know, and he had planned to tell her, but he had dreaded the revelation, knowing that it would make her sad.

James saw the sadness now and knew that Allison had already been told.

"You know about Gweneth, don't you?"

"Yes."

"Did Eve tell you?"

"No. Maylene did."

James scowled. "I wonder why."

"It was because of something I said. I had assumed that the two of you were involved."

"And what did Maylene say?"

"That you were friends." All the fluttering until now had been merely slow motion, the most languid of heartbeats, so casual, so calm. Allison tried to take a steadying breath, but the frantic fluttering in her chest drove it away. "And that you were committed to your work . . . and to Gweneth's memory."

"That's right, Allison," James affirmed quietly. I have nothing to offer you, lovely butterfly. I have only my nightmares, and my rage, and a deadly enemy who may one day appear from the shadows to strike again. "That's how I've decided to live my life."

Like hers, his eyes had been illuminated by candlelight, silver dappled with gold. And, like hers, the true light had come from deep within . . . and now, even the brilliant gold of the dancing flames could not brighten the sudden darkness of the silver.

James knew what his eyes looked like now. They were ice-cold, as desolate and as barren as his heart would have been had it not been for Hong Kong. He was a silver-eyed panther, intent on destruction, and surely in the face of such fierceness the delicate butterfly would gracefully—and gratefully—fly away.

But she didn't. Her eyes held his without wavering, and, astonishingly, the green seemed to shine more brightly than ever.

Don't care about me, Allison. It was a silent command, a silent warning, and it was fortified with the greatest ferocity of all as James permitted his mind and heart to fill with fiery images of a night in Wales. *It would be dangerous to care . . . and quite futile.*

And still the emerald eyes did not waver. They merely glowed, shy—and yet so determined—and remarkably unafraid. Had James been harboring any lingering thoughts that Allison was involved in a mystical collaboration with the spirits of Hong Kong, the thoughts would now have been vanquished once and for all. Confronted with the fearsomeness of his gaze, even the boldest of phantoms would have promptly scurried away.

Allison Parish Whitaker was acting on her own, and now her shining eyes sent their own fearless message.

I understand the rules, James. You are married to Gweneth, and always will be. But we could still be friends . . . *couldn't we?*

PART FIVE

CHAPTER 18

Lloyd-Ashton Centre
Wednesday, September 1, 1993

When Sir Geoffrey Lloyd-Ashton returned to his office following his 1:00 P.M. address to the Legislative Council, he noticed at once the blinking green light on the small black device that lay on his desk. Usually the device was without life. But now, because it signaled activity, Geoffrey strode across the Ming carpet to the eleventh-century armoire. Both were works of art, prized possession of ancient emperors.

The armoire was far more than decorative. Behind its ornate hand-carved doors was the most modern of surveillance equipment. From his penthouse office, Geoffrey could monitor every square inch of Peak Castle and its grounds, and, of course, all telephone calls were routinely recorded. The equipment in the armoire was a tiny version of that which existed in the castle itself. Here, he had only a single television screen and VCR, but in the castle, in a room adjacent to his study and concealed behind a wall of books, there were enough machines to enable him to record simultaneously all activity taking place in the castle.

The surveillance system had been installed when the castle was built, before Geoffrey ever met his bride-to-be. Hong Kong's most powerful resident had known that he would be hosting parties for the territory's elite. He wanted access to his guests' most intimate conversations, to know what they said, in whispers, when they believed no one could overhear—intriguing tidbits of impending mergers and private scandals. Since the arrival of Governor Patten, the information to be secretly gleaned was even more important. Business and politics had become entwined and sides were being taken. Some believed Hong Kong's long-term economic survival could be assured only by swift democratic reform, while others had already made lucrative deals with the government in Beijing.

Over the years Geoffrey's surveillance system had proven invaluable, affording him an extraordinary advantage in any number of business pursuits. But since his marriage to Eve, it was the personal surveillance that gave him the greatest pleasure. He was able to watch his wife every moment of every day if he wished, observing her when she believed she was alone, invading every privacy.

Eve never did anything dramatic. She ate almost nothing, drank only small amounts of tea, and the pills she ingested many times a day were only aspirin, taken in an attempt to lessen the severity of the headaches she had because of the oral contraceptives he insisted that she take. With Eve on birth-control pills, Geoffrey could claim his bride wherever and whenever he chose—and without delay; and pills were also the most reliable way to prevent a permanent—and unwanted—mingling of his blue-blooded genes with her wretchedly common ones.

Eve was always a portrait of stillness. Indeed, she was sometimes so still, so quiet, that the system that on electronic command would swiftly find the room in which there was motion could not even detect her presence. Geoffrey would have to search for her, clicking from screen to screen until she was found. Eve would be in the great room, reading, or outside, standing at the edge of the cliff and staring into space.

There were times, rare but real, when the expression on her face seemed almost happy, almost peaceful, as if she had journeyed to a faraway dream. It was then that Geoffrey would cancel his appointments and rush home, startling her, shattering her peace and reminding her with brutal force that she belonged to him and always would.

Sir Geoffrey Lloyd-Ashton had not become Hong Kong's wealthiest taipan by wasting time watching the motionlessness of his wife, nor did he need to program the cameras in the castle to record her every move while he was away. Neither was necessary. The small black device on his desk alerted him to any unusual activity.

Now, as he unlocked the doors of the armoire, he saw that two lights were flashing. One, which blinked twice per beat, signaled that two phone calls had been recorded, and the other indicated that there was a stranger in the castle, a voice that the preprogrammed electronic sensors didn't identify as belonging either to Eve or to the maids, chauffeurs, gardeners, and cooks who came and went on an erratic schedule controlled entirely by him.

A visitor to Peak Castle, to Eve, was Geoffrey's top priority. As the image on the monitor came into perfect focus, he discovered the identity of today's guest: Allison Whitaker, appearing precisely when he himself had invited her to—when, at last, the skies over Hong Kong had changed from azure to gray.

Geoffrey assumed that the recorded telephone calls would be between Eve and Allison, and he churned with anger when they were not. It meant that the two women had spoken on Monday, when Eve was away from the castle and using a telephone that he could not control.

The first call was from a man, a physician who identified himself as Lily Kai's cardiologist. After profuse apologies for bothering Eve at home, the doctor's voice became even more tentative as he launched into the reason for such an intrusion.

"I've just finished seeing Lily."

"Is she all right?"

"What? Oh, yes. It was just a routine office visit. But I'm afraid a rather awkward situation has developed and I thought you should be forewarned. It seems that little Lily has imagined that you've promised her that you'll be at the hospital on the day of her surgery. It's not unusual for a five-year-old to make something like this up, but—"

"Lily isn't imagining anything, Doctor. I did promise her that I would be there."

"You did?"

"Yes. I mentioned the promise to the nurses on Ward Three, and they were going to let me know as soon as the surgery date had been set."

"We set it today. We're planning for Monday, December thirteenth."

"Do you have a time? I told Lily that I would see her just before she goes to surgery."

"She's scheduled to be the second case of the day. The surgeons estimate that they'll call for her at about ten that morning."

"So if I arrived at the hospital at eight, I'd be able to see her?"

"Certainly."

"And after? I also told her that I would see her again when she awakens."

"If all goes well, she should be awake—and alert—by late afternoon."

"If all goes well . . . do you expect problems?"

"No, we really don't. But one can never take open-heart surgery lightly. There's always the possibility of an intraoperative catastrophe. The procedure itself, however, is quite straightforward—placing a patch over the defect—and, for Lily, it should be a cure."

"So once she's safely out of surgery, she'll be fine?"

"She should be. Well, I've taken enough of your time. Thank you again, Lady Lloyd-Ashton. This is really terribly nice of you, and it obviously means a great deal to Lily, as well as to her parents."

Lily, Geoffrey mused. The little Chinese girl for whom Eve had subjected herself to numerous needle sticks. He wondered when Eve planned to tell him about the promise she had made. Perhaps never. By sheer chance, Lily's surgery had been scheduled for Monday, Eve's usual hospital day, and if her luck held, he would have no other plans for her that day. She would be able to see Lily before and after surgery—and he would never need to know.

But now I know.

Geoffrey wanted Eve to keep her promise, of course. Happy ending or not, the Princess of Peak Castle's compassion would make a compelling story for the local media. A perfect human-interest story for Cynthia, Geoffrey thought with amusement, knowing how Cynthia despised such "non"-news—but knowing as well that she would do this story *for him*. Cynthia would be at the hospital that day, as would he, supporting his princess whether she told him about the promise or not.

The second recorded telephone call was an outgoing one, placed just twenty minutes earlier, from Eve to Juliana Kwan at the Pearl Moon boutique.

"It's Eve, Juliana. Do you remember my mentioning Allison Whitaker? The photographer for the Jade Palace who owns the rainbow-sequined gown you designed?"

"Yes, of course I remember."

"Well, she's here with me now and has just told me that she's hoping to find another Pearl Moon gown to wear for the hotel's grand opening. I thought it would be nice if she met with you directly. Would that be possible?"

"Absolutely. I'd be delighted. Please tell her that I'd also be happy to design a gown for her especially for that night."

"How lovely. When should she come to see you?"

"Let me look at my book." There was a brief silence in the recording before Juliana spoke again. "I have an opening this Friday at eleven. Would that be convenient for her?"

As Geoffrey idly listened to Eve confirm the date and time with Allison before saying good-bye to Juliana, his thoughts drifted to the telephone conversation between Eve and Juliana that had been recorded in June—and to the intriguing disclosure that Juliana and Maylene were mother and daughter.

Oh, the secrets you keep from me, my princess. With a smile, Geoffrey amended, The secrets you *try* to keep. But there are no secrets, my love, not from me.

Geoffrey focused then on the video screen, turning up the sound so that he could hear the words being spoken now at Peak Castle. Allison was raving about her recent visit to Po Lin Monastery on Lantau Island, a contagious joy that had clearly spread to Eve. Her sapphire eyes glowed, and she looked so young, so happy, and so free.

"What a lovely afternoon, Eve," Allison enthused as she stood with her hostess at the front door of the castle. "Thank you so much."

"Thank you so much for coming, Allison. I loved having you. Are you certain I can't have someone drive you back to the Trade Winds?"

"Oh, no." Allison smiled. "I'm going to enjoy wandering through the mist."

The mist—and the magic, Allison embellished silently as she

walked down Mount Austin Road toward the tram terminus located within Peak Tower.

Dark clouds had loomed over Hong Kong since Sunday, and today the misting had begun, and soon there would be rain at last. But for now, Victoria Peak was an enchanted drama cast in silver and black, mist and magic, as if great billowing puffs of smoke were drifting from the immense jaws of its blinded dragon.

As Allison walked her thoughts drifted like the mist to another dramatic black-and-silver portrait . . . and to the magical candlelit evenings that she and James had spent together since July. They saw each other only once each week, a carefully rationed rendezvous that began with his appreciative perusal of her latest pictures, followed by dinner—and sometimes, in breathtaking moments, his appreciative perusal *of her*.

Most of the time his eyes were guarded. Polite, yes, and interested as a friend's would be—but a little distant, slightly remote. And his strong hands, heated from the fires banked deep within, touched her only to protect, guiding her safely through doorways and across streets.

But there were times when James seemed to forget his own rules, if only for a moment . . . and it was then that Allison saw what looked like hunger—for her.

But was hopelessly unsophisticated Allison Parish Whitaker truly the object of James Drake's hunger? Or was it that by some extraordinary coincidence she reminded him of Gweneth?

Allison had no idea that Eve herself had been wanted only because of her resemblance to another woman. She knew only that when she asked Eve to tell her about Gweneth, Eve seemed to understand what she was truly asking, and had taken great care to assure her that there was really no similarity between the two of them at all.

Which meant that the magic was real. The intense desire Allison saw in the silver panther eyes—the hunger, the longing, and the need—were, astonishingly, for her.

Even though it was only six o'clock, and Allison had learned from James that the Jade Palace's gifted architect normally worked at Drake Towers until late into the night, the impeccably dressed figure walking ahead of her on Chater Road was definitely Maylene. Her model-perfect posture, the graceful gait despite her stiletto-spiked heels, and the tightly coiled topknot of shining black hair were unmistakable.

Still, Allison hesitated before calling out, her words stalled by memories of the conflicting—and confusing—messages she had gotten from Maylene. The quiet little butterfly who had spent her life tightly swaddled in her cocoon of love was not accustomed to evoking responses from strangers. Whenever she did, however, the responses were usually as bland as she—and as positive—a warm smile, a friendly hello . . . certainly never dark glowers, as if, somehow, she were a *threat*.

But, from the very first, the reactions she seemed to evoke in Maylene were anything but bland. They were extreme, in both directions. In her entire life, Allison had never felt more welcome than she had during those first moments at the airport. It was as if Maylene had been waiting forever to meet her, as if they were already connected, long-lost friends reunited at last.

But then, at the apartment, she had caught Maylene's troubled jade-green eyes staring at her . . . and even though Maylene later confessed that she had been worrying about a blueprint, Allison couldn't shake the feeling that Maylene's intense glower had been quite personal—as if Allison had done something to harm her. And it had felt personal, too, on that July dawn when, just as she had been on the verge of suggesting that they get together, Maylene had suddenly cut her off.

More than once, as Allison had replayed in her mind those bewildering scenes, she had reminded herself of the truth: Maylene Kwan was in the midst of an extraordinary—and extremely challenging—project. Her moodiness was to be expected. It was unlikely, not to mention *presumptuous* to imagine, that a bland little butterfly, a virtual stranger, would incite any reaction at all—much less such a strongly negative one.

Or strongly positive one, Allison thought as she recalled those first—unforgettable—moments at the airport. Had the happiness she believed she had seen in Maylene's eyes been purely an illusion? Had her own rose-colored vision been tinting everything a gloriously friendly pink? If so, it was a very powerful illusion, and it went way beyond the visual. There were feelings as well, strange and compelling ones. Several times during the summer Allison had awakened from a deep sleep, not groggy at all and with an almost overwhelming urge to call Maylene, to see if she was wakeful, too, and in the mood for a late-night chat.

Allison had always resisted those surprising urges. But now, on this afternoon of mist and magic, she called out, "Maylene?"

Allison's voice was soft, but Maylene heard it, and as Allison closed the gap between them, the sisters took stock of the changes that had occurred since their chance meeting in July.

The changes Maylene saw in her golden sister were entirely reassuring ones. Allison's hair was longer, a lush tangle of moonbeams and fire curling exuberantly in the dampness of the mist, and her face was slightly tanned, and gently freckled, and her emerald eyes seemed to glow even more brightly than before.

The changes Allison saw in Maylene were at once magnificent and troubling. The mist had brought magic to the lustrous black hair, dotting it with a thousand tiny diamonds, and her beauty was stunning still, but slightly ravaged. Dark circles rimmed her jade-green eyes, and the eyes themselves seemed terribly anxious. Allison understood the fatigue—the relentlessness with which both Sam and Maylene had been working on the hotel was explanation enough—but not the anxiety. According to James, everything about the Jade Palace was progressing flawlessly.

After exchanging hellos, Allison asked, "Are you through for the day, Maylene?"

Maylene nodded, a dance of diamonds on midnight-black silk, and then shrugged. "I wasn't accomplishing anything. How about you?"

"I'm through, too. In fact, I took the entire day off. I shopped this morning and visited this afternoon with Eve." Allison had planned to spend the evening in her darkroom, of course, but now those plans no longer mattered. Maylene mattered. "I wonder, since we've both called it a day, would you like to have dinner with me?" When Maylene's response was an instant frown, Allison offered quietly, "You probably already have plans."

"No, I don't." Then, with a voice that, to Allison, sounded more brave than confident, Maylene said, "I'd like to have dinner with you, Allison."

"Shall we do something informal? Room service in my apartment?"

"Yes. That sounds good."

CHAPTER 19

"Please excuse the clutter," Allison said as she escorted Maylene into her living room. "I'm in the midst of assembling a package to send to my family."

The clutter was colorful, a rainbowed potpourri of Hong Kong offerings: delicate porcelain figurines; cloisonné bud vases adorned with peacocks, dragons, flowers, and butterflies; silk ties and cashmere sweaters. They were lovely gifts, lovingly selected, and just by looking at them, Maylene learned about the recipients. One grandmother was pastel, muted and soft, and the other was vivid, bright and bold, and of the three men in Allison's family, at least one of them was willing to take fashion risks.

Pointing to a particularly flamboyant silk tie, Maylene asked, "Who's this one for? Your father?"

"No. For my grandfather, my mother's father." Allison gave the tie a critical look and admitted, "It may be a bit flashy even for him."

In response to Allison's words, Maylene allowed her delicate fingers to gently touch the silk of one of the more conservative ties. *Allowed* them to? No, the foolish fingers moved of their own accord, suddenly wanting, needing, to touch something that would be worn by Garrett Whitaker ... or, perhaps, by her grandfather.

The thought of her grandfather took Maylene completely by surprise. She had missed, and loved, and mourned Juliana's parents, the grandmother and grandfather who had been swallowed by the wind-tossed sea. But until this moment she had never really thought about the grandparents who were alive.

Her grandfather would wear one of the ties she was touching now. And her grandmother? Maylene's hands drifted thoughtfully from the silk ties to the cashmere sweaters. And, as if her fingers knew the answer even before she asked the question, they came to rest on pale pink, not brilliant flame. "Is it your maternal grandmother who wears the bright colors?"

Allison nodded. "The Whitakers tend to be far more traditional than the Parishes."

Traditional. The word pierced Maylene's heart like a jagged-edged knife, plunging deep, ripping tender flesh. As her old wounds screamed with fresh pain, tormenting thoughts danced in her mind. *An illegitimate half-Chinese daughter doesn't really fit the description of traditional, does she? Do you honestly think that your Whitaker grandparents would be happy if they knew that you had so lovingly, and so foolishly, caressed the garments they would one day wear? Dream on! They would wear the clothes still, of course, gifts from their golden granddaughter—but first they would have them cleaned, purified.*

The soft cashmere beneath her fingertips suddenly felt like spun glass, its sharp fibers cutting into her delicate flesh, and in hope of balming all her screaming wounds, Maylene reached for the small stack of photographs that lay beside the porcelain figurines. The first was so soothing—a golden sunrise awakening over Victoria Harbour—that she moved eagerly to the next, and the next. It was working, she was feeling ever more calm, and soon the actress within her would be in control again, and she would be able to look up, and smile, and . . . and then she came to the final photograph in the stack—and the fragile calm was shattered.

Hong Kong had recently celebrated the Festival of the Hungry Ghosts. The Chinese equivalent of Halloween, it was a time when the gates of the underworld were opened, for twenty-four hours only, and the *Yen Lo*, the hungry ghosts, were permitted to roam the earth. To keep the wandering spirits happy, so that they would not wreak havoc on the living, lavish offerings of food and clothing were made, and incense, joss sticks, and imitation money were burned.

The festive party for the visitors from the underworld ended with the launching of a fleet of miniature "ghost ships" into the sea. In the hold of each tiny boat burned a small candle, and the cumulative light from all the ships was enough to illuminate the banner on the last one. *Hsun-feng Teh-li*, it read: Temper the winds and gain profits.

As Maylene stared at Allison's lovely photograph of the candlelit flotilla of ghost ships, she felt the stirring of ever more anguished memories: that fateful day when she had learned the truth about her father—and when the very best parts of her had died. From the ashes, her own angry ghosts had risen, cruel phantoms that hungered to strike out and hurt as she herself had been hurt.

Maylene had once permitted her hungry ghosts to roam, wreaking havoc on her beloved mother. But they weren't content with just one day of freedom, nor had they sailed into a candlelit sunset never to harm again. They lived within her still, she knew they did. And that, she had vowed, was precisely where they would remain. Never again would she allow the gates of her own underworld to open.

Drawing strength from that brave vow, Maylene looked up at

last, and smiled, and said softly, truthfully, to her golden sister, "These are wonderful, Allison. I'd love to see more. Or are all the others in the vault downstairs?"

"No, nothing's there." Allison shrugged. "I keep the negatives in the asbestos file cabinets, but even that seems an unnecessary precaution. So if you'd like to see them . . ."

"Yes. I definitely would."

They spent almost an hour in Allison's workroom, and even though some of Allison's photographs of Hong Kong triggered ancient memories of pain, Maylene managed to stay focused on the present, on her sister's magnificent talent . . . and by the time they began the short journey from workroom to living room, to make tea and call room service, Maylene's heart was racing with hope.

I can do this. I can be with Allison—where I want to be—and I can control my pain, and . . .

During the few moments of the short journey, the gray-black skies over Hong Kong had finally opened. The rain fell in thick heavy sheets, blurring the lights of the city, running all the colors together.

"Look at this rain!" Allison exclaimed. "How cozy."

"*Cozy?*" Maylene echoed incredulously, cringing at the tone in her own voice and terrified at its meaning. She had been feeling so confident, so hopeful, so in control. And now? Had one of her hungry ghosts escaped after all? *No*, she told herself. It was something else. But it had caused harm, she realized as she saw the sudden confusion on Allison's face. It reminded Maylene of Juliana's confusion, her startled disbelief that the daughter who had always been so loving had suddenly become so cruel. After a moment Maylene heard herself saying to her sister the words that she hoped, one day, she would find the courage to say to her mother. "I'm *sorry*, Allison."

"It's okay!"

"No, it's not." Maylene frowned. "I probably should have said no to doing anything tonight. I should have known I'd be terrible company."

"Why, Maylene?" Allison asked softly. "Has something happened with the Jade Palace?"

"No. It's just me. My period's due." Her frown deepened and she added hastily, "PMS is not an excuse, I *know* that. In fact, as far as I'm concerned, it's a weakness . . . a major design flaw."

"It *may* be a design flaw," Allison conceded with a lovely smile. "But, Maylene, it's *not* a weakness. It's something that happens . . . something that's very real."

"I'd actually been wondering just how real it was. Since the feelings I get are so emotional—so *crazy*—I'd almost concluded that it was all in my head. But this afternoon, just when I'd decided that the past two weeks of blueprints were utterly hopeless and was about to feed them into the shredder, I happened to notice the date on the calender and realized that I'm due again."

"That must have been a relief."

"Well, it was a stay of execution for the blueprints. I'll look at them again in a few days."

"And you'll see that they're just fine."

"I hope so. What about you, Allison, do you get PMS?"

"I don't get it now, and I don't remember if I ever did. I've been on birth-control pills since I was eighteen. I imagine that evens out the hormonal swings."

Somehow Maylene managed to suppress her surprise that Allison was taking birth-control pills. Although twenty-seven-year-old virgins were vanishingly rare, she had decided that if anyone would be that wondrously innocent, that joyously pure, it would be Allison. Maylene had believed that her sister would give herself only to the man she would love forever, but obviously that belief was wrong. Sometime during the same year when Maylene Kwan had left Hong Kong, loathing herself so much that it seemed beyond imagination that any man would ever want to touch her, her sister had begun using birth control. Men had wanted to touch Maylene, of course, and she had permitted them to, even after she had learned the truth about herself, how icy she was, how awkward, how destined to disappoint.

Was this—sex—something that sisters discussed? And was making love such a wonderful pleasure for Allison that she wanted it often, and sometimes so impulsively, that birth-control pills were the only practical approach?

Maylene broached the subject cautiously. "Eighteen seems young to have gone on the pill."

"Yes, although in my case, I should have started taking it much sooner. My periods were excessively heavy, but since I'd never discussed the subject with anyone, I didn't know what was usual. A week before I was supposed to begin college, I collapsed."

"Was that why you needed the blood transfusion?"

Allison nodded. "When the doctors discovered that transfusions weren't possible, they gave me iron and birth-control pills instead. They were skeptical that the pills would actually control the bleeding, but they have, so now I'm on them forever. Well," Allison amended softly, "until it's time to get pregnant."

Maylene saw the sudden determination in Allison's eyes, the *defiance*. "Is it safe for you to go off the pills, Allison? Mightn't you bleed too heavily before you become pregnant?"

"Maybe . . . although what my doctors—and my family—are more concerned about is childbirth itself. There's no solid medical evidence that I would have the same complications that my mother did, but even the remote possibility, given my inability to receive blood, has made them all conclude that I should never have children."

"But you don't agree."

"I don't know the medical answer, of course, only the emotional one. I will want to have children with the man I love."

"But *not* if it might cost you your life!"

"That's what it cost my mother, Maylene," Allison said softly. "But she gave my father the baby he wanted."

The baby he wanted. The words tore at the heart of the baby Garrett Whitaker did not want. But Maylene scarcely noticed *that* pain. It was familiar, an ancient scream, and now there were new emotions tearing at her as she imagined her sister dying during childbirth—dying *ever*.

Allison can't die. The soft plea was followed by a defiant vow. I won't *let* her die.

Maylene Kwan was only half Whitaker, half traditional, and as her heart made its solemn pledge, she found herself envisioning something decidedly avant-garde. In this era of *in vitro* fertilization and surrogacy, it was possible to find a woman willing to carry another woman's child . . . someone who already had her babies, *or who knew that she never would*, but who wanted to help a mother who should.

Someone like me.

It was an exhilarating thought, liberating and hopeful—until it crashed. The baby would be Allison's, with her pure golden genes, but for nine months it would dwell within Maylene. What nurturing could she promise a tiny life surrounded by hungry ghosts? What if, while growing inside her, Allison's child of love was transformed into a modern-day Rosemary's baby?

This definitely is my fault, Allison thought as, for the second time this evening, Maylene's expression became deeply troubled. The dark torment had been there earlier, when Maylene had stared—glowered—at her photograph of the flotilla of ghost ships—and it was back now. Allison wished she could attribute it to the monthly whimsy of hormones, or to some lurking worry about the Jade Palace, but this time there could be no doubt. It was personal, something *she* had said.

Earlier, just seconds before Allison would have asked if she had unwittingly violated some unwritten rule that forbade the photographing of the tiny ghost ships on the sea, the jade-green storm in Maylene's eyes had suddenly cleared. And now, just as Allison was finding the courage to ask what she had done, this time, to make Maylene so upset, the turbulence vanished yet again.

They had finished their dinner, a Szechuan feast from the Wild Ginger, and were sharing a pot of freshly brewed jasmine tea when Maylene returned their conversation to the weather. Her voice held a soft apology, as if she wanted to be given a second chance to discuss—civilly—that particular topic.

"Tell me why you like the rain so much."

"Because . . . it really does feel cozy to me."

It feels cozy to me, too, Maylene realized. Why on earth would that be? Whatever the reason, it definitely had nothing to do with her life in London. The drizzle there always felt so cold, depressing and dreary. Was there, then, something cozy about the tropical rains of Hong Kong? *Yes.* Maylene couldn't remember what it was, only that, astonishingly, it felt like being safe . . . like being loved.

"I also like going for long walks in the rain," Allison continued, encouraged by the sudden gentleness of Maylene's expression. "It makes my hair completely unruly, of course, but there's something about rainwater that also leaves it feeling very soft."

"I've never tried it."

"Really? Downpours like this are typical in Hong Kong, aren't they? From the dinner conversation at Peak Castle, I gathered that you had been raised here."

"I was." Maylene shrugged. Then, with a smile, she added, "I guess I always carried an umbrella."

"Do you have family here? Sisters and brothers?"

"I have a sister," Maylene admitted, staring into her teacup so that Allison could not read her unspoken thought: And yes, she is here. "She doesn't know about me, though."

"She doesn't? Why not?"

"My—our—father was an American. He was in Hong Kong just long enough to get my mother pregnant. He told her that he loved her, of course, but it was just an expedient lie. He returned to the States and never looked back."

"Did he know that your mother was pregnant?"

"Oh, yes. The last time she spoke to him was two days after I was born."

"Oh, Maylene," Allison said softly. "I'm sorry."

Maylene looked from the porcelain teacup to the freckled porcelain of her sister's sympathetic face. "What do you think of a man like that, Allison?"

"I . . . What do *you* think?"

"That he's despicable, dishonorable, beneath contempt." This was so dangerous, this dance with pain. Maylene had vowed to keep the gates of her own underworld closed forever, *and she would*, but there were questions that her wounded heart needed to ask. "Can you imagine your father doing something like that, Allison?"

"*My* father? No. Never." The empathic shake of Allison's head eloquently underscored her words. "You said he has another daughter . . . your sister?"

"Yes." Maylene bravely met her sister's earnest green eyes. "She knows nothing about me, has no idea that I even exist."

"Have you ever thought about trying to get in touch with her?"

"I've thought about it a lot," Maylene confessed, then paused, needing to. But Maylene Kwan needed answers even more than she needed to calm her racing heart. "What do you think, Allison? Do you think she would want to know about me?"

"Of course! Why wouldn't she? You're her *sister*."

"Yes . . . but both of her parents are Caucasian. Don't you think it might be a little shocking for her to discover that she has a half-Asian sister? Don't you think that's something she might prefer not to know?"

Allison's fire-gold head shook again, slowly this time, even more emphatic in its deliberateness, and her luminous eyes shone with solemn confidence. "I think she would definitely want to know."

She's quite color-blind, Maylene realized. Color-blind, race-blind, free from prejudice of any kind.

Tell her, Maylene's heart whispered. It's safe. You know it is. Allison would never turn away in disgust. You know the words. You've rehearsed them a thousand times, over and over, in the middle of the night. Say them now: *You're my sister, Allison, my sister! And I'm so very proud of you, and—*

No! Don't you dare speak those words of love! Maylene expected the sudden—and powerful—protest to come from one of her hungry ghosts, enraged at being imprisoned for so long, with only their captor herself—Maylene—upon whom to wreak their cruel havoc. She expected harsh reminders from them now. How tarnished she was, how unworthy, how impure.

But the vehement protest came not from a ghost, but from the deepest recesses of her heart. You can't tell Allison the truth, not now—and not *ever*. Such a revelation would be far too devastating. Oh, yes, she would gain a sister—and because she is Allison, she would graciously overlook even your most grievous flaws—but in the process she would lose the father she loves, and trusts, and believes to be a man of great honor. You can't shatter Allison's fantasy. You, of all people, know too well the anguish of discovering the bitter truths about a parent you love. You cannot—you will not—cause Allison such pain. *You are not that cruel.*

"Maylene?"

You are not that cruel. The brave pronouncement sang in her heart, with nary a rebuttal from a hungry ghost, and whether the silence of the ghosts was because they agreed, or merely because they were momentarily stunned, it didn't matter. Her entire being trembled with hope—and when the jade-green eyes met the emerald ones, they were brilliantly clear, and shimmering. *It's not the right time to tell her.*

Allison nodded, unable for a moment to speak. The brightness of Maylene's eyes—the glittering hopefulness—reminded her of those first moments at Kai Tak. We *are* destined to be friends, Allison thought. Maylene wants it, too. It's not just my rose-colored illusion. The journey toward friendship will likely be difficult, and confusing, as it already has been . . . but it's what we both want.

With a lovely smile, and eyes that shimmered, too, Allison bravely ventured a little farther into the emotional territory where the fragile roots of their friendship would try to find a nurturing home.

"What about your mother, Maylene? Is she in Hong Kong?"

"Yes," Maylene answered softly. "She's here, but I haven't seen her. We drifted apart years ago."

"Do you know how she is?"

"Oh, yes. She's fine. Terrific actually. Hugely successful."

"But you haven't spoken to her?"

"Not for nine years," Maylene said quietly to the sister who had spent her life wishing for a mother. "Not all relationships between parents and children are as wonderful as yours is with your father. My mother told me more lies than I could bear, and I said things to her that I could never expect her to forgive. It was best—for both of us—that we went our separate ways."

"You're certain?"

"Absolutely." I'm absolutely certain that she's better off without me. *But I miss her.*

It took Sam a moment to realize that there were two watery sounds in the hotel's Eden Health Spa—the torrential rain splashed on the atrium windows above, and a more distant sound, a rhythmic splashing, that came from the pool. It was 1:00 A.M., and even though Sam knew how compulsive businesspeople of the nineties were about fitness, he had imagined that he would be alone. Sam wasn't exercising, of course. His body remained lean, taut, powerful simply from the way he wandered the planet.

Not particularly curious, but because looking again at the design of the pool area was part of why he was here, Sam wandered in the direction of the smooth, rhythmic splashes. At the sight of the woman swimming in the pool, he drew a sharp breath into lungs that no longer burned from smoke but now gnawed with hunger as the mouths of the tiny demons within clamored to be fed their daily dose of destruction.

It was Maylene, Sam was positive, even though her face was mostly buried in water. She was swimming with the form and speed of a champion, and the one-piece swimsuit she wore further confirmed the image. Her hair, however, was wrong for a champion. Instead of being tightly confined in a cap, it trailed behind her, a long black braid that skimmed along the aquamarine water as sleekly as she.

Sam recognized the braid. Maylene had worn it every time she visited the construction site since mid-July. She was a silken cowgirl: blue jeans, cowboy boots, black silk braid, and soft silk blouses. Sam had encouraged her to stop by at least once a week, and she had willingly complied, but the visits were hardly necessary. He hadn't truly needed her input to construct the skeleton of gleaming steel. Beginning next week, however, Sam would need her almost every day.

Need her . . . want her . . . every day.

So far everything with the Jade Palace had gone beautifully, way ahead of schedule and with far fewer modifications than Sam had anticipated. But they weren't home free yet, not by a long shot. The trickiest part loomed ahead, the layering of the alabaster flesh onto the silver skeleton. The trickiest time for Sam and Maylene lay ahead as well. Could they work together, weathering the difficult decisions and not letting the inevitable professional setbacks become personal ones?

Sam hoped so.

He hoped for so much more.

"Oh! You."

"Hi," he greeted softly.

She was in the middle of the pool, treading water in the long dark shadow cast by Sam.

"Why are you here, Cowboy?"

"I wanted to take a look at the atrium. I think a variation on the same idea will do very well in the Palace, don't you?"

"Yes." Maylene frowned. "How long have you been here?"

"Just long enough to see how well you swim. Did you swim competitively?"

"No."

"Then why do you swim so well?"

"I suppose because I learned to swim even before I could walk." Maylene had been wondering, as she swam, if the faraway memory of coziness that had been triggered by the tropical rainstorm was merely a memory of being immersed in the warm waters of a swimming pool. She decided that it wasn't. Yes, swimming felt safe, and there was even love blended in, but it was a different emotion than the one evoked by the pelting rain. "My mother insisted on it."

"Was she a champion?"

"No. She couldn't swim at all, even though she spent the first thirteen years of her life on a boat in Aberdeen Harbour."

"She came ashore when she was thirteen?"

"There was a typhoon. Her entire family was lost."

"But she was rescued."

"She rescued herself," Maylene said quietly. It was the truth, she realized, despite the fact that Juliana had never given herself any credit at all. In Juliana's recounting of the story of her life, it was the plank from *Pearl Moon* that had rescued her, in concert with the gods, and then the kindly truck driver, and then Vivian, and then, five years later, the most important rescuer of all: Garrett Whitaker.

Maylene was in the middle of the pool still, treading water, and the aquamarine drops on her long inky-black lashes sparkled like diamonds. But Sam saw beyond the shimmering diamonds to the sudden dark shadows in her jade-green eyes.

"I will give you a few hundred thousand U.S. dollars for that thought, Maylene."

"It's not worth it!"

"Let me be the judge."

"It's not worth it."

"All right." Sam smiled. "Twenty Hong Kong dollars then."

Maylene shook her head no, a small tight shake that was more plea than defiance. With the gesture, the diamonds from her lashes splashed onto her cheeks like glittering tears.

"Okay," Sam assured her very gently. "The thought remains with you. I just wanted to be sure there hadn't been any recidivism."

"Recidivism?"

"I know, it's a big word for a cowboy. But I think I've used it correctly. I just wanted to be sure that you hadn't lapsed back into whatever self-destructive habit it was you gave up six weeks ago."

"You haven't lapsed?"

"Not a puff."

"You must not have been a serious smoker."

"I was a very serious smoker, Jade. I was also very serious about the deal we made."

Her lashes dropped, spilling more diamonds. Sam allowed his eyes to follow their shimmering path as far as her lips, but no lower. Beneath the aquamarine water, her lovely body was thinly veiled, he knew, but Maylene had not invited his eyes to travel there. So he stopped at the lush lips, which themselves sometimes sent dazzling invitations, perhaps without her permission. They were trembling now—and dusky.

"You're cold," Sam said. "And you're probably not about to get out with me standing here, are you?"

Maylene looked up, her blue-tinged lips smiling slightly. "I need to swim some more laps. That will warm me up."

"All right. Good night, Jade."

"Good night, Cowboy."

Sam started to turn away, but stopped for a final impulsive question. "What do you think of the rain?"

"I think it's cozy." But I don't know why.

CHAPTER 20

Thursday, September 2, 1993

aylene walked, retracing the footsteps of her childhood, the pouring rain drenching the long black hair
that she wore unrestrained. She looked like a madwoman, she supposed, a specter in cowboy boots and jeans, walking into the storm instead of seeking shelter from it, her face
washed fresh, her jade-green eyes searching for some truth hidden amid the raindrops.

She drew stares, but she was oblivious to them. She was on a
quest for a memory, illusory, invisible—and yet terribly important and real.

Her storm-tossed journey took her to the places made magical by her mother during their first thirteen years together, the
places of love and lies and fairy tales. From the silver-tipped
waves of the harbor, to the lush green serenity of Victoria Park, to
the top of the Peak itself, she wandered. There, at the precise
place on the Hong Kong Trail where her mother and father had
met beneath the April moon, Maylene lingered the longest in the
fiercely punishing rain. She and Juliana had come here so many
times. But never on a day like this, when the rain pelted and the

wind swirled. There were memories here, but none that could explain the coziness of the rain.

Maylene's soggy journey commenced at dawn and ended five hours later without an answer. She couldn't find the memory of love and rain. It was a phantom, she decided. Or perhaps it was merely a wish to share something with her sister, to feel the same joyful wonder that Allison felt.

But the memory Maylene sought was, in fact, quite real, even though her conscious mind would never be able to recall it. It would remain forever a feeling not a thought, a memory of the senses made by a tiny infant who had been tenderly cradled in her mother's arms during a rainy February twenty-eight years before. The mother was young and starving and cold and afraid, but all her baby daughter knew was warmth, despite the rain . . . and love, despite her mother's fear.

"We can't sail today, Eve," Tyler had said when she reached him by telephone at nine. He had added, very softly, "I've leased an apartment in the Mid Levels, for us, for days like this."

They couldn't go to his suite at the Regent. In the hotel's elegant lobby, her brightly colored disguise would draw too many stares. But the apartment building on Robinson Road was quite safe. Its other residents would be away, at work in Central, from dawn till dusk.

Now, three hours later, as Tyler waited for Eve to arrive, he wondered—and worried—about the afternoon that lay ahead. They had sailed almost weekly since mid-July, enchanted afternoons of glowing sapphire eyes and soft words and softer smiles. They spoke only of the present—the forest-green islands, the graceful flight of seabirds overhead, the silent power of the boat in full sail, the sun's golden rays on the blue and emerald waves.

Eve and Tyler marveled at the splendor around then, but the greatest splendor of all was what Tyler beheld when he gazed at Eve. With each passing moment, he believed, her lovely blue eyes seemed to see more clearly his love . . . and their dream.

And yet, even though they had loved with eyes and smiles, they had never kissed. Indeed, the only time they ever touched at all was when he helped her onto the *Seven Seas'* bobbing deck . . . and Eve always seemed a little confused by his gentle caress, as if she couldn't even feel it, as if her delicate flesh was quite numb— or as if, perhaps, it belonged to someone else entirely.

She *was so afraid.* He wouldn't push her, of course. Even though they would be in a private apartment, not sailing on the open sea, Tyler would wait for her to make the first move.

Eve couldn't tell him why she was so fearful of intimacy, couldn't confess to him that the only memories she had of making love were violent ones. She had to conceal from Tyler Geoffrey's sexual brutality, just as when they eventually discussed her life with Geoffrey, she would have to portray her marriage as loveless but tolerable.

At the moment such a portrayal would be more truth than falsehood. Living with Geoffrey *was* tolerable. He seemed oddly euphoric, strangely energized, and he hadn't come near her for weeks. Eve was certain that he was involved with Cynthia Andrews, but she was equally confident that it was not his new mistress who made him feel so exhilarated. Quite probably it was an impending business deal. He was undoubtedly on the verge of some great financial triumph. The anticipatory gleam she saw in his eyes was that of a predator about to go in for the kill.

Eve knew the gleam of imminent conquest all too well. It was precisely the way Geoffrey's dark eyes looked just before he violently claimed her fragile body.

What if Tyler's eyes, gleaming with desire, triggered terrifying memories of Geoffrey?

She had to hide her fear.

She had to.

As Eve neared the apartment building on Robinson Road, she saw him standing in the pouring rain, waiting for her. He was drenched, but his blue eyes smiled with love and welcome . . . and it was then, quite suddenly, that Eve began to hear the most remarkable sound.

She had absolutely no idea what it was, only that it came from deep within, and it grew louder, ever louder, as she and Tyler rode the elevator to the apartment he had found for them. Then they were inside, and his eyes found hers, and the desire Eve saw in them was pure love, without a glimmer of conquest, and the mysterious sound suddenly became gloriously clear.

It was singing, *singing*, a chorus of hope that came from the body that for so very long had called to her only with screams of pain—and that had betrayed her by being beautiful, the object of a cruel, dark desire. Eve had long ago abandoned the traitorous shell in which she dwelled; but that exquisite shell was imploring her now, pleading with her to be allowed to be joined again with its heart.

At first, Eve interpreted the plea as merely a wish for a shift in sovereignty, from Geoffrey to Tyler. But that was wrong. The body from which she had so long been estranged wanted to belong to *her*. Then, when she was whole at last, invisible no more, she could give herself to the man she loved.

"Oh, Eve," Tyler said with gentle sadness when he saw her sudden tears. "Darling, we're only here because it's raining. I'll make tea and we'll talk, just like on the boat."

Eve answered with a soft smile and blue eyes that shimmered brightly beneath the tears. "Make love to me, Tyler."

"Evangeline," he whispered as he, too, began to hear the remarkable sound. It was a duet now, and even before his lips tenderly greeted hers, and even before their loving bodies joyfully became one, their hearts sang in perfect harmony. *"Evangeline."*

As nourishing raindrops spilled from the dark skies outside, nourishing tears of pure joy spilled within. *I love you.* The wondrous words were carried on whispered kisses, and soft laughs, and astonished sighs, and they were gift-wrapped with tender caresses of eyes and hands and lips.

But now, as Eve whispered the words, Tyler heard a wistful note of despair, and he saw that the glow in her luminous sapphire eyes was beginning to fade, as it always did when their afternoons together were drawing to a close.

Now, as then, Eve attempted to offset her sadness by forcing cheeriness into her voice. "I guess it's time for me to don my plumage."

"Your plumage?" Tyler echoed softly.

With a lovely smile, Eve told him about the Festival of the Maidens, a time when the girls of Hong Kong celebrated their hope for good marriages. As with all Chinese celebrations, she explained, the Maidens' Festival was based on legend—in this instance, an ancient tale of love, of lovers condemned by the gods to forever live far apart, each on a different star. The Birds of Heaven took pity on the couple, however, and once a year they flew together, so close that wing touched wing, thus creating a great bridge of feathers to connect the distant stars.

"We're like those star-crossed lovers," Eve said. "The bridge of brilliant plumage that enables us to be together is the wardrobe of vibrant costumes made by Juliana. She even uses feathery colors, peacock and canary and—"

"We're not star-crossed, Evangeline."

Tyler's words were quiet, yet almost fierce, and with them the cheeriness that Eve had been forcing swiftly vanished, as did the remaining glow in her eyes.

"Yes, we are," she whispered quietly, and fiercely, too.

"No." Tyler cupped her face in his hands, gently compelling her sad eyes not to look away. "I love you, Eve, and I believe that you love me, and it's not a love destined to be held together only by a bridge of feathers. I want to spend my life with you, every day of my life, for the rest of my life."

"Oh, Tyler. I want that, too. But . . ."

"Unless you love Geoffrey more than me, there are no buts."

Her cloudy eyes flashed then, a sudden spark of life—of love—for him. "I don't love Geoffrey at all! You can't believe that I do!"

Tyler smiled softly. "Then stay with me, beginning right now. I'll be more than happy to explain the situation to Geoffrey, or we can do it together."

"It's not that easy."

"Yes, it is. You don't owe him anything, Eve. Not a thing."

Now it was she who smiled. "Oh, but I do owe Geoffrey. If it weren't for him, if he hadn't brought me to Hong Kong"—*and imprisoned me here*—"you and I would never have met."

"We would have met," Tyler countered with solemn confidence. Then, with wonder, he embellished, "I had spent my entire life searching for you, and I would have kept on searching until you were found. But I've found you now, my love, we've found each other. Isn't it time for us to make plans to be together?"

For seven years, because of Geoffrey, Eve's sable-brown hair had been short-cropped, exposing her face, making her feel naked and vulnerable. That same face was now framed by gentle hands of love, and Eve felt naked no more, only loved, only strong. She placed her hands over his, twining her delicate fingers with his powerful ones. After several moments she took his hands away, but held them still, as she sat up.

Tyler's heart didn't die as Eve pulled away. There was a determined glimmer now in her sapphire-blue eyes, a flicker of light, as if a golden beacon deep within her was at last enabling her to see a way to their future.

"Geoffrey cares very much about image," Eve began, speaking softly to their dream. "He enjoys our status as Hong Kong's royal couple. I couldn't leave him and remain in Hong Kong."

"Then we'll leave Hong Kong. We'll sail until we find a place we want to live. Or, my love, we'll just sail forever."

Was this really happening? Eve wondered. Was she really making plans for happiness, for love?

Yes, her heart sang. Yes you are.

Just like Rosalind did. The sudden icy thought stunned—and chilled—her. Eve had never felt the slightest closeness to the woman with whom she shared an outer shell. But now she did. Rosalind, too, had undoubtedly discovered the brutal truths about Geoffrey. She, too, had planned to leave him for someone she truly loved.

Had Rosalind's heart sung with joy as she made plans to leave Geoffrey? And had she been so consumed with her own happiness that she became careless, foolishly telling Geoffrey of those joyful plans, as if he would understand? *Yes.* And Geoffrey hadn't understood, hadn't wished for her happiness. He had raged at her, chased after her . . . and during her frantic flight, Rosalind had died.

"Eve, darling, you look so afraid."

"It's just . . . I was thinking about Geoffrey. He isn't going to be gracious about this, Tyler. He doesn't like to lose, doesn't know how to."

"That's too bad. Maybe it's about time for him to learn."

Eve found a smile then, for him, and, for him, she even banished the fear from her eyes. But it lingered in her heart as she thought about Rosalind, who had been so happy—and so careless. Eve tried to keep the fear from her voice as she said, "Geoffrey can't know, or even suspect, anything about us until after we're gone."

"All right," Tyler agreed, even though such secrecy would not have been his choice. But it was obviously very important to Eve, and he wanted no worries, no fears, to cloud her vision of their future. "When will we leave, Evangeline? When will we sail into our dream?"

Tyler knew the answer even before she spoke.

"In December."

"After Lily's surgery."

"Yes."

Tyler smiled lovingly at the woman who had made a solemn promise to a little girl, and who would never break that promise, even if it meant postponing her own dreams. They would leave in three months, and it was such a short time, really, compared with a lifetime of happiness, and he would never try to convince her to break her promise. But still . . . "I hate the thought of your living with him until then."

"It doesn't matter," Eve said softly, and it didn't, not to her. She could endure anything for three months. *Anything.* But if Tyler knew the truth of her life with Geoffrey . . . Eve drew a steadying breath, and then lied to the man she loved. "Except in public, Geoffrey and I live totally separate lives."

An hour later, just before leaving the ladies' room at the Hilton, where she had made the transformation from a tourist with bright plumage to Lady Lloyd-Ashton, Eve cast a glance at the mirror. The glance was routine, to make certain that her hair and makeup were as they should be, but when she saw the image that looked back at her, Eve's eyes widened with astonishment.

It wasn't beauty she saw, and perhaps that was something she would never see. Nor did it matter. For what Eve saw was far more wondrous: *happiness*, radiant and glowing, where always before she had only seen despair.

Had Tyler Vaughn been standing before a mirror in their apartment on Robinson Road, he, too, would have seen for the first time in his entire life what happiness looked like on his handsome face. But Tyler was standing before a window, and as he stared outside, the happiness faded to a frown.

How he had wished for this day, when Eve would believe in herself, and in his love, and would be able to see with brilliant clarity the path to their future. And now she did . . . *but he didn't.*

Before she left the apartment, Eve had described with quiet joy the day in mid-December when they would set sail. It would be a truly glorious day, she said. The skies would be bright blue, and the tropical breezes would be warm and dry, and the rays of the winter sun would gleam a burnished gold on the aquamarine waves.

The image of that gold-and-sapphire day had danced in Tyler's mind since July. But now, on this day when it should have shone more brightly than ever, the image was in hiding, veiled by a mysterious darkness that was as opaque—and as ominous—as the storm clouds that now cloaked Hong Kong.

Eve and I will sail into our dream, Tyler vowed as he glowered at gray-black skies that merely glowered back. Nothing will stand in our way. *I won't let it.*

Finally, with sheer love, sheer will, Tyler's mind compelled the menacing gray-black skies to part . . . but when they did, he no longer saw the familiar image of blue and gold, but a new one, a sparkling tableau of stars and moon. His frown lingered for several moments, but as the celestial scene came into clearer focus, he smiled. He saw the sea at last, and rippling across its night-black waves was the silver ribbon of moonlight that they would follow to the horizon—and beyond . . . to their dream.

CHAPTER 21

Trade Winds Hotel
Thursday, September 2, 1993

For the second day in a row Maylene and Allison returned to the Trade Winds at precisely the same time. Today as yesterday Maylene looked model perfect despite the rain, and today as yesterday Allison's golden-red hair was a barometer of Hong Kong's weather. Gently misted yesterday, it was dripping wet now.

"I've just made a mad dash from Cat Street," Allison explained as they strolled through the hotel lobby toward the elevator. "Feel free to pretend that you don't know me."

Maylene smiled. "I took a long walk myself this morning. The concierge made a not-so-discreet point of looking the other way when I came back." With a thoughtful tilt of her shining black head, she added, "You're right about rainwater, Allison. It makes your hair feel very soft."

When they reached their floor and the brightly polished brass doors of the elevator opened, they were suddenly face-to-face with the hotel's chief of security. His already troubled expression became more grave when he saw Allison. Instantly abandoning his plans to board the elevator, he greeted, "Miss Whitaker."

"What's wrong?" Maylene demanded as a quick glance down

the corridor revealed that the door to Allison's apartment was wide-open. "What's happened?"

"I'm afraid there's been an act of vandalism in Miss Whitaker's apartment," the security chief explained as they walked down the hallway. "It was discovered about two hours ago, when the butler let himself in to restock the kitchen. He notified me and I called Mr. Drake and the police."

"The police?"

"They haven't found anything helpful. No fingerprints at all. The vandal undoubtedly wore gloves." He turned to Allison. "And you must not have been back since the apartment was cleaned at nine this morning."

"No, that's right. I haven't. What was vandalized?"

Allison's soft question was answered, very softly, by James. He appeared in the doorway of her apartment, a portrait of elegance—and of darkness—in his black silk tuxedo. "Your photographs, Allison."

"Oh, no," she whispered as she swept past him through the doorway and into the living room.

The bright clutter was gone, the colorful gifts to her family shipped this morning from the Connaught Place post office, and in its place was celluloid clutter, a confetti of film, negatives, and photographs. The scattered bits of her talent had been neatly sliced, victims of the sharpest of blades, a coldly calculated act of violence, not a heated impulse of emotion.

The clutter in the living room was the end of a trail of destruction that began in her workroom. Allison followed the trail in search of even a lone survivor. But everything was destroyed. The drawers of the asbestos cabinets where the negatives had been carefully filed, protected from both an unlikely blaze and the sprinklers that would swiftly reply, were wide-open, gaping, as if shocked by the willful carnage.

"Oh, Allison," Maylene whispered with soft despair. Then,

with sudden hope, she reminded, "You sent photographs to your family."

"Yes, but only a few, and without the original negatives it would be impossible to do quality enlargements." Without warning, Allison began to shiver. It was a natural response of rain-drenched skin suddenly exposed to air-conditioned chill—and a natural response, too, of a heart exposed to the emotional chill of such meticulous destruction.

"You're freezing," James said gently. "Why don't you take a hot shower? The police are almost finished, and as soon as they're gone, I'll give housekeeping a call. Everything should be cleaned up by the time you're through."

"No." The words came quickly, through trembling lips. "Thank you, James, but I'd really prefer to do the cleaning up myself."

"After a hot shower."

Allison nodded, a gesture that caused a splatter of raindrops, like the iciest of tears, to spill to her cheeks from her storm-soaked hair. Embarrassed, her eyes fell—to his tuxedo. Remembering what he had told her over candlelight on Tuesday evening at Lai Ching Heen, she said, "This is the night that you're addressing the Chamber of Commerce. You'd better go. You're probably already late. As soon as I get warmed up, I'll be fine."

"And I'll stay, Allison, if you like," Maylene offered. "I could make a pot of tea."

Allison's trembling lips curled into a wobbly smile. "Yes, thank you, Maylene. That would be very nice."

By the time Maylene returned to the living room with the freshly brewed tea, everyone was gone. The room was silent, and quite dark. The storm outside had imposed an early nightfall on Hong Kong, and the room was now cast in shadows. But still

Maylene saw the sliced remnants of her sister's magnificent art, and her heart ached anew at the devastation. Who could have done something this wantonly destructive, this brazenly cruel?

Maylene realized then that she was not alone after all. James stood by the window, staring out, absolutely still. He was a midnight shadow, long and dark and cold. Only his coal-black hair held any color, reflected glitter from lights outside. Maylene couldn't see his face, but his body spoke eloquently of his rage. Even in its motionlessness, the power was immense. The panther was ready to spring . . . and to destroy.

"I thought you'd gone," she said softly, wondering as she did if the sound of her voice would startle him.

But James Drake was not a man easily startled. It was several moments before he moved, and when he did, when he turned slowly to face her, it was a motion of pure grace, despite his fury. His face was mostly shadowed still, but Maylene saw his anger nonetheless. The fires of rage that he always kept so carefully banked deep within were blazing now, hot and bright, a gleaming inferno in his silver eyes.

"There's something I need to discuss with Allison," he said. Despite the fury that smoldered in the molten silver, his voice was cool, and as still—and as dangerous—as his powerful body. "Privately."

Maylene understood his fury, she felt it, too, but why did James want to speak with Allison in private? Why was he dismissing *her*?

Because he thinks you're responsible, of course. The inner voice belonged to a hungry ghost. Maylene's ravenous phantoms had been taunting her all day, deriding her foolish search for coziness in the chilling rain . . . and for the even greater foolishness that had begun last night: the fantasy that she and Allison might become friends. *We can,* she defiantly told her taunting ghosts. *It's what we both want.*

Maylene had spent the day fighting a battle within herself. Strident reminders of her past unworthiness warred—thundered—against the brave whispers of hope. The hopeful whispers had seemed vastly outmatched. But they had been *winning*—until now.

Now her ghosts tasted blood—and fear—and they weren't going to relent until all her foolish longings were crushed forever. Have no doubt, they admonished, James remembers clearly your vehement opposition to his selection of Allison for the Jade Palace. How could he not remember such a scene? And it will not have escaped the notice of James Drake's discerning eyes that the destruction of Allison's photographs was meticulous, flawless, impeccably neat—like you are—as if executed by an X-Acto knife, an architect's preferred tool. And he also knows that it was almost noon before you arrived at Drake Towers today—because, on this day of all days, he left a message at 9:00 A.M. that he wanted to see you as soon as you came in.

And, most importantly, this man who is himself an expert on rage—and the cruelty that may escape from it—has sensed the rage and the cruelty that dwell within you.

James believes that you are responsible for this viciousness, and, unworthy and foolish Number One Daughter, it is going to be very difficult for you to prove him wrong.

Always fastidious Maylene Kwan had spent the morning walking in a rainstorm, chasing illusory memories of love. Yes, the concierge had seen her return, but that proved absolutely nothing. Mere minutes in today's downpour—like the amount of time required to leave the hotel to dispose of an X-Acto knife and gloves—would have left her utterly soaked. And if anyone in Hong Kong *had* happened to catch a glimpse of her this morning, a madwoman in quest of an illusion, such a witness would doubtless have concluded that she was crazy—and, therefore, quite likely to have committed an act of such willful and wanton destruction.

Maylene was trembling now, chilled to the bone with pure fear. But maybe she was wrong. *Please.* On that evening in June, James had expressed such surprising faith in her, believing her then to be fully capable of controlling—and perhaps even conquering—her own demons. Was that faith shattered now?

Maylene saw the glinting silver fury. But was it for her, or for some nameless vandal? She couldn't be absolutely certain. She needed to see more of his darkly shadowed face. With trembling fingers she switched on a nearby lamp.

But the sudden glow was far too bright. It glared at her, as if she were already the number-one suspect, being questioned in the harsh light of a tiny interrogation room.

"I didn't do this, James," she pleaded softly, blindly, into darkness. "Yes, in the beginning, I was opposed to having Allison be part of the Jade Palace. But that was *before* I met her. I believed the photographer should be either British or Chinese, that's all. It had nothing to do with her. You have to believe—" Maylene stopped abruptly as she sensed a new presence. She spun from James and the shadows to the room's arched entryway. There were no shadows there, only her sister, brightly illuminated by lamplight. *"Allison."*

Her bulky bathrobe was cinched tightly at her slender waist, and her golden-red hair was still slightly damp, and her lovely face was freshly scrubbed. She looked delicate, and young, and she might have been an innocent girl ready for a bedtime story—had it not been for her eyes. The magnificent green was stricken—by the destruction she had beheld earlier . . . and by the even greater destruction she was witnessing now.

"Maylene is not responsible for destroying my photographs, James. She may not have wanted me to take the photographs for the Palace but . . ." Allison faltered, shaken and bewildered by what she had overheard. *She had been right after all.* There had been something quite personal in the dark glowers of the jade-green eyes. Now it was confirmed. But, last night, there had been the fragile beginnings of friendship, hadn't there? *Yes,* and now Maylene was looking at her with such hope—and such gratitude—that she had so swiftly come to her defense. When Allison spoke again, her voice was strong. "Maylene did *not* do this."

"I know that," James answered quietly as he stepped from the shadows into the light.

There was no fury in his eyes now, only gentleness—for both of the women who stood before him. James had, of course, considered the possibility that Maylene was to blame for the destruction of Allison's work. Given the facts, it would have been impossible not to. But he had dismissed the possibility, a decision of the heart, for Maylene; but a decision that, he realized now, mattered very much to Allison as well.

Now, to Allison, James said, "I never suggested that she did." And softly, to Maylene, he added, "And I never would have."

"Thank you."

Maylene's voice was a whisper of relief, and of gratitude, to both James and Allison. James answered with a gentle smile, and Allison, smiling, too, admonished, "Don't be silly!" Then solemnly, wanting to close the door firmly—and forever—on even the slightest suggestion that Maylene might have been to blame, she said, "While I was showering, I thought about who might have done this."

"And?" James asked. "Do you have an idea?"

"Not specifically, no. But it's obvious that I took a picture I shouldn't have. Maybe I inadvertently caught a couple involved in an illicit affair, or maybe a criminal who was in hiding."

"You've told me that you always make a point of asking permission before photographing anyone."

"Yes, I do. But there was probably someone in the background, someone who wasn't really recognizable but believed they might have been. That's the only thing that makes sense, and it *does* make sense."

"Except that everything was destroyed. Not just one or two shots."

"Whoever did this was obviously very annoyed. He was making a point, teaching me a lesson. And now I've learned. In the future I'll be even more careful about people who might be in the background, and I'll keep extra copies of all the negatives in the vault downstairs." Allison stopped with a shiver. Something she had said caused a sudden change in James's eyes. All the gentleness had vanished, and what remained was so dark, so tormented . . . she shivered again. "I guess I'm still a little cold. Tea will help."

Maylene also saw the ominous change in the silver, and she remembered his ominous tone when he told her that he wanted to speak with Allison—privately. Maylene didn't want to leave. She, too, wanted private time with Allison, to explain again what Allison had overheard, to make very certain that Allison knew that she never would have done something so cruel.

But Maylene owed a great deal to the man who, from the very beginning, had had such faith in her—and who hadn't permitted that faith to shatter, even when he might have. And now she heard herself say, "I think I'll leave you two alone. But I'll be in my apartment all evening, Allison, so if you'd like help cleaning up . . ."

James walked Maylene to the door, and when he returned to the living room, he found Allison standing amid the devastation, seeing it anew and finally truly understanding the magnitude of what had been lost, the irreplaceable images of this unique summer during which the humid air had shimmered for months with unspilled tears.

Allison's own tears began to spill then, and a moment later she was curled in his arms, and even though she was wrapped in the thick layer of down, she felt his heat and his strength. James felt her warmth as well, her lovely softness, and as he pulled her even closer he felt the fluttering of her heart.

"Oh, Allison," he whispered, his lips softly caressing her freshly washed hair.

Allison had never heard such a whisper before, one filled with such raw longing, but her heart recognized it instantly, and when she looked up at him and saw pure desire glittering in his silver eyes, her lips trembled with joy as they waited to welcome him.

But James didn't kiss her. Before her eyes, the desire vanished, replaced by a torment that was even more raw than his longing had been, and when James spoke again, his voice was harsh.

"I want you to leave Hong Kong."

Allison wasn't certain what happened next, whether he released her or she backed away in shock. But, suddenly, they were apart.

"Leave Hong Kong, James?" Leave *you*?

"Whoever did this, whoever is responsible for this coldly calculated violence, is still out there. You must go, Allison. It's far too dangerous for you to stay."

"The danger's over! Every photograph is gone."

James didn't seem to hear her words and his eyes had become dark smoke.

"You have to go, Allison," he repeated quietly. Then, even more quietly, almost to himself, he said, "If anything ever happened to you . . ."

As Allison saw his anguish she experienced again the improbable impression that something was caging him. But what could imprison a man like James? True, his heart could be held captive by memories of the love he had lost. But that imprisonment would have been a gentle sadness—and what smoldered now in his fierce gray eyes looked like a savage rage.

It came to her then, the reason for his imprisonment, and she asked softly, "You blame yourself for Gweneth's accident, don't you? You blame yourself for not being able to save her."

"Yes." His voice was dangerously soft. "I blame myself."

"But you shouldn't, James. There was absolutely nothing—"

"Gweneth's death wasn't an accident, Allison. She was murdered. I was the intended victim, but she was the one who died."

"Oh, James." Allison whispered. "I had no idea. Neither Maylene nor Eve—"

"They don't know."

"The murderer hasn't been caught, has he?" she asked with sudden comprehension. The caged—and so ravenous—panther was hungry for revenge, starving for it, pacing with restless torment until the day that it was his. "You believe he's in Hong Kong, don't you? That's why you're here."

"Yes, Allison." The softness, but not the danger, was gone from his voice. It was stark now, and as empty as death. "That's why I'm here."

"Who is he, James? Do you know?"

The frustration Allison saw gave her the answer even before he spoke. "No. I don't know. I've assumed that he was a land developer, someone who felt threatened by the prospect of my moving to Hong Kong. I've spent the past four years trying to get him to show his face, but he's remained in hiding."

Allison tugged thoughtfully at her lower lip. "Maybe he isn't here."

"He's here," James said quietly, and with his solemn words he focused beyond her, on his prey, his expression eloquent, and so deadly, in its intent.

"Is that why you want me to leave, James?" Allison asked

softly of the faraway—and murderous—eyes. "Because you believe he might be the one responsible for destroying my photographs?"

Allison's soft question drew James back from his future vision of death, but it was still a few moments before he answered. Earlier, when he had walked into her apartment and seen the slashed remnants of her magnificent art, it felt as if the knife-sharp blade were carving into his own heart. And now, for the first time ever, James wondered if, on that night in Wales, Gweneth had been the intended target after all. By killing her, the murderer had killed him as well, in a way that was far more punishing than his own death would have been.

Was the monster coming out of the shadows at last, to harm yet again a woman he loved?

No, James decided. No one knew that he had fallen in love with Allison. It was a truth that he had tried very hard to keep hidden even from himself.

But it *was* the truth.

Finally, to the woman he loved, and to whom he must say good-bye, James answered, "My guess is that it's not him. But, Allison, it's still far too dangerous for you to stay."

"I'm not afraid, James."

It was then that James saw the breathtaking proof of Allison's courage. She wasn't frightened of the vandal, even if he was a murderer, but that was a trivial conquest of fear compared with the rest. She wasn't afraid of James himself, his icy heart, his fiery rage, his lethal hands.

"Oh, Allison," he whispered.

The emotion in his voice gave her hope. "I'm going to stay, James."

James had believed that no one in Hong Kong knew that he had fallen in love with Allison. But now he realized that it wasn't true. *She* knew. And now her glowing emerald eyes were bravely confessing her love for him, too, and they were sparkling with happiness as they envisioned all the joy that the two of them would share.

For a wondrous, indulgent moment James allowed himself to see the joyous future through her hopeful eyes. But, too swiftly, the image of love was engulfed in flames of death. And when he spoke again, all emotion had vanished from his voice.

"Mrs. Leong will arrange for you to be on tomorrow morning's eleven o'clock flight for San Francisco."

"I'm sorry, James," Allison countered with soft defiance. "But I have a very important appointment tomorrow morning at eleven. And, as soon as it's over, I'm going to start taking pictures again. This time I'll make copies of the negatives to keep in the vault downstairs."

"I'm not going to display your work in the Palace, Allison. All the morning papers will carry articles to that effect—that you are no longer involved with the hotel."

Or with you, her heart cried as she realized that even if she remained in Hong Kong, everything would be different. To protect her, on the off chance that the vandalism was in some way connected to him or his hotel, James was severing their professional relationship. And their personal one? The icy resolve in his mist-colored eyes told Allison with devastating clarity that that magic was over as well.

James stood before her, a towering monolith of granite and steel. His eyes were ice-cold, but, as always, an aura of heat shimmered around him. Allison now knew the source of that heat, the impassioned fires of rage that blazed within.

And if she reached for James now? Could she get beyond that invisible wall of flames?

No, she realized as she gazed at the harsh shadows of resolve in his handsome face. Not now. Not *yet*.

"You don't have to use any of my pictures, James. But you'll have them on December eleventh, just as we agreed. I'm going to honor the commitment I made to you, just as I will honor the commitment I made to my publisher."

His face was so hard, his eyes so dark, that Allison wondered if he had heard her.

But he had, because just before leaving to deliver the important address that had been all but forgotten, he said, very softly, "Please be careful."

After James left, Allison stared at what remained of her two months in Hong Kong: neatly carved slices of celluloid, nothing more.

No, that wasn't true. It might have been the case for the *old* Allison, the one who had been an observer only, the woman who, since childhood, had viewed the world from a vantage point of safe detachment. Her photography had merely made such distancing official. Oh, yes, her lenses were quite rose-colored, and she was a most interested and hopeful chronicler of the scenes she beheld; but for a very long time her photographs had been far more bright, more vivid and vibrant and bold, than Allison herself. They, not she, were proof of her passion—proof of *her*.

And now Allison's photographs of this extraordinary Hong Kong summer had been destroyed. But . . . but her magical memories lived still, vivid and vibrant and bold. And there was something else, the reason for which she had come to Hong Kong in the first place. Allison Parish Whitaker had found her wings.

True, the discovery had been made because of James, and the soaring had been so effortless because of him. And now that he was gone? Was the delicate butterfly going to come crashing to earth?

No, Allison vowed. It was a brave vow, but the new Allison was confident that it was a promise she would keep—because, she knew, much more had been unfurled this summer than her delicate wings. And those powerful emotions, awakened at last and fluttering now with such valiance, were demanding their chance to live . . . to fly.

James was gone, but she would soar still, a solitary flight, becoming stronger every day . . . until her wings were so strong, so invincible, that she could swoop through the invisible wall of flames. She would journey then to his heart, to the cage of fury in which it dwelled, and once there, she would find a way to transform that prison of rage into a cocoon of love.

Allison might have cleaned up the tiny remnants of her art, then spent the rest of the evening staring at the rain-blurred lights of Hong Kong as she reaffirmed her solemn promises to the fluttering emotions deep within. It seemed a night to be alone, to begin to find her solitary strength.

But Allison could not forget the expression in Maylene's eyes just before she left. She seemed so uncertain, and almost fearful, as if afraid that Allison might have lingering doubts about her innocence. Nor could Allison forget her own wish that she and Maylene become friends.

So Allison made a phone call, and when the tentative voice answered on the first ring, she greeted, "Maylene? It's Allison. Will you come help me?"

CHAPTER 22

Peak Castle
Friday, September 3, 1993

"I've just learned something rather distressing," Sir Geoffrey Lloyd-Ashton said to his wife shortly before leaving for the day. It wasn't yet eight, but he had been in his study since six, as always, drinking coffee as he scanned morning newspapers from around the world.

"Oh?" Eve asked, hiding her fear, praying that there hadn't been mention of a rainy rendezvous between a flamboyantly dressed mystery woman and Hong Kong's famous race-car driver turned shipping tycoon.

Whatever the item was, Geoffrey had discovered it in the *South China Daily Post.* He handed the pertinent page to Eve as he explained, "There was a break-in at the Trade Winds. Allison Whitaker's apartment."

"Oh, no. Was she there? Was she hurt?"

"She wasn't there, but apparently all her work was, including the negatives. Evidently, everything she's done in the past two months was destroyed."

"But why?"

"My guess is that she unwittingly took a picture she shouldn't have, a clandestine meeting between a triad member and a prominent banker, something like that."

"She must be devastated."

"I imagine she'll be leaving Hong Kong."

Eve frowned. "Really?"

"I should think James would insist on it. In fact, I think he already has. According to the article, James has decided not to use her photographs for the Jade Palace after all. Why don't you give her a call, Eve? To say good-bye."

"No, Eve, I'm not leaving! I know the article says that I'm no longer involved with the Jade Palace, but that's just James, being very cautious, in case the vandalism was done to protest the fact that a virtual stranger to Hong Kong has been chosen to take the photographs. I'm going to retrace my steps, making certain that I don't accidentally photograph anyone who doesn't want to be. This batch will be a little rainier, of course, but that will just add its own drama."

"So much work, Allison. You told me that, as it was, you would be working almost every day to make the December deadline."

"Now I'll just have to amend the *almost* to *absolutely*. But that's fine." Allison added cheerily, "I still plan to have time to meet you for lunch, Eve, and before I do anything else, I'm keeping this morning's appointment with Juliana Kwan."

One hour later two of Hong Kong's most powerful men were in closed-door meetings in their respective penthouse offices. The purpose of the two meetings was superficially the same: to hire experts in surveillance, specialists who would not lose track of their quarry even in the fast-paced crowds of Hong Kong.

Although being hired for essentially the same task, the experts in question had quite different credentials. Robert McLaren was an ex-cop, a detective who had been forced to retire from the Royal Hong Kong Police following a gunshot wound. He had a good pension, but liked to work, and was now making a comfortable living providing security to Hong Kong's elite.

The other man, John Wu, was a successful businessman. He'd become modestly wealthy through several lawful enterprises and vastly wealthy through a number of illegal ones. John Wu commanded a small army of criminals, all of whom were quite willing to do his bidding, whatever it happened to be, for a price. His soldiers were well paid, discreet, and absolutely loyal.

"Her name is Allison Whitaker," James told the man who had served ethically and honorably with the Royal Hong Kong Police.

Robert studied Allison's photograph on the dustcover of *Lone Star Serenade*. "When we spoke last night, you said you wanted her watched twenty-four hours a day seven days a week."

"That's right," James confirmed. "You have a team of people working for you, don't you?"

"Of course. Now, what kind of written reports do you want? By the minute? The hour?"

"I don't want any reports at all. I don't care what she does. I just want her to be safe."

"You believe she's still in danger?"

"I honestly don't know. If I had to guess, I suppose I'd say that what happened yesterday was an isolated incident. But since I can't be certain of that, I want to make sure she's protected at all times."

The instructions given to John Wu were quite different.

"She only needs to be followed on Mondays and Thursdays, but on those days I don't want her out of your sight, not for a second, and I want a detailed accounting of everything she does."

"No problem, Sir Geoffrey," John Wu assured, concealing his own smugness. This was truly easy money. Lady Lloyd-Ashton stuck out like a sore thumb. She couldn't hide even if she wanted to. He would give this assignment to his teenage nephews. It would teach them discipline and patience, because this was going to be extremely tedious. "Anything else?"

"Yes. I want to know immediately if she goes to the airport, and if she starts to board a plane, even a small one, I want her detained."

As she was dressing for her appointment with Juliana Kwan, Allison made a frightening discovery. The ivory silk gown with its shimmering rainbow sequins had also fallen prey to yesterday's intruder. A casual look into her closet, the kind the police undoubtedly had made, would not have revealed the destruction. The gown hung on its hanger still, and in its motionlessness looked quite intact. But when touched, as Allison did as she withdrew another dress, the truth was revealed: the ivory silk had been slashed as meticulously as her photographs had been, in thin, even, perfect strips—like shredded flesh.

Allison shivered, then swept her hands through the closet, searching for other victims. But there were none. The lovely gown of rainbows had been singled out.

But why? It made no sense. There seemed no possible connection between the Pearl Moon evening gown purchased in Dallas and the photographs taken in Hong Kong.

Then she had it: there *was* no connection. The spacious closet was simply where the vandal had hidden until the maid left, and while waiting, he had amused himself by making neat, silent slices through the silk. Allison shivered again, but at least the mystery was solved.

Or so she thought. . . .

In June, when Mrs. Leong had put her in touch with Susan Kwan of the Hong Kong Tourist Association, Allison had already known that Kwan was one of the most common surnames in Hong Kong. But still she had idly wondered if Susan and Maylene might be related. By September, Allison had encountered so many Kwans that when Eve told her that Pearl Moon's talented designer was named Juliana Kwan, the thought that Juliana might be related to Maylene did not even cross her mind.

But within moments of meeting Juliana, Allison was certain that she had just met Maylene's mother. It was a knowledge of the heart. It could be nothing else. Despite the extraordinary beauty of both mother and daughter, there was virtually no physical resemblance between them. Juliana's beauty was classically Chinese, subtle and serene, whereas Maylene's was absolutely unique, striking, sultry, sensational.

So how could Allison be so sure? Because of the way Juliana looked at *her*, with a mother's loving caress, as if it were Allison who was her long-lost daughter. The look was for Maylene, of course. Juliana was searching for her own daughter, uncertain how to go about it, yet hopeful that Allison could help.

Allison had spent her entire life missing her mother, and even though she knew that Juliana's gentle maternal gaze was for Maylene, not for her, she felt its wonderful embracing warmth nonetheless. The warmth enveloped her, a lovely cloak, while they discussed the gown that Juliana would make for her for New Year's Eve, and Allison was warmed, still, as she left the boutique.

But then, quite suddenly, she felt chilled. It had nothing whatsoever to do with the cool, wet wind that greeted her. This bitter-cold storm swirled within, and it came with thunder as turbulent memories from the past two days crashed together.

On Wednesday, Maylene had confessed to feeling so emotionally raw that she felt a compulsion to destroy. She had, after all, come very close to shredding two weeks of blueprints. That night, she had also spoken of the mother from whom she was irrevocably—and mysteriously—estranged.

On Thursday, all of Allison's photographs were meticulously destroyed, *shredded*, as was the romantic gown of rainbows designed by Juliana Kwan. And that evening, Allison had learned the bewildering truth that Maylene had opposed her selection as the photographer for the Jade Palace.

Was Maylene responsible after all? Had she willfully and with such coolly calculated violence destroyed both the photographs and the gown? It seemed impossible, but . . .

But if she had, it was because she was so desperately sad. And with reason: Maylene had been abandoned by her father, and she was estranged from her mother, and even though she wanted to approach her long-lost sister, Maylene was afraid, fearful of rejection yet again.

Maylene Kwan needed a friend, and Allison wanted to be that friend. I *am* that friend, Allison told herself. No matter what.

And, she thought, even though I may not be able to do anything about Maylene's father or sister, somehow I will find a way to reunite Maylene with the mother who obviously misses her so much.

"Good evening. I'm Cynthia Andrews. Welcome to *Newsmaker Interview*. My guest tonight is Juliana Kwan."

Maylene spun in the direction of the television. She'd been getting ready for bed, listening to the eleven o'clock news, and now, suddenly, here was the mother she had not seen for over nine years.

As Cynthia Andrews provided a brief biographical sketch of Juliana Kwan—Hong Kong native, renowned fashion designer, outspoken advocate for swift democratization of the territory—Maylene stared at the image on the screen.

She had forgotten her mother's delicacy. Juliana looked like a porcelain doll, fragile and proud, her back straight, her hands folded, her slender legs crossed demurely at her ankles. The suit she wore was dark blue, a creation that artfully blended understated elegance and daring style. Maylene owned the same suit in both lavender and flame. In London, where no one knew of their relationship and there was no chance that Juliana might hear of her daughter's foolish sentimentality, Maylene Kwan always wore Pearl Moon.

When Cynthia's introduction was finished, she turned from the camera to her guest. "Many of Hong Kong's most powerful businesspeople oppose Governor Patten's attempts to bring democracy to Hong Kong more quickly than what is prescribed in the Basic Law. You, however, feel that the governor's proposals aren't aggressive enough. Is that correct?"

"Yes, that's a correct representation of how I feel," Juliana replied, her voice soft, regal, gracious—and yet firm. "I'm not sure, though, about the accuracy of your assertion that many of Hong Kong's most powerful oppose the governor."

"Why don't I speak specifically then? Sir Geoffrey Lloyd-Ashton, indisputably the most powerful man in Hong Kong, is quite outspoken in his opposition."

"Yes, he is. But there are others, such as James Drake and Tyler Vaughn, who have been equally outspoken in their support."

"True," Cynthia conceded. "They've been labeled as idealists."

"But we *should* aspire for the ideal for Hong Kong and its future, shouldn't we?"

"Are you saying that those who stand in opposition to rapid democratization don't care about Hong Kong?"

"I'm saying that their reluctance to provoke Beijing is motivated by self-interest, not by a commitment to Hong Kong—because, in general, they are not permanent residents of Hong Kong. They are expatriates, or are in possession of full British passports, not merely second-class ones, and, as such, they are quite free to leave whenever they wish, to move their families and businesses elsewhere. Moreover, many already have substantial investments in China and will profit immensely if the relationship with Beijing remains friendly. Such people will survive without democracy, Miss Andrews, but Hong Kong itself cannot."

Cynthia Andrews was obviously delighted that her demure guest was so deliciously outspoken. Hoping for more dangerous revelations, she said, "The Basic Law provides for universal suffrage by the year 2007, as well as for the rule of law, freedom of the press, an independent judiciary, and one country with two systems. This is a solemn agreement made between Britain and China. Are you saying that you don't trust it?"

"I'm saying that the sooner we bring full democracy to Hong Kong, the safer it will be for everyone."

"I've heard that you're planning to run for a seat in the Legislative Council in the next election. Is that right?"

"That is my plan."

"Some have suggested that Beijing will not permit anyone who's been outspoken against the provisions of the Basic Law to serve on LegCo after the turnover in 1997. There's even been the suggestion that such people, like yourself, will be labeled counter-revolutionaries."

"And thrown into prison for their free speech? That doesn't sound like a government which respects democracy, does it?"

Cynthia Andrews didn't have to answer Juliana's question. The time allotted for the *Newsmaker Interview* was over. Turning her violet eyes back to the camera, she said, "I'm afraid that's all the time we have tonight. Next Friday I will be speaking with Sir Geoffrey Lloyd-Ashton, who, as has already been mentioned, holds an entirely different view from the one just expressed by Miss Kwan."

The television image of Juliana vanished, but Maylene saw

her mother still. She had forgotten her delicacy, and she had forgotten, too, her courage. The girl who had rescued herself from the sea was alive within Juliana still, clinging to lofty ideals as tenaciously as she had clung to the plank of *Pearl Moon* during the raging typhoon. Maylene wasn't surprised. The mother she had known, and loved, had always been a dreamer. Juliana had, after all, spun a sordid affair with a sailor into a magical tale of boundless love.

Long ago, because of her own immense pain, Maylene had mocked her mother's lovely romanticism. But now, astonishingly, Maylene found herself imagining a magical scenario of her own. In her mind's eye, she saw a family of freedom fighters—a mother, a father, and two sisters. They stood together, united by love, as they fought valiantly for democracy . . . for a future Hong Kong that glittered brightly still.

Fantasy! an inner voice screamed, shattering the glorious images of family—and of freedom—and leaving Maylene to face the splintered shards of what was real: she had been so cruel to her mother. Juliana must have been tremendously relieved when Maylene left Hong Kong. Just look at how much she had accomplished in the nine years without her spiteful daughter.

Maylene's heart swelled with pride for the brave orphan of the sea who had achieved so much—and then it contracted with fear. Juliana's outspoken commitment to democracy was admirable, courageous, but terribly dangerous. Tonight, in effect, in front of millions, Juliana Kwan had said that she didn't really trust the government of Beijing—the same government that, in less than four years, would be in control of Hong Kong . . . and that, already, was undoubtedly keeping track of its potentially rebellious future citizens.

Had Juliana no memory of Tiananmen Square?

"Oh, Mother," Maylene whispered softly. "Please be careful."

Allison didn't see the *Newsmaker Interview*. She spent the thirty minutes from 11:00 to 11:30 talking to her father. The Friday-night conversations weren't the only weekly ones that Allison had with her family in Dallas, but they were the only ones during which father and daughter could talk without the loving inter-ruptions—and loving concerns—of her grandparents.

Allison had approached tonight's call with apprehension. She wasn't going to lie to her father, of course. She was merely going to omit a few events of the past week, skipping over not only the *least* important one—the destruction of all her work—but the truly significant ones as well: James holding her, his eyes glittering with desire, before commanding that she leave Hong Kong; her bold defiance of that harsh command; the worry that the compli-cated woman with whom, perhaps, she was beginning to forge a friendship might have slashed the photographs and shredded the silken gown of rainbows; the confident belief that Maylene was Juliana Kwan's daughter.

Allison had worried that her voice might betray her by sounding either surprisingly hesitant or excessively cheerful, but what she heard was her own strength, her resolute conviction that, despite everything, Hong Kong was where she belonged.

There was hesitancy during the phone call, however, but it came from Dallas, not from Hong Kong. When Allison shared with her father her hope that she and the Jade Palace's gifted ar-chitect might possibly become friends, it took a few beats longer than Allison would have expected to hear him say that he hoped so, too; and when she told him about the romantic gown of jade silk that Juliana Kwan was designing for her to wear on New Year's Eve, there was yet another pause.

"It seems as if our voices are bouncing off a few extra satellites tonight," Allison observed finally.

Garrett heard her at once, but allowed a few seconds to elapse before saying, "I guess so."

"Well, then, I'll leave you with a question I *know* you'll want to delay answering. Have you given any more thought to coming to Hong Kong? Any time would be wonderful, of course, but once I've met my December eleventh deadline, I'll be much less busy."

Long after the call ended, Garrett was still at the desk in his study, replaying the conversation in his mind. Allison and Maylene were becoming friends. Allison and Juliana had met. Both revelations had caused a flood of emotion that had stalled his words. But what had almost drowned his heart was what Allison didn't say: that the architect who was becoming her friend and the designer who was creating her gown were mother and daughter.

Why didn't Allison know that? There was an obvious, painful answer: Maylene and Juliana were estranged. Something had severed the bond between the Daughter of Greatest Love and the woman he would love forever.

Garrett began the letter to Juliana then, although in truth he had been composing it in his heart since June. It was far easier to write in that gentle place of love than on the stark whiteness of paper. Even the greeting was difficult. The words he wanted to write—*My dearest Juliana, my darling love*—were hopelessly presumptuous.

For all he knew, Juliana was happily married. But that was what he wished for her, wasn't it? Happiness? And love? Yes, of course.

Dear Juliana, he decided, and then set about the impossible task of writing the rest. He wrote pages and pages of emotional words that he knew he could never send. He wrote of his love, his longing, and of his powerful belief that their lives were now fated to become entwined anew . . . as if destiny were rewarding them at last for their good behavior. Garrett couldn't send such emotional words. Nor were they necessary. The woman he loved would already know them all.

In the end, he wrote, simply:

Dear Juliana,

I promised you that I would never return to Hong Kong. But circumstances have changed now, haven't they? I would like to come in December, to see you on the tenth and surprise Allison with my visit the following day. But I can come whenever you want, Juliana, and I will do nothing without your permission. Please let me know.

Garrett

Garrett's letter, marked *Personal and Confidential*, arrived at the Pearl Moon boutique during Hong Kong's most beautiful celebration—Chung Chui, the Festival of the Moon. It was a time to worship the wonders of nature, and to give thanks for a bountiful autumnal harvest, and on that night, as if in homage to the moon, the dark clouds that had shrouded Hong Kong for the past week parted to reveal its full, golden splendor.

Thousands of paper lanterns adorned the territory. Brightly colored, the lanterns came in a myriad of shapes—butterflies, flowers, dragons, and fish. As the sun fell and the moon rose, parades of celebrants, each carrying a lighted lantern, descended on Hong Kong's beaches and parks.

Allison and Maylene were among those who journeyed to the beach at Stanley. They sat on the snow-white sand, amid elaborate sandcastles illuminated by candles, and searched for the images of Chang O and the Jade Rabbit in the moon above.

It was then, as their daughters marveled at the lustrous amber of the autumn moon, and shared the delicious sweetness of a mooncake, that Juliana began to write her reply.

She had read Garrett's letter a thousand times, sometimes

imagining an infinity of glorious words—of love and of wonder—between the lines; and then, on rereading, concluding that
the written words were all there were. Juliana wanted to send an
infinity of wondrous words in reply, but in the end her response
was as matter-of-fact as his. Indeed, it was even more busi-
nesslike, because the location she proposed for their luncheon
rendezvous was a favorite haunt of the world's most successful
entrepreneurs.

Dear Garrett,
   Yes, please come. I shall meet you at one o'clock on
December 10 at the Captain's Bar in the Mandarin Orien-
tal Hotel.

Juliana

PART SIX

CHAPTER 23

Drake Towers
Wednesday, October 27, 1993

"Your lady is really extraordinary."

James's inscrutable granite eyes studied Robert McLaren as he considered the ex-cop's statement. That Allison Whitaker was extraordinary was beyond dispute. But she was hardly *his* lady—despite the fact that he dreamed about her nightly.

Because of Allison, the images that drove James gasping from sleep had taken on new layers of terror. The fiery nightmare of Gweneth and their son was with him still, blazing hot and bright, but it had become even more tormented. Now, when he ran into the inferno, two flaming silhouettes awaited him, calling his name, pleading for his help . . . and for his love. By moving to save one, he was condemning the other to certain death, and by making no move at all, both beloved women would perish in the flames. James always awakened before making a choice, but the torment remained with him as his body spent the remainder of the night practicing its deadly moves against the faceless enemy who had destroyed so much.

There was the old nightmare, worse now, and since September there was a new nightmare as well. Allison was alone in the flames, her lovely face bewildered as she stared at the blood that flowed from her meticulously shredded flesh. The fire didn't prevent him from reaching her. He was able to enfold her in the safe haven of his arms as he urged her to let him take her to a hospital. But in response to his gentle urging, her head of golden flames would always shake no, splattering crimson drops of blood on him as it did. Then, in slow motion, she would raise one of her slender, blood-streaked arms and he would be blinded by the shining silver bracelet that promised death to her if anyone ever tried to give her blood.

James slept less than ever before, but sometimes he was rewarded with a dream, a floating vision of emerald eyes and flushed pink cheeks and beckoning lips. The dream of Allison drove him gasping from sleep as surely as his nightmares did, but with a different torment—the deep, intense aching of longing and of love.

Except in his dreams, James hadn't seen Allison since she had softly defied his harsh command that she leave Hong Kong. From both Robert McLaren and the security staff at the hotel, James knew that she was quite safe. Nothing worrisome had been detected at all. The Hong Kong police had reached the same conclusion that Allison had regarding the destruction in her apartment—an isolated act of vandalism—but James worried still. Today, although he and Robert had spoken often over the phone, he wanted to meet face-to-face to hear more details.

"I know she's extraordinary," James replied finally. "What makes you say so?"

"She's absolutely tireless. She leaves the hotel every day at dawn and doesn't return until nightfall. Quite frankly, my men and I are glad that with each passing day there's a little less daylight. When I was forced to retire because of the gunshot wound to my leg, I thought the decision was ridiculous. But after following Allison up every hill in Hong Kong, I've realized that my leg's not as good as new after all. Of course, she has some old injury as well."

"What do you mean?"

"By the end of the day, she's limping. It doesn't stop her, not for long anyway, although occasionally she'll stand very still, as if debating whether or not to go on. She always keeps going."

James remembered the brightness of her candlelit eyes when she told him what a soothing balm Hong Kong's tropical heat was for her creaky joints. The skies overhead were clear once again, but the steamy humidity was gone, and Allison was pushing herself even harder than before, reshooting the pictures that had been slashed and taking all the new ones she had planned. For her book? Yes, although that deadline was far away. The more immediate deadline was December 11, for the Jade Palace, a commitment she was going to honor despite what he had said.

James wanted to go to her, to hold her so tightly against him that the fires that burned within him enveloped her, warming her, easing the aching in her joints . . . and in her heart. That was what James Drake wanted for himself—and for her? He still wanted Allison to leave Hong Kong. Even if there was no longer any danger from some unknown vandal, there was the ever-increasing danger *from him*. With each passing day, it became ever harder for him to stay away.

But what did he have to offer lovely Allison? James demanded harshly of himself. His love, yes, and so much more: his nightmares . . . his rage . . . and his deadly enemy.

"Does she ever take time off?"

"Not much. She spends almost every evening in her apartment, presumably in the darkroom, because each morning before she leaves for the day, she delivers a new batch of negatives to the vault. She and Maylene Kwan get together once or twice a week, usually in the hotel, and beyond that she's had a few lunches with her other friends."

James had vowed not to spy on Allison, caring only that she was safe, but now, still searching for clues of lurking menace, he asked, "Her other friends?"

"Hong Kong's best—Lady Lloyd-Ashton and Juliana Kwan."

The muscles in James's jaw rippled in response to Juliana's name. He respected her immensely, of course, and during the past few months, as she had become even more outspoken, he had made a special point of publicly agreeing with every politically dangerous comment she made. By his wholehearted endorsement of Juliana's views, James hoped to share the burden with her. Indeed, he wished he could shift it entirely to himself, to assume all the risk. But of course he never could. He was British, and therefore immune from retribution. No matter how outspoken his words, because he was not Chinese, James Drake could never be considered a traitor to China.

But Juliana Kwan could.

"Juliana Kwan," he echoed softly.

Robert McLaren correctly interpreted James's concern. "I think Allison's relationship with Juliana has very little to do with politics. Juliana is Hong Kong's top designer, after all, as well as being its most courageous revolutionary. Yesterday Allison left the Pearl Moon boutique with a long garment bag—presumably a gown—and whenever she and Juliana meet for lunch, the conversation looks personal. I'm quite confident they're not rewriting the Basic Law."

"Is Juliana being followed?"

"Definitely not. Why would she be? She's hiding nothing. Both her beliefs and her willingness to express them are on the record. When Lady Lloyd-Ashton is present, however, we do have an extra pair of eyes, sometimes two extra pairs."

"Eve is being watched?"

"You bet. It's not surprising, is it? She's such an obvious target for kidnapping. Can you imagine the ransom? Sir Geoffrey would pay it, of course, but I think he's very wise to try to prevent anything from happening to his princess."

If they hadn't been his sister's sons, John Wu would have had his nephews killed. For almost six weeks they had lied to him, submitting detailed reports of the activities of Lady Lloyd-Ashton that were clever fictions at best.

John Wu's discovery of his nephews' lies was sheer luck. On October 8, as he was reviewing the week's summary before submitting it to Sir Geoffrey, his eyes fell on a three-hour lunch that Eve had allegedly spent with Juliana Kwan the day before. Juliana's name appeared frequently on the reports, as did Allison Whitaker's. Indeed, with occasional exceptions, it seemed that all Lady Lloyd-Ashton ever did was shop at Pearl Moon, work at the hospital, and dine with Allison or Juliana.

But hadn't there been an article in this morning's *Standard* regarding a luncheon address given yesterday by Juliana Kwan? Hadn't the fashion designer–turned-revolutionary been expressing her views to a group of bankers at the Plume, not dining with the Princess of Peak Castle at Au Trou Normand?

John Wu found the article and confronted his nephews, who promptly confessed all. There were days, they admitted, at least once a week, when Lady Lloyd-Ashton simply vanished. She would go into the hospital or Pearl Moon and never come out. Frantic, they would spend the afternoon at the tram station on Garden Road, praying she would reappear, and when she did, they would follow her home, clocking the precise moment that she returned to the castle. Then they would create scenarios for the unwitnessed hours based on what she had done on the few afternoons when they hadn't lost her.

John Wu's nephews were lucky he hadn't killed them, and he himself was lucky to have discovered the fraud before Sir Geoffrey did, and it was the greatest luck of all that wherever Lady Lloyd-Ashton had vanished to, it wasn't, apparently, the airport.

She had never truly vanished, John Wu decided. His nephews were merely lazy and careless. But when he put his best men on the task, Lady Lloyd-Ashton eluded them as well, and for the weeks of October 11 and 18, John Wu himself was forced to create fictional luncheons with Allison and Juliana as well. Finally, on Monday the twenty-fifth, his men tracked the disguised princess to a condominium building in the Mid Levels where she was greeted by Tyler Vaughn.

John Wu's relief was instantly overshadowed by what lay ahead: revealing to Hong Kong's most powerful taipan what appeared to be his cherished wife's clandestine affair.

"There must be a problem," Sir Geoffrey Lloyd-Ashton said as he greeted John Wu. "Your reports usually come to me by courier. Or are you here to demand more money because the task of keeping track of my wife is so difficult?"

"We found something."

"Tell me." Geoffrey's casualness was very far from the churning impatience he felt. "Would you like a drink, John?"

"No. Thank you."

"All right. Go ahead, then. Tell me."

John Wu used more words than he needed to, as if somehow the excess verbiage would cushion the shock and attenuate the taipan's rage. He recounted first the normal events of Monday morning: Lady Lloyd-Ashton's arrival, on time, at the hospital and the four hours she spent there with the children on Ward Three. Then, as if it were normal, he described her disappearance into the ladies' room in the hospital lobby and her emergence moments later lavishly disguised. He gave vivid details of her vivid outfit and with matching thoroughness chronicled her journey from Wanchai to the Mid Levels: from Causeway Bay to Central on the MTR, disembarking at Pedder Street, then on foot from Wyndham to Glenealy to Upper Albert to . . .

The excessive description gave Geoffrey the opportunity to anticipate what was coming and to reflect that it hadn't just started two days before. Since having Eve followed, he had made a habit of asking about her days away from the castle. Only twice had she mentioned lunching with Allison, and although she described weekly visits to Pearl Moon, she recounted dining with Juliana just once. Geoffrey had reconciled the discrepancies between Eve's words and John Wu's reports by assuming that it was Eve who had lied, hiding from him her friendship with both women—especially the American pilot. But now, as Geoffrey saw clearly where John Wu's meandering words were leading, he realized it was the reports that had been false.

By the time he learned the name of the man for whom his wife had gone through such an elaborate charade, Sir Geoffrey Lloyd-Ashton was in complete control. In fact, he was smiling.

"Well, old chap, it's about time." His grin became sheepish. "I'm afraid you've been the unwitting victim of a wager between a husband and wife."

"A wager?"

"My princess may not be Chinese, but she loves to gamble. She bet me that she could become invisible in Hong Kong, that even if I hired the best people to follow her, she could elude detection. I didn't believe it was possible, of course, not even one time, but I decided to humor her. She did very well, didn't she?"

"Very well," John Wu murmured, confirming what Geoffrey had already guessed, that although Eve's affair had been discovered on Monday, it had clearly been going on all this time.

Geoffrey laughed. "She's had a grand time. She's been to the airport twice, and not a soul noticed her at the Temple of Ten Thousand Buddhas, and this isn't even the first time that Tyler's been in on the joke. Don't worry, my friend! Your secret is safe with me. Your men are still the best in Hong Kong. I won't tell a soul that my pampered princess tricked them. I will, however, have to buy her a particular diamond-and-emerald necklace she's been wanting." Geoffrey waved a dismissive hand. "Well, why not? She's earned it."

"You certainly don't have to pay me, Sir Geoffrey."

"Nonsense!" With that Geoffrey withdrew his checkbook and wrote an extravagant check. As he handed it over he said, "Thank you, John. This adventure was really very important to Lady Lloyd-Ashton, and therefore to me. She's spoiled, but who wouldn't spoil her? Now, if you'll excuse me, I need to call my mistress of disguise to tell her the jig is up—and that I'm on my way to the castle with her necklace."

As soon as John Wu was gone, all vestiges of humor left Geoffrey's face. He unlocked the armoire, pressed the buttons that caused the silent search of his silent home, and finally found her. She was at the window, looking down at the rooftops of the high-rise buildings below.

Was she staring at the condominium where she met Tyler Vaughn? Geoffrey wondered. That place of sin where she committed her unforgivable acts of betrayal?

What a mistake you have made, my princess.

The first authentic smile of the afternoon touched Geoffrey's face. He would take such pleasure in her pain. With a little careful planning, he would find a way for Eve to watch Tyler die. Better yet—so *much* better—he would have Eve's pale, thin fingers pull the trigger that launched the bullet into her lover's heart.

The image filled Geoffrey with intense desire. Soon, very soon, he would return to Peak Castle, startling Eve from her traitorous reverie and then ravaging her with such passion that she would not begin to suspect that he knew the truth.

It was too bad, Geoffrey mused, that Eve would have to die. It would have been most amusing to watch her suffer after Tyler's death. He had learned, quite by accident, how very entertaining such grief could be.

But Eve was going to die. She would simply have to do her suffering in advance. Well, that was easy. There was still plenty of time to savor her pain. Geoffrey was confident that his hopelessly compassionate wife would never break the promise she had made to the little Chinese girl. Always before he had privately felt contempt for such compassion.

But now it made him smile.

Because of Lily Kai's damaged heart, he had at least six weeks in which to inflict damage on his unfaithful wife. Six glorious weeks of torture and torment. And if he did it right, despite her anguish, Eve would hold on to the glimmer of hope—the fantasy of escape—until the very end.

And Geoffrey would do it right. This time.

You will pay for disloyalty, my princess . . . my rose.

How you will pay.

CHAPTER 24

Trade Winds Hotel
Wednesday, October 27, 1993

"**Y**ou're limping!"

Allison smiled at Maylene. "Nothing that a little rest won't cure." She gestured to the couch in her living room where they would sit, talk, and eat the dinner that room service would provide. "I plan to be a couch potato all evening."

"Beginning when?" Maylene teased as Allison limped right past the couch toward the kitchen.

"We need tea, don't we?"

"I'll make it. Sit."

"In a minute. There's something I want to show you first—in my bedroom."

Maylene would have cast a glance of fond exasperation at her sister had Allison's expression not suddenly become so serious.

"Why don't I go get whatever it is?"

"No," Allison replied firmly. "Let's go together."

With that she turned and led the way, trying not to limp yet limping nonetheless—a faltering gait that was trivial compared with the stumbling uneasiness of her heart.

The evening gown was on the bed, where Allison had laid it in anticipation of this monumental moment. An exquisite creation of jade silk, its slender bodice was adorned with emerald-and-silver beaded butterflies and its flowing skirt was dotted with more silver beads, tiny sparkles that glittered like stars in a jade-green sky.

"Do you remember the gown I wore to the party at Peak Castle?" Allison asked softly, praying that Maylene wouldn't glance furtively toward the closet where the gown of rainbows had been shredded. *And she didn't.* Maylene merely nodded, her solemn eyes never leaving the gown that lay on the bed. "It was made by a Hong Kong designer, and over the past two months she's made this for me as well, to wear for the grand opening of the Jade Palace."

Maylene's mind swirled. Had her mother approached Allison? Had Juliana been so eager to meet the beloved daughter of the man she loved that she had somehow orchestrated a chance meeting? Speaking to an emerald-and-silver butterfly delicately embroidered on silk, she asked, "How did that happen?"

"Eve arranged it for me. What about you, Maylene? Have you decided what you're going to wear that night?"

"Black satin," Maylene murmured. "Chanel."

"I'm sure that would be stunning, but why don't you ask Pearl Moon's designer to make something for you instead? There's still time, and it would be nice, wouldn't it, to wear something designed in Hong Kong, and I know she'd be delighted." Maylene looked up then, and her expression confirmed what Allison had long since guessed. "Juliana Kwan is your mother, isn't she?"

"Did she tell you?"

Allison wanted to lie. Maylene suddenly seemed so hopeful.

But she answered truthfully. "Not in words, no. But from the moment we met, I knew. It seemed as if she was searching for you, trying to get to you through me. I know you said that the two of you are estranged, and that it's best for both of you, but I guess I don't agree. Don't you want to see her again, Maylene? I know she wants to see you."

"You *don't* know that, Allison," Maylene countered swiftly. "You said she's never admitted our relationship."

"But I do know, Maylene. She's always so interested when I mention your name. I thought, maybe, we could have tea together, the three of us—or better yet, just you two. A leisurely tea . . . at the Peninsula . . . wouldn't that be nice?"

Allison's emerald eyes shimmered as she envisioned the mother–daughter reunion, so blissfully oblivious to the devastating truth of what had happened twenty-eight years before at the stately hotel.

Maylene left her sister's shimmering green eyes, and as she gazed down at the shimmering green gown made by her mother, her hand moved to gently touch a sparkle of silver. After a moment Allison followed suit, touching another, more distant bead . . . and as the sisters talked, their hands grew ever closer, journeying from star to star across the silken jade-green sky.

"You have time for afternoon tea now, don't you?" Allison asked softly. "I dropped by the construction site yesterday and Sam seemed so pleased. The illusion is going to work beautifully—*perfectly.*"

"It's *probably* going to work. We won't know for sure until the netting is removed."

"But still, you definitely have time for tea. Your mother's wonderful, Maylene. You're so lucky."

Lucky. Maylene's hand froze on a sparkling bead. In truth, she had never felt luckier. Over the past two months she had shared a magical friendship with Allison . . . and there had been an entirely different kind of magic during the long hours spent working with Sam.

Maylene felt so very lucky . . . and because she believed herself to be undeserving of such good fortune, she also felt so very precarious.

"You *are* going to see your mother, aren't you? Sometime?"

"I don't know, Allison. I've thought, maybe, when the Jade Palace is finished—and successful—I would see her."

"Oh, Maylene," Allison whispered. "She doesn't care about that. You don't have to prove yourself to your mother."

Maylene shrugged. "I guess I feel that I do. The things I said to her were very cruel . . . unforgivably cruel."

"Whatever they were, Maylene, I know she'll forgive you. In fact, I'm sure she already has." Allison hesitated, frowning thoughtfully, then murmured, "I wonder . . ."

Maylene looked up then, from the hand that had frozen on a silver star to her sister's uncertain—and yet shining—emerald eyes.

"What do you wonder, Allison?" *Do you wonder, since I have no relationship with my wonderful mother, and since you long ago lost your own, if Juliana could be your mother? If so, the answer is yes. Yes! It's what she wants, has always wanted . . . a daughter who is loved and cherished by Garrett Whitaker.* "Tell me."

It was a command, harsh and anguished, and the sudden torment in Maylene's voice was mirrored in her beautiful eyes. Over the past two months such jade-green storms had appeared less and less frequently, but had not entirely gone away, and when they came, Allison had learned to weather them with silence. And now?

Now, Allison decided, I am going to tell Maylene what I was wondering—despite the fact that it's presumptuous, as if we were the very best of friends, as if we were truly free to speak such personal words to one another. . . .

The journey of Allison's fingers across the jade-green silk stalled then, five sparkling silver stars away from Maylene, and that was as far as the journey of hands would go tonight. But with Allison's bold and gentle words, the hearts of the sisters journeyed ever closer.

"I wonder, Maylene, if it's you who needs to forgive yourself."

"Good morning, my love." Geoffrey's deep voice was wrapped with tenderness as he greeted his awakening wife.

Eve lay naked and ravaged in their satin-sheeted bed. Geoffrey, fully dressed, loomed over her. The world outside their bedroom was charcoal gray, the pale rays of the autumn dawn just beginning to mingle with the blackness of night.

It had been the blackest of nights at Dragon's Eyes. Geoffrey had wanted. And he had taken. His desire for Eve had never been darker, his passion for her never more intense. He had apologized for his insatiable need, and for his careless neglect of her over the past few months.

There was apology now, still, as he spoke. "You look exhausted, my darling. Why don't you stay here today? In the castle—and in bed. Don't worry, I won't surprise you this afternoon. But be warned, Eve. You'll need your rest. Now that I've discovered you again, my princess, I can't get enough of you." His smile was tender, his eyes dark with desire. "You don't have anything important scheduled for today, do you?"

"An appointment at Pearl Moon." *An entire day of love with Tyler.*

"Well, you can easily cancel that. At the moment I couldn't care less if you ever dressed again." He leaned over then, his hand dipping beneath the satin sheet to cup a breast as his mouth claimed lips that were swollen still from his harsh possession. Then, with a promise that felt to Eve like an ominous warning, he whispered, "I'll see you tonight."

Eve had assumed that eventually Geoffrey would want her again. It was for that reason that she had long since stopped taking aspirin for her headaches. The medicine caused her delicate flesh to bruise too easily, and she knew from experience that even if

Geoffrey took her between satin sheets, his brutal passion always left marks. She wanted the lingering symbols of his fierce desire to be small and readily explainable: a minor stumble in the garden, perhaps, or the clumsy snagging of a high heel in plush carpet— nothing that would alert Tyler to the truth about her marriage.

But now, even without aspirin, the bruises from last night's "love" were larger than ever before, huge red and purple blotches on her snow-white skin. It would be a very long time before these bruises disappeared, a time during which she dared not make love with Tyler.

Eve's body ached from all the places where it had been crushed, but those were tiny hurts, inconsequential ones compared with the screams of her heart. In September, her heart and body had been joyfully reunited, and since then she had learned to feel and trust and give and love. But now she was torn apart again, severed perhaps beyond repair, and the dream that was only six weeks away seemed impossible.

Leave today, *now*, her ravaged body pleaded. You think you're too weak to walk down Mount Austin Road, but you're not. Besides, Tyler will come get you, and he'll drive you to Lily Kai's home, and you'll gently explain to the little girl that, astonishingly, she was right: that somehow, as long ago as June, she had known that you would not be in Hong Kong in December. You'll tell her that she'll do just fine without you, her surgery will be a stunning success, and that even though you won't be with her on that all-important day, your heart will be . . . it will float to her from wherever you are.

Lily will survive, you know she will, *she has to*—but you may not, unless you leave *now*.

But I *will* survive, Eve vowed bravely. I will keep my promise to Lily . . . and after her surgery Tyler and I will sail into our dream.

It felt so strange to phone Tyler from the castle. Eve rarely made personal calls from the place that was supposed to be her home. Peak Castle was Geoffrey's, not hers, and even when she was alone, she never felt comfortable. Indeed, sometimes, she felt as if she were being watched—which, she supposed, in a way she was. At any moment a cook or housekeeper might suddenly appear. Their schedules seemed random, without predictability of any kind, as if Geoffrey wanted her always to be on guard, always fearful of doing anything that might be seen or overheard.

"I won't be able to see you today," she told Tyler, cringing at the flatness of her voice. She was canceling their day of love in the same polite, matter-of-fact tone with which she would cancel an appointment.

"What's wrong, Eve?"

"Nothing. I have the flu, that's all."

"Then let me take care of you. I'll come get you, and tuck you into our bed, and make soup for you, and—"

"No," she interjected. Then, softly, she added, "Thank you. I need to be here. Geoffrey knows that I'm ill and will probably be calling to check on me. I have to go now. I think I hear the cook."

"I love you."

"I . . . me, too."

CHAPTER 25

The Jade Palace
Friday, October 29, 1993

The bamboo scaffolding and emerald netting that cloaked the Jade Palace would not be removed until early December. Only then would Hong Kong know whether James Drake's most ambitious project was glittering treasure or glaring folly.

But Sam Coulter knew now. Just as he had been able to see the building before the ground was ever broken, he could make invisible the green-and-bamboo cloak—and what he saw was even more magnificent than he had dared to dream.

But the magnificent dream paled by comparison with what he saw when he entered the trailer that Friday afternoon: his cowgirl, with her jeans and boots and long black braid, gazing out the window, her lovely face glowing with happiness.

Maylene didn't hear him come in, nor did she sense his stealthy approach.

"We did it," he said softly when he stood very close.

She spun, met his smiling dark blue eyes, and asked, "You think so?"

"I know so. Don't you?"

Her face glowed still, but she shrugged. "I guess I won't be absolutely certain until it's unwrapped."

"Well, I'm absolutely certain now. Which is why I think it's time to start celebrating." His expression became serious, intense and intimate, and when her beautiful eyes shimmered bravely with welcome, he gently moved from beside the luminous jade a renegade strand of black silk that had escaped during her wind-tossed ferry ride across Victoria Harbour. "I've wanted to do that for a very long time."

"Move my hair away from my eyes?" Maylene asked, breathless now and trembling deep inside from the exquisite tenderness of his caress.

"Touch you," Sam clarified softly. Clarifying further, he kissed the place where the midnight silk had been, and after a lingering journey of kisses brought him to where he had put it, behind her ear, he whispered, "And kiss you."

"I've wanted you to."

Even as his lips were making wondrous discoveries of the fragrant satin of her graceful neck, Sam somehow forced his mind to make swift calculations. He would leave the site shortly after ten. Twenty-five minutes later he would reach his apartment at the Trade Winds, where he would shower and change, so . . .

"Invite me to your apartment, Jade, at about eleven-fifteen tonight."

Maylene stiffened in response to his words, and when Sam looked at her eyes, he saw dark shadows of worry amid the brilliant desire.

"Invite me to *your* apartment, Cowboy."

That wasn't how Sam Coulter played, not ever. He always went to the woman's home. That way he could leave precisely when he chose, long before demands were made of his heart.

Now Maylene was asking him to change his absolute rule, to

play by some shadowy dictum of her own. Sam wanted no rules with her, no games, no playing at all.

"Okay, Jade," he said softly. "You're invited."

It might have taken Maylene forever to decide what to wear, but early in the debate a voice within hissed a mocking reminder. It doesn't *matter* what you wear! It's not your clothes he's interested in. Choose something that's easy to get off—and even easier to put back on. No tiny buttons to slow you down after it's over. You'll want to escape very quickly from the deafening silence of his disappointment.

But, her heart whispered, maybe he won't be disappointed.

Excuse me? Where have you been all your adult life? You're as sexy as ice, remember?

Yes, but when Sam touched me I felt warm, wonderful—

That's because *he* is so sexy—which is all the more reason that he's going to be terribly disappointed when he discovers the truth about *you.*

"I brought champagne," she said when Sam opened his apartment door to her at precisely 11:15. "I know you don't drink much."

"I don't drink at all," Sam amended quietly. He took the champagne bottle from her hands, waited until her eyes met his, and added softly, "And you don't need this—not tonight."

Then, because she didn't quite seem to believe that, Sam set the champagne bottle down, freeing both of his talented hands for her. Gently cupping her face, he repeated, "Not tonight."

At his touch, the magical dance of desire began anew, as if not a second had passed, much less hours. The warm, wonderful sensations deep inside her responded instantly—and with such joy—to his gentle caresses, twirling, leaping, without the slightest falter.

Sam kissed her eyelids, her temples, her cheeks, savoring places that other men had never even sampled. Whereas others had wanted only the sultry promise of her lush lips, Sam Coulter seemed to want everything, every tiny patch of her silken flesh. It was as if he was trying to learn all there was to know about her, as if he actually cared, and there was even more: his tenderness seeming to be telling her that he would cherish every discovery, every secret, no matter how shameful it was.

The ice within her was long gone, melted by the dancing fires ignited by him. But still, just moments before his mouth greeted hers for the first time, she shivered.

"What are you afraid of?" Sam asked softly when he found her eyes and saw shadows of fear amid the brilliant jade-green desire.

"Nothing." *Everything.* But at the moment what Maylene feared most was that she would lose this chance, perhaps the only one she would ever have, to feel what it was like to be loved. Sam's desire for all of her, not just her provocative body, was merely an illusion. She *knew* that. But still she could pretend, couldn't she? Just for a while, just long enough to permit herself this most daring dance, this most magnificent pas de deux?

Sam saw the urgency of her desire and was acutely aware of the immense power of his own. He had wanted her so much, and for so long, but he wanted their intimate discovery of each other to be lingering, careful, leisurely—an unshatterable foundation upon which they would build and build.

"Are we in a hurry?"

"Yes."

She seemed so worried, as if the magic might suddenly vanish, and even though Sam knew it wasn't true, he took her hand and led her to his bedroom.

As Sam moved to turn on the bedroom light, Maylene whispered, "No."

A ripple of worry shot through him. She wanted their loving to be in darkness, and that was what he had always preferred—before, when sex had been for pleasure not for love.

But tonight was different.

"I want to see you when I make love to you, Jade."

"No, Cowboy."

Her voice was soft, laced with regret and with such fear that once again Sam acceded to her request.

Maylene's wish to hurry was born of pure fear, and Sam's was born of pure desire, but still he did not rush. He possessed a confidence that Maylene lacked—the absolute certainty that their loving was a magnificent reality not a fragile mirage.

He undressed her slowly, kissing each shadowed discovery, learning all that could be learned without his eyes. Maylene had blinded him as surely as Sir Geoffrey Lloyd-Ashton had blinded Hong Kong's most revered dragon, but the midnight darkness merely made Sam's remaining senses all the more acute. She was made of fragrant, intoxicating, trembling satin; and for many moments the only sounds he heard were the soft astonished sighs of her desire; and then with a surprised and breathless whisper, he heard her ask, "What are you doing?"

Loving you. "Unbraiding your hair. What are you doing?"

"Undressing you."

When her hands reached for the buttons of his shirt, Sam realized with a rush of tenderness that she wasn't an expert at this at all . . . and the surprising uncertainty of her light eager touch made him want her all the more—to love her, protect her, cherish her.

As the brave yet awkward caresses of her delicate fingers conspired to further fuel his desire and undermine his control, Sam stopped fighting at last. This first time they would make love with

335

all the urgency they both felt, and next time, or perhaps the time after that, they would go more slowly.

Maylene's desire was as powerful as his, as bold, as demanding, as brave. And yet, in that astonishing moment when they became one, even their breathless desire held its breath in reverent wonder as they were joined in this, the most magnificent creation of all.

Sam searched for her eyes in the shadows, wanting to see in the luminous jade a joy that surely mirrored his own, but the darkness was impenetrable. He found her eyes with his lips instead, tenderly caressing the corners when they were open and the lids when they fluttered closed. And even when the fires of their passion compelled them to resume their dance of love, and even as the flames exploded into glittering shards of gold, Sam kissed, still, the jade-green eyes that he could not see.

His arms cradled her, gentle and strong, and her head lay softly on his chest, and she could hear his heart thundering still from the power of their passion.

But there was another thunder, deep within her. It had been muted into stunned silence during their joyous loving—but was silent no more.

You really fooled him! the voice proclaimed. At least he *seemed* to enjoy himself. Don't forget, he's been working nonstop for four months. That's a lot of abstinence for a man as sexy as Sam Coulter. *Any* woman would have done quite nicely. Even you couldn't disappoint.

But he's done with you now. And even though for you it was more wondrous than you'd ever imagined, when he reflects on it, he'll undoubtedly remember all the mistakes you made, how awkward you were, how trembling and uncertain . . . and yet how unashamed—and desperate—in your need.

Hear his heart? It's slowing already, far more quickly than yours. Unlike you, he's obviously quite accustomed to this sort of passion. It's routine for him, a preferred form of exercise. Very soon his well-conditioned lover's heart will be beating at its normal pace, as slow and leisurely as a Texas drawl. He'll let go of you then, and he'll probably roll away for a cigarette. Oh, you thought he'd really given them up? For *you*? Forever? Have no doubt, he'll light up tonight. He's had you now. The seduction is over.

Any second you'll feel him pull away, like every man before him always has. If you were in *your* apartment, he would leave. But that's why you're here, remember? So you can make the first move. You'd better hurry, though. His heartbeat is getting slower, ever slower.

She didn't want to pull away! She wanted to spend the rest of her life exactly like this, cradled in his arms, pretending that the tenderness of his caresses had been a manifestation of love not merely expertise. But she'd already indulged in enough fantasy tonight. She must leave the sanctuary of his arms *now*, before he let her go. It was her only hope of preserving the illusion that it had been for him, as it had been for her, a rare and wondrous dance of love, not merely a routine union of lust.

The moment Sam sensed Maylene's move for freedom, he released her. He had been holding her far too tightly, he knew. He had wanted her to be as close to him as she could possibly be, but his strong yet gentle grasp had undoubtedly impeded the lungs that were still recovering from their breathless loving.

Sam expected her to breathe, stretch, and then return to his arms. They would then entwine more loosely, and whisper between kisses . . . until, again, they needed desperately to be one.

But Maylene was getting out of bed, and in the darkness that had so recently hummed with soft sighs of desire, Sam heard the sounds of her getting dressed.

Then there was a new sound, his own voice, and from it

came a question that he had heard many times but had never asked. Always before, it had been asked *of* him, by a lover, as he was making his swift—but never this swift—escape. "Are you leaving?"

"Yes."

Please stay. The plea formed in Sam's mind but never journeyed to his lips. Maylene wanted to leave now, just as, in the past, he had always wanted to. Like him, until now, she had merely wanted pleasure, nothing more—and now she was restless for privacy, for solitude, for escape.

Had the women whose beds he had left so precipitously felt such fury? Sam wondered. He had never pretended to offer more than passion, of course. But, he realized, neither had Maylene. Indeed, from her insistence that they meet in his apartment to her request that their loving be in absolute darkness, she had behaved precisely as he usually did.

Now, quite obviously—quite urgently—she wanted to leave. She was, it seemed, far more eager to put distance between the act of sex and the emotions of intimacy than he ever had been.

Maylene clearly wanted no more from him than pleasure, breathless loving without love, explicit intimacy without affection, fiercely demanding desire without the gentler demands of the heart.

Sam had been looking for such a passionate—and dispassionate—lover all his life.

At last he had found her.

But as Maylene vanished into the darkness Sam couldn't imagine touching her ever again.

R*ecidivism.* Maylene remembered the sexy gleam in his indigo eyes when he confessed that it was a mighty big word for a cowboy. He had been seducing her then, luring her ever closer to his bed.

And now she had been there, and he had allowed her to leave without even a good-bye, and now the memory was so drenched in pain, the fragile illusion so irreparably shattered, that she wished the night of pretending to be loved had never happened at all.

Maylene Kwan had relapsed completely—a total surrender to recidivism. Every self-destructive urge she possessed was on full alert, searching for ways to punish herself even further for her foolishness.

She did not need to go to the Jade Palace construction site, not today, not ever. The on-site decisions between builder and architect were now a thing of the past. Indeed, she realized miserably, Sam had precisely timed his ultimate seduction so that, if they chose, their paths need never cross again. His involvement with the hotel would be completed within days of its early-December unveiling, several weeks before the grand opening. What remained to be done after that would be cosmetic, not structural, and was already in the capable hands of the same designer who had been responsible for the Trade Winds's elegant decor.

It seemed unlikely that Sam would even stay for the grand opening. He had more buildings to build, more challenges to meet, more women to seduce. In six weeks he would be gone. Between now and then Maylene could send the final blueprints for the hotel's lavish interior to him by courier.

But on the Monday following their brief union of passion, Maylene went to the site anyway. She dressed as she had before the seduction began: in a silk suit by Dior with matching stiletto heels, her lustrous black hair pulled into a tight knot atop her head.

Sam was standing in front of the Palace's main entrance, talking to Chan Peng, when Maylene arrived. He was facing away from her, but he turned, sensing her presence despite the vast expanse of the white marble drive. Maylene felt his eyes follow her to the trailer and knew that he would join her there when he'd finished speaking with Peng.

It didn't take long, and then he was there, and there seemed to be a flicker of worry when he first saw her. It vanished quickly, though, replaced by a mocking glint as his insolent gaze slowly appraised her attire.

"I see you're not planning to climb up on any beams with me today."

I will if you want me to! the cry came from her heart, from a foolish place that clung, still, to the hope of love. Maylene crushed the foolishness swiftly—or so she thought. It bounced back almost immediately, reminding her of another lost love, and as if she'd actually had the courage to agree to Allison's plan for a mother–daughter reunion, she lied, "I'm meeting someone for tea at the Peninsula. I'm a little early, so . . ."

"So you thought you'd drop by to ask me how my weekend was?"

Maylene lifted her chin in proud defiance as she met his contemptuous blue eyes. "Yes."

"Well, let's see. It actually began quite promisingly. But, unfortunately, it deteriorated rather rapidly to disappointment. How was your weekend, Maylene? Completely satisfying? Everything you dreamed it could be?"

Sam was disappointed, just as she had known he would be. Even though his heart had thundered with passion, he had not even been satisfied by her. Somehow, proudly still, she answered, "It was fine."

"All that you wanted?"

"Did you want more?"

"Sure." His lazy cowboy smile was seductive now—and predatory. "I wasn't through with you, not by a long shot."

What did that mean? That he wanted to see her again? To touch her and kiss her and give her another chance despite how disappointing she'd been? And if that *was* what Sam wanted, would she agree?

Of course she would. Every self-destructive cell in her body was still searching for more ways to be hurt . . . and there was that tiny, hopeful place in her heart that was still looking for love.

"Did you want to get together again, Cowboy?"

Her voice was as vulnerable as her eyes. Proof positive, Sam mused, of her gifts as an actress *and* her impeccable insight into him. She must have realized that her abrupt departure from his bed had annoyed him immensely, and now, because she wanted more pleasure from him, here she was, trying to bewitch, quite aware that he was far more enchanted by her in the role of uncertain courtesan than confident seductress.

She was very good. Sam had to give her that. As he moved toward her she even managed to cast shadows of pain in the already vulnerable jade.

As Maylene Kwan had left his bed Sam Coulter couldn't imagine ever touching her again. But now he couldn't resist. Cupping her lovely face, he caressed her gently with his eyes until he saw uncertain hope and shimmering desire.

It was then, when her beautiful eyes so eloquently confessed that she wanted more breathless yet dispassionate passion, that Sam said, very softly, "No, Jade. I don't want to get together again."

PART SEVEN

CHAPTER 26

The Jade Palace
Monday, December 6, 1993

The crew at the Jade Palace worked throughout the night, removing the cloak of bamboo and mesh, and when the first pale yellow rays of winter dawn stretched across Victoria Harbour, there it was, completely revealed, a shimmering jewel in the soft golden light.

On that glorious Monday, time stood still. The relentless pace dictated by the uncertainties of Hong Kong's future was forgotten. The financiers in Central left their billion-dollar deals to join the throngs on Blake Pier. Some played hooky even longer, riding a Star ferry across to Kowloon for a closer look. Word traveled swiftly throughout the territory, and even though the hotel would stand forever—and its grand opening was still three and a half weeks away—everyone wanted to see the remarkable work of art *now*.

From Chai Wan they came, and Tai O and San Tin and Cloudy Hill. Within hours of the unveiling, Hong Kong's ever-alert entrepreneurs had already begun to capitalize on what had clearly become a pilgrimage. Junks, sampans, and walla-wallas lined the seawalls on both sides of the harbor, each promising to provide paying passengers with the closest possible Palace view. The sight-seeing offered by private boats was a relief to the suddenly overloaded Star ferry system, but it was also a nightmare. The already busy harbor was busier than ever and near accidents were commonplace as even the most experienced skippers became mesmerized by the jade-and-alabaster illusion at water's edge.

Enterprising photographers instantly created postcards of the dazzling new landmark, on sale everywhere by early Monday afternoon, and by Tuesday morning Jade Palace souvenirs—from T-shirts to cloisonné—had become Hong Kong's most rapidly growing cottage industry.

The frenzied interest only increased with each passing day. New visitors came, as did those who had already seen it once, twice, three times. They wanted to see it again and again, a daily ritual. Thursday morning brought a dramatic change in weather, from sunny warmth to misting cool, but despite the unseasonably chilling dampness, the waters in front of the hotel and the sidewalks of Salisbury Road were even more congested than on Monday.

Hong Kong had a new temple, a glittering shrine to itself, its splendor, its courage, its heart, its soul. It seemed impossible that the brilliant luster would ever fade.

But it did. By Thursday's stark winter twilight, the Jade Palace was a hated thing. No longer a reverent celebration of harmony, it became a harsh reminder of the ancient bitterness from which the Crown Colony had sprung: the exploitation of the native Chinese by the *gweilos*, the foreign devils who had come to make their fortunes—and then to leave.

The dream began to unravel at two o'clock Thursday afternoon when James received the phone call, followed immediately by faxed copies of the damning documents. At 2:20, he instructed Mrs. Leong to arrange a 3:30 meeting in his office.

"What if one of them isn't available at such short notice?"

"That isn't an option," James said. "They both must be here. If there's a problem, let me know."

Sam bristled slightly at what sounded like an imperious command, even translated through the polite voice of Mrs. Leong. But the timing could not have been better. She had caught him just as he was leaving the construction site for the last time, his job successfully completed.

Tyler bristled more than slightly. He was at the condominium waiting for Eve when his secretary paged him.

"Mrs. Leong says that you *must* be there."

"But she didn't say why?"

"No, not even a clue."

The scowl that darkened Tyler's face as he replaced the receiver had nothing to do with any concern about the mysterious meeting at Drake Towers. Rather, it had to do with Eve, the precious time with her that would be preempted if he went.

Since early November he had seen her less than once a week, and their time together had been measured in minutes, not hours. Eve had frequent appointments, luncheons and teas, scheduled by Geoffrey. Tyler was frustrated by their limited moments together, but what truly troubled him was what happened during those rare interludes of love.

During September and October he and Eve had made joyous plans for their new life together: when they would marry, where they would live, the children they would have. But for the past month Eve had been obsessed with their escape itself, needing to repeat each carefully planned detail over and over, like a mantra—and yet not soothed even then, as if some sixth sense told her that there was a hidden—and fatal—flaw lurking in those careful plans.

Eve's unspoken yet obvious fear that something would pre-

vent them from sailing into their dream had nothing whatsoever to do with Lily's surgery. Eve seemed to believe, as Lily did,
that as long as Eve was there, as long as the promise was kept,
everything would be just fine. Eve never raised the specter of an
intraoperative catastrophe—as if, Tyler decided, Eve simply would
not permit herself to imagine such a tragedy befalling the brave
little girl.

If all went well, by early Monday evening Lily would be out of
danger. Which meant, Tyler told Eve, that they could leave Hong
Kong Tuesday morning. Eve seemed so tempted by that suggestion, but in the end she said that she would prefer to wait until
Thursday. That was her usual day away from Peak Castle, she explained, and if they were lucky, Geoffrey wouldn't miss her,
wouldn't even begin to realize that she was gone, until he returned home late that night.

Eve would leave him a note, she decided, a polite announcement that she had flown to England, and that her lawyers would
be contacting him regarding a divorce, and that she wanted nothing from him but her freedom. On Thursday morning, moments
before they set sail, Eve would phone Juliana, who—at the last
minute—would cancel any engagements Geoffrey had made for
her for that day; and on the following Monday, Juliana would no-
tify the director of volunteers at the hospital—as well as Lily and
her parents—that a personal emergency had compelled Lady
Lloyd-Ashton to return to London indefinitely.

It was carefully planned, and by the time Geoffrey missed her,
she would be far away, and if he tried to find her, his search
would take him to England, not to the aquamarine sea . . . but
still Eve worried. And she was panicky, too, about her passport—
or lack thereof.

"You're a British citizen in good standing, whether or not
you have the document in your possession," Tyler had lovingly explained. "We'll sail to Australia first, go immediately to the British

consulate, and in a matter of days, a new passport will arrive. You're not a criminal, Eve. This is not going to be a problem."

Tyler and Eve didn't discuss her worries just one time, but every time they were together, with almost exactly the same words, hers anxious, his patient, loving, and calm—despite his own ever-crescendoing concerns about both her anxiety and her health.

The flu that had kept them apart for the first ten days of November had left Eve more thin than ever, and strikingly pale, and they hadn't made love since before her illness. She seemed far too fragile for even the most gentle of loving, and although she curled against him as he whispered reassurances about their escape, and the dream that lay beyond, she made no move for greater intimacy.

Tyler had tried gently, often, and without success to convince Eve to live with him until they left Hong Kong. But now, today, he planned simply to issue a command of love. They would have an hour together, from three, when she hoped to arrive, until four, when she needed to return to Peak Castle to prepare for the party she was hostessing this evening; and during that hour Tyler intended to tell her that they were leaving Hong Kong on Monday night, as soon as Lily was awake and Eve had said to her little friend the words she needed to say.

That was how Tyler planned to spend this afternoon's precious hour with Eve. And now?

Now James Drake had called a mysterious meeting . . . and now Tyler placed a call in return.

"This is Tyler Vaughn, Mrs. Leong. I need to speak with him."

"One moment please, Mr. Vaughn."

The tonelessness of the voice that greeted Tyler a few seconds later eloquently communicated the seriousness of the proposed meeting. Still, with matching solemnity, Tyler said, "Three-thirty is not convenient for me, James."

"Make it convenient."

Tyler answered the stony command with one of his own. "Tell me what this is about."

"If you honestly don't know, Tyler, then it's all the more important that you're here."

"Hello, my love," Tyler greeted moments later.

Eve saw his love . . . and his worry. "What's wrong, Tyler?"

"James wants to meet with me in half an hour. I don't know the reason for the meeting, but I'm afraid I'm going to have to go. I want to say something to you first, though." Tyler took her cool, thin hands in his warm, strong ones, gazed lovingly into her anxious eyes, and said, "I want us to leave Hong Kong this Monday, Eve, as soon as Lily's out of surgery and you've spoken to her."

"We'd sail at night?"

"Yes." Quite suddenly Tyler remembered that September afternoon when his mind had willed the storm clouds to part. The image that had come to him then had been a nighttime one, a sky bright with stars and a ribbon of silver moonlight rippling on the night-black sea. Clouds shrouded Hong Kong now, again, but in four days the opaque gray curtain would open—just for them— and they would sail into that heavenly scene. With quiet wonder, Tyler elaborated, "We'll follow the moon and the stars. We'll let them guide us to our dream."

For the past month Eve's sapphire eyes had been haunted by a secret fear that there was a fatal flaw in their careful plans for escape; and the beautiful blue had tried so hard to discover that hidden flaw, straining to see it before it was too late. And now, just in time, it was found. They weren't meant to leave Hong Kong on the glorious blue-and-gold day that they had envisioned together a thousand times. Instead, the lovers—not star-crossed after all—were meant to sail beneath a black velvet sky alight with starshine and moonglow.

This was what Eve had been trying to see; and now, as she did, her eyes glowed with hope.

"Evangeline?"

"Yes." It was a whisper of pure joy. "We will leave Hong Kong this Monday night."

It was an impulse, which meant that as Maylene made the short walk from her office to his, she needed to make swift plans. She would demand that James have dinner with her, she decided. They would go to the Verandah, where they would be recognized at once, the owner and architect of Hong Kong's glittering new shrine. With all eyes watching, James would be compelled to engage in smiling conversation—even when she artfully guided the topic to Allison.

A week ago Allison had quietly confessed her feelings for James, her *love* for him, and as Maylene had listened to her sister describe her magical summer of candlelit dinners with James, she realized that James cared very deeply for Allison as well. Maylene had been an eyewitness to his happiness during the summer— and to his dark torment ever since.

Allison had entrusted Maylene with this bold secret of her heart, and Maylene would do nothing to betray that sacred trust. She would broach the subject of Allison carefully, and casually. Perhaps, quite innocently, she would ask when James was planning to keep the promise he'd made at Peak Castle to have Allison drive him to Aberdeen for dinner on a floating restaurant.

The memory of James's promise to Allison triggered Maylene's own memories of that evening. Sam had come to her rescue twice, as if he knew her secrets and cared about her anguish, her shame, *her.*

It was all just a clever seduction! Maylene reminded herself. Just a passing illusion to keep Sam amused while he built the permanent one.

Maylene hadn't seen Sam, not even during the past four days when Hong Kong had been celebrating their triumph. According to James, Sam would be leaving soon, and he had no plans to return for the grand opening. Maybe, once he was truly gone, her heart would stop its foolish fantasies, its revising of history, as if there had been for Sam—as there had been for her—something far more than disappointment.

It was at just that moment, as Maylene was thinking about the fantasies of her heart, that she entered the reception area outside James's office and found herself face-to-face with the cowboy himself.

"Oh!"

"Hello, Maylene," Sam greeted quietly.

"Hello," she murmured. Then, realizing that Sam wasn't surprised to see her, and that Tyler was there as well, she asked, "What's going on?"

"We don't know any more than you do, Maylene," Tyler said. "Just that it's a command performance."

"Command performance?" Maylene repeated, just as the door opened behind her.

Maylene turned—and saw pure granite. His eyes, his face, his sleek and stylish body were as cold, as unyielding—and as unreadable—as stone.

"James?" she asked softly. "What's happened?"

For the briefest of moments the stone-hard silver of his eyes softened slightly—for her. Maylene was an innocent victim. He had been intending to gently tell her the devastating news following his meeting with Tyler and Sam.

But that was wrong, James realized. She deserved to hear everything now, firsthand. "Why don't you join us, Maylene?"

"We have a problem," James began. His voice was calm, controlled, as always. "An hour and a half ago I got a phone call from the building commissioner. He's received two letters claiming that the quality of the materials used for the Palace was substandard."

"What materials?" Tyler demanded.

"The concrete, the steel, the glass."

"That about covers it, doesn't it?" Sam scoffed. "We just wanted to make damn sure the thing blew over in the first strong wind. Oh, and don't forget the shards of jade-colored glass scattered all over Kowloon. Let me guess, the letters were anonymous."

"Actually they weren't, although at the moment no one seems willing to share the names with me. Both men have been interviewed and both stand firmly by their stories. They don't know each other, nor does there appear to be a common link, and neither has ever been implicated in any criminal activity. One is a member of the construction crew and the other works on the loading docks at Grand Prix."

"Tyler and I are the criminals, is that it?" Sam greeted his own question with disgust—and disbelief. "And it gets worse, doesn't it, because I made such a special point of requesting that Grand Prix supply all the materials for the Palace."

"Is that really where this discussion is leading, James?" Tyler's voice was quiet, and cold, with anger. "Are you actually suggesting that Sam and I are conspirators in fraud, that I billed you for top-of-the-line materials but delivered garbage instead? For what? A few million dollars?"

"More than a few."

"For what purpose? Greed?"

"A motive as old as time."

"You *cannot* believe this, James."

The jaw muscles rippled in James Drake's granite face, but neither his stone-gray eyes nor his rock-steady voice would be read.

"What I believe hardly matters," he replied evenly. "And

given the disasters that have occurred in Hong Kong over the years as a result of construction fraud, the building commission has no choice but to call a halt to all further work on the building. They've been told by two independent—and apparently unimpeachable—sources that the foundation of the Jade Palace is about as dependable as quicksand."

"Quicksand?" Sam echoed. His tone was fierce—and fiercely controlled. "Has anyone bothered to talk to Chan Peng? Because we're foreigners, Tyler and I may be suspect, but Peng's a native. His commitment to the people of Hong Kong is beyond question. Ask him, James. He'll tell you we built the Jade Palace to last forever."

"He has been asked. He says he wasn't there when the foundation was poured." James was speaking to Sam, but out of the corner of an eye, he sensed Maylene's reaction. "What, Maylene?"

"Peng wasn't there," she confirmed softly, looking at Sam, because somehow he had commanded her to. "He was ill."

"And I told him to go home," Sam embellished, his voice dangerously calm. "I assured him that I could supervise the pouring of concrete." He paused then, allowing his dark blue eyes to remind Maylene what else had happened on that day: the cowboy boots he'd given her; his multilayered confession of need for her; his gentle assertion that yes, if she wanted, she could be a cowgirl—*his* cowgirl. When he was certain that Maylene remembered all the intimate promises of that summer day, he asked, very softly, "Do you believe that I poisoned him, Jade?"

Do you believe that I so willfully destroyed your extraordinary dream?

No, of course I don't believe that! Maylene's heart cried.

But as she struggled to find the courage to let this man who had only been playing with her see the truth of her love, what danced in Maylene's jade-green eyes were dark shadows of uncertainty—and to Sam the uncertain shadows were just as damning as her unequivocal belief in his guilt would have been.

At that moment all Sam Coulter wanted to do was get the hell out of Hong Kong, and he would as soon as possible, but his expression betrayed none of his urgency. His eyes lingered on Maylene, seductive and mocking, and only when her vulnerability—the most extraordinary illusion of all—reminded him of his own foolish wishes, did he slowly look away.

"What now, James?" he asked.

"What do you suggest?"

"Other than a typhoon, you mean? I think you should tear down part of the building, any part you want, and take a good look. The quality is impeccable throughout."

"I'll make that suggestion to the building commission," James said. "But it may be a while before it's implemented. At the moment they aren't too interested in my ideas. The assumption seems to be that the three of us conspired to defraud the bank, not to mention the people of Hong Kong."

"So we all go down together."

"So it would seem."

CHAPTER 27

Allison responded reluctantly to the insistent ringing of her doorbell. December 11 was only two days away, and she was in her darkroom, developing the photographs that would be given to James—to Mrs. Leong—on that morning, as promised.

But when Allison saw Maylene's expression she regretted even a moment's hesitation. "What is it, Maylene? What's happened?"

The picture window in Allison's living room provided a view across the harbor to the Jade Palace. Maylene stood with her back to the window, never even glancing toward the hotel as she spoke, but in looking at Maylene, Allison saw as well the jade-and-alabaster structure. The Palace shone brightly despite the dark gray December sky, as if quite oblivious to the clouds that shrouded Hong Kong—and to the dark cloud of scandal that was now its own somber cloak.

"Someone else is responsible," Allison said quietly when Maylene had finished. "I don't really know Tyler, but he couldn't have done anything without Sam's help, and Sam would never do anything so dishonest, so *destructive*. You believe that, don't you?"

"Yes," Maylene confessed, desperately wishing that she'd had the courage to let Sam see her absolute confidence in his innocence. So what if he had been amused by her foolish admission of love? A memory of glinting blue would have been far better than the memory she had: the indelible image of Sam's contempt.

"And what about James? He can't truly believe that Sam and Tyler are guilty."

"I'm not sure what James believes. He must have been angry, enraged, but as always he was calm and controlled. They *all* were." Maylene frowned. "The Jade Palace meant *so much* to James."

"I know it did," Allison said softly. "And it also meant so much to you."

Allison felt great anger at whomever had so callously tarnished James and Maylene's glittering triumph; but quite suddenly and far more powerfully, her fury turned toward James and Maylene themselves, for putting so much—their hearts, their passion, and their dreams—into something as inconsequential as steel and stone.

"It really couldn't matter *less* whether the Jade Palace ever opens."

"*What?* Allison, what are you saying?"

"Have you ever read *The Wizard of Oz*?"

Maylene's startled frown deepened at the non sequitur. "Yes, of course, but—"

"Well, then, you'll remember why Dorothy and the Scarecrow and the Tin Woodman and the Cowardly Lion all journeyed to the Emerald City. They believed that the Wizard would give them what was missing from their lives. But the Wizard was merely an illusion. He had no power to give them anything. That power lay entirely within themselves. The Jade Palace is just an illusion, Maylene, just a *symbol*. For James, it represents the promise he made to Gweneth. He's like the Woodman, I suppose. He believes that he has no heart, that the hotel *is* his heart. And even though when I first arrived in Hong Kong I felt like Dorothy, I've decided that I'm really more like the Lion, searching for the courage to be who I am." *And to fight for what I believe—and for the people I love.* Allison was fighting now, for the people she loved, and when she paused, flushed and breathless, her eyes were as brilliant as the dazzling city of Oz.

Perhaps the emerald was too bright, blindingly earnest, or perhaps with her breathlessly impassioned words she had finally pushed too far the limits of their friendship. Whatever the reason, Maylene abruptly turned away, from the dazzling emerald of Allison's eyes to the illusory jade structure across the water.

Allison held her breath, and the apology she might have spoken, hoping, waiting. . . .

And at last Maylene spoke, a soft query of wonder and hope. "*I'm* Dorothy, aren't I?"

"I think so," Allison answered with matching softness—and hope. "You're searching for your home, the place where you belong. The Jade Palace was just an excuse for returning to Hong Kong. The real reason you came back was because of your mother . . . wasn't it?"

"Yes. I guess it was." Maylene turned then, from the shattered dream across the harbor to the sister who knew the only dream that truly mattered. "I've been thinking about going to see her— at least from a distance—tomorrow night."

"Oh, good, Maylene. I'm so glad. From a distance?"

"There's an open meeting tomorrow night at the Coliseum." With loving pride, she explained, "My mother, the revolutionary, will be on stage. It's not really the right setting for a reunion— there may be thousands of people there—but . . ."

"It's a first step. Would you like company?"

"No, thank you." Maylene's jade-green eyes shimmered with gratitude. "But may I borrow a little of your courage?"

"Hello, Mrs. Leong, it's Allison Whitaker. I'm sure that Mr. Drake is deluged with calls right now, but I wonder if I might leave a message for him?"

"Certainly."

"Would you please ask him if he's free to have dinner with me tonight? I thought I'd have DuMaurier's send something to my apartment, but even though we'll be dining in, I'd like the evening to be black tie."

Mrs. Leong promised to deliver Allison's message as soon as James was off the phone and that she would call with his reply. For the next thirty minutes Allison paced like a lioness, cowardly no more. She knew who she was, and what she believed . . . and she would fight for the people she loved.

Finally the return call came, but not from Mrs. Leong.

"You just aren't afraid of me, are you?" he greeted softly.

"James? Afraid of you?"

"There aren't many people in Hong Kong—with the possible exception of a few reporters—who would want to spend this evening with me."

"I'm not afraid."

"Can we make it a nightcap instead of dinner? It may be midnight before I can get there."

"Yes, of course, a nightcap's fine . . . midnight's fine."

"And Mrs. Leong said something about black tie?"

"Yes, but if you'd rather not—"

"I'd rather."

At 11:30 P.M., Eve slipped away from her guests to make a brief, necessary phone call. He was in his office at Grand Prix, fielding anxious and angry calls from around the world, but Eve got through right away, on the private line that he kept open, always, for her.

"Eve?"

"Oh, Tyler," she whispered. "I'm so sorry."

"It's okay. At least half of the people I've spoken to are willing to trust Grand Prix still—for a discount, of course."

"You sound so tired."

"I'm all right." The fatigue vanished from his voice as he added softly, "All that really matters is that on Monday night Lily will be safely out of surgery and you and I will set sail for Australia."

Eve had spent the evening listening to Geoffrey and their dinner guests discussing the Jade Palace scandal and the now clouded futures of James Drake, Tyler Vaughn, and Sam Coulter. To his credit, Geoffrey had staunchly defended all three. But, he had added solemnly, from this point on their every move would be watched. Their behavior had to be beyond reproach. Sam must return to his San Antonio office right away, Geoffrey said, to put out fires there, and James and Tyler needed to remain in Hong Kong, doing the same thing, convincing creditors and customers alike that their businesses were strong, solvent, and above suspicion.

Eve knew that Tyler could not leave Hong Kong on Monday night with the wife of the territory's most powerful taipan. Grand Prix would never recover. Surely Tyler knew that, too. And yet there wasn't anything but love in the voice that had just reaffirmed his plan to follow the stars and the moon to their dream.

"Here's *my* plan," Eve countered softly. "As of Monday night, I'm going to begin living in our condominium with you."

"In hiding, Eve?"

"It won't feel like hiding, Tyler. It will feel like love. Please? We can sail to Australia any old time."

"Are you sure this is what you want?"

"I'm positive."

"I love you, Evangeline."

"I love you, too, Tyler," she whispered. "I'll see you Monday."

At precisely midnight Allison opened the door to the man she loved. The events of the day had cast dark shadows across his face, and her panther seemed more caged than ever, more ravenous and more fierce, but Allison felt no fear.

"You look ravaged," she said softly.

"And you look ravishing."

"Juliana Kwan designed this gown for me to wear on New Year's Eve."

"I wasn't talking about the gown, Allison," James said quietly. "I was talking about you."

Champagne awaited them in the living room. As soon as James finished filling their crystal flutes, Allison raised hers in toast. "To the Jade Palace."

James hesitated a beat, then touched crystal to crystal and echoed, "To the Jade Palace."

After they had each taken a sip of the honey-gold bubbly, Allison drew a steadying breath and began, "Maylene told me that at the end of this afternoon's meeting you said, 'If I'm the cause of all this, please know how deeply sorry I am.' She didn't know what you meant by that, but I've wondered if you believe that the man responsible for Gweneth's death is also responsible for sabotaging the hotel?"

For a long while James simply looked at her. How very brave she was, he thought. How very lovely.

"That's why you invited me here tonight, isn't it?" he asked softly. "You knew that there was no one else with whom I could discuss this, and you imagined that it was something I might very much need to discuss."

Allison's nod caused curling wisps of golden-red hair to caress her face, and as if the curls were dancing flames, her cheeks flushed pink in reply. "It was something you could have discussed with the inspector at Scotland Yard. Have you?"

"Yes."

Allison's breath caught. "So you *do* think that her . . . murderer . . . is to blame?"

"I think it's possible. But, Allison, there are any number of developers in Hong Kong who would like to see me discredited, even temporarily, so that certain lucrative contracts would come their way. And there are any number of taipans who would be delighted to see Tyler take a fall for the same reason. What I do know, though, is that whoever orchestrated this did so very carefully. It was probably planned before construction on the Palace ever began."

"Maylene told me about Chan Peng's illness in July. Do you think he was poisoned?"

"Yes, I do. Incapacitating Peng during the pouring of the foundation took careful planning, but it was easy compared to finding the two men who wrote the damning letters. From all accounts, they are solid citizens. Neither would have been tempted by bribery. In the name of family honor, however, to protect a loved one from scandal, they might have been susceptible to blackmail."

"Is there evidence of scandal in their families?"

"Not yet." James smiled wryly. "But as of about an hour ago, a discreet investigation was begun." His smile faded. "Even if we discover that they were being blackmailed, the trail to the mastermind will not be easy. He'll undoubtedly have protected himself with many layers of middlemen. The only hope is to allow the entire scenario to play out."

"The entire scenario?"

"The bank has already called in my loan. Instead of paying it off, I'll let them have the hotel. They'll put it on the auction block and somebody will get it very cheap."

"And that somebody will be the murderer?" Even as she asked the hopeful question Allison frowned. It seemed unlikely that

James's deadly—and clever—enemy would show his hand in such an obvious way.

"If we're very lucky," James said, his tone conveying what Allison already knew: they weren't going to be that lucky.

Even if Gweneth's murderer was behind the scheme to discredit the Jade Palace—and therefore James—he wasn't going to claim the hotel as booty. The end of James Drake's dominion over the best land in Hong Kong was prize enough. The monster, quite pleased with his latest foray, had undoubtedly already returned to his sanctuary in the shadows.

Once before, James Drake had been gravely wounded. But on learning the truth about the death of his wife and unborn son, he had miraculously recovered, empowered by his hunger for revenge. He was wounded now, again—at least his empire was. He could rebuild, and in a few years the murderer might feel threatened, and he would emerge to cause more harm, and then he would vanish anew, and . . .

"Are you going to spend your entire life waiting for a chance for revenge that may never come?"

"No," James answered softly. "I'm not."

"You're not?"

"No." James smiled gently at her bright, lovely eyes. Allison didn't fully understand the meaning of his words, not yet, but she felt hopeful—for him. After a moment he continued solemnly, "I want him to be caught and punished for what he did. I'll never stop wanting that, Allison, not ever. But I'm going to stop envisioning my role in that punishment."

"You'd always planned to kill him yourself," Allison said quietly, a statement not a question, because she knew it was true. "I'm glad you're letting go of that plan, James. Even though he's unspeakably evil, I think it would be very difficult . . . emotionally . . . for you to do that."

"Perhaps," he conceded, although he believed without a

flicker of doubt that he could murder the monster without re-morse. "But it's not because of myself that I'm promising to let it go. It's because of you, Allison . . . because of us."

His voice was soft, and the sensuous silver glittered with love, and as Allison began to understand at last what he was truly say-ing, her emerald eyes shimmered with happiness.

"Us, James?"

"I love you, Allison. I didn't believe it would be possible for me to fall in love again, but I have, with you."

"And I love you, James." Her heart was soaring now, and it should have been a flight of pure joy, but . . . "In September, you wanted me to leave Hong Kong."

"I believed it wasn't safe for you here."

"But now it is? Because of what happened to the Jade Palace? What if—"

James stopped her worry with a loving smile. "I wasn't going to let you leave without telling you of my love and of my plans to keep you safe. Long before today I'd decided to cut back on my projects, to stop trying to provoke him." James gazed at her, this woman who had never been afraid to love him, not even when he had so harshly warned her away. After a moment the bare hands that for so long had yearned only to kill, and that now pledged themselves solely to love, tenderly touched her lovely face. "Will you marry me, Allison? Will you be my bride?"

"Oh, James," she whispered. "Oh, yes."

She was a fragile and delicate butterfly.

And he was a strong and powerful panther.

Because of him, she had found her wings and learned to fly.

And because of her, he was no longer imprisoned in his cage.

But James was hungry still, *ravenous*, for her.

Her jade-green gown of silver stars and emerald butterflies lay

gently on a nearby chair, and his black tuxedo was lost somewhere in the shadows, and they were in her bed, kissing, touching, whispering words of love.

Their eyes, brilliant with love, were perfect mirror images of
silver and green . . . until, quite suddenly, James saw flickers of
uncertainty.

"Allison?"

"I've never made love before, James. I just thought you
should know."

The revelation was stunning, at once joyous and solemn. Allison had been engaged to be married, so he had assumed . . .

With exquisite tenderness, his once lethal hands moved a
love-tangled curl of moon-kissed fire away from her lovely eyes.

"You were waiting for your wedding night, weren't you?" he
asked gently. Then, even more gently, he suggested, "Why don't
we wait until then?"

"No," Allison whispered. All flickers of uncertainty were
gone, and her emerald eyes had never been more glowing—or
more fearless. "It wasn't my wedding night I was waiting for,
James . . . it was you."

Maylene returned to the Trade Winds shortly after 1:00 A.M.
She had been walking for hours in the bitter-cold wind, and now
she was going to swim for hours in the warm aquamarine waters
of the hotel's heated pool, and she might never go to bed. Her entire being was expectant, on alert, restless and eager.

Her plan to be part of an audience of thousands tomorrow
night, near her mother but far away, was reason enough to make
her feel this way. And yet it seemed to Maylene as if there was
something else, something that, unbelievably, was even more
monumental. . . .

Across Victoria Harbour, Garrett Whitaker's entire being was on alert, too, as he walked into the Peninsula Hotel. He was here, again, at long last—and just barely. The storm that was brewing in the South China Sea wasn't the only unseasonably violent weather system on the planet. Torrential rains and howling winds plagued San Francisco as well, closing runways and causing long delays. For almost six hours it had appeared that his flight to Hong Kong would be canceled.

But now he was here, and in only twelve hours he would see Juliana, and Garrett knew that he would not sleep tonight. His restless heart sensed what his daughter's did: that something truly astonishing was about to happen.

CHAPTER 28

The Captain's Bar
Mandarin Oriental Hotel
Friday, December 10, 1993

Her hands were trembling. Her heart was trembling. And trembling thoughts filled her mind. She was going to see Garrett again, after all these years, and even though the exhilaration she felt was beyond words, what Juliana felt now, mostly, was fear.

Their love was the greatest truth of her life. It was her essence, who she was and who she wanted to be: the woman who had been loved by Garrett Whitaker. The six days of their love had illuminated her soul, and the brilliant luminescence was there still, a golden light that had sustained her all these years.

But what if that flame was about to be extinguished? What if she was about to learn that Garrett had long since viewed those enchanted days as merely a crazy infatuation? A pleasurable—yet ultimately inconsequential—interlude? A sailor's lustful escape from the horrors of war?

Juliana did not want to know. But she seemed powerless to prevent her mind from imagining the scene that might unfold today, *soon*: the dark green eyes she loved glittering with amusement as he remembered the desperation of their passion—and their desperately foolish words of love. With that image, Juliana felt flickers of darkness, of blackness, deep inside, a somber signal from the golden flame that, with such a revelation, it would surely die.

Garrett did *not* need to love her still. That was far too much even to dream. Juliana only prayed that he wouldn't shatter her memory of what their love had been.

And what if her prayers were answered? What if Garrett's memory of those days was, like hers, a memory of pure magic? Even that prospect filled Juliana with fear—because his recollection would be of an eighteen-year-old girl, not a forty-six-year-old woman.

Juliana looked at that forty-six-year-old woman now. She had to. The short journey from Pearl Moon to the Mandarin had been a wind-tossed one, as she had known it would be. That was why she had arrived early, to repair the damage to her hair. And now, as she returned errant strands of black—and silver—to the soft knot at her nape, she saw the tiny lines around her eyes, and the bitter truth of her trembling hands.

Her once delicate fingers, slightly swollen from years spent creating enchantments of sequins and beads, seemed quite grotesque to her now, ugly and gnarled—and so very far away from the hands that Garrett would remember. Oh, what hands those had been. *Dancing* hands. Shy yet bold, they had caressed him with grace and joy; and in discovering him, in touching him and loving him, Juliana's talented hands had created their greatest enchantment of all.

I can't see him. I *can't!*

But you have to. For your daughter. Go now. It's still early. You can convince the maître d' to seat you, and you can study the menu in advance, and long before Garrett arrives you can have replaced your reading glasses in your purse, and for this luncheon, during which it will be impossible, anyway, for you to eat, you will toy with your food with your left hand, because of the two once graceful hands, the left is the least ugly, the least gnarled, the least *old.*

Garrett Whitaker's heart trembled, too. With exhilaration—and with fear. For months he had allowed his mind to wander to a most glorious fantasy: that he would be returning to *their* Hong Kong, that private place of magic, and to their love.

But except for the Peninsula Hotel and the Star ferries, the Hong Kong of twenty-eight years ago had simply vanished. At the time it had seemed so bustling, and so very modern, but compared with this new Hong Kong, the old one had been sleepy— and charmingly archaic.

As he'd ridden the *Twinkling Star* across Victoria Harbour's choppy waters, Garrett had stared at the foreign skyline. Skyscrapers of pure gold now shone like gigantic ingots against the steel-gray sky, and even Victoria Peak wore a new pearl-white crown.

Where were Juliana and Garrett? he had wondered. What had become of the innocent eighteen-year-old girl and the jaded twenty-four-year-old pilot who, because of her, had discovered the joyous innocence of love? And where, *where,* were the magical places of their love?

Gone. All of them—the girl and her pilot, and the places where they had loved. Like this new Hong Kong, Garrett and Juliana had grown up. Both were spectacularly successful now, and it was more than appropriate that for their reunion they were meeting at a place renowned for billion-dollar business deals negotiated over lunch.

Now, as Garrett neared the Mandarin Hotel, a great sadness washed over him. He had not wanted Juliana and Garrett to die. In his heart, they would always be alive, joyous and young—and whenever he thought about her, he was young again, still, always, and the entire world shimmered with possibilities.

Garrett's gait suddenly slowed. Was this all a terrible mistake? Mightn't it have been far better to live forever with the memories—and the fantasy of what might have been? He had believed, his heart had convinced him, that the astonishing coincidences of the past few months had been orchestrated by the fates, that he and Juliana had finally paid all their dues, and at last, at last . . .

But destiny had never been kind to the love of Garrett and Juliana. What if this was the most cruel twist of all?

She was already in the restaurant, seated on a plushly upholstered rust-and-gold brocade sofa and separated from the other diners by partitions of intricately etched glass. And she was not alone. An elegantly dressed woman had stopped to chat—which gave Garrett a moment to gaze at her before she realized that he was there.

She was his Juliana, the woman he loved. Yes, the black velvet hair that had barely caressed her shoulders was longer now, and swirled into a soft chignon. And, like his, it was laced with threads of silver. There were fine lines around her eyes, as there were around his, and when her hands gestured gracefully as she spoke, Garrett saw that the slender fingers that had loved him with such delicacy were delicate still, but slightly swollen.

But she was Juliana, and now she was looking at him, and even though it seemed as if she was trying to fight her joy, a glorious light shone brightly in her eyes.

Garrett remembered that light.

He had never forgotten it, and he never would.

"Juliana," he greeted softly.

"Hello, Garrett." *My love, my love!* He hadn't changed, except that he was even more handsome, his dark green eyes even more intense, and he was smiling at her . . . as if nothing had changed

. . . as if she had never sold her soul, or lost the precious gift of love that he had entrusted to her care.

Juliana frowned then, and Garrett prayed that it was only because she had suddenly remembered that they were not alone. But even after the other woman was gone, Juliana seemed tense still, and then someone else stopped to say hello, and this time, when Juliana politely introduced Garrett, his name was recognized, too—he owned Whitaker Enterprises, after all—and the girl and her pilot were gone . . . dead . . . *no.*

"Are you hungry, Juliana?"

She had anticipated a thousand different questions from Garrett, but never this one, and with a soft startled laugh, she confessed, "No, not at all."

"Then let's go."

"Go?"

"Please, Juliana. Please come with me."

The winds that greeted them on Garden Road blew in harsh, cold gusts. But the chilly air didn't deter Garrett in the least. Indeed, it merely assured him of the privacy he wanted when they reached their destination.

The Peak Tram was almost empty, and the few hardy tourists who made the journey to the summit remained inside Peak Tower's sheltering warmth. The Hong Kong Trail belonged to Garrett and Juliana alone.

Over the past twenty-eight years Juliana had been here countless times. She had spent endless hours standing in the precise spot where Garrett had found her, waiting for him, in a silver pool of moonlight.

Juliana knew exactly where she had been standing at the silvery moment when her entire life changed; but now, as they neared that magical spot, it was Garrett who slowed first, remembering it, recognizing it, even after all these years.

And then his dark green eyes glittered with wonder, as they had on that April night, and when Juliana's eyes met his, and mirrored the remembered wonder—and the remembered love—he greeted softly, just as he had then, "I'm Garrett."

And in reply, as she had replied then, she whispered, "I'm Juliana."

And magically, magically, she was *there*. It was that long-ago night once again, and she was reliving its splendor, and now she even felt anew what she had felt then—that it was destiny, that every event of her eighteen years, however tragic, had a single purpose: to bring her to this place, at this moonlit moment, to him.

The chill of the winter day vanished, and Juliana was flooded with warmth, and even the color of the sky overhead changed from ominous gray to glowing silver . . . and she wanted never to leave this magic, to dwell for eternity in the soft light of the silver moon and the loving light of his dark green eyes.

Garrett remembered their love, just as she had prayed he would. Their love, the magic, the promises they had made.

Something lashed her face then, a harsh gust of the winter wind, and with its cold fingers came a stern reminder, a swirling strand of her black-and-silver hair. It's December, not April, the wind hissed. And it's now, not then. And there is no silver moon, only the silver of your hair . . . and there is no magic, only the secrets he does not know.

You must tell him those secrets—even though, when you do, the memory of magic may not survive.

"Oh, Garrett," she whispered. "There's so much you don't know."

"Tell me, Juliana. Tell me everything."

He stepped closer to her, and it seemed as if in another instant his arms might have been around her, cloaking her against the bitter wind while she told him the bitter truths.

How she wanted his arms around her. How she needed his touch.

But how she would die when he withdrew his arms. How very cold she would be when, as he learned the truth, he took his warmth away.

Juliana turned from him, facing the icy wind as she uttered the words that, surely, would chill forever even the most magnificent memories. She began with the first lie that she had told him. She was not, she confessed, an heiress whose parents had been lost in a yachting accident. Rather, she was a child of the sea, and then its orphan, born to poverty. Then she explained her true relationship to Vivian, a bond of the heart not of blood, and then she told him about Vivian's will . . . and then about Miles Burton, the man to whom she had sold her body—and her soul.

Juliana whispered her words into the wind, and they were carried behind her, on that harshness, to Garrett. And when she stopped speaking, she heard only the wind. It seemed to be crying now, howling, and its anguish was so loud that it had surely hidden the sound of his footsteps as, in disgust, he had left forever their place of magic, and its memories, and her.

Juliana was certain that he was gone, and she was about to turn, she couldn't stop herself, needing to see him still—even as he was walking away from her. But then she heard his voice, and it sounded at once warm and cold, as if he was caught somewhere between that spring night of love and this wintry afternoon of secrets.

"Did you try to reach me, Juliana? Did you phone only to have my parents refuse to let you speak to me?"

"No, Garrett, I didn't try. You know what I believed about our love, how dangerous it was."

"But . . . *Juliana.*"

She heard only the coldness now, as fierce and icy as the wind. "I'm sorry! I know what I did . . . what it makes me."

"What it makes you?"

"I sold my body. That makes me a prost—"

"That makes you a mother. Juliana? Please look at me."

And now there was only warmth, and such tenderness, and when she turned to him, a graceful pirouette of pure hope, she met dark green eyes that were gentle with sadness. "You saved our baby's life, Juliana. What you did, you did for her, for our daughter. *I'm* the one who's sorry. I hate that you had to endure . . . that."

"It . . . he wasn't cruel, Garrett, and after nine months he returned to England and never came back." Oh, if only that were all she needed to confess to him. If only she could let him touch her. He wanted to, his dark eyes were telling her how much, but . . . "There's more, Garrett, things you need to know about Maylene."

"Maylene," he echoed, his voice as soft now as it had been when Juliana had told him that he had a daughter . . . another daughter. "Maylene?"

"About her childhood," Juliana whispered, remembering clearly Garrett's quiet joy when she had told him about his baby . . . and remembering, too, his anguish when she had made him promise that he would never be part of his daughter's life. Juliana had excluded Garrett from Maylene's childhood, and now she had to tell him the enormous price their daughter had paid for that promise. "I believed that she was happy, but she was such a gifted actress. She hid her pain so well that until she was thirteen, even I didn't know about it."

"What pain, Juliana?"

"She has your green eyes, Garrett, and her skin is snow-white, and she's very beautiful, but her classmates taunted her for being different, for being only half Chinese. Oh, I should have *known* about the prejudice against Eurasians! During my own childhood in Aberdeen Harbour, I had been taught to hate all *gweilos*. I had even been told that those Chinese who were foolish enough to mingle their blood with the blood of foreigners were viewed with arch disdain. But I had *forgotten* those lessons of hatred. I had fallen in love with you, and Maylene was our daughter, and I thought only about love, not intolerance."

"The way the world should be," Garrett gently assured even as his heart ached for the daughter whose rare beauty had not, for her, been proof of a joyous truth—that she was the Daughter of Greatest Love—but rather had been a symbol of great shame. "Tell me what happened when Maylene was thirteen."

Juliana drew a breath, hoping to steady herself, but inhaling only an icy chill. "There was an article about you in *Fortune* magazine. I had told her that you were British, and that you'd died before she was born, and that you would have loved her with all your heart. But I also told her your name. It made you more real to her, and she needed you to be real, and it seemed so unlikely, so impossible really, that a little girl in Hong Kong—"

"What are you telling me, Juliana? That Maylene knows I'm alive? That she's known since she was thirteen and has hated me ever since?"

"She's hated both of us. I told her the truth about our love, and about my fears, but she didn't believe that we ever truly loved each other. She was too young, too hurt, and with so many hidden hurts. She didn't understand."

"I don't understand either, Juliana." All tenderness was gone from Garrett's voice, and all warmth. It was as cold as the wind— and as filled with the promise of a violent storm. "You should have let me know. I would have come to Hong Kong. I needed to be told that my daughter knew I was alive."

"I was afraid to tell you!"

"Because of retribution from an angry dragon?"

"*Yes.*" Juliana was face-to-face with that enraged dragon now, and she feared his retribution most of all. There was only one way that Garrett could harm her, by revoking the wondrous memories of their love, and that was precisely what was happening. She felt the darkness now, as the flame within her began to flicker. The tiny blaze was struggling, a valiant effort but a futile one, its strength pathetic against the immense storm in his eyes. Soon, she knew, the golden flame would be extinguished, and Juliana Kwan would disappear, and she would watch it happen, bearing witness to her own death, as, long ago, Tranquil Sea had watched her loved ones vanish into the sea. "I was afraid, Garrett. I was *afraid.*"

He didn't hear her fear. He was lost in his own swirling feelings, a kaleidoscope of them, image upon image, emotion upon emotion, worry upon worry. . . .

"If Maylene knows that I'm her father, then she must know that Allison is her sister."

"Yes. But she would never tell Allison. Maylene isn't cruel . . . except to herself."

Garrett had come to Hong Kong with plans, wishes, and dreams. He would meet Maylene, of course, the gifted architect who was Allison's friend. That in itself was a dream come true. But his heart had wished for more: that somehow there could be a way to reveal the truth without causing pain.

But Maylene already knew the truth, and for fifteen years the revelation had caused her great pain, and . . .

"I need to see her." His voice was urgent now, hoarse with emotion and soft with despair. "I need to see the daughter who believes that I never loved her."

"You can tell her that I'm to blame, Garrett! I should have let you know. It's all my fault."

At last, at last, Garrett heard Juliana's anguish. He focused sharply—and then so gently—on her lovely, devastated face; and as he heard the echoes of his own harshness and realized how far away from her he was standing, he narrowed the gap—only to have her recoil from him.

This woman he loved, who was afraid of destiny and dragons, seemed now to be afraid, most of all, of him.

"Oh, Juliana," he whispered. *"I love you."*

"You love me?" she echoed. "How can you possibly love me?"

"I can," he answered softly. "And I do. Then, now, always."

There was no fierceness in his green eyes now, only love, only love . . . and as the golden flame within her glowed with its small bright fire, never to flicker again, the disbelief vanished from her eyes . . . and there was love, only love.

"Oh, Garrett, I love you, too."

"Then, my Juliana, my love, may I touch you? Please? May I hold you?"

Then she was in his arms, where she belonged, and for a very long time they scarcely moved, scarcely breathed, overwhelmed by this wonder—and feeling anew the power of a love that was so strong that it could shut out the world.

But they could not shut out the world now, nor did they want to. There was a precious daughter who needed their love.

Garrett held Juliana still, they held each other, as they talked.

"I won't deny my anger, Juliana, but it's directed at myself, not at you. I could have called you. At any time in the past twenty-eight years, I could have picked up the phone and called."

"But you promised me that you never would."

"I could have called you," he repeated solemnly. "I *should* have. It's time for the truth, Juliana. I want both of our daughters to know everything. I need to see Maylene first, to talk to her, to explain. Should I do that alone, or should we go to her together?"

It was then, in the loving sanctuary of his arms, that Juliana told Garrett of her estrangement from Maylene, and of her hope that Maylene's decision to return to Hong Kong meant that they might see each other again, and that she had vowed to wait for Maylene to make the first move.

"But last night I broke that vow. Not that she knows. I was never able to reach her. But I had to try. I knew how terribly upset she would be about the Jade Palace."

"The Jade Palace?"

Garrett didn't know what had happened to the hotel. Even though news of the scandal had been shouted from the headlines of all of the day's papers, he had been lost in memories . . . and in dreams.

"I know Sam Coulter," Garrett said after Juliana told him about the claim that substandard materials had been used in construction of the Palace. "He would never be involved in fraud."

"I don't know Sam, but I have the same conviction about James Drake and Tyler Vaughn. Still, until the matter's resolved, all work has been suspended indefinitely. The hotel may never open."

"I wonder if Allison's on her way home to Dallas."

"No, she's not. In fact, Garrett, she stopped by the boutique this morning to make a rather special request. She wants me to design a wedding dress for her."

"A wedding dress? Is she marrying James?" When Juliana nodded, Garrett answered with a smile of happiness—and relief. "She talked about him during the summer, and there was such love in her voice when she did, but for the past few months, not a word, just quiet sadness."

"The love is definitely back in her voice now," Juliana assured. Then, her own voice filling with love, she added, "I'm fairly confident that your lovely daughter has guessed the truth about Maylene and me. Whenever we're together, she always makes a special point of mentioning Maylene. And today . . . I think the real reason Allison came by the boutique was to tell me that she was going to ask Maylene to be her maid of honor, in case I was worrying that Maylene might be about to return to England."

"Allison is *your* lovely daughter, too, Juliana. That's a relationship I'd like to make official as soon as possible."

"Oh, Garrett."

"We've spent all these years obeying the commands of the fates. How can we stop now? The fates have brought us all to Hong Kong, and it's time—at last—that we become a family."

"That sounds so wonderful, but . . . it won't be easy, Garrett, not with Maylene, and perhaps not even with Allison. And what about your parents? And Beth's parents?"

"At this moment all four of them are on a cruise ship in the South Pacific. They're scheduled to arrive in Hong Kong on the twenty-fourth, and when they do, we'll invite them to be part of our family." Garrett saw her worry, and he worried, too, about both the daughter who had hated him for fifteen years and the one who had loved him for twenty-eight. But, for Juliana, he smiled and added confidently, "We *will* be a family by then, Juliana. I promise. Now, my love, it's really very cold up here. Will you come to the Peninsula with me?"

"I can't, not until tonight." Juliana shrugged. "I have appointments at the boutique all afternoon. I made them so I would have something to come back to, to occupy my mind, after seeing you. And this evening there's a meeting I must attend about the future of democracy in Hong Kong." With another shrug, she confessed, "I've become a bit of a spokesperson for reforms that are even more radical than what Governor Patten has in mind."

"Isn't that dangerous?"

"Not as dangerous as Hong Kong without such reforms."

"Will this be an open meeting?"

"Yes." Juliana tilted her head. "Do you think you'd like to come?"

"I know I would." Garrett smiled. "Does this mean we're going to live in Hong Kong?"

"Oh . . . I . . ."

"We'll live wherever you want to live, Juliana."

"Then here, in this magical place where we fell in love, and where Allison has fallen in love . . ." Her lovely face filled with sadness.

"There must have been some magic here for Maylene as well, Juliana," Garrett said softly. "I've seen the Jade Palace. It wasn't designed by someone who hates Hong Kong. Shall I try to see her this afternoon?"

Juliana considered the question for several long, thoughtful moments.

"I don't think so," she answered finally. "I'm not sure what's best, exactly how you should approach her, but I don't think it should be a surprise. Let me think about it and we'll decide tonight."

"All right," Garrett agreed, fighting his own restlessness to see his daughter with the knowledge that Juliana was undoubtedly right. After a moment he echoed softly, "Tonight."

The soft word hummed with layers of meaning. Tonight, in the privacy of his suite at the Peninsula, Garrett and Juliana would be parents, solemnly making decisions of the heart for the daughter of their love.

And, tonight, Garrett and Juliana would be lovers, again, after twenty-eight years.

"Oh, Garrett, I wish I were still eighteen for you."

Earlier, Garrett had startled Juliana by asking if she was hungry. Now it was she who startled him, with words about a different kind of hunger entirely, and to his amazement, Garrett saw that she was serious. He answered first with a gentle smile, and then, as he tenderly moved a strand of black-and-silver hair away from her lovely, worried eyes, his own eyes became solemn with love—and with a promise: his hunger for her, his passion and his desire, were as strong now as they had been then. In fact, the intense dark green amended, they were even stronger, as was their love.

Garrett found her hands then, and when slowly, and so lovingly, he kissed the swollen joints, Juliana's heart began to dance—and, she realized with joy, her dancing hands would dance anew. And finally, just before his lips greeted hers, just before they became lost again in that all-consuming wonder, he said, "The woman I love, Juliana, the woman who I want and who I need, is forty-six years old."

CHAPTER 29

Trade Winds Hotel
Friday, December 10, 1993

"Miss Whitaker? This is Alex, Mrs. Leong's assistant."

"Oh, yes?"

"Mr. Drake wonders if you would be willing to meet him at five o'clock this evening outside Drake Towers. He would like you to bring his Jaguar and drive him to Aberdeen for dinner on one of the floating restaurants. Would that be possible for you?"

"Yes, absolutely." Allison's soft voice smiled with love. James had left her bed at dawn, following a night in which neither had slept, neither had wanted to. Allison knew that his day would be steeped with problems, and that it would be at least midnight before she saw him again, but now, despite everything, James had chosen today to keep the promise he had made at the party at Peak Castle. She would drive the six blocks to the Towers, she decided, and then she would turn the wheel over to him. She needed to prove nothing to the man she loved, and with James driving, they could safely hold hands. "That's perfect."

"Excellent. I shall let him know. Oh, one more thing. Mr.

Drake wanted me to remind you to please remember to fasten your seat belt."

Allison swept through the Trade Winds's revolving front door at 4:45. At precisely the same moment Maylene stepped into a brass-and-mirror elevator that was already—and only—occupied by Sam Coulter.

"Oh!"

A slow, mocking smile touched his sexy lips. "Come now, Maylene. Surely we can think of something to say for forty-eight floors."

The hotel's elevators were swift, Maylene knew. The ride would be short. Merely an intimate eternity of dark blue eyes that devoured her with a blend of seduction and disgust.

"I thought you'd be in Texas by now."

"I should be. But there's a storm system in California. I can't get out of here until tomorrow." His shrug was easy, nonchalant, betraying none of the churning frustration he felt at being trapped in Hong Kong when he needed to be in San Antonio. "So, Jade, maybe we should get together tonight? For old times' sake? We could meet at my place."

"You make it sound like you don't have anything better to do."

"I don't. I can't begin my next embezzlement scheme until I get back to Texas, and even then it's going to be a little tough. No one's too eager to hire me at the moment. In fact, my next two projects have already been canceled."

I'm sorry, her heart whispered. And I'm so sorry, too, that you believe I don't trust you.

"So, what do you say, Maylene? We could drink champagne, and I could teach you how to smoke, and one thing might lead to another, and you might even tell me who the hell you really are beneath all the disguises. It might be fun, and besides, what do you have to lose? After tonight, you'll never see me again."

Maylene wondered if Sam had already been drinking, but what she saw in his brilliantly clear and undeniably sober blue eyes was far more dangerous. Sam Coulter was, quite simply, very angry. Years ago, when Garrett Whitaker had rescued him from the sea, Sam had vowed to change his life into one worth saving. And he had. But now, everything he'd fought so hard to achieve was being taken away. And now, his fury was as cold—and as violent—as the storm in which he had nearly drowned.

"You're scaring me, Cowboy."

In response to her hushed words, the ice-blue fury relented, just for her, and when Sam spoke again, his voice was very gentle.

"Understand this, Jade—I would never hurt you."

The elevator door opened then, and another passenger stepped in, and the remainder of the swift trip to the lobby was made in silence.

"Are you a gambler?" Sam asked as he and Maylene walked together toward the revolving door that led outside.

"No."

"Well, why don't you come to Macau with me tonight anyway? I'll teach you how to play twenty-one. I'll teach you how to win."

For a tantalizing moment Maylene allowed herself to imagine an evening in a casino gambling with Sam. She would be seated at the gaming table, and he would be standing behind her, his hands resting gently on her bare shoulders, his lips lightly caressing her temple as he whispered to her what she should do: double her bet, draw a card, stand pat with what she was dealt.

She would be betting Sam's money, thousands of dollars on every hand, perhaps tens of thousands. When she won, she would see calm satisfaction in his dark blue eyes. And when she lost, and turned to him with anxious apology? The sexy half smile would greet her, and he would wink, a reminder not to panic . . . because, in the end, he *always* won.

Tonight Sam Coulter would be wild, reckless, fueled by fury. And tomorrow?

"You're going to convince the people who canceled your next two projects to change their minds, aren't you?"

"You bet. At least I'm sure as hell going to try."

Tomorrow Sam Coulter would set his dark blue gaze on salvaging his dreams. But tonight that dark and dangerous gaze would be focused solely on her—if she wanted it to be. Maylene knew that Sam was promising her nothing more—and nothing less—than a night of pure pleasure, of wild passion and reckless desire. And she knew, too, that on this night any woman would do.

I would never hurt you, he had vowed, and despite the violence that was now a shimmering aura around his taut body, Maylene knew it was true. Sam wouldn't hurt her—not physically. On this night when his dreams were shattered, and he needed desperately to fill the emptiness inside, he would be fiercely—and exquisitely—tender.

And tomorrow he would leave, and Maylene would never see him again, and it was sheer self-destruction even to consider his offer. Besides, she had other plans for this evening, perhaps equally self-destructive, to see her mother.

Maylene hadn't slept at all last night, and she had spent the entire day roaming around Hong Kong, but if her body was exhausted, she didn't know it. Restlessness churned within her still, energizing her and propelling her ever onward to the all-important destination that was, as yet, hidden from her.

Was it the Coliseum? Maylene wondered. Was that where the monumental event would occur? Despite the vastness of the crowd, would Juliana find her? And with eyes alight with love—and forgiveness— would she implore her wayward daughter to join her courageous crusade for freedom?

Or was her true destination Macau, with Sam, courageously gambling on loving him just one last time?

Or was the restlessness she felt compelling her toward yet another destination entirely?

Allison smiled at the white-gloved valet who arrived with the Jaguar. He set the parking brake, but left the motor running, hopped out, and held the door for Allison as she climbed in.

She was eager to be on her way, to be with James, but years of keeping herself safe for those she loved imposed caution. Her safety was more important now than ever, because now a man who had once lost a woman he loved was allowing his heart to love again.

Allison carefully studied the car's control panel, discovering how to operate the horn, the turn signal, and on this misting day, the windshield wipers. She adjusted the rearview mirror and, with the parking brake still set, depressed the clutch and moved the stick shift through all its gears.

Then she was ready, and the purring car was ready, too, and there was only the final caution, James's loving reminder to fasten her seat belt. That accomplished, she was just about to release the parking brake when she caught sight of Maylene and Sam.

Impulsively unfastening the seat belt, Allison got out of the car and began walking toward them.

"May—"

Allison's half sister's name was torn in half by the sudden explosion of James Drake's gleaming silver Jaguar. As metal fragments shot high into the air they were followed, even higher, by brilliant red-orange flames and feathery plumes of dark gray smoke.

"*Allison!*"

Sam and Maylene rushed to her, to the place where she lay

motionless and bleeding. The explosion had hurled her with merciless—and yet merciful—force far away from the inferno. Her
own magnificent golden-red curls were the only flames nearby.

"Allison," Maylene whispered, kneeling on the pavement,
gently touching the pale white face. "Allison, *please.*"

In response to Maylene's soft plea, Allison's emerald eyes
fluttered open and a lovely smile touched her ashen lips.

"Maylene," she murmured dreamily, "James and I are getting
married. We want you to be our maid of honor."

Allison lost consciousness before hearing Maylene's loving
reply, but Maylene spoke to her still. In soft whispers, she told Allison of her love, and what a wonderful wedding it would be, and
how lucky James was, the luckiest man on earth.

While Maylene cradled Allison and the hotel personnel summoned help, Sam searched for a way to prevent Allison's death.
The ghostly whiteness of her face was solemn testimony to the
fact that she was losing blood, lots of it. If only he could find an
external source for the blood loss, one that could be controlled by
a tourniquet . . .

Allison's limbs were bloodied, but Sam's swift yet careful
search failed to reveal a pulsing spill of crimson from a lacerated
artery. There were scrapes only, superficial abrasions caused by
the harsh collision of delicate flesh and jagged concrete. Allison's
life-threatening blood loss was internal, and with every frantic
heartbeat, she moved ever closer to death.

The air screamed with high-pitched sirens . . . and then there
was a deeper sound, quiet, anguished, primal, raw.

"*Allison.*"

Maylene looked up at James's stricken face, and as he knelt
their hands touched. James needed to be where she was, cradling
the woman he loved, whispering his love to her. Maylene yielded
to James's need, but she touched her sister still as she quietly explained, "She was in the Jaguar, about to leave, but when she saw

us, she got out and . . ." Maylene frowned, disbelieving still. "The car exploded, James. It just exploded."

"Allison was in the Jaguar?" It was a whisper of grief—and of rage.

Allison had been in his car, just as Gweneth had been in his bed, and now the sky was filled with flames and smoke, just as it had on that night in Wales. If Allison were in the fiery carcass of his car now, that was where James would be, trying to save her, even though it would have been impossible. But, miraculously, Allison was here, away from the burning metal, and she was alive—barely.

She is going to live, James told his screaming heart. *She will live.*

"She was conscious for a few moments," Maylene said softly, her heart screaming, too, as she struggled against the truth that both she and James saw: the ever-increasing pallor of Allison's face. "She told me that you're getting married and asked me to be her maid of honor. I will be, James . . . and it will be the most romantic wedding *ever.*"

"Yes it will be," James said softly, responding to Maylene's words but speaking to his bride-to-be. His lips caressed Allison's temple as he spoke, and it took all of his love to keep the fear from his voice. Her skin was so very cold. "Do you hear me, my love? Our wedding is going to be so romantic, but that romance will be nothing compared to our life together. I love you, Allison. Fight, my darling, please fight."

"We're taking her to the operating room now." The announcement was made by Dr. Pamela Lau, a trauma surgeon, and it came less than seven minutes after Allison reached the emergency room. "She's bleeding internally, probably from a ruptured spleen. I need to ask if any of you know her medical history. The medical-alert bracelet she's wearing warns against blood transfusions."

Maylene, James, and Sam all knew Allison's medical history. Allison had shared it with her sister and the man she loved, and Sam had been told by Garrett Whitaker.

It was James who answered the surgeon's question. After listening to his solemn revelation that a blood transfusion could be fatal, Dr. Lau countered with matching solemnity, "I don't believe she can survive without one."

"But you're going to stop the internal bleeding."

"Yes, but she's already lost so much blood that her heart is beginning to fail. It's beating as fast as it can to circulate what limited blood she has. We *must* transfuse her. We really have no choice. We'll simply have to manage any untoward reaction as best we can."

"Can you do that?"

"We can try."

Maylene spoke then, urgent words in rapid Cantonese, and when she stopped, Dr. Lau explained, in English, to Sam and James, "She has just offered to donate her blood."

"And I'm offering mine," Sam responded swiftly. "I'm Type O, universal donor, and I have more pints to give than Maylene does." He looked at Maylene, his dark blue eyes silently yet eloquently conveying the most important reason of all: I'm not going to let you do this, Jade. I'm not going to let you spend your life feeling responsible for your friend's death. Without leaving the darkly shadowed green, he commanded, "Use my blood, Doctor."

"She can't," James said softly, understanding the Cantonese—and so much more. "She can't use your blood, Sam, and she can't use mine. Not when she can use Maylene's."

"I don't want Allison to know, James," Maylene said, her voice now as urgent in its regal English as it had been in its musical Cantonese. "*Please.* She never needs to know."

"But *I* need to know," Sam said quietly. "Maylene? James?"

It was Maylene who answered, Maylene who told Sam Coulter what he had always wanted to know: who she really was beneath all the disguises.

"Allison is my sister. Garrett Whitaker is my father, too."

With that revelation Sam, like James, began to understand the secret fears and lovely vulnerability of the complicated woman with whom he had fallen in love. He would need time to sort it all out, and that would happen later, hopefully *with her*, but right now Sam's top priority was to protect Maylene from further harm.

"That's all the more reason for you *not* to do this," he said gently to the determined jade-green eyes. To the doctor, he added, "When Garrett Whitaker told me about Allison's transfusion reaction, he also said that both his blood and that of Allison's grandparents had been tested, and had been shown to trigger the dangerous response. That means, doesn't it, that Maylene's blood would very likely trigger it, too?"

"Not necessarily," Dr. Lau countered, suddenly as determined as Maylene. "In fact, as Allison's sister, Maylene is undoubtedly her best hope."

Juliana had phoned Garrett in his room at the Peninsula three times in the two hours since he had kissed her good-bye at the Pearl Moon boutique. The calls were brief, moments of pure joy wedged in between appointments. They had last spoken ten minutes ago. Juliana claimed that it would be her final call, their last words of love until after the town meeting at the Coliseum. In less than five minutes she would be leaving to plan the evening's events with the other speakers.

Garrett decided to go for a walk along Nathan Road, Hong Kong's "Golden Mile." He was almost out the door when the phone trilled. He answered with a smile in his voice—for her.

But the caller wasn't Juliana. It was Sam. Garrett's answering service in Dallas had provided Sam with the number in Hong Kong where Garrett could be reached.

"There's been an accident, Garrett. Allison has internal injuries that require emergency surgery. She's on her way to the operating room now. The doctors believe that it's absolutely essential that she be given blood."

"She *can't* be given blood, not unless it's tested first. Her doctor in Dallas—"

"There's no time for testing, Garrett. Allison needs to be transfused immediately. Maylene is here. She's offered to donate her blood."

"Oh, Sam." Garrett's anguished whisper held love—and worry—for both of his daughters.

"Maylene wants to do this, Garrett. And the doctors all agree that it's Allison's best chance."

CHAPTER 30

Doctor Lau's face was so grave that Maylene felt the death of her sister even before the doctor spoke.

"Allison accepted your blood as if it were her own."

Already lost in grief, her own heart dying, Maylene needed several moments to truly hear the words. "She did? But . . . it was too late? She . . . died . . . anyway?"

"Allison is alive, and the bleeding has stopped, but her heart is still failing."

"She needs more blood."

"Yes."

Maylene extended her slender white arms, palms up. "Then *take* more!"

"According to hospital policy, we're not permitted to take more than one unit from any donor."

Even as the doctor dutifully reiterated the policy her grave expression became more hopeful. In another lifetime, pure-blooded Chinese Pamela Lau might have been a classmate who taunted Maylene Kwan for her green eyes and white skin. But now Pamela and Maylene shared a common goal. Both were determined to do whatever was necessary to save Allison's life. And they both knew that by giving Allison blood in spite of the medical-alert bracelet, far more stringent rules had already been broken.

"Take my blood, Dr. Lau. Take as much as you need . . . as much as Allison needs."

Without a heartbeat's hesitation, Pamela Lau prepared Maylene's arm for its second assault. The needle she chose was larger than what was customarily used for blood donations. Maylene's rare and precious blood needed to be collected as quickly as possible.

Once the needle was secured and the crimson was flowing, Pamela Lau said, "Both Mr. Drake and Mr. Coulter would like to see you. And, Maylene, your father is here. He wants very much to see you, too."

"My father? He's *here*?"

"Apparently he arrived late last night."

"He—they—don't know where I am, do they?"

"No, they don't know," Dr. Lau said, quietly confirming that she had, of course, honored Maylene's impassioned request for absolute privacy while she waited to hear if her blood had been lethal or lifesaving for her sister. "But now we know that your blood is compatible with Allison's, and with this next transfusion I truly believe she'll be out of danger, so isn't it time for you to see them? They're all quite eager to see you."

"No . . . not yet . . . please."

When Dr. Lau returned an hour later, she was smiling.

"Your sister's heart rate has slowed dramatically," she said as her lean fingers curled instinctively around Maylene's wrist. "In fact, her pulse is stronger—and much less rapid—than yours."

"She's going to be all right?"

"She's going to be fine. Now, there are three men who want to see you."

Maylene shook her head, a gesture that caused waves of dizziness, a vivid reminder of her own loss of blood.

"These are determined men, Maylene," Dr. Lau said. "So far, they've been honorable about not following me. But next time—"

"There won't *be* a next time." Maylene sat up, too quickly. Her whole body whirled. "I'm leaving."

"You're in no condition to go anywhere. You've just lost a great deal of blood. It may have happened in a hospital, in a controlled way, but to your body that makes absolutely no difference. I want you at bed rest and on IVs overnight."

"I've donated blood before," Maylene said, willing her pale fingers not to tremble as she began to pull at the edges of the paper tape that secured her intravenous line.

Pamela Lau put her light gold fingers on top of Maylene's pale white ones. "This wasn't a typical blood donation."

"No." Maylene smiled softly. "No, it wasn't." Her smile faded. "I need to go. Please. I won't go far, and I'll call you as soon as I get there, and if you give me iron pills, I'll take a handful of them, and I'll put myself on strict bed rest."

The doctor sensed, correctly, that Maylene was going to leave with or without her blessing. "Where will you go?"

Maylene thought about her apartment at the Trade Winds and rejected it. They would look for her there. Besides, the Hilton was even closer. She would be nearby, in case Allison needed more blood.

"I'll be just across the street at the Hilton." Maylene paused, thought about the smart and determined men who might be looking for her, and decided she needed another name. I already have another name, she realized, the name my sister gave me. It was the right name, too, the perfect name. She was searching for where she belonged . . . and it seemed, perhaps, as if she was getting ever closer to home. "I'll register as Dorothy . . ."

"Dorothy who?"

Yesterday Maylene might not have remembered the last name of the fictional heroine of *The Wizard of Oz*. But now it came to her. And it, too, was perfect. On this night when Hong Kong was being assaulted by powerful winter winds, and when Maylene's own heart was a turbulent swirl of emotions, and when she seemed to sense that Dorothy would need to weather even more storms before she was truly home, what better name could there be?

"Gale," she replied softly. "I'll be registered as Dorothy Gale."

After calling Dr. Lau to report that Dorothy had made it safely across wind-tossed Garden Road and was now in her room at the Hilton, Maylene reached for the Hong Kong telephone directory. She knew that there was a listing for J. Kwan on Mount Cameron Road. The discovery had been made months ago, shortly after her return to Hong Kong, but Maylene had allowed herself only a partial glance at her mother's telephone number. She feared that if she knew the number by heart, long before the time was right, she might make an impulsive phone call of love.

Maylene was calling now because of love, but tonight's message was quite different from the one that one day—soon—she would find the courage to speak. And, Maylene knew, Juliana wouldn't even be home. She was at the Coliseum. Maylene would leave her important message on Juliana's answering machine . . . assuming Juliana even had such a device.

The phone was answered, electronically, on the fourth ring. As she heard the delicate hopefulness of her mother's recorded voice, imploring the caller to please leave a message, Maylene wondered if the answering machine was new. Had it, perhaps, been acquired since June? So that in the event that her daughter called, that long-awaited moment would not be lost?

The wonderful thought stole from Maylene the calm with which she had planned to deliver the carefully rehearsed words. They came haltingly now, trembling with emotion.

"Mother . . . it's me. I know you're at the Coliseum, but when you return home, if you turn on the news, you'll hear about Allison. She's *fine*. There was an accident, but everything's all right. Well . . . not completely all right. Garrett Whitaker is in Hong Kong, and he's probably very angry. I gave Allison my blood, you see, and because of that . . . Mother, he knows that I know the truth, that Allison is my sister. I know how you feel about him, but . . . don't go to the hospital, *please*." That, in essence, was what Maylene had called to say, a warning to Juliana that Garrett Whitaker was in Hong Kong and was undoubtedly furious that his secret had been revealed. But there had not yet been a beep signaling that her time was up, and the hopefulness in her mother's recorded voice still echoed within her, and . . . "Mother? *I'm so sorry.*"

While Allison and Maylene slept, gaining strength, the storm in the South China Sea gained strength as well. By noon Saturday, the people of Hong Kong were told to brace themselves for the most powerful typhoon in more than three decades. The residents of Kowloon received a special warning: according to the sophisticated storm-tracking system, landfall was expected shortly before midnight at the peninsula's southernmost tip—or, to be even more precise, at the Jade Palace.

Maylene awakened, disoriented, at two Saturday afternoon. She had been asleep for nearly eighteen hours, she realized, a deep, dreamless—and uninterrupted—sleep. Fumbling for the bedside telephone, she dialed the hospital and requested that Dr. Lau be paged right away.

"It's Maylene," she said when the doctor came on the line. "Is Allison all right?"

"Yes, absolutely. She's a little groggy, which is to be expected, but she's fine—out of danger. How are *you*?"

Maylene reflected briefly on the question. She felt weak still, dizzy and fatigued despite her long rest. But, she decided, on balance the symptoms related to her blood loss were improved, or maybe it was just that they paled in comparison with her new symptom: the gnawing ache that resulted from taking a handful of iron pills on an empty stomach.

"A little groggy, but fine," she murmured. *Just like my sister.*

"May I tell them that? It didn't take long for them to figure out that you'd left the hospital, and they've been worrying."

"Please tell them not to worry," Maylene said softly, wondering who *they* were—and who among them truly worried about her welfare. James? Yes, her future brother-in-law would most definitely care. Garrett Whitaker might care as well, but his *real* concern would be for her secret, not for her. And what about Sam? Maylene realized then that Sam wasn't even among the *they* at the hospital. It was Saturday afternoon. His flight to Texas had left hours ago. "Mr. Coulter is gone, isn't he?"

"He left last night, shortly after deciding that you were no longer in the hospital. But Mr. Drake and your fath—"

"Please tell them I'm fine," Maylene interjected. "But that I need a little more rest . . . and privacy."

"I hope you'll remain right where you are until the typhoon passes."

"The *typhoon*?"

As Maylene learned about the devastating winds that were howling toward Hong Kong, and precisely where they were expected to inflict their most violent assault, her dizziness was all but forgotten, as were the journeys she would make when she was stronger—to her mother, her sister, and perhaps even her father. Her family would be safe, far away from the typhoon's deadly path.

And where would Dorothy be during the raging storm? The answer came with amazing calm and a wondrous sense of peace. For the first time in her entire life, Maylene Kwan knew exactly where she belonged.

PART EIGHT

CHAPTER 31

The Jade Palace
Saturday, December 11, 1993

H e was watching the drama of the wind-battered harbor. The emerald water churned, and the blowing gusts cast its silver-tipped waves high into the air, creating a glittering rainfall of diamonds.

The Star ferries, having long since made their final voyages before the storm, were snuggled tightly in their berths. But there were other, smaller boats on the harbor still. The captains, whose lucrative Jade Palace sight-seeing excursions had vanished forty-eight hours before, were making money again, shuttling passengers away from the Jade Palace this time, from Kowloon Peninsula to Hong Kong Island. Strong winds would be felt throughout the island, but the typhoon's most ferocious blows were forecast to affect only its westernmost tip—Aberdeen, Victoria Peak, and Kennedy Town—as it moved relentlessly toward Kowloon, where the greatest devastation was predicted to occur.

After boarding up their homes and businesses, many Kowloon residents had crossed the churning green waters to Hong Kong Island, to weather the storm with friends and family there. Most had made the trip hours before, by Star ferry or MTR, and for the past hour Sam had watched the last of the stragglers climb into the private boats that had lined the seawall of the harborside esplanade. The promenade was quite empty now, except for the spray of diamonds, and most of the small fleet of sampans and walla-wallas was well on its way to the safe haven of the Yau Ma Tei typhoon shelter.

Indeed, only a single sampan remained. Sam had been vaguely aware of its bobbing voyage across the harbor, but now it was snuggling close to the seawall, as if about to let someone off . . . someone as crazy as Sam . . . someone who had chosen to spend the night here, directly in the typhoon's deadly path.

She rose like Venus from the sea, a vision in blue jeans and cowboy boots. The wind punished her slender body, and her black silk hair, long and unrestrained, lashed mercilessly against her face.

Sam had been watching from the Imperial Suite.

By the time he reached the lobby, Maylene was at the harborside door, punching the alarm system's numbered code into the white keypad. She gasped when he opened the door, and Sam himself drew a sharp, startled breath.

She was so pale, a delicate porcelain doll.

So *fragile*, he thought, and yet so strong. Her jade-green eyes had never been brighter.

"You're a gambler after all," he greeted softly. *And you're willing to bet your life on my integrity.*

"You're not on your way back to Texas," Maylene murmured, realizing then that, deep inside, she had known—her heart had known—that Sam Coulter would be here.

"Not a chance. When I heard that the Jade Palace was about to be put to the ultimate test, I had to be here." Sam's smile caressed her very gently as he added, "Just like you."

Maylene trembled then, an icy shiver that came without warning.

As he moved a cold, wet strand of hair away from her eyes, Sam said, "Come with me, Jade."

The Building Commission's decision to suspend all work on the hotel had come just minutes after boxes containing jade-green towels and robes, each embroidered with the hotel's logo, had been delivered to the lobby. Sam grabbed several towels for Maylene's sea-dampened hair, and a large, lush robe for her sea-drenched body. Then he escorted her to the Imperial Suite.

The suite, intended to be the Jade Palace's most lavish, was completely unfurnished. The baby grand piano, hand-carved four-poster bed, and elegant ensembles of sofas and chairs were still in storage at Grand Prix. But the paint on the walls had long since dried, and the thick wall-to-wall carpeting had been installed, and . . .

"We have lots of ashtrays," Maylene observed as her eyes fell on a small stack of them—a colorful assortment of Florentine marble—that lay on the floor. "That's good."

"It is?" Sam asked. "Don't tell me you've taken up smoking."

"No. But . . ." But two nights ago you asked me to go gambling with you. We would drink champagne, you said, and you'd teach me how to smoke, and . . . "I thought that you would want to."

"I don't smoke, Jade. I quit last summer—forever." Sam's dark blue eyes embellished his solemn words. I quit, last summer, for you. "Remember?"

"Yes," she whispered. Her heart could remember everything, without his help, but now his eyes were drifting to her lips.

"And I'm very glad that I quit," Sam added with the caressing tenderness of a kiss . . . a kiss that tasted of her, of their loving, not of his cigarettes. Sam might have kissed her then. He wanted to, and her lovely lips smiled softly with welcome—but those lovely, welcoming lips were also tinged faintly blue. "Why don't you change out of your wet clothes while I do a little more foraging?"

Sam returned twenty minutes later, his arms filled with plush bedding taken from the pallets that lined the subterranean corridor outside what was to have been the hotel's central laundry.

Maylene was sitting on the soft, thick carpet. Her wet clothes lay neatly on the floor, as did her cowboy boots, and she was now luxuriantly cloaked in the bulky jade-green robe. But an unfolded towel lay on her lap and her silken black hair glistened still with diamonds from the silver-tipped waves.

She seemed to be resting, needing rest, as if the effort of changing had exhausted her and it would be a very long time before the arms from which so much of her blood had been drained would be able to take on the task of drying her hair.

"Let me," Sam offered as he took the towel from her pale white hands. "Let me know if I'm being too rough."

Sam wasn't rough at all, of course. The strong hands that coaxed the chilling dampness from her hair were exquisitely gentle. Despite the gentleness of his touch, however, he sensed her extreme weakness, how she was struggling to find even the energy to sit.

"Are you dizzy, Maylene?"

She had been dizzy since awakening in her room at the Hilton, and the whirling had only increased as she compelled the body that needed rest—*pleaded* for rest—on a journey that took her first to her apartment at the Trade Winds, where she showered and changed, then to Blake Pier, where she found the last sampan before the storm, and finally across Victoria Harbour, amid winds that seemed intent on blowing her into the sea.

Yes, she was dizzy, but now there was a new dizziness—a wondrous one—because of Sam. Maylene's heart wanted to float to him, but the body that had been pushed too far already threatened, quite simply, to collapse.

"I'm a little tired," she admitted. "I slept for hours last night, but . . ."

"You donated a great deal of blood." Sam gently parted the black veil of silk that curtained her face. "Why don't you take a nap? The real show isn't going to begin for a few more hours."

"I suppose I should."

"Okay. Let me get your bed ready for you."

What Sam made for Maylene was more nest than bed, a thick, cozy, enveloping swirl of sheets, blankets, and comforters. When her nest was ready, Sam returned to her and reached for her pale hands. Maylene swayed as she stood, but was instantly steadied by a strong and gentle arm.

"Thank you. I'm still a little wobbly."

"Sleep will help."

Sam wanted to tuck her in, and Maylene didn't resist, and when she was curled into the lush nest, and he asked if she would like to hear a bedtime story, her lips answered with a soft dreamy smile.

"Once upon a time, there was a beautiful princess. Her eyes were the color of jade, and she was very lovely, in so many ways— *all* ways—and yet . . ." His exhausted princess was already fast asleep, but still, as he softly kissed her pale white temple, Sam whispered, "And yet, she didn't seem to understand how lovely she was . . . or how loved."

The violence inside Peak Castle began just as the curtain of darkness fell over Hong Kong. It lasted less than an hour, but it was far more devastating than anything that had come before.

There was no pretense of passion this time, just raw, brutal punishment.

And when it was over, Eve fought desperately to remain conscious, to keep her own private curtain of darkness from falling.

Had Geoffrey slammed her head against the marble staircase? she wondered vaguely as her thoughts floated in the graying haze. Perhaps. Or maybe so much blood had pooled in her bruises that there wasn't enough left for her brain. Or, quite possibly, there was a far deeper injury. Perhaps her heart had shattered, having long since realized the truth to which only now her floating thoughts were drifting: Geoffrey was going to kill her.

Tonight. *Soon.*

Eve was in the great room, naked and bruised. Moments before, Geoffrey had left her without a word. But he was somewhere in the castle, and he would be back.

But, Eve vowed, by the time he returns, I'll be gone. Somehow I'll dash up the marble staircase, and then down the two flights of stairs outside. It doesn't matter that I'm naked. Nothing matters . . . except getting to Tyler.

She began her escape then, her bruised and battered body moving valiantly toward the promise of Tyler. And when she heard Geoffrey's ugly laugh behind her? Eve willed her trembling legs to climb ever faster.

But Geoffrey's laugh grew closer, and uglier, and just as Eve reached the foyer he caught a thin arm and spun her to him.

"You can't go anywhere, Eve." Sir Geoffrey Lloyd-Ashton was smiling and his voice was terrifyingly calm. "We're expecting company. Here," he said as he shoved a sheer silk negligee at her. "I brought you something to wear. Not that it's really necessary."

"What do you mean?"

Geoffrey relished the terror in her beautiful blue eyes. "Why don't you come listen to the phone call I've just made? It's recorded, of course, as all calls to and from the castle always are."

As Eve's eyes widened with growing comprehension and fright, Geoffrey added, "You didn't know that, did you, Eve . . . or should I say *Evangeline*?"

Geoffrey's fist imprisoned her arm, crushing her delicate flesh all the way to the bone, but Eve was empowered by fear—and by love. She twisted away, surprising and delighting him. He permitted her three precious steps toward freedom before recapturing her.

"Let's go listen to the phone call, princess."

In the room hidden behind bookshelves in his study, Geoffrey spent five minutes regaling Eve with the wonders of his surveillance system before torturing her further with the recording of the phone call he had made.

"Hello," the beloved voice greeted, hopeful, filled with love, because Eve alone knew the unlisted number of the condominium on Robinson Road.

"Hello, Tyler," the hated voice replied. "It's Geoffrey. I imagine you're wondering how I got this number? Eve gave it to me, of course. In fact, I'm calling for Eve. She's told me everything, Tyler, and although to say I'm displeased would be an understatement, Eve's made it quite clear that I have no choice but to accept the situation as gracefully as possible." To that point, Geoffrey's tone had been congenial. It cooled considerably as he continued, "Frankly, old chap, I'm sufficiently annoyed that I want Eve to leave the castle tonight instead of Monday. She's packing her things right now, and we'd both appreciate it if you would come get her. The winds are already very strong up here, but you're a pro at driving faster than the wind . . . aren't you, Tyler?"

"May I speak with—"

The tape continued to move, but there were no more words, only a hissing, whistling noise. After a moment Geoffrey pressed a button that simultaneously activated both "Rewind" and "Erase."

Arching an eyebrow at his stricken and still-naked wife, he queried, "I'd call that propitious *feng shui*, wouldn't you? The phone went dead at the precise moment that Tyler wanted to speak with you. What do you think, Eve? Did he believe me? Not that it really matters. I'm quite certain that our hero will be arriving at any moment, aren't you?"

"What are you planning to do, Geoffrey?"

He answered her with a smile, and his eyes gleamed ominously with the anticipation she knew so well, the eagerness of a predator about to savage his prey. "You'll find out. It's going to be wonderful, Eve. You and your lover are going to get everything you deserve." Geoffrey's smile faded and his eyes glowered at the diaphanous gown she still clutched in her hands. The gown was provocative, to be worn especially for a lover. Through its transparent silk every naked secret was revealed—and on this night, Eve's lover would see as well the huge bruises that adorned her snow-white skin. "Now get dressed."

"Hello, my precious love."

"James," Allison whispered.

For almost twenty-four hours this had been the extent of their dialogue. Allison's eyes would flutter open, and she would see his loving smile, and whisper his name, and then, smiling softly, she would drift back to the sleep that was so necessary for her healing body.

But two hours earlier, just as she was drifting away, Allison had whispered a word that had almost stopped his heart. "Seat belt," she had murmured, smiling as she did, as if for her the word triggered memories of love, not of terror.

For James, however, *seat belt* meant death. That there had been a bomb in his Jaguar had been obvious from the moment of the explosion. The police had confirmed that easily, and more: the detonator had been connected to the seat-belt buckle, programmed to send its deadly impulse to the bomb twenty seconds after the belt was fastened. It was the only sure way, they surmised, that the intended victim, not the hotel's valet, would be killed.

For two hours James had waited restlessly for Allison to awaken, and now she had—but, already, her eyelids were beginning to flutter closed.

"Allison?"

With effort, with love, she opened her eyes. "Yes, James?"

"Do you have the energy for a few questions?"

"I'll try."

"Good. These questions may seem obvious, too easy, but the doctors want me to test your memory. So, let's see. Do you remember why you were in the Jaguar?"

"Of course I remember," Allison answered softly. "You wanted me to drive you to Aberdeen . . . for dinner on one of the floating restaurants . . . just as you'd promised in June."

At her words, restless power suddenly flooded his deadly hands, and his heart began to pump with pure rage. But, for Allison, James smiled, and his lethal fingers were exquisitely gentle as they touched her beloved face, and with effort, with love, he even kept his murderous thoughts from blazing in his silver eyes.

"Did I call you to make those plans?"

"No." Allison frowned briefly, searching her foggy memory. Then she smiled. "Alex did."

"Who is Alex?"

James thought that she might not answer. Despite her valiant efforts, the powerful magnet of sleep was about to win. But then she spoke.

"Mrs. Leong's assistant," she murmured.

"Very good," he said softly. "Now, just one last question. Did Alex specifically remind you to fasten the seat belt?"

As Allison nodded her reply her eyelids fluttered down over

her beautiful emerald eyes. Before leaving her, James kissed her lips and whispered, "Sleep well, my love."

And while you sleep, my love, I will find the man who did this to you—and I will deal with him.

E ight people had been present when James made his promise to Allison of a December dinner in Aberdeen. Even before leaving her bedside, James had reduced the list of those who could have tampered with the car to two: Geoffrey and Tyler.

Tyler was the more likely. The onetime race-car driver was an expert mechanic—and just yesterday James had raised the possibility that he had intentionally supplied faulty materials for the Jade Palace. But James had never truly believed that Tyler was responsible for sabotaging the hotel, and by the time he reached the street outside the hospital, Tyler was no longer on his short list of suspects.

Geoffrey was the monster. Even the winds seemed to howl his name. And, with their vicious gusts, they shrieked another truth: Geoffrey was a new enemy—and an old one.

And, the cold winds hissed, Gweneth had known all along.

"I don't like him, James," she had confided during their Christmastime visit to Hong Kong.

"Really? Why not? Has Eve said something?"

"No. But I don't think she's happy with him. I hope I'm dead wrong, James. Geoffrey seems so charming, and maybe I'm just being cynical, but . . ."

But Gweneth Drake had not been dead wrong about Sir Geoffrey Lloyd-Ashton.

CHAPTER 32

Dragon's Eyes
Saturday, December 11, 1993

The barrel of the gun was pressed against Eve's temple, and the hammer was fully cocked, and Geoffrey's finger was curled around the trigger. He held Eve with his other arm, a crushing embrace that stretched the negligee's sheer silk tightly across her battered torso.

"Do you like these bruises, Tyler?" Geoffrey's eyes glittered. "From what I can tell, you didn't have enough *fun* with Eve. You were gentle with her, weren't you? Too bad. She loves pain, *begs* for it. Don't you, my princess?"

"Let her go, Geoffrey." Despite his anger—and his fear for Eve—Tyler's tone was quiet, conciliatory. He must keep the madman calm, he decided. Calm, and talking—and the instant Geoffrey dropped his guard, Tyler would make his move for the gun. "If you have a problem, it's with me, not with Eve."

"You mean *Evangeline*," Geoffrey hissed. Then, smiling, he clarified, "Actually, Tyler, my problem is with both of you. You'll be pleased to know that I have a solution. It's not all that I'd hoped, mind you, but things got a bit rushed when Eve decided to leave on Monday despite the Jade Palace fiasco. Frankly,

I'd counted on that little disaster giving me more time rather than less."

"More time for what, Geoffrey?" Tyler asked.

Geoffrey feigned surprise. "To *punish* her, of course. It was really going to be quite amusing watching Eve suffer as an endless series of tragedies befell her precious friends. Oh, well, one has to be flexible, doesn't—" The doorbell sounded then. Geoffrey seemed intrigued by the interruption, and not the least bit alarmed. "I wonder who that could be?"

The answer to Geoffrey's question was instantly visible on the great room's closed circuit monitor.

"Why, it's James," Geoffrey observed, his wild eyes gleaming with delight. "I imagine that our little Allison has recalled a telephone conversation with a mystery man named Alex which took place shortly before her accident. James is more than welcome to join our party, of course, although his presence will pose a slight problem."

Geoffrey didn't elaborate on the potential problem.

He merely solved it.

In a fluid motion, he took the gun from Eve's head and fired.

The bullet struck Tyler in the chest. But Tyler did not fall. He *would not* fall.

Instead, moving toward Geoffrey, knowing that he would die and caring only for Eve's safety, Tyler whispered, "Run, Eve. *Run.*"

But Eve couldn't run. Geoffrey's arm imprisoned her still. And, had she been free, Eve would have run to Tyler, not to safety.

Geoffrey greeted Tyler's brave approach with an anticipatory smile. The second bullet, fired at close range, would find Tyler's heart. But at the last instant Geoffrey remembered his plan to force Eve to pull the trigger for that lethal shot—and the immense pleasure that would be his in watching.

He fired at Tyler's left leg instead, striking bone midthigh and shattering it. Tyler tried, still, to walk. But it was impossible. After a few staggering steps, he fell to the floor.

Eve struggled to be free, to be with Tyler, and without hesitation Geoffrey released her. As Eve dropped to her knees beside the man she loved, Tyler reached to caress her beloved face. For several heartbeats their eyes held and they journeyed far away . . . to their dream.

The moment ended quickly, as Eve felt the warmth of Tyler's blood pooling on the cold marble floor beside her. But even before she began ripping strips of silk from her negligee, to make a tourniquet for him, Tyler was removing his jacket for her—to cloak her nakedness, to give her privacy, dignity, even as his own life was slipping away.

"This is as pathetic as *Romeo and Juliet*," Geoffrey scoffed. "Go ahead, Eve. Tourniquet his leg, but do it quickly. James is waiting."

"Let James go, Geoffrey!"

"You just don't get it, do you, my princess? James has undoubtedly figured everything out—and you haven't even begun to. James isn't about to leave. Hurry up, Eve. Our guest is waiting."

Eve tied the pure silk tourniquet around Tyler's bloodied leg, kissed him softly on the lips, then returned to Geoffrey. She had no choice. The next bullet would have been in Tyler's heart.

As soon as she was imprisoned again, the gun barrel wedged against the purple bruise that had formed on her temple, Geoffrey instructed her to press the button that unbolted the castle's front door.

James didn't hear the gunshots. The fury of the winds, and of his own thundering thoughts, drowned out all else. And if he *had* heard the shots? It would not have deterred him. Nothing would have.

When the castle door flew open, James entered without the slightest hesitation—even though he realized that he might be about to confront *two* mortal enemies. Tyler Vaughn's Lamborghini was parked outside, raising the possibility that his instincts about Tyler, his belief in his integrity, had been wrong.

It didn't matter if Tyler and Geoffrey were partners in crime. James Drake's heart and body were fully prepared to kill them both.

As soon as James began his descent of the marble staircase, however, he saw the truth. Only one mortal enemy awaited him in the great room below.

"James," Geoffrey greeted. His voice was warm and friendly, as if absolutely untroubled by the fact that a man lay dying at his feet and that he himself was holding a cocked gun to his own wife's head. "What a pleasant surprise. Devilish night to be out and about, isn't it?"

James's only answer to Geoffrey's greeting was the deadly intent in his silver eyes. With graceful yet measured power, he moved toward his enemy, stopping only when he reached the precise spot on the shining white marble that was exactly the right distance away from Geoffrey. As he looked at the murderous taipan James made a silent assessment of the gun at Eve's temple—and of himself. He could do this. In a single motion, and so swiftly that Geoffrey would never realize what was happening, he could kick the gun from Geoffrey's hand and snap Geoffrey's neck.

The panther needed a few moments to ready himself to make the lethal move. Every cell in his entire body must be focused, ready to spring, to become airborne. James had rehearsed such flight a thousand times.

But did he have time, now, to prepare properly? Yes, James realized. Sir Geoffrey Lloyd-Ashton was in no hurry to bring to a close his deadly party. He was enjoying himself far too much—and he believed himself to be in absolute control.

"Is there anything you'd like to ask me, James? Let's face it, this is an opportune time. Wouldn't you like to know about Gweneth?"

"Oh, no," Eve whispered. "Oh, James . . ."

"You're finally beginning to understand, aren't you, Eve?" Geoffrey mocked. "There was no way I could permit Gweneth Drake to move to Hong Kong. And do you know why? Because of you, my love. You were far too happy when Gweneth was here. *Far* too happy."

"Oh, James." Eve turned her head then, and the gun barrel sunk even deeper into her bruised temple, and the sudden movement might have caused Geoffrey to pull the trigger. But Eve didn't care. She needed to see James. *"I'm so sorry."*

James hesitated a moment before speaking. He would spend tomorrow, the next day—as long as it took—trying to convince Eve that she was not to blame. But if there wasn't a tomorrow? Then she needed to know, to believe, *now.*

His eyes became gentle, filled for that moment with love not with death, and he said, very softly, "It's not your fault, Eve. You couldn't possibly have known . . . or even imagined. It's *not* your fault."

Instantly impatient—and annoyed—with the exchange between Eve and James, Geoffrey taunted, "You believed that *you* were the target, didn't you, James? How terribly arrogant of you. But I'll tell you the truth—you were partially right. You and Gweneth were both supposed to die in Wales. It was a botched job, and I was furious when I first learned of it, but it really worked out rather well." His expression became one of smug satisfaction. "I've enjoyed immensely watching your grief. *Most* entertaining." His smugness suddenly dissolved into a glower. "After a while, however, you began to annoy me. As long as I'd spared your life, the least you could have done was to build the Jade Palace for me. But it took you *forever* to get around to it, didn't it?"

Geoffrey shrugged dismissively. "Well, I'm willing to let by-gones be bygones. Especially now that the hotel is going to be mine. I'd been concerned that it might be awkward for me to buy it, a bit too obvious, but now . . . well . . . it will make perfect sense to everyone in Hong Kong that I would want to dedicate such a spectacular shrine to the loving memory of my cherished princess and our dear friend James." For a moment Geoffrey's face became solemn, as if imagining the eulogy he would deliver at the grand opening of his Jade Palace. Then he smiled, beaming with sheer madness as he announced, "I'm afraid we're going to have a bloodbath, right here, all over this pristine white marble. This wasn't exactly the scene I had planned, but I think it will work out rather nicely."

Geoffrey became a director then, explaining to each of his assembled actors the motivations for their respective roles in his deadly scenario. "You'll have come here tonight, James, in pur-suit of Tyler. You'll have discovered that indeed he *was* cheating you. There will be a fight. Eve, our little heroine, will bravely try to intercede." He sighed dramatically. "But, alas, her efforts will be to no avail. In fact, she'll be caught in the cross fire as the two of you fight to the death. When I return home to my castle, I'll find three dead bodies. *Splendid*, don't you think?"

It was time, James realized. Geoffrey's crazed eyes seemed eager to actually *see* the crimson carnage he had so gleefully described.

And James was ready to kill.

In eight seconds, he decided, Sir Geoffrey Lloyd-Ashton would be dead. Eight—for luck. The silent countdown to death would begin as soon as James finished asking a final question.

"Why did you try to kill Allison?"

Eight.

Geoffrey shrugged. "Why not?"

Seven.

"She was a bloody nuisance. She could have left Hong Kong without a scratch, but *no*, the brave little pilot had to stay."

Six.

"You were responsible for the destruction of her photographs, weren't you, Geoffrey?"

Five.

Geoffrey grinned wickedly. "Of course I was."

Four.

"Speaking of nuisances, I'm truly sorry that you'll all miss the plans I have for Juliana Kwan."

Three.

"I so enjoy having people left behind, you see," Geoffrey explained. "The suffering, you know, the *mourning*."

Two.

"Oh well, perhaps Juliana's half-breed daughter's green eyes will fill with tears."

James Drake's sleekly muscled body was about to become a lethal weapon.

But just before he silently counted off the final second, there was an extraordinary sound. It was far too immense to be human, and even though at precisely the same instant the winds outside began their most savage howling yet, the fearsome sound seemed quite distinct from the noises made by the raging typhoon.

It was something else—it sounded almost like a roar—and it seemed to come from within the castle itself.

The roar came again, and this time the walls of the castle shuddered and shook, and then ground on which they stood began to tremble, and before their eyes, the white marble floor beneath them opened.

The crack was huge, gaping, and its marble edges were jagged and sharp, like massive white teeth, and it was so wide that Geoffrey was suddenly far away from James, separated by the deep abyss and out of danger, for the moment, from James's deadly leap.

But there was new danger for Geoffrey. The floor had opened just beneath his feet, leaving him teetering on the very edge of the gaping hole. To maintain his balance, he released his crushing grasp of Eve. The maneuver worked. His balance was instantly restored—but only for a moment.

The roar sounded yet again, even louder this time, a thunderous bellow that seemed to come from deep within the hole, and the earth trembled anew, and now the great jaws of white marble were beginning close, and as they did they took Sir Geoffrey Lloyd-Ashton with them, pitching him into the abyss . . . and swallowing him whole.

Then there was silence.

And even the winds outside were still.

And for a very long time none of them spoke. Indeed, it was something about which none of them would ever speak. The world would believe that the colossal winds had shaken the castle to its very foundation, as indeed they had.

But those who had been there knew the truth.

The blinded dragon had exacted its revenge.

CHAPTER 33

S am was amazed by the noise. The walls of the Jade Palace were thick and well insulated, and the glass had been specifically designed to withstand the most ferocious of storms, but it still sounded exactly the way hurricanes were supposed to—as if a freight train were speeding its way into the room.

More amazing than the sound was the fact that Maylene was sleeping so peacefully. Sam had made her nest in a secluded alcove, far away from the wall-to-ceiling window. At the very worst, of course, the top-quality glass was only supposed to crack, not shatter. Sam didn't doubt the quality of the glass. But had it really ever been tested against anything so fierce as this typhoon?

Even if the glass did shatter, he reasoned, Maylene's nest in the alcove should be well out of harm's way. Still, to be sure, Sam had become a human shield, positioning himself between her and the window.

Maylene stirred then, a graceful uncurling of her long pale limbs, the first time she had moved at all in nearly five hours. Sam assumed that she wouldn't awaken, but as he watched, the long inky-black lashes fluttered open.

Her jade-green eyes seemed even brighter now, and her lips smiled softly as she searched the shadows and found him.

"Hi," he greeted.

"Hi." Her eyes widened. "What's that noise? The typhoon?"

"The prelude to the typhoon. Unless it's picked up speed along the way, its full force won't reach Kowloon for another hour."

"Is it that late? Almost midnight?"

"Almost. You slept very well. You obviously needed the rest. How do you feel now?"

Her bright eyes sparkled. "Rested."

And stronger, she amended silently. And brave, she added as she rose then from her nest and began to walk toward the protective body of the cowboy.

She had almost reached him when the lights went out.

"Oh, Sam, *look*," she whispered. "Look at the window."

Sam believed he already knew what he would see: rivulets of water that streaked horizontally, not vertically, across the glass. The typhoonal winds, it seemed, had no regard whatsoever for the laws of gravity. Torrential rains that didn't fall to earth were remarkable enough, but the effect was even more dazzling because of the watery blur of lights from the island beyond.

As Sam turned he expected to see again the magnificent play of wind and rain and color. But what he saw surpassed all else: the window itself was aglow. Rippled by the wind, the glass gave off its own inner light, a luminous blend of emerald and jade.

Maylene walked in awe toward the glowing glass, unable to resist. She was Dorothy after all, and this wall of green shimmered like the Emerald City of Oz.

"This is the best glass on earth," Sam said as he moved beside her. "But these may also be the strongest winds the planet has ever known."

"I'm not afraid." Maylene smiled as she extended a graceful

hand toward the window. "It's unbelievable, isn't it? You see it, don't you? The two colors glowing together?"

"I see it," Sam answered softly. "But it's something I've seen before . . . and I don't mean tonight while you were sleeping. The jade in this glass is the precise color of your eyes. Maybe you don't know that. And maybe you don't know, either, that when you're happy, there are sparkles of emerald in your jade-green eyes. Look at me, Jade."

Maylene followed his gentle command, turning from the glowing window to him. And when her lovely eyes met his, Sam saw glowing jade-and-emerald still, shimmering together, as one.

"I see both colors now. Are you happy now, Jade? Are you glad to be here?"

"Yes." *This is where I belong . . . with you.*

Moments earlier Maylene's graceful hands had reached for the window, to touch the brilliant illusion of emerald and jade, and now, so bravely, those same delicate hands reached gracefully for him.

Sam Coulter was an illusion, too. She knew that. But at this moment his dark blue eyes were promising her the most magnificent illusion of all, an entire night of love, with him.

As Maylene reached to touch his chest Sam gently caught her hands, welcoming them, drawing them higher, around his neck, and when they rested there, he tenderly encircled her waist.

"Dance with me, Jade."

They danced, their swaying silhouettes illuminated by their glowing green moon. Outside, the typhoon thundered ever louder, crescendoing with ever more ferocious breaths. But inside, Sam and Maylene heard a different sound entirely, and they danced to it, the joyous music made by hearts joined together in the splendor of love.

And as they danced they kissed, and eventually their dancing desires compelled them to journey from the soft glow of their window to the dark shadows of the secluded alcove.

"Make love to me, Sam," Maylene whispered when it seemed, suddenly, as if he might be merely planning to tuck her gently into her nest.

"Are you sure?" he asked softly. "I don't want to hurt you."

"You won't."

And he didn't, of course. He was very careful with her, exquisitely gentle with the delicate woman who had recently given so much of herself for her sister. Maylene's passion—Maylene's love—were far stronger than her body. Much too quickly, even Sam's wondrously tender loving exhausted her. She fell asleep in his arms without ever hearing his whispered words of love.

Sam listened to the wailing storm send frantic warnings to all in its path that soon, very soon, the world might come to an end. But, he thought, for us, the world is just beginning. He planned to stay awake all night, holding her, keeping vigil while she slept. But more than once, Maylene awakened, wanting him, needing him, welcoming him with soft sighs of pure joy.

The electricity announced its return just as dawn was announcing itself with a pale pink sky. The former came with a surprising amount of noise as lights, elevators, and furnaces whirred back to life all at once. Maylene was curled against him, facing away, and when he sensed that the noise had awakened her, Sam waited for her to turn to him yet again.

Last night's loving had been in shadows, in darkness, the secluded alcove hidden even from the soft beams of light cast by their glowing green moon. But now, at last, they would be able to see each other while they loved. Sam would see her lovely jade-and-emerald eyes, and Maylene would see the love in his, and Sam would tell her of his love, to be very certain that she knew.

But Maylene didn't turn to him. Instead, with careful movements that were clearly intended not to awaken him, she left their love nest and began to dress. In moments she was a cowgirl again—minus her cowboy boots and her long black braid. Her love-tangled hair fell free, a cascade of softly curling silk. She wasn't going to take the time to braid it, Sam realized, and now she was picking up her boots, about to leave, her getaway swift and silent.

Sam Coulter's anger was not in control, not by a long shot, but this time he wanted words from Maylene Kwan as she left his bed.

"Where are you going?"

The slender body that had danced with him throughout the night, moving with his with such grace and such love, suddenly became stiff. Maylene didn't turn. She stared instead at the window. Hours before, it had glowed like her eyes, but now it was clear again, just another pane of glass.

"I don't see any Star ferries, but there are already lots of sampans in the harbor. I want to find James, to tell him that the Jade Palace survived the typhoon." Maylene's voice faltered as she spoke the obvious lie. No one needed to tell James Drake that his hotel hadn't been built on quicksand. The moment he looked across the harbor, James would know. And he would look. All of Hong Kong would—and they would see at a glance that their magnificent shrine glittered still.

But what truth *could* Maylene speak to Sam? There was only one truth in her heart—*I love you*—and only moments before Allison's accident, Sam had very clearly spelled out exactly what he wanted from her. One final night of passion, nothing more, after which they would never see each other again.

"You probably won't have any trouble getting your next two projects back."

"Probably not," Sam conceded quietly as his heart raged.

Why had Maylene decided to spend last night at the hotel? Sam had convinced himself it was because she trusted him, because she *loved* him. But now he wondered. Had it been, for her, just the ultimate reckless pleasure, tender loving amid the merciless violence of a devastating storm?

"I imagine Kai Tak will open soon." Maylene spoke to the crystal-clear glass. "You'll probably be able to leave Hong Kong today."

"I imagine so."

Maylene needed to leave him *now*, before he heard her tears.

"Well," she said softly. "Good-bye, Cowboy."

"So long, Jade."

Sam watched as Maylene made her way to the harborside esplanade and climbed onto a varnished launch that rocked gently beside the seawall. Victoria Harbour was flat calm on this pale pink winter morning. Even its silver-tipped waves were hidden beneath its mirror-smooth surface.

Maylene did not look back, not once. When she was halfway across the harbor, Sam's fist unclenched just long enough to curl around one of the marble ashtrays from Florence.

Had he been thinking, it would have occurred to him how foolish the gesture was—and how futile. But Sam wasn't thinking. He was only feeling. And, at long last, the violence that had lived within him all these years was going to be permitted one small escape.

Sam had the rest of his life to punish himself for falling in love with Maylene Kwan—and he would. No matter how much violence escaped now, there would be plenty left inside.

For the first time ever, Sam Coulter took aim at something outside himself: the crystal-clear glass that hours before had been their private moon.

Even as he was hurling the alabaster marble at the window, Sam chided himself. The window would be unscathed. The marble would bounce back onto the plush carpet, mocking him.

The marble did bounce back. Everything that had been promised about the quality of the glass was true: even in the face of the most extreme violence nature could offer, it might crack—but it would not shatter.

Nature had spent most of the night trying to put even the tiniest line in the tinted jade glass . . . and had failed. But the violent power of Sam Coulter's fury surpassed even that of the monstrous typhoon.

Before his eyes appeared not just a single line, but thousands of them, a gigantic spiderweb, its delicate gossamer threads emerald and jade against the pale pink sky.

Sam waited an hour before making his own journey across Victoria Harbour. The decision was designed to avoid seeing Maylene, and it brought him face-to-face with James.

Both men were returning to the Trade Winds for the first time since the typhoon. Both were unshaven, and neither had slept, and although Sam felt the ravages of internal trauma, only James was covered with blood.

"What happened?" Sam asked. Then, instantly worried about both sisters, he asked softly, "Allison?"

"Allison's fine," James assured. "This is Tyler's blood."

As they crossed the lobby toward the elevator James gave Sam a brief sketch of what had transpired at Peak Castle. "It was almost four this morning before the winds had subsided enough for us to drive down the mountain. Tyler had lost a great deal of blood by then—*too* much, it seemed—but he's at the hospital now and the doctors say he's going to survive. It will be a while, though, before he walks again. They're going to have to remove all the shattered bone from his leg and replace the missing length with a steel rod."

"When do they plan to do that?"

"This evening, assuming his chest wound and blood count have stabilized."

"Is he awake?"

"He never lost consciousness." James's eyes and voice were solemn with remembrance. It had been, he decided, an act of pure love. Tyler hadn't believed that he would live. He wanted to be with Eve, telling her of his love, for as long as he could.

"I think I'll drop by and see him before I leave."

"You're leaving today, Sam?"

"If I can get a flight out. Oh, James, just so you know—what happened to the window in the Imperial Suite had nothing to do with the typhoon and I'll pay to have it replaced."

James waved a dismissive hand. "You've already been to the hotel?"

"I spent the night there. As did Maylene."

"So you've seen her this morning, and she's all right?"

"Maylene?" Sam heard the bitterness in his own voice. "Oh, yes, she's perfectly fine."

Just moments before the varnished launch would have reached Blake Pier on Hong Kong Island, Maylene impulsively dug deep into her jeans pockets for what remained of the money she had stuffed there yesterday afternoon before beginning her journey to the Jade Palace. Expecting that it might be quite difficult to convince anyone to take her across the choppy waters, she had taken all the cash she had in her apartment. But despite the cost of that wind-tossed voyage, there was still quite a bit left.

As she extracted two one-hundred-dollar notes she asked, in

Cantonese, "Will you take me to Aberdeen Harbour? I'll pay you two hundred dollars."

It was a fair price, but this was Hong Kong, and even within hours of a typhoon, negotiations were expected.

"Four hundred," the boat's skipper countered.

"Three hundred," Maylene offered.

The man smiled, satisfied with the deal. "Three hundred."

As soon as Maylene handed him the money, they were on their way to Aberdeen.

CHAPTER 34

Aberdeen Harbour
Sunday, December 12, 1993

L ast night's typhoon had been more powerful than the one that had destroyed Tranquil Sea's world more than thirty years before. But this time Tin Hau had chosen to protect those who dwelled on the floating city of junks. At the last moment the ferocious puffs had swept up to Victoria Peak, before descending down to the Jade Palace, and except for a green blizzard of palm fronds and eucalyptus leaves, Aberdeen had been mercifully spared.

Maylene didn't know what had compelled her to journey here, to this place that once had been Juliana's home, but now, as she wandered along the shoreline, an astonishing thought began to dance in her mind: she and her mother were very much alike.

For a long time Maylene resisted the wonderful—yet improbable—thought. True, as young girls, both Tranquil Sea and Maylene Kwan had been torn between two worlds. Juliana was a child of the sea who dreamed of life on land, and Maylene was a child of two races who dreamed that, someday, just one of the two would accept her. And, for both girls, at age thirteen, their lives were changed forever.

But . . . but Juliana was so courageous, so loving, so strong.

The girl who had rescued herself from a typhoon had grown into a woman capable of great love. She fell in love with Garrett Whitaker, deeply and forever, and even though her love had not been returned, what Juliana had felt in her own heart was wondrous—and very real. She had cloaked her daughter with her own joyous memories of that imaginary love, and for thirteen years her magical words had been an invisible shield, protecting Maylene's young heart from even the cruelest taunts.

Juliana's lies had been lies of love. She had wanted only—and always—to protect her beloved daughter from every sadness and every harm.

Just as I would protect my own baby, Maylene realized. Just as I *will* protect her.

It was then, as Maylene stood at water's edge, with teak junks floating before her and emerald dragons towering behind, that she became aware of the way she was standing. Her posture was model perfect, as always, straight and tall, but her delicate hands rested gently on her lower abdomen, as if they were already caressing—and protecting—a tiny new life that dwelled inside.

I have loved you with all my heart from the moment I knew you were alive inside me. Do you know when that was, my darling? Just hours after you were conceived, before your father even left Hong Kong. Maylene had so cruelly dismissed her mother's impassioned words. It was only additional proof, she had taunted, of Juliana's romantic delusions.

But now . . . now Maylene felt a new life inside her. Only a few hours old, already it needed all her protection and all her love. Was the little life growing inside a child of lust? To Sam, yes, but not to her. To Maylene, this baby was the child of greatest love.

And what would she tell her baby about its father? The truth: that he was gentle, and loving, and kind. And the lie: that he would have spent his life with them, loving them, if only he could have . . . but that he had died.

"Oh, Mother," Maylene whispered softly to the shining emerald sea. "We are so very much alike."

"May-May," Juliana whispered with joy when she opened the front door of her Happy Valley home. It was almost twilight. The winter sky glowed lavender and gold and the fragrant evening air was beginning to chill. As Juliana opened the door wider, welcoming her long-lost daughter inside, she whispered again, *"May-May."*

"Mother . . . I've come to ask for your forgiveness."

"*My* forgiveness?" For a moment Juliana's joy faltered. She had believed that Maylene had heard all her words, and had remembered them all but . . . "*I'm* the one who needs to be forgiven. I'm the one who lied. Don't you remember? The last thing I said to you before you left Hong Kong was that I hoped one day you could understand—and forgive."

"I remember, but . . . you never meant to hurt me . . . and I was so cruel to you."

"Oh, my darling." Juliana touched her then, a maternal gesture as old as time, tenderly moving a strand of hair away from precious eyes that she needed to see. "You'd spent your life being hurt, and hiding your pain to protect me, and when you learned the truth of what I had done, you felt so very betrayed. I wanted you to understand. But how could you? You were so young, my May-May, just a girl, a loving little girl who had always been so brave. You were never cruel, my love, you were only so terribly hurt."

Juliana held her arms open then, for her daughter, and when Maylene moved gratefully into her mother's loving embrace, Juliana whispered, "I love you, my May-May. I love you."

"Oh, Mother, I love you, too."

Many moments later Maylene pulled away, just a little, just enough to see her mother's beloved face.

"And," she said softly, "now I *do* understand. I understand everything."

Juliana heard the softness of Maylene's words, and saw the hope—and the sadness—in her daughter's jade-green eyes, but before she could ask about the man with whom Maylene had fallen in love, another voice spoke.

"You don't understand everything."

Maylene Kwan had spent her lifetime wondering what a father's voice would sound like when it filled with love for his daughter . . . and now she knew. The loving voice came from behind her, and now it was speaking again, and this time, in flawless Cantonese perfected by twenty-eight years of practice, it was whispering her name—Daughter of Greatest Love.

Maylene wanted to turn to him, but her limbs were frozen. This final journey of love, it seemed, would be impossible for her to make.

But the Daughter of Greatest Love didn't have to make the journey alone. Juliana was there, holding her hand, just as she had held it all those times when mother and daughter had wandered through Hong Kong, sharing together Juliana's magical memories of love.

Gently encouraged by Juliana, Maylene turned to her father, and what greeted her when she did were dark green eyes that were soft with love—just as Maylene's own dark green eyes would one day soften, always soften, for her own baby.

"Everything your mother told you about us was true." Garrett's voice was deep with emotion. "We loved each other deeply, forever, and we would have spent our lives together . . . loving you . . . if we had believed that we could."

Garrett began walking toward her then, and somehow Maylene's hand was already reaching out for his.

For so many years, when she and her mother had walked, hand in hand, through the streets of Hong Kong, Maylene had felt his hand, too, loving her, protecting her. And now that loving hand was there, entwined with hers, and as Garrett's other arm curled around both mother and daughter, they became a circle of love . . . they became a family.

The sky was alight with stars by the time they made the short journey from the house overlooking Happy Valley to the hospital.

"Allison never needs to know," Maylene had told her parents. "You can pretend that you've just met, and fallen in love, and—"

"Allison already knows," Garrett had interjected softly. "I told her this morning . . . and she can't wait to see her sister."

Garrett's words echoed in Maylene's mind, giving her strength, but still, as she approached Allison's room, her heart raced with apprehension. Garrett and Juliana and James were all discreetly absent, in the nearby waiting room. The sisters would be alone, with each other . . . and the truth.

Then Maylene was there, in the doorway, but even before she made a sound, Allison's magnificent curls of fire and moonbeams were turning toward her, and then their green eyes met and held—and at that moment jade and emerald wore identical expressions of uncertainty and hope. And then, at the same instant, as if remembering that the hard part was over, that they were already friends, they smiled.

Six months earlier, at the airport, Maylene had felt herself gliding, floating, toward Allison, as if pulled by a magnet deep within the golden girl. Maylene was gliding again now; but it seemed as if the once tarnished sister now had her own magnet of gold deep within, because Allison seemed to be pulled toward her as well, reaching out to her with pale slender arms.

"Maylene," Allison whispered with welcome, and joy, as Maylene neared.

"I think you should call me Dorothy, Lion."

"You're home now, aren't you?"

"Almost." Maylene reached Allison then, and as she embraced her sister she added softly, "Now I am."

After their gentle hug ended, their hands touched still, at last completing the brave journey that had begun weeks before on a gown of jade-green silk and silver stars.

"You're so pale," Allison said.

"But I'm fine. I was a little wobbly at first, but now I'm fine ... and you're fine ... and if you ever need blood again you know where you can get it."

"Thank you." Allison tilted her golden-red head. "You saved my life, Maylene."

"Well," Maylene countered quietly, "I think you saved mine, too. And Allison? About your babies? I can carry them for you, as a surrogate. I *want* to."

And, Maylene thought, your babies will be safe within me— because sometime in the past two days, all the hungry ghosts have vanished forever.

"Oh, Maylene."

"I mean it, Allison. If anything ever happened to you ..."

"It *won't*. I promise. Before becoming pregnant, James and I will talk to the doctors. The monitoring they can do now is so much more sophisticated than what was available twenty-eight years ago. I'm sure everything will be fine."

"But if not, Allison, if it seems too risky, let me do it. Please?"

"Yes," Allison answered softly, gratefully. "Yes."

"Good." Maylene smiled, then shrugged, then confessed, "I couldn't be a surrogate for you right away, though."

Allison's eyes widened with comprehension. "You're pregnant?"

"I think so, even though it seems impossible to know this soon."

"But you do know."

"Yes, I do."

"And Sam? Does he know?"

"Sam?"

"I know how you feel about Sam," Allison said. And then, with what was meant to have been a loving tease, but which trembled with emotion, she added, "It's my *job* to know such things. I'm your sister, after all."

Your sister, your sister!

For several moments all that spoke were shining eyes and wobbly smiles. Then wanting—and needing—to talk to her sister about the secret that Allison already knew, Maylene said, "I assume that Sam Coulter is halfway back to Texas by now."

"Yes, he is," Allison confirmed quietly. "He stopped by this morning to say good-bye. I thought he seemed very sad."

"I doubt that."

"He seemed sad to me," Allison repeated firmly. And, firmly still, and with green eyes that were thoughtful, and earnest, and perhaps even wise, she offered, "If you're pregnant with his baby, Sam needs to know, just as, I think, he needs to know how you feel about him. You're not home, Dorothy, not all the way home, until you tell Sam everything."

By Christmas Eve, when the luxury liner carrying the Whitakers and Parishes docked at Ocean Terminal in Kowloon, Lily Kai was dazzling her parents with her newfound energy. She had sailed through surgery, a voyage that had begun and ended, as promised, by visits from Eve.

And, by Christmas Eve, Tyler Vaughn was dazzling his doctors—and his bride-to-be—with his remarkable recovery. And Hong Kong was dazzled as well, by the speed with which Peak Castle was being torn down. For the first time in years Victoria Peak's dragon would be able to enjoy the spectacular fireworks that lighted the midnight sky on New Year's Eve.

Garrett didn't go to Ocean Terminal to meet the cruise ship.

There was a ritual involved in arriving by boat in Hong Kong. Passengers were met by Rolls-Royce limousines and whisked in luxurious style to their luxurious hotels.

Only after his parents and in-laws were settled comfortably into their adjoining suites at the Regent did Garrett appear.

"Where's Allison?" Pauline Whitaker asked even as she embraced her son.

"Just next door, at the Jade Palace, overseeing the placement of her murals. She'll be here later. First, though, there's something I need to tell you."

"Is Allison all right, Garrett? You look so serious."

"Allison's just fine, Dad. In fact, she's never been happier. But we do have something serious to discuss, something that involves you all." *Something that may be too difficult for you to accept.* "Why don't you all sit down?"

Because it was abundantly clear that Garrett would not speak again until all four had obeyed his command, they sat . . . and he remained standing . . . and then he began.

"I need to tell you about the week when Blake was killed and I was in Hong Kong."

"Oh, Garrett, no! We're here now, isn't that enough? Why do we have to bring up the sadnesses of the past?"

"Because they have a bearing on the present . . . and on the future. I'm sorry, but you really must hear what I have to say." He drew a soft breath. "I was here, in Hong Kong, but I wasn't alone. I was with a Chinese woman named Juliana. . . ."

Garrett told them about that week, his love for Juliana, her resolute belief that their love could never be, and her insistence that he not wait for her, that he find someone else to love, to marry.

"Beth never knew about Juliana," he quietly assured Robert and Iris Parish. "And she never would have known. I loved Beth. You know I did."

For many heartbeats it seemed that they would not answer.

This was all too shocking, too painful—and now they had journeyed from memories of the death of the beloved son to the death of the beloved daughter.

But at last Iris Parish whispered, "Yes, Garrett, we know that."

"And now, Garrett, *no more*. Please!" The entreaty came from Pauline Whitaker, and was met by apologetic—yet resolute—green eyes that told her there *was* more, and that he was going to tell them. Her gaze fell away, from her son's determined face to his hands . . . and when Pauline saw the glitter of gold, it was she who moved the unwanted conversation from the past to the present—with a horrified gasp. "You're wearing a wedding ring!"

"Juliana and I were married six days ago."

"But why, Garrett? Why after all this time?"

"Because, after all this time, we love each other still. In fact, we love each other even more."

"But why marriage? And why so quickly?"

"Because people who love each other the way Juliana and I do want to be married. And because, for our daughter, we want everyone to know of our love."

"You mean this hasty marriage was Allison's idea?"

In fact, it had been. They had all been at the house overlooking Happy Valley. Juliana had been sewing Allison's wedding gown, stitching onto the ivory silk the iridescent seed pearls—each with its own rainbow—which, when they were all in place, would be a garden of butterflies and roses. *Stop*, Allison had commanded as she gently placed her own hand over Juliana's. Please make your own wedding gown first.

"Actually," Garrett admitted, "it was Allison who insisted that we marry so soon. But when I said our daughter, I was referring to Maylene." His solemn eyes met his parents' startled ones as he added quietly, "Your *other* granddaughter, the child Juliana and I conceived during that week twenty-eight years ago."

"You and Juliana . . . ?"

How Garrett wished that he could not read his parents' unspoken thoughts. How he wished that he could not see their prejudice toward the half-Asian daughter their son had fathered. How he wished he could be forever blind to the truth: *they didn't want her.*

His heart thundered with rage, but Garrett fought it, contained it. He would not leave until he had said everything he had come to say—because the words that remained, the most important ones of all, were about Maylene.

And so he spoke them, telling his parents how difficult Maylene's life had been, and how very much he loved her. Garrett never mentioned how beautiful Maylene was, or that she was the gifted architect who had designed Hong Kong's most extraordinary landmark. Nor did he even tell them of Allison's joy—and Maylene's—that they were sisters.

Garrett wanted his parents to accept Maylene unconditionally, because she was their granddaughter, not because she had credentials that might persuade them to see beyond their prejudice.

But it was too much to ask, he realized as he saw their expressions of disbelief—and denial. Still, he said every one of the words he had planned, finishing with the most significant words of all.

"Maylene is every bit as much your granddaughter as Allison is. Allison and Maylene are sisters, and Juliana and I are husband and wife, and we want very much for you to be part of our family—if you wish."

But it *wasn't* what they wished. Garrett saw that clearly. His parents' hatred for all that was Asian was as deep and strong as was his own love for Juliana and Maylene. They couldn't accept what he had told them—which meant that he would try to understand . . . but that he would also say good-bye.

It seemed, however, that Douglas Whitaker was going to say good-bye first. Douglas stood, and as Garrett watched his father struggle to find the words with which he would forsake his only living son, Garrett's heart screamed with pain. Garrett Whitaker was a grown man. He had a wife, and two daughters, his own family of love. But still Garrett felt the anguish of a child being abandoned by his parent—by his *father.*

The pain was quite remarkable, quite excruciating . . . but it was trivial, so very trivial, compared with what a thirteen-year-old girl would have felt when she discovered that the father who she had loved so much had betrayed that love.

Garrett turned away then. He needed to be with that girl, that beloved daughter who had been so hurt. He needed to tell her again how sorry he was, and to love her and help her as she struggled with this latest rejection. He strode swiftly across the plush carpet, and the hand that bore his shining wedding band was just reaching for the doorknob when he was stopped by the voice of his father.

"Garrett."

He faced his father then, and saw a face flushed with emotion. Garrett waited, steeling himself for his father's farewell.

But Douglas Whitaker did not say good-bye. Instead, the father who Garrett had always loved, and trusted, and admired, said softly to his only son, "I would like to meet my granddaughter."

Pauline Whitaker stood then, and even though Garrett's image of her was slightly blurred, he heard her words loud and clear. "So would I."

And now it was Iris Parish who spoke. "What about us, Garrett? Would you be willing . . . would it be possible . . . could Maylene be our granddaughter, too?"

CHAPTER 35

The Jade Palace
December 31, 1993

She stood on the harborside esplanade, in the precise place where, on that day in June, she and Sam had been able to see what no one else could—their hotel, already built, glorious and triumphant.

The Jade Palace glittered tonight. Its clear-glass lobby was a sea of people who had come to celebrate its grand opening, and perhaps some of Kowloon's dragons had dropped by as well. But she was here, alone, marveling at the brightly twinkling lights of Hong Kong reflected off the smooth, black mirror of Victoria Harbour.

It was almost midnight. The winter moon was the color of champagne and the night air was fragrant and warm. She wore a gold brocade cheongsam, a Pearl Moon design, and her shining black hair, which had for so long known the tight constraint of a sleek chignon, was now a crown of soft, loose curls atop her head. And, as she stood gazing at the jewel-bright splendor, her hands rested gracefully on her lower abdomen.

"Happy New Year, Jade."

Maylene believed that she was hearing things, hopeful whispers that came from her own heart. She had been thinking about him, of course, and about his baby—when and how she would tell him. But in her fantasy she had not imagined "Happy New Year, Jade," spoken so softly. Indeed, she had not yet dared to dream *any* gentle words that Sam might speak.

The words she heard now *were* gentle, as caressing as the warm night air, and then there was more warmth as the strong cowboy body moved beside her.

"Sam," she whispered. "You decided to come."

"I couldn't stay away." For a moment Maylene's eyes shone more brightly than all the lights of Hong Kong. But, too quickly, Sam saw a dark jade shadow. "I take it you're not too happy to see me."

"Did one of my family ask you to come?"

"No." It was the truth, and when Maylene seemed relieved, Sam smiled. "You have a family now, don't you?"

"Yes," she said softly. "I have a wonderful family now."

"And a protective one," he added. "All save one seemed to have mixed emotions about telling me where to find you."

"But not Allison."

"But not Allison," Sam affirmed. "In fact, your sister took me by the hand, led me to the window, and made certain that you were still here before turning me loose."

That's because Allison believes in fairy tales, Maylene thought. Fairy tales—complete with happy endings.

And there was something else in which Allison Parish Whitaker had unshakable confidence: her sister. Sam *loves* you, Allison had insisted a thousand times during the past three weeks. How could he not?

Allison's relentless and loving refrain had almost convinced Maylene to fly to San Antonio, where she would appear at Sam's ranch, Stetson in hand, boots on her feet, and after greeting him with, "Happy New Year, Cowboy," she would confess her love.

What's the *worst* that could happen? Allison had asked as, together, the sisters envisioned the scenario in Texas. He could break my heart, Maylene replied. To which, Allison countered softly, Your heart is already broken.

But now Sam Coulter was here, and he had braved her fiercely protective family to find her, and . . .

"I've missed you, Jade."

"You have?"

"I imagine it's usual to miss someone you love, but I don't really know. I've never been in love . . . until now." Sam hadn't known how Maylene would respond. He knew only that he couldn't spend the rest of his life missing her, loving her, and wondering how she truly felt beneath all the disguises. Nothing was disguised now. Her jade-green eyes shimmered with brilliant emerald sparkles of pure hope. "I love you, Maylene Kwan. I should have told you long ago. I thought you were playing with me, but you weren't, were you? You were just terribly uncertain."

"You love me?" Maylene echoed.

"I love you." Sam's tender words floated in the night air, enveloping her with their warmth and their love, and when all the shadows of uncertainty vanished from her lovely eyes, he said, "And I want to spend my life with you." He withdrew a small red cardboard box from his pocket. "Open it, Jade. I'm exercising my gift giver's prerogative."

The jeweler's Christmastime gift box happened to be a brilliant red, but wanting all the luck he could get, Sam had embellished a little more. After discarding the ring's purple satin home, the man who had created a special nest for Maylene on the night of the typhoon, created yet another one—quite small this time and made of bright red tissue paper.

The diamond was perfectly round and absolutely flawless, and it danced with inner fire in its six-pronged Tiffany setting. As Maylene stared at it, unable for the moment to speak, Sam offered quietly, "It's very traditional, and if you'd prefer something else . . ."

"No," she answered softly, "We Whitakers are very traditional."

Maylene touched the diamond then, her delicate fingers as reverent now as they had been on the night of the typhoon, when Dorothy had reached to touch their jade-and-emerald moon. The glowing glass had been an illusion, and this was real, but it was still so hard to believe that it could truly be happening to her.

"Does that mean you like it?" Sam asked. "And that you will marry me?"

"I love it." Looking up from the diamond to dark blue eyes that glittered with love, she whispered, "I love *you*."

They needed all hands free to touch each other, but there was still the matter of the small red box with its brightly sparkling jewel. Removing the diamond ring from its nest, Sam slipped it gently onto her trembling finger.

For a moment it seemed to Maylene as if his hands trembled, too. But *that* surely was an illusion.

Then the ring was on her hand, and it fit perfectly, made just for her. "You were pretty sure I'd say yes, weren't you, Cowboy?"

It was a soft tease, to keep herself from dissolving into tears of joy, but his dark blue eyes did not smile. They only became even more intense.

"I wasn't sure at all," he said quietly. "I only hoped, with all my heart, that you would. I still haven't officially heard your answer."

"Yes, Sam, *yes*, I will marry you."

Maylene's tears spilled then, and Sam kissed them all, and long after the tears had stopped flowing, he kissed her still.

Finally, between kisses, he whispered, "When, Jade? When will you marry me?"

"Whenever you want me to. James and Allison are getting married tomorrow."

"On your birthday. We could get married on Allison's birthday, if you like—assuming it's sometime very soon."

"It's today, actually, and in about ten minutes it will be over."

Sam considered for several moments before saying the next. Then, very gently, he began, "Well, let's see. Allison is getting married on the first day of the Western New Year, so we could get married a month from now, just as the Chinese New Year begins. Or . . ."

Sam paused, hoping he would see on her lovely face that she understood what he was really saying—and he did. Her green eyes sparkled, and her alabaster cheeks glowed a soft pink, and it was obvious that she was no longer merely a gifted actress feigning happiness when all she truly felt was pain.

She was a child of two worlds, and at long last, Maylene Kwan was proud of who she was.

"Or," she finished with quiet joy, "we could get married halfway in between."

They kissed again, long, lingering caresses of love.

Eventually, with a tender smile, and a voice laced with need, Sam said, "We may have to start thinking about where we're going to spend the night." But before she could reply, and suddenly wanting to make far more permanent plans, he asked, "Where will we live? Where will your family be?"

"They'll be here, including, for long stretches, my grandparents. I'm afraid we've become a family of freedom fighters."

"I think I have a little of that in my Texan blood. So, we'll live in Hong Kong. Do you suppose we could convince James to let us collaborate on a few more of his buildings?"

"I *suppose* so." Maylene's expression went from teasing to serious. "But you have those two other projects to do first, don't you?"

"No." Sam smiled at her surprise. "They did call me. I told them I'd let them know after the first of the year . . . after seeing you."

"You could still do them. I'd go with you."

Sam had no intention of taking the woman he loved away from her family. "I'd rather stay here. I'm looking forward to finding a beach, and a couple of horses, and teaching you how to ride." In response to her sudden frown of worry, Sam swiftly assured, "Riding isn't an absolute essential for a cowgirl, but I think you'd enjoy it."

"Yes . . . but not right away."

It came to him then, as he remembered the way she had been standing when he arrived, the graceful hands that had rested so gently, so protectively, on her abdomen. At the time he had been struck by how lovely she looked, how breathtaking in that unusual—and yet so compelling—pose.

And now Sam realized something even more breathtaking: the gracefully protective gesture that he had seen was distinctly— and gloriously—maternal.

Softly, so softly, he asked, "Are we having a baby?"

Maylene looked at dark blue eyes filled with love—and with joy—and told him, "We're having a little typhoon."

"Are you all right?"

"I'm wonderful, Sam. I just whirl every so often."

"You were whirling when I met you."

"And you didn't let me fall."

"I will never let you fall."

Sam Coulter's strong hands trembled then. It was no illusion, merely reverent wonder, as, so gently, he touched her abdomen. And, as Maylene's delicate hands entwined with his strong ones, they both knew the truth about the gesture.

It was distinctly maternal *and* distinctly paternal . . . the solemn yet joyous promise of both parents to cherish forever the tiny gift of love that was growing deep inside.